HEIR
TO THE
SILVER
CROSS

HEIR
TO THE
SILVER
CROSS

CHRIS PERRY

atmosphere press

for brittney

CHAPTER 0

"Alana," a voice whispered in the dark. "Alana, your father will die tonight."

Alana sat bolt upright in her bed and looked around her room in a cold sweat.

"Who's there?" she said. She looked around her, glancing from shadow to shadow, scared of what she would see.

Nothing.

She got up hesitantly and walked over to look out the window. A fading light in the west told her she hadn't been asleep long. Slowly she crept back to bed, careful to avoid any shadows, and lay her head down to rest, keeping her eyes wide open and scanning the room.

Everything was still. Down distant halls she faintly heard servants and attendants readying the palace. She heard movement in the bedroom of the king and queen. But no voices.

Her heart began to relax, and the panic subsided into exhaustion.

Alana shook her head. "Must have been a dream," she mumbled, and took in a nice deep breath. She closed her eyes to try to get back to sleep.

"Alana, Alana," the voice called again. "Alana..."

"You are so lucky I'm cremating you," Jane grunted as she pushed the huge body onto the bier. "There's no way I would have kept you intact if they wanted me to haul your giganticness to some distant grave."

"I sure don't think," Olivier panted, "that he's feeling particularly," he wheezed, "lucky."

It had taken them the better part of ten minutes to move the corpse from the wagon onto the ceremonial display in front of all the mourners, and Olivier was beginning to panic after hefting his true mass. "Will the mechanism even hold such a load?" he muttered under his breath. "Will that flimsy boat collapse?" He shrugged his shoulders. "Surely Jane knows what she's doing," he thought.

The sun was dropping in the west, the sunset glinting off the waters of the Andaluvian as it slowly worked its way downstream. Crowds were gathering nearby as they awaited the sendoff, and Jane wiped her brow, happily surveying their success.

"Okay, scram," Jane whispered to Olivier, "it's showtime."

"At your service, miss," Olivier whispered.

"Doctor!" Jane hissed.

Olivier smiled and waved patronizingly as he walked back to the wagon.

The crowd of loved ones, friends, and random passersby crowded around the giant man's bier and bowed their heads.

His wife gave a brief address muddled with tears. A few of his children spoke their peace. And just as Jane was starting to get bored, she saw a priest of Apollo wend his way through the crowd and take the front.

"This should be interesting!" she thought. Funerals were oh so boring, especially given how many she was asked to officiate.

The old priest was covered from head to toe in a brilliant orange robe. A hood hid all of his features save his craggy nose.

The priest clasped his hands together under the long sleeves of the robe and began his speech.

"The great Apollo will take this man to his home in the beyond," the priest stated, "and from thence he will be embraced in the arms of his loved ones."

The priest pulled his hands apart and rubbed his fingers together, creating a spark in the air.

"He will not be stuck in the realm of the dead!" the priest abruptly shouted, causing the front row of mourners to pull back in fright. The priest waved his hands about in the air, turning the spark into fire and drawing an intricate symbol in the air. Each stroke burned and hovered like it was drawn on paper.

"He will rise to greet the mighty gods on Olympus herself!" he shouted with a flourish and finished his fiery symbol. It burned brightly and hung in the air in front of the astonished crowd.

Jane took a few steps to the left to get a good angle on the symbol and smiled. "Absolution," she muttered, "of course."

"And from there he will find rest and peace in the eternities," the priest finished. He clasped his hands back together under the long sleeves and shuffled off into the crowd as the symbol melted away into wisps of smoke.

Jane stood watching the man leave. "I've never seen that before," she said. "Most impressive."

Olivier hissed and motioned towards her from the back of the crowd and pointed at the bier.

"Oh right," she said, and Jane jumped into action. From behind the bier she lit two torches and carried them around front to the crowd. She waved them in the air, then threw and caught them.

"Taka Valhalla!" she screamed. "Taka Valhalla!"

She drew many stares from the crowd: most of the

mourners had never seen someone with such pale skin; they had never come across a foreigner from the west.

"Eg radasta theo taka Valhalla!" she screamed out in the language of the ancients of her people, and with that she threw her torches onto the bier. It exploded with flames racing for the sky and embers bursting like fireworks in the air high above.

She kicked out a support, and the bier flopped down onto a dry reed boat, which, to Olivier's astonishment, miraculously held. Jane pushed the boat down a ramp and into the current, taking care not to get singed. Downriver went that great man, burning into the night.

Jane gingerly stepped back onto the beach holding the torch to her side and surveyed the beautiful sight. Plumes of grey smoke rose high into the twilight.

"Next stop, Valhalla," Jane said, and taking care to not expose it to the others, she whisked out a small green emerald from inside her necklace. She held it in her hand and focused downriver.

The crowd erupted into screams and moans as the last bit of light in the west extinguished and the flaming boat bobbed down the Andaluvian.

"Now off to Valhalla before you get stuck downstream," Jane whispered, and she threw out her arm towards the boat and whispered. A pale green light erupted from the emerald and threw itself onto the river. It bent and swirled around to create a fiery green circle which encased utter blackness. The darkness inside the lit green circle seemed to suck in any nearby light as it pulsed menacingly.

The crowd shouted in shock and stared at the ink-black circle as the flaming boat floated into the circle and disappeared beyond sight.

And just as the boat entered, from within the same dark circle three cloaked beings emerged, and slowly floated over the water towards Jane.

6

"Oh no," she said. "Oh no."

Alana walked the halls of the palace, trying to avoid the servants and emissaries tidying up from a long day. She knew they would whisk her off to bed, but that was the last place she wanted to be right now, what with the ghost voice going on and on whenever she closed her eyes.

The candlelight flickered in the palace, casting eerie shadows on the walls. Here and there electric lights buzzed wherever they had been installed and blinked and pulsed as they shone their unnatural light.

Alana wrapped herself in her robe and shivered. A cold breeze blew through the palace and from the river she heard dark whispers and the faint roar of a crowd.

"Whatever are the commoners up to now?" she said, trying her best to see out one of the windows in the hallway, inching up on her tiptoes to peer down capitol hill to the river below.

My father asked Alana about this night a few times, and he said initially he felt she held something back. In her official statements, she didn't see anything of interest when she went to the window. But in her most unguarded moments when they were better friends, she told him what she thought she saw as a child but refused to believe as an adult. She could only ever bring herself to talk about the dark figures in hushed tones, far away from the prying ears of those who might doubt her.

"Get back to the eternal pit!" Jane screamed on the beach. The panicked crowd dispersed in a frenzy and left the bearer of the dead alone to face the dark figures. Jane picked up and lit a torch with her left hand and whipped out an ink-black dagger with her right. "You have no power here!" she hollered.

The figures attempted to go around her, but Jane walked up and down the river, waving her torch.

"Get back," she said, "or I'll send you back myself the old-fashioned way!"

The first figure held out an empty sleeve and motioned for her to move, but Jane shook her head.

"Over my dead body," she spat out.

The figure shrugged its empty shoulders and headed straight for Jane, eerily hovering above the water as it went. As it reached the beach, Jane ran towards it screaming ancient curses, brought her dagger up, and buried it deep in the figure's chest.

It didn't react to the attack until the dagger pressed in, and then the arms flapped around in panic, and the figure let out a horrific screech and puffed away.

The other two figures hovering over the water looked at Jane in what could only be shock.

"Get back to the eternal pit, you monsters!" she hollered, "This is not your kingdom!" Jane screamed at the top of her lungs, pumped full of adrenaline. "You can go back with him!"

The second figure sped directly at Jane and whipped up a furious wind, throwing sand and water as he came. He came like a whirlwind and blew out the torch, but circled around Jane, avoiding the ancient black dagger, and then began to motion towards the boulders on the riverside, lifting them up through some unknown power.

Jane held her left arm in front of her eyes to block the sand and wind, and seeing the boulders moving, she flipped her dagger around to the point, and threw it with all her might into the second figure which vanished in a squeal.

The third figure looked at Jane, then up to the palace, then back at Jane, and flew up the hill, totally ignoring her.

"Oh no you don't!" Jane shouted at the figure in flight. She ran down the beach and picked up her dagger, then looked around towards her wagon.

"Olivier, Olivier!" she shouted.

"Y-y-y-yes?" a stunned Olivier called out from beneath the wagon.

"Tell my husband I'll be back late!" she shouted.

Jane whipped the green gem out of her necklace and traced a circle in front of her, burning a green light above the beach, and stepped through the portal.

Alana watched in shock as a fiery green circle appeared in front of her and grew until a woman stepped through onto the stone floor.

The woman put a green gem in her necklace, lowered a black dagger, and looked at Alana. "Where'd he go?" she asked.

Alana stared up at her. "Did she hear the voice too?" she wondered.

"Have you seen anything strange?" Jane asked Alana.

Alana stuttered, "I-I-I," the girl stuttered in panic, "I heard a voice," she said.

"What happened?" Jane asked impatiently.

"I heard something tonight," Alana replied nervously.

"Little girl, let me tell you, it is of utmost importance you tell me what you heard," Jane said, "it's the only way I can help."

Alana started to cry. "It said my dad was going to die tonight!" she blurted out.

Jane scrunched up her face and looked at her. "Who's your dad?" she said.

"King Titus!" Alana bawled.

Jane's eyes opened in fear. "I was really hoping you wouldn't say that," she said. "Which way to his room?!"

Alana pointed down the hall. "Up those stairs—it's the door on the right-hand side!"

Jane was already halfway down the hallway. "Thank you!" she shouted.

The first door was a closet. The second was locked. "WHICH door on the right?" Jane cursed.

From down the hall she heard a shriek. "Bingo!" she yelled, and in four steps she was bursting through the double doors into the royal bedroom.

King Titus lay in bed with the dark figure above him, his soul being sucked out of his body as his wife lay screaming in panic.

"I said go back to the eternal pit!" Jane shouted and lunged at the figure.

The dark figure held out its hand and motioned to one of the ropes on the curtains, which sprang to life and wrapped itself around Jane's neck. The dark figure moved his arm upwards, and the rope moved up and lifted her high into the air. Jane grasped at the rope and squirmed in the air as she struggled to breathe.

The dark figure screeched at Titus in an unholy high-pitched yell of a banshee as it pulled him into the kingdom of the dead.

From the door a set of personal guards arrived, and seeing the dark figure, leveled their revolvers and fired shot after shot at the hovering figure. The figure quickly twisted Jane into the path of gunfire, and the shots fired into her legs as she hovered horizontally in the air between the window and bed.

She screamed in agony. "You demon!" she managed to grunt through her choking neck. With her right hand she used the emerald to open a portal next to the figure, and with her left she reached through with the dagger, slashing at its head.

The figure immediately let the rope drop, and Jane fell, slamming into the bed on top of the startled couple. Her dagger dropped to the bedside.

Seeing an unconscious Titus lying beside her, Jane noticed his own necklace. She could see a leather band laced with gold and silver thread reflecting in the dim candlelight. And on the end, there was a pouch. Not just any pouch! On it was branded a cross encircled by a serpent eating its own tail. Anyone would recognize that iconography. Anyone would be shocked to see it.

"The Silver Cross," Jane said reverently, "I thought it was lost," and having no other weapon, she ripped open the pouch to face the demon.

It was empty.

The demon laughed above them, and with a flourish, stole the soul of Titus. The man rose a moment, then fell back down on the bed, lifeless.

"No!!!" screamed Jane, and she flung herself to the side of the bed to grab the dagger, but the dark figure pointed at a guard. The man dropped his aim and pointed the revolver directly at Jane. His finger twitched on the trigger.

"No!" she screamed again, waving her hands, "don't shoot!"

"I'm trying!" the guard screamed.

Jane lifted the emerald and drew one last fiery green circle, throwing the gem in by itself into the dark abyss, and as the green circle disappeared, the shot fired, and the dark figure disappeared out the window and into the night.

Darkness enveloped Jane. Alana approached[1] the large doors thrown askew and saw the guards helpless, her mother in hysterics, and her father dead. Jane lay on the floor dying, crying, "Ethan! Ethan!"

And so fell the spark that would burn down the five nations.

---

[1] Alana always claimed she arrived after the fight but carried such an in-depth understanding of how it played out, I have never quite believed it.

CHAPTER 1

Thunder boomed in the distance, and rain dumped another deluge on the hillside. A flash of mud came streaming down the road in a torrent, hitting the long wagon train snaking up the hill. They were barely moving against the elements, but slowly and almost imperceptibly the train inched forward up one of the last approaches to the capital.

Alana looked up at the line of red lanterns. Their attempt to light the night was fruitless as they rocked in the wind and fought to glow into the rain. Lightning flashed, closer this time.

"Keep moving," she yelled. "What's the hold up?"

"Oh, shut up already! We're trying! Old Jakratha up in front can't handle his ox, apparently," one of her commanders called back.

Alana smiled at the gruff reply. She loved this. Everything about it.

"Tell him I'll send him back to Cairn if he can't get a move on!" she hollered back up the line.

"No good," another soldier hollered back. "That's exactly what a lazy snail like him is looking for. Better to threaten him with driving the wagon in front of yours!"

"Quiet!" she said laughing, her white teeth shining, and her thick wavy hair plastered against her dark skin, "Or I'll have you driving my wagon and you'll never hear the end of me."

"For one year I haven't heard the end of you—another hour isn't going to hurt!" he shouted over the wind.

Alana laughed and shut up. There was nothing like a good hard trek to cheer her up. She and the rest of the artillery were practically ecstatic to be out and moving again after their long posting at the southern fortress at Cairn.

So here she stood, ankle deep in mud, a heavy spring storm giving her company a thrashing, and having the absolute time of her life.

"Keep it up" she shouted. "We're not far now, keep it moving!"

Her men grumbled and pushed on as they slipped and braced their way up the hill.

Her wagon was pulled by two strong horses, but even their strength was no match for the elements. The wagon fishtailed this way and that as it skidded through the slippery conditions. Alana threw her strong shoulders into the rear to stabilize the wagon against the shifting mud currents, her high dark leather boots giving her traction the horses lacked, and her six-foot frame giving her ample leverage as she pushed against the incline. Each step was a struggle up the hill. The horses strained against their harnesses and slowly beat back the mud, inch by inch gaining their ground. Up and over the hill they went.

The red lanterns bobbed and weaved in a giant line, occasionally disappearing through thick fog and rain, but coming back in sight as the rain changed from pouring to drizzle.

At the last hill she paused and looked out over the valley as the clouds lifted. The storm clouds blew over dark green fields and, in the distance, dim lights from a giant city spread out along the open plain. White-capped mountains stood at the far northern end, just within sight. The rain released fragrances trapped in the earth all winter, and the whole world stopped for just one moment as she inhaled the beautiful springtime scene.

They approached one of the outer bridges. On the far side sat one of the old-school priests of Apollo—you can always pick them out with their signature long orange hooded robes. The priest perked up from his boredom when he saw the group draw near and stood to light their path. As the first soldiers passed him, he began pronouncing blessings on each and every one.

"The spirit of Apollo rest upon you," he said as they passed. He waved a wand of burning embers that traced yellow arcs into symbols that hung and burned in the air in the dimming light. "The spirit of Apollo rest upon you, and may you be borne up by the everlasting light," he said as he waved his blessings.

"Thank you, brother," they mumbled as they walked by, staring at Apollo's light weaving in the darkness. Most had never seen it so close.

The young priest largely kept his head down, and only allowed himself the occasional peek down the road as he looked over the group. The rain had soaked his robes, and his hood hung dripping onto the ground as he waved his wand again and again. "The spirit of Apollo rest upon you."

"Thank you, brother."

The priest was scanning the soldiers. Looking for someone.

"The spirit of Apollo rest upon you," he said and waved again. The amber patterns hung in the air, suspended in a trance-like state for a few seconds before they puffed away into darkness. He peeked down the group and saw the last few soldiers. There she was at the end: Alana always proved easy to find in any crowd. He knew she claimed six feet in height, but also knew she could sometimes...embellish the truth. Not that he could look down on her—she was much taller than him. And it wasn't just height either; she carried a spirit of power in her frame.

"Apollo himself carry you!" he shouted as she approached. He removed his hood and began gesticulating wildly with his amber wand, drawing patterns with the light in the grey mists. He stepped into her path and drew ancient symbols of power and protection that hung in the air. A few of the soldiers reached for their sidearms. They weren't about to let some religious madman attack anyone in the company, even if the greatest perceived threat was a severe eye poking.

Alana motioned for them to relax. "Rafael!" she said warmly. "I haven't seen you for what, four years?"

Rafael finished off his symbology with a flair, the wiry frames of light hanging in the air for a moment before they disappeared. He smiled and bowed deeply to the ground. "Welcome, my liege," he said. "and not to correct you, but I do believe you left the palace some five years ago now."

The other soldiers gave him some serious side eye, but seeing that Alana somehow knew this crazy person, continued on. She gave him a huge hug.

"Holy one, how nice to see you on such an unholy day." Alana said.

"I heard there were some unholy masses passing through," he paused as he pulled back and surveyed the damage of touching her and solemnly brushed off as much mud as he possibly could.

"Unholy masses passing through," he said as he finished brushing, "that need some holy cleansing performed!" and with a look of self-righteousness, he flicked and twirled his wand high up in the air. "Cleanliness!" he shouted.

"Oh brother, I mean priest," she replied, "I thank you for the declaration of cleanliness." She quickly flicked off any mud she could see on herself. "But I am quite all right and shall prepare myself adequately before I present at the temple...which is why I assume you're here? I, of course, had every intention of paying my respects to the fathers and gods the minute I had a moment of leave."

She, of course, did not previously have those intentions.

"I am sent to offer blessings for our queen," he said, as he flicked his wand again. He kept his eyes focused on her as he dramatically waved his right arm out and flicked his wand in indecipherable randomness. "Blessings!" he shouted as he stared at her.

Alana curtsied, and took the chance to not-so-surreptitiously scrape off as much mud as she could from her boots. "And I thank thee for the blessings, old friend."

Rafael bowed and said, "But of course, my queen."

"No no no no," Alana immediately replied, "princess, sure, but no crown, no queen. I'm just here on army business. Not queen business."

"But you must know, my queen," Rafael started.

"Princess!" Alana insisted.

"You must know, my princess," he said quietly as he looked around anxiously, "you are not welcome here."

"What in the name of Hades are you talking about?" Alana said with a hint of anger.

"Queen you must become, because as princess you are definitely not welcome here," he whispered.

"So, it's treason." Alana said. "And from such an old friend like yourself! What do you even mean?"

Rafael looked all around him, checking for people he didn't see, and took her to the side of the bridge. He stood up on tiptoe and whispered in her ear, shielding his words from the passing traffic with his hand. "My liege, my old friend," he said, looking around.

"They are going to kill you."

Alana's mouth dropped and her eyes exploded, and she

roughly grabbed and with both hands held Rafael against the stone of the bridge, staring down at him. "Who?" she said. "Who says such things?"

"Your majesty," he said, "I do not know, but I was told from someone I trust, you must leave at once, there are plots against you."

Alana rolled her eyes. "This again?" she said. "More conspiracy theories?"

It was Rafael's turn to get mad. "You'll never let that go, will you?" he said. "This is nothing like that. I'm telling you: they will kill you! I heard it from my own ears."

Alana shook her head. "Nobody is going to kill me," she said. "Have you not watched the stars? They are moving my way. Venus is ascending. I've waited and watched their movements for years, and I see how everything is slowly coming to work in my favor. It is not death you divine, it is my rebirth into my divine right." She let go of him with a bit of a push against the stone and stepped back. "Yes. It is not my death you have heard; it is my rebirth. Not now, but soon. The time is coming."

Rafael shook his head. It had been a long time since they were friends, a long time since they had seen each other. He knew the same old dynamics would kick in, but for a moment he had hoped that she could drop her prejudices just once, just for this. "You don't know what you're doing," he said. "You're walking into a trap."

"Nobody can trap me," she said tapping the crown of her head, "Divine right of kings."

"Princess!" Rafael corrected her.

"Whatever," Alana said, and with that she turned and chased after her group.

"At least," he shouted after her before catching himself and jogging to reach her and whispering to her over the din, "at least don't sleep in the palace, the barracks will be much safer."

"Okay, okay," she said, "now bugger off, I've got work to do."

Alana marched off with the rest of her unit, her feeling of hope just the smallest bit dampened. "Couldn't hurt to listen to him," she thought, "maybe he's right..."

"Be careful!" Rafael shouted as he watched her disappear into the mist. With the last bit of emotional stamina, he had after such a letdown, he drew a symbol into the mist with his burning amber wand that charmed the rest of the passersby. It was a single intricate character, weaved through a dazzling series of strokes and counterstrokes. It stood for one thing:

Redemption.

And it faded.

Alana, daughter of Titus II, had returned. To what end, he did not know.

Far, far to the southeast on the edges of civilization, a woman in a grey robe descended a steep hillside in the fading light, stretching her hands out on either side to feel the sunflowers as she walked down. Every path up the hills was lined several feet deep by rows and rows of them, drawing yellow lines up and down the dry mountains, which were otherwise covered in scrub and sagebrush.

A brief glint of steel caught her eyes as she calmly walked down, but it had been so long since anyone had come for her, she didn't even think twice. Besides, she was done running.

The setting sun cast red and yellow hues across the desert valley spread out before her and she could see tiny dots of light blinking on for miles and miles. As shadows from the far mountains crawled across the broad valley, each family lit a candle or fire to extend their daylight. There was a tiny crossroads several miles in the distance with a few buildings crammed together, but otherwise the valley was sparsely populated by squatters like herself, trying to stay alive through any number of means. Most of them, like herself, had pasts they didn't care to acknowledge. It made neighborhood get-togethers awkward and infrequent.

She reached home and let herself in. Dark figures slowly approached along the makeshift path, up the wash to her house. She had just started boiling some water for tea so she could drink away her hunger when she heard pounding on the door outside.

"Federal police! Open up!" they shouted.

Her heart sank.

"Federal police! Open up!" they shouted again.

They had finally found her.

Alana slept in her dormitory in the officer's section of the barracks that night. Like all soldiers since time immemorial, she had learned to sleep anywhere, anytime, and was totally and completely zonked out by the time her head hit the pillow. She entered a deep and dreamless sleep after a week on the road.

But somewhere as she swam in the inky darkness something was not quite right. A long curling black hand unfolded from the eternal pit below and its wiry fingers slowly tightened around her. In her otherwise featureless sleep, she felt panic.

Alana awoke, paralyzed. She opened her eyes in her dark room.

It was the darkest part of the night, and it seemed as though there was an endless hole in front of her, sucking any sound she might make or any emotion she could feel into an unreachable beyond.

She gasped as she saw in front of her a hooded dark figure that hovered over the foot of her bed and beckoned.

Alana froze and searched her mind. Where had she left that black dagger? How could she be so careless?

There was a noise and the hooded figure looked around and vanished, and from behind its floating robes out walked a man.

Alana screamed into the abyss.

The man vaulted onto the bed and stopped her scream with a heavy, oily hand. His gruesome face snarled. "Shh..." he hissed.

She immediately lifted her left arm up, but it was pushed down by his. She brought her right arm to bear, and he quickly moved his hand to push that arm down, rendering her totally immobile.

As she let out a scream, he threw his body over onto the bed, and with his right knee he clamped down her left arm again and once again cupped his hand around her mouth to muffle her cries.

With his other leg he trapped her other arm, and quick as a flash produced a roll of tape and wrapped it around and around her mouth and head.

The gruesome face came back within inches of her and smiled. He breathed putrid beer-scented air into her nose and she mumble-shouted through the tape. His saliva dripped down onto her face.

Alana had no idea what was going on. She briefly wondered if this was a dream. Her arms had lost feeling and she could barely breathe through her nose, and no, this was definitely not a dream. A nightmare, sure. A dream, no.

He brought his face down next to hers again. "If you don't struggle this'll be a lot easier on the both of us," he said.

"I'm sure it would," she tried to mouth through the tape, her voice trapped in her throat. In desperation, she head-butted the face as hard as she could, twisting her entire body to bring up force from the edges of her toes all the way through her glutes and back. She smashed her forehead into his nose with a hollow crunch. He fell back groaning, rolling off her and the bed and onto the floor.

Suddenly, her left arm was free. The blood rushed in and a thousand needles stabbed their way towards her freedom.

She wrenched her semi-lifeless arm over her body and onto her right side and blessed her instincts for giving her the presence of mind to wake up in the last moment of possibility.

Before she could get up with her limp arms, the man stood up, this time fully enraged. Blood dripped off his broken nose and into his mouth outlining his teeth as he bared them in primal fury. He swung out a huge knife, flipped it and caught it pointing downwards, and, kicking himself for not just doing the job the moment he got there, he drove the knife to her heart.

In the light of the moon, Alana saw the flash of a blade as the strike came down. She rolled over and threw herself on the far side of the bed. He slashed into the mattress and feathers flew everywhere. He yawped with primeval rage and cocked again to slash. She threw herself to the left this time and he came down on the far side. He went high, she slipped low, he went low, she slipped high, and in the brief span of fifteen seconds he had slashed her mattress in a half dozen places and feathers exploded through the room like a circus.

He came down again, and this time she spun her legs up, kicking them fully free from her blankets. Spinning around, she kicked him in the face and wrapped her legs around his stabbing arm, twisting it with her entire strength. He let go of the knife and she threw him down on the bed.

From his position under her legs, he anchored against the end of the bed and threw her entire body against the top of the bed, smashing her against the wall. She dropped the knife on the floor and crumpled up in agony. Swinging his arms loose, he began to beat her with his fists, wildly swinging, tangled up as they were. She braced against the headboard and, with the force of her powerful legs, launched him off the bed onto the floor.

She jumped off the bed and ran for the door. Her entire head was bound up in tape still covering her mouth, but if she could make it down the hall into one of the common rooms for the enlisted men, she could get all the help in the world. As an added plus, choosing the right common room would literally call in the cavalry.

The man picked himself up off the floor and was hot on her tail inches away. She threw herself against her door. It only gave an inch before hitting an unseen barrier. She smacked hard up against the door and crashed back onto the ground. Someone had barricaded it from the other side!

The man kicked her with all his strength as she lay on the ground. He kicked again and again, hitting her ribs, her face, legs, you name it. He sprained at least a couple of her fingers with one kick. She was bruised and bleeding on the floor as he wound up for another kick...and she rolled aside. He nailed the flimsy door, kicking out the bottom panel clean through.

Alana saw her chance and sprung at him, hitting him like a linebacker from the side. She laid into him with the last bit of force she could muster, and his body went left, but his leg, stuck in the door, stayed where it was. With another sickening crunch, she heard his knee pop out of its socket.

But Alana wasn't waiting around to find out what happened next. She pushed him out of the way as he writhed in agony, then scraped and scrambled and forced her way through the bottom of the door into the dark hallway. Above her she could see someone had hastily secured a makeshift beam on her door, preventing any escape.

With no time to question anything, she limped down the hall, bruised and bleeding through her long underwear, the only clothes in which she slept. Her vision was partially obscured by her hair, as it had been hastily taped into position by the man. Down the hall, she could hear his screams had stopped and he was shuffling through the hole in the door. But that didn't matter to her because she had reached the nearest door and she knew behind that door she would find her men, and all would be...

Empty.

She swung the door open and the bunks were, to a bed, empty. Her jaw would have dropped, but as you'll recall it was taped in place.

She ran to the next door.

Empty.

From behind her a shot rang out down the hallway, and she heard a bullet whiz by her ear.

Next door.

Empty.

The entire building, the entire regiment had disappeared in the middle of the night. She was totally and utterly alone.

Well, almost.

Another shot rang out. The man was limping down the hall, nose bleeding, knee hastily bent back into place, and with pain in every step his hulking frame came slowly down the hall. Alana frantically opened door after door to find zero help for Atlas' royal daughter.

She couldn't believe her eyes, couldn't believe what was happening. She was quickly going into shock. From his shaking hands the man pulled the trigger on his revolver and managed, through a miracle of randomness, to shoot through her left foot as she turned a corner. Alana gasped in pain as she fell on the ground. She wrapped it as best she could with a nearby rag and began hopping her way to freedom as the unstoppable force of a gruesome man slowly hobbled towards her.

Alana hopped her way out of the barracks into a world cloaked in blackness and silence, and not far behind her came lumbering an incredibly angry and somewhat disabled assassin. The barracks sat by the government buildings near the top of the hill, but there was no one to be found at this time of night. There was an eerie stillness aside from the two figures on a desperate, if comically slow, chase.

Alana grit her teeth and ran towards the palace. There were guards on duty all night long, and even if the army had failed her, she was sure to find protection in her old home.

But as she rounded a corner, she saw the dark hooded figure again. She gasped in horror and fell backwards. On the ground, she could feel sound and light and soul being sucked into the emptiness inside as it approached her slowly.

Alana scrambled up and ran back towards her attacker, the two of them colliding in the dark street as she ran back. Alana elbowed him in the face, and with her adrenaline pumping she jumped up to run.

She ran, but was running out of options. The dark figure calmly approached, and the gunman fired another wild shot. Alana didn't have much hope left. Her blood smattered on the cobblestones from her injury, and her assailants gained: the dark figure seemed unstoppable as it hovered over the ground, and the gunman still had at least two more shots in that revolver.

Reality seemed to melt into the dark figure itself, giving her no hope of being saved by anyone who might hear the scuffle or screams.[2]

She went uphill, further up towards the dead end of the cliffs of capitol hill overlooking the Andaluvian. Alana hopped up a set of stairs, clinging desperately to the rail to try and lift herself faster. There wasn't much space left for her to run...er...hop. In her current state, climbing down a rocky cliff face wasn't really an option, and even if it were, being immobile on a cliff face has the bad side effect of making you a super easy target.

She arrived at the top of the stairs and reached out with her heart to the stars above. "Help me," she pleaded. Hadn't the stars been moving her way?

From below she could hear the man coming up the stairs.

---

[2] Though, to be fair, this is Alana we're talking about, who famously refused help even when needed, so I very much doubt spontaneous rescue was on her mind.

She was out of options. This was it.

Except, as you know, it wasn't it.

Alana was saved by laziness.

Some poor enlisted soldier on mail duty, tired of carrying mail from the barracks, down the hill, through the city, down to the docks, and then back up again, finally got fed up enough that he, along with some buddies, strung up a line. The wire ran from the top of the hill all the way down to the docks below. All one needs to do is hook a mail bag on the line, push it over the edge, and voila, it would zip line its way down to the docks below for collection by ship. Each bag had a rope attached which they'd use to haul it back up the line for collecting any return mail from the docks. It was labor saving, it was fun, and delivering mail was now the best job in the regiment.

Alana spied the line in the low moonlight and hopped her way over to the edge. She couldn't see the end of the line: it just trailed off into blackness. But as the man came up to the top of the stairs and aimed for the last time, she didn't have a choice. Hooking on a nearby bag, she jumped over the edge and held the burlap sack as she sailed away from certain death.

She picked up an amazing amount of speed as she flew down the wire. Below her she started to make out the shapes of the buildings along the river below. Sparks flew off the wire as the metal hook scraped against the wire. She flew like a bird in the air. "Was this a dream," she thought? No longer a nightmare, it must be a dream.

Alas, the hook snapped. The weight of a human was too much for such a flimsy affair, and she found herself no longer flying, but holding the bag and falling into the inky darkness below. Luckily, she was over the river, and in a moment the cold dark waters of the Andaluvian came up and slapped the wind out of her and she sank.

The man watched her go over the edge and down the line.

He was furious at himself: he should have dispensed with the dramatics and killed her so much faster. A bullet would have been louder but also have guaranteed success.

He never noticed the dark figure, though he did mention he felt a weight lift from around him after she sped away, and he looked around and noted the world was just a little bit louder and less dark after Alana disappeared.

He cursed into the night and hobbled back down to his horse. Now he was going to pay for this. He was really going to pay for this if he couldn't find her right now. He made his way down to the river.

Apollo was harnessing his horses in the east for his daily run when the limping man made it to the riverside on his horse. A dull glimmer of light began to fill the sky. He searched the docks, searched the banks, searched the water, but could not find any signs of life. He was down there for an hour, searching up and down, his face covered in scabs, his knee swollen to twice its size. He stayed out there until the fishermen began to disembark, until the longshoremen began arriving, until the crowds began to fill in for the day. He could not for the life of himself find her, and he knew this was unbelievably bad. He had never botched a job before, but to botch this job, this was unforgivable. He hung his head and returned to the slums to find his handler and deliver the bad news. He held out the tiniest bit of hope that she had died in the fall, but he remained unsettled.

As he should have been. Far up on the cliff face overlooking the Andaluvian a woman held onto the rocks and crags, unnoticed in the din of the day. She was covered in mud and blood, wearing naught but grey woolen long underwear, and slowly making her way up the cliff face, holding onto her savior: the bit of rope they used to haul the bag back in, still attached to the top of the cliff. She used that to help her scale all the way up to the top, and by the beginning of the day, she had climbed her way back up the imposing hill to where she had begun. She paused and stood triumphantly next to the barracks and took a deep satisfied breath.

She was alive.

CHAPTER 2

A sweaty, rotund little man walked into the room to find the woman in grey seated under house arrest. In the east the sky began to lighten a little, and with the smallest amount of pale light he could see bruising on her face. It had taken him a little longer than he anticipated to traverse the valley in the night, and it appeared that the federals had their hands full in keeping her subdued.

"Zara," he said as he rubbed his sweaty hands together again and again with muted glee. "We meet at last."

Zara looked up under her grey hood. "And you must be Scipio, the little weasel. I should have known you were behind this, what with the lack of tact and imagination."

"To think that for all these years you were right here," Scipio said as he looked around her tiny home, and then glanced out a window and looked into the sagebrush-covered hillsides stretching out into the great beyond and shuddered. "To think you've been waiting for us all this time." He stopped rubbing his hands to pull out a pipe, and Zara noticed his hands shaking as he tried to light it. He succeeded on the third try and puffed smoke into the room. "To think all this time you've been waiting for me," he continued.

"This really truly has been an honor," Zara said, "but I'm afraid I need to get going." She tried to stand but a bruised federal put his hand on her shoulder and tried to force her back down. "Life on the run can be somewhat busy, you know."

Scipio instantly drew out his gold-handled revolver and shot above both of her shoulders, the bullets screaming out of the house as they blasted holes in the thin walls. "Sit down," he said.

Zara blinked and slowly sat back down in her chair. Scipio calmly pulled up a chair and sat opposite her, putting his gun away.

"Tell me," Scipio said. "Where is it?"

Zara stared at him with dead eyes. "I have no idea what you're talking about," she said.

"Tell me where it is," he said again.

"Please?" Zara said.

"What?" he replied.

"PLEASE tell me where it is?" Zara said.

The soldiers had to muffle a laugh behind Scipio. He looked backward and glared at them.

"Tell me where it is...or else," he said.

"Please tell me where it is or else what?" Zara said.

Scipio ignored the muted laughs this time.

"Or else I shoot," he said, pulling out his revolver again, spinning it in his hand nervously.

"Or else you shoot what? The wall? You might as well, I'm going to have to mend it anyway." she said.

"I'll shoot you!" he shouted back in reply.

"Sure, you can try, but last time you did you hit the wall, remember?" Zara said.

She defiantly glared directly into his tiny eyes, which were encased in a layer of flesh that bulged around his eye sockets, the fat barely restrained by a tight layer of skin as it bubbled up on his entire face. He stared back for a moment and then started shooting again, firing wildly on either side of her until all of the chambers were empty and the click, click, click of the firing pin was the only noise they could hear.

"Told you so," Zara said. "I've got nothing to say to you."

He put away his revolver and, holding out his hands, lunged for her neck, but she slid down and out of her chair, catching his legs with her feet, tripping and toppling him over behind her. His pipe fell out and burning tobacco leaves sprayed over the back wall. Little by little, small fires began to form.

A federal jumped to grab Zara's legs, but she kicked out, and scrambled up to run out the door. Scipio tried to roll himself back over on the ground screamed, "Stop her!", and as Zara reached and opened the door just the slightest bit, from the other side a federal heaved his full weight against it, body slamming her and sending her airborne several feet back into the house. She crashed into Scipio just as he stood, causing the two of them to fall to the ground in a tumble once again.

The federals, no longer laughing, calmly subdued her on the ground, and Scipio, with concerted effort, lumbered up and stood over her as she lay flat on the floor and dazed. He stepped over her legs, heaving his immense rotundity to precariously stand over her, and he shouted with his face beet red, "For the last time, where is it?"

"Go to hell," Zara said, squinting as she looked up, coughing from the smoke. The small fires grew in the background.

"We'll wait outside until you're ready to tell us," Scipio said, and he motioned for the others to follow. "Barricade it," he said as they walked out the door.

And all along the back wall, flames grew and grew.

Alana lurched into parliament, heaving the double doors

open before her. The doors slammed against the walls, pressing against their hinges. The entire room immediately hushed and stared.

From the far side of the long room, Alana limped her way with royalty and grace past the rows and rows of tiny desks towards the prime minister's office in the front of the building. Pages and assistants stood frozen mid-action as they watched her with wide eyes. Papers hung from their fists mid handoff, telegraph operators ignored their buzzing, and various ministers sat at their desks with jaws agape.

All across her face and up her arms there were scratches and blood stains. Purple bruises strung across her neck and face. Alana's hair was covered in dried mud, naturally windblown from her climb up the cliffside. She had stol...borrowed... an overcoat from the coatroom in the front, tightly buttoned around her body, but at her shins her long underwear showed through on every step as she walked, brown from mud and grit that she had swum and climbed through. She held her head high and proud as she walked barefoot, save a scarlet bandage. It was soaked through with her blood and it dragged and stained the floor behind her red.

One of the younger pages ran up and offered her a shoulder to lean on, as she clearly struggled to walk, but she waved him off, in total silence in front of what was likely forty or fifty people. They stared at this unlikely figure, the princess of Atlas. She could tell through the searing stares that she was not welcome there. She could tell that many of them, in fact, did not expect to see her ever again. But she did not care what they thought of her.

When she reached the entrance to the prime minister's chambers, she swiveled around on her good foot, and with an elegance reserved solely for royalty, she gave a quick bow and threw out her hand. "As you were," she declared, and entered the offices beyond. Slowly, very slowly, the activity began back up anew. Though there were not a few who began investigating why the plan of the morning had failed so badly, most everyone else went about their business, except the poor janitor who looked at the muddy bloody trail across the room and cursed the day. "Not again," he said, and went to work.

The door said "Wallay", the current prime minister, but everyone knew who really ran the government, and he made clear his seniority by perpetually occupying the place of power. Alana brushed off a secretary who tried to intercede, and she threw open the door. "JACQUES!" she yelled into the dank smoky office.

There were five or six old men in the office, smoking cigars, and dressed in the finest suits. There was only a lamp or two in the office producing a dull yellow light which barely pressed through the thick haze of cigar smoke to illuminate the room. Immediately opposite Alana sat Jacques LePen, caretaker of Atlas, or true holder of power, in absentia of the king. He was at the desk in a large upholstered leather chair, and opposite him sat the prime minister, along with a number of high-ranking ministers.

Jacques didn't lose a beat. He stood up, totally unperturbed, apparently completely unaware of Alana's uncomely appearance and said, "of course, Alana, please, do come in," as slimily and debonair as could be. He took out his cigar and motioned for her to sit at another chair, and its existing occupant quickly jumped up and to the side to vacate her seat.

"Why are you trying to kill me?" she demanded.

"It looks like you're already having a go at it, why would I try?" Jacques said as he sat down and shuffled his papers.

"Don't give me that, I know this is your doing, it has all the hallmarks of your own brand of incompetence," Alana grunted.

"Poppycock," he replied, "nobody is trying to kill anybody. Please, do come in," Jacques replied, "I know it's rather early, but from the looks of it you could use a drink."

Alana stumbled into the room, her face red with rage. "Don't poppycock me you throne-usurping treasonous rebel," she said, "you gave the order for my entire regiment to go on exercises in the middle of the night."

"Of course I did, the safety of the nation is in my hands, and we are not safe," Jacques replied.

"And then," she stuttered with rage, "you ordered that I was to be left alone!"

"Of course I did, I felt your rest was paramount to obtain with the safety of the nation at stake," Jacques said nonchalantly.

Jacques was such a smooth operator he could have passed a lie detector test while in the act of stealing actual candy from an actual baby, and not even flinch. Jacques LePen had nerves of steel.

"And the assassination attempt of the future queen, WHICH IS ME I MIGHT ADD, just happened to be PERFECTLY PLANNED FOR JUST SUCH AN OCCASION?" she shouted.

The rest of the men blushed in the room and looked away; their eyes filled with shame. Jacques stood firm and refused to be moved. "Your assassination?" he declared with feigned care, "Who would do such a thing?" he asked. "I'll search the ends of the earth until I can track down the perpetrator of such a...such a...crime." he said in a low monotone. Jacques was a career politician, a caretaker of power for his entire life. He wasn't going to lose his cool to an inexperienced upstart, even if that upstart was filled with passion. Passion doesn't get votes, doesn't change minds, only self-interest can do that, and Jacques' primary gift in life was to understand exactly what motivated everyone he met, and with this power he could manage anyone. That's why I think Titus liked him so much. He could always deliver.

And it's also why he sat on one side of the desk, and Alana the other.

Alana seethed with rage, but Jacques calmly smiled. "I

apologize my dearest, but my valet can assist you in finding clothes," he said as he looked her up and down with disgust, "and back to your quarters, however you require," he snapped his fingers and from an unseen corner a man appeared by her side.

"No, no, no," Alana said, "you're not going to just snap and get rid of me that easily. Nobody is going to get rid of me easily. I am your future queen! Do you hear that? I am your future ruler! This is regicide! This is rebellion! What kind of spineless cockroaches are you?" she shouted fruitlessly like kicking back at the wall after you stub your toe. Getting angrier and angrier at the lack of response, she yelled again, "at least have the guts to look at me if you're going to kill me!" and the men in the room with their heads bowed sheepishly looked up, unintentionally providing some confirmation of her accusations.

Jacques stood his ground. "Of course, my dear, of course, nobody is going to get rid of you," he said with his flat, sarcastic monotone. "You are our princess after all. What am I saying? Our queen. We want nothing more than to be ruled by you," he continued dryly, "that is, just as soon as you've cleaned yourself up," he said, "nobody wants a dirty queen now do they?"

The men quietly chuckled and Alana grumbled.

"Now about these baseless accusations you make," Jacques continued, "I would be happy to investigate. The gods know how seriously I take the security of every citizen of Atlas, so please head down to the nearest police station by way of the nearest bath, and report your experiences to the sergeant major in charge, and we will be sure to assign a detective to the case just as soon as we are able to free up from all of the other high-profile cases we are tracking." he said. "In the meantime, try to avoid swimming in your underwear, it's unladylike." The other men in the room could barely contain their laughter.

Alana was stuck up a creek without a paddle, and Jacques knew it. It was naive of her to assume that she'd just walk in and the power structure would just magically grant all her wishes, but she didn't really know what else she would have done.

She could see now that she had another problem: there was no intention of crowning her queen in any event. All this talk about her being the "future" queen would always be reserved for the future tense.

Alana left the room to the stifled laughter and started figuring out her next approach. This meant war, and she had never lost a fight.

"Matty! Matty!" Alana shouted down the hallway. She was on her way out, but as luck would have it, there was her friend.

Matty continued quickly walking with an air of self-importance.

"Matty!" she raised her voice such that everyone nearby stopped and looked, including an obviously embarrassed Matty.

He offered a pale smile and replied quietly, "It's Mateo," he said firmly, and continued blandly, "why Alana, it's been so long, so nice to see you."

Alana hobbled up to him amid stares of passersby, lowered her voice and continued, "Well okay then MA-TE-O, it's been so long since I've seen you; what five years?"

"It has been ever so long; I haven't even counted the days" he replied haltingly as he looked around. "But they have been many." Mateo said.

"How have you been? How are you doing?" Alana asked.

"You know, just plugging away, getting stuff done you know," Mateo said, constantly scanning the horizon.

"Congratulations on the job here, this is amazing. I never pegged you for a parliamentarian," she said with withering excitement. As each of her sentences were met with bland stoicism the level of enthusiasm in her voice died down with each statement.

"Thanks, I just got lucky." Mateo said.

Which was a bald-faced lie, and Alana knew it. Mateo had no capacity to avail himself of luck. And had no need of it either; he was an old friend of Alana's because his family was politically connected going back hundreds of years. The man could walk into any politician's office, say, in this case, the Prime Minister's office and be employed solely because his father had been prime minister for two separate terms, and his mother the daughter of a famous opposition leader.[3] He wasn't lucky, he was a warm body with a name. He didn't realize that, of course, he firmly believed to his dying day that all that he achieved in life was due to his diligent hard work,[4] and none was a result of luck, or of nepotistic connections.

His eyes darted back and forth between offices as they walked, and he quickly followed up with, "what can I do for you? I'm late for a subcommittee meeting, so I should be on my way soon..." Mateo said.

Alana could already see she was going to get nowhere with Mateo but tried anyway. "Mateo, who is trying to kill me?" she said with a whisper.

"Kill you?!" Mateo said in shock. "N-nobody is trying to kill you."

"Mateo you dummy, can't you see?" she asked.

"I dunno, but I sure can smell," he said as he crinkled his nose.

Alana had yet to bathe. It was patently obvious to anyone nearby. Honestly, this was a common theme in her life. I kind

---

[3] There's more of a pedigree here, but you get the point.

[4] A self-serving self-deception if there ever was one. The man worked long hours, sure, but about half of his time was spent in an armchair drinking or pouring drinks for some compatriot, whereupon they would gossip for hours and ratchet it up to "work".

of think she may have lacked a well-defined sense of smell.

"No, you dummy, someone tried to kill me last night," she said.

"Why would someone want to kill you?" he said as ignorantly as he could possibly muster.

"Et tu Mateo?" she said.

Mateo said nothing in return but mumbled an apology and walked off.

Alana looked after him and wondered how the entire world went crazy.

Alana left parliament by the side entrance soon after, off to mend and heal. The bullet from last night had taken a chunk out of her foot, but it passed through flesh, and the rest of her injuries were largely superficial, so she figured the surgeon would make short work of her. The bigger problem of how to not die would have to wait.

Or not.

From a nearby rooftop a desperate shot rang out, and the stone adornment behind her exploded. "For the love of everything holy," she said, and dropped to the ground just as another explosion sounded in the distance, and a shot ricocheted on the ground just behind her. This was bad.

People were screaming and running in parliament square as mass hysteria took hold, and any guards around parliament were quickly distracted by the pressing onslaught of humans. Everyone who could run ran. And those who couldn't...

Alana crawled behind a low-slung brick wall which made up a raised planter box filled with newly budding flowers and a large cherry tree in full bloom. It only offered a foot or two of protection. She squeezed herself down into the ground and hugged that wall for dear life. Another shot came through, exploding the top layer of bricks above her, and she was showered with shards of brick, handfuls of dirt, and tulip petals. The shots stopped for a moment. Alana hazarded a look around and checked her bearings. The planter box was probably enough to survive another few shots before she became totally exposed, but the assassin wasn't going to wait that long. The rooftop on which he stood ran the length of the square, and she saw a figure darting along the roof to get a better angle. A clear shot.

In a few seconds she would be in sight again. She looked around in panic. The box was flush against parliament, there was no way for her to maneuver another angle. She looked up and down, left and right, anywhere in those few moments and saw nothing but a granite rock desolation. There was nowhere to hide, nothing to do. It was the end all right.

Alana sat up, her back against the short wall. She wasn't going to die hobbling away like some wounded rabbit. She held her back straight and defiant, ignoring the many bleeding wounds opened by her scramble which puddled below her. She saw the assassin pick his way to another spot and quickly level his rifle, steadying himself for the shot.

She held her back straight and looked up and to the right: she looked into the gunsight of her assassin and into his eyes. With fire in her eyes, she made a few obscene gestures and shouted at the top of her lungs, "burn in hades, traitor!"

There was an explosion, and Alana closed her eyes to return to her father.

A hand grabbed her and shook her shoulder. "Alana!" a voice shouted over more explosions.

"So this is death," Alana thought.

"Alana!" it shouted again.

She opened her eyes and looked straight into the face of one of the commanders in her artillery company.

"Alana are you hit?" he said.

Confused, she patted her hands up and down her body, and then lifted to her head to check that it was intact as well. "No?" she said.

Another commander ran up. "We've been looking

everywhere for you," he said. "Hop on, we're getting out of here. Let's get back to the barracks."

"This time with the rest of you I hope?" Alana said.

"With the rest of us," he laughed.

The first commander picked her up and lifted her onto the back of the second, and the three of them scurried to cover. As they ran, Alana saw dozens of soldiers running through and securing the square. Her carriers ran her through a barrier of riflemen who had just finished peppering the opposing rooftop with fire, just to be on the safe side. She looked up behind her on the roof and saw him: her assassin was dead. They had come just in time.

"Thanks commander," Alana said, and the exhaustion and stress overcame her, and she blacked out.

CHAPTER 3

The Golden Temple of Apollo was built a mile due east of parliament, on a smaller hill from which the sunrise could first be seen over the capital. It was one of the great wonders of Atlas. Originally built using marble hauled from a quarry near Olympus, it was surrounded by bas relief sculptures covered in thin gold leaf depicting the epic series in the life of Apollo. Each panel was almost twice as tall as the average adult, yielding gods that stood over ten feet high in their prime. It was an absolutely exhilarating and totally intimidating experience to enter the temple in the presence of such gilded marbled majesty.

Every morning an elite cadre of priests prepared the sunrise rituals to Apollo, patron god of Atlas. He was a big deal, and they made sure to show their devotion to him; the sunrise ritual had been performed every day for over two hundred years uninterrupted. The priests clambered up a huge tower in the middle of a complex series of pillars purpose-built to track the sun, and just as first light hit the horizon, they lit a huge bonfire with their torches and chanted greetings to the bearer of the sun as he raced with his chariot pulling the sun across the sky.

In a society where you'd consider the most atheist among them to be hugely and superstitiously religious, Apollo governed even the smallest natural movements in their lives. Being a priest set up to greet and placate him was a huge honor.

And Rafael had made it.

This morning, like all others, he followed up the senior priests and lit the fires, careful to watch for embers on his robe, or worse, the robes of his superiors, and with religious ecstasy belted out the chants. He felt his whole heart and soul join with the sun god as one.

The sun moved up and out from behind the earth and, if he squinted, he thought he could almost see his idol up there, racing along with the sun as it moved up into the sky and its rays started warming up the platform.

After the fire died down, Rafael walked down the steps, sweating a bit from the heat and exertion, once again proud of what he had achieved. He didn't come from a particularly outwardly religious family, so it was a bit of a shock to everyone when he applied for and was accepted into The Order. The fourth of five brothers, he watched his older brothers head off to sea as merchants, join the engineering trade, or follow his father into business, but nobody had taken a second thought for the priesthood of Apollo.

He walked down the steps replaying in his head over and over again what his supervisors said about his dedication, how they appreciated his hard work. And over and over again he tried to put out of his mind how absolutely and unexpectedly indifferent his parents were when he told them he had been accepted into the most elite religious order on the planet. He had finally achieved something they could be proud of, and yet they didn't seem proud at all...

"Rafa!" Alana said.

The other priests, startled by the interjection, immediately turned their hooded heads in unison. Rafael waved at them to relax. "Alana," he said, bowing deeply, his loose hood hanging over his entire head. A gold medallion on a chain swung down and out of his deep orange robes. He moved two fingers in front of his head in a geometric pattern and continued, "the spirit of Apollo rest upon you."

Alana quickly and awkwardly bowed. "and on you," she said. She hobbled over to him, gingerly avoiding placing weight on her damaged foot, holding herself up with a cane as she walked over the granite tiles.

Rafael motioned for her to follow him down the colonnade to a bench along the wall, and she followed.

"I'm sorry," he said, deeply embarrassed, "I see I did not help my friend as I thought I would."

"You were right," she said, gritting her teeth as an angle caught her healing foot the wrong way. "You were right."

"Not right enough to save you," he said, "not right enough to save you. I'm just so happy they misjudged you terribly. It takes a lot more than that to kill a princess." They sat down on a marble bench to continue. "I can't believe the gall of those people! In your own bed!" he continued.

"How did you know?" Alana asked. "How did you know? This thing, this plot, this goes all the way to the very top!" They say she was near hysterics with him, but since that feels vaguely sexist, let's just say she was exceptionally animated. Which was, after all, understandable given the situation.

Rafael put his finger to his lips and looked around the empty gallery. "One learns many things by keeping one's ears open and mouth shut in here," he said. "I'm not sure who it was, but I am sure of the message."

Deep in the caverns below they heard deep chanting and singing.

"What am I to do?" she said. It had only been a few days, but her bruises were still visible. Her entire neck was purple, and she had scabs all over her body. She looked at him pleading in a way that she never plead with anyone. Rafael had known about the trouble she was getting into, and maybe he knew how to get out of it.

"This is a troublesome plot you've fallen into Alana!" he said with a resigned smile, "you're being outmaneuvered by people who spend their entire life lusting for power. These are hard days here in Atlas. The old ways are crumbling, and some new power arises. I always considered that you would naturally ascend to the throne when you reached the age, and Jacques as caretaker would step down peacefully. But it appears clear that is not to be. The future is hazy to me and the priests here, I can only see one day at a time."

Alana sighed disappointedly. This was the Rafael she remembered. Kind, loyal, hardworking, totally devoid of any shred of insight or creativity.

"What do you think is the right course of action?" he said, trying to resurrect his reputation in even a small way.

Alana sat looking this way and that. Her men had taken turns being round-the-clock guards for her, but this couldn't last forever. Something was going to give, and she had to figure out a way that the thing that gave wasn't her life. "What do you think," she said, with some hesitation, "what do you think is the will of the gods?" She pursued her lips in the tiniest bit of rage at being reduced to asking another authority what an absent authority thought about her.

"Honestly Alana, I don't know if they care," Rafael said.

Alana looked at him in disbelief. "Of course they care about you, dummy," she said, "otherwise why would they go to the trouble of ordaining my ancestor, Minos the Conqueror, as our king? Why would they have visited my grandfather, King Leo, in his moment of despair to bring about our salvation? Why would they have walked the road with each of my predecessors, but then suddenly stop caring now?" Alana looked at him in disgust. "No, that's not how these things work. They care all right. They care about me. There has been no revocation of my right to rule, let alone my right to live! In five hundred years we have preserved this people, this empire. I have a divine right passed onto me in an unbroken line." Alana struggled, but stood with some pain and brought herself to full height, standing into a beam of light that was now passing through the stained-glass windows into the temple. "I am the queen to be," she said, "and I intend to exercise my right to lead and guide this nation. The stars are moving my way. They can't kill me off."

Rafael looked down so she wouldn't see him rolling his eyes. Alana stood for another moment before it got awkward and Rafael looked up. "You done yet?" he said.

"I'm good," she said, and sat back down.

"Alana," Rafael said, "I do not think you will find your answers here. The plot against you is deadly, and we cannot divine who is friend or foe. I think," and he flinched anticipating her reaction to his next sentence, "I think you need to speak with your oldest ally."

Alana's temper was legendary, but she managed to hold it in enough to ask, "who?" though she could guess.

"Someone who can point you to other allies, other loyalists in the government." He said.

"Surely you don't mean to suggest..." she said.

Rafael replied, "that you should go see your mo..."

"Mother?" Alana interjected. "No."

"Yes." Rafael said.

Alana bit her tongue and pursed her lips. She was really, really hoping he wouldn't say that. Like some serious hope. She and her mom weren't exactly best of friends. Alana was her only child so it's not like there was any internecine conflict there, it's just her mom was...

"My mom is a total nutjob!" she released. "She's a religious fanatic!" she shouted to the confusion of priests within earshot.

"No offense intended, of course," she quickly added.

"None taken," Rafael lied again.

"You know what happened when my father died. She was catatonic for a week; I still haven't been able to get her to tell me everything that happened without her babbling about some dark plot from Hades to ascend and consume humanity. Ever since she woke up, she's never been the same. Why she is so devoted to the Oracle to this day she consults her on her meal choices. It's totally bizarre!" Alana caught herself before she talked about her mom's habit of reading entrails and crap like that (pun intended).

"In her defense, she did at least get you good care and education," Rafael offered.

"And immediately absconded to Delphi and stopped contact," Alana retorted.

"Maybe she just really loves the gods?" Rafael suggested.

"Let's put it this way: I wouldn't bet on her mental faculties," Alana said.

"I don't know what to tell you Alana," Rafael replied.

Alana looked at Rafael long and hard, and he shrugged and gave her the most sympathetic glance he could muster when he had nary an ounce of sympathy in his body, but Alana knew he was right. She didn't really have any other choice.

"Well, thanks," she said, and stood and walked back to the entrance, where a soldier waited to accompany her back to the barracks.

"You're welcome," Rafael said. "Who's to say what the gods want anyway? You should stop by the Oracle while you're there!"

"Hmph!" Alana grunted.

But she knew he was right, so Alana emotionally prepared herself for a reunion with someone she had secretly hoped to never see again. She got back to the barracks and packed a few things that day, then went down to the central station and caught a train north to Delphi, at the base of Mount Olympus to the north.

Alana figured she could visit the Oracle without any prior scheduling, given that the Oracle, I dunno, was an Oracle. She arrived at Delphi in the late afternoon.

Delphi today is a sprawling city with planned suburbs spreading out from an old town center, but in those days it was a small backwater: a small central temple for the Oracle up on the primary hill, with a small cow-infested settlement spread out haphazardly on the hillside below, which comprises the old town you may be familiar with. They say that the winding narrow streets of the old town were cow paths they turned into roads, but I wouldn't really believe they put even that amount of effort into planning it.

Several soldiers from her unit had come for this trip; they were fiercely loyal to their leader, and her taking a trip so far away from them made them nervous. The group of them reached the outer gates of the temple complex just as the spring sun started meandering down towards the horizon.

Massive marble walls looked down on them, fully encircling temple hill. There was but one gate to enter, and guarding the entrance stood a phalanx of female soldiers, specially trained temple guards.

"They can't come through here!" the commander shouted at Alana, pointing at her soldiers.

"I know, I know, they're just getting me this far," she said, and looked at her men, "stay nearby. I'll be safe inside; they don't let anyone dangerous in here."

"You mean they don't let men in!" one of her soldiers corrected her.

"Same thing!" she said with a smile and ducked through the phalanx into the gates and into the temple at Delphi.

Alana made her way through the complex quickly, and in the fading light she was just able to find the dwelling place of one of the Oracle's most famous disciples.

Alana knocked on the somewhat makeshift door. "Mom?"

she shouted in.

She could hear some whispered chanting, so she waited a minute before she knocked again. "Mom? It's me, Alana."

The whispering continued.

"Uh, are you in there?"

Whispers.

"Helllllooooooo"

"YOU HEATHEN IT IS EVENPRAYER SO PLEASE MAINTAIN SILENCE IN THE FACE OF THE GODS ZEUS AND HERA AND APOLLO AND HEPH...HEPHAES...THE VOLCANO ONE!" a woman inside screeched out at the top of her lungs.

Alana smiled sheepishly to a few startled passersby. "That's my mom!" she said. "I'm just a chip off the regular ol' block."

A few more minutes passed, and an older silver-haired woman opened the door with forced grace. She was wearing light white robes, and she moved with outlandish gestures, apparently trying her best to appear both regal and humble, a queen mother and a servant to the Oracle at the same time. It just ended up looking like a writhing elf.

"Welcome, daughter of earth and sky, child of Gaia and Uranus," her mom said. "I am Diana, daughter of..."

Alana cut her off at this point and said, "Wait, are you being serious? You're my mom, remember? We're like related and I know you and you haven't seen me for years so maybe we could cut it with the sh..."

At this point Diana cut her off to continue her title, "daughter of Boz, wife of Titus II, inheritor of the throne of King of the Five Nations from Leo the Great,"

Alana rolled her eyes and stood clearly nodding her head right and left, signaling her desire for speed.

Which went totally unheeded by Diana.[5]

---

[5] Later in life dad loved to do his best impression of Alana mimicking her mother from this interaction. It would always bring down the house.

"...but now servant to the Great Oracle," Diana continued, "communicator with the gods, and pronouncer of proclamations, visionary of visions! Welcome, Alana, welcome to my home and servant's quarters. Tell me, are you pure?"

Alana's eye roll could be seen from space at this point.

"Yes mother, I am pure."

Diana pressed on, "but are you pure from the crawlers of the earth and the fowl of the air? Have you spoilt yourself by eating the messengers from the Gods? Have you kept yourself worthy of your station as flower of the earth? Have you trodden in the forbidden holy lands? Are your prayers heard in the heavens? Are you yet heathen? It is just my most sacred desire to see you serve the gods until the day when you are safely dead and outside of temptations' power."

Alana cringed. Her mom always threw in a "safely dead" for good measure, just to remind her she'd rather Alana be dead than irreligious.

Alana raised her tone to a more feminine pitch, and, with a curtsey, replied in the most saccharine way possible, "why yes, I am free of guilt from the death of those messengers from above, I abstain from the beings from beneath, and I have not spoiled the holy lands with my footsteps, and my prayers are frequent and heard."

The power dynamics with a strong-willed mother and strong-willed daughter are always awkward, but especially when the mother insists on treating the adult daughter like a subservient, and Alana figured if this was the way it was going to be, it was the way it was going to be. She had to live after all.

Diana smiled and said, "Well then my daughter, please return to me with honor." And she stepped out of the way to unveil her tiny living quarters, and Alana entered.

"But they're trying to kill me!" Alana objected to her mother's silence after she finished her story.

"Obviously not trying hard enough..." Diana muttered.

"I heard that!" Alana shouted.

"Oh, come on Ally, you've tried to kill me thousands of times over the years. And I'm still alive, aren't I? You're fine, stop blowing things out of proportion." Diana said.

"Blowing things out of proportion?" Alana shouted, "look at me! I could pass for a rainbow trout with all of these bruises."

"I told you not to join the army," Diana said.

"THE ARMY ISN'T TRYING TO KILL ME," she said, "JACQUES IS."

"Oh, come on," Diana said, "you leave Jacques out of this. He's a very good man you know."

"A good man who is trying to kill your daughter, yeah a very good man. Who also, by the way, has no right to rule in the throne of my father...and your husband!" Alana said.

Diana slowly sipped her tea with both hands tight around the cup. "Sure he does," she said, "he's the custodian."

"Custodian being the operative word in that sentence," Alana said. "Jacques is usurping the throne. For good. No more Queen Alana. In fact, if you'll recall, no more Alana."

"Well at least I could explain the lack of letters at that point," Diana said.

Alana ignored the last jab. "Mother," she said, "this is treason. T-R-E-A"

"I can spell treason, you're the one who can't write," Diana said as she swirled her tea some more. "But you have to admit, it wouldn't be the worst thing in the world."

"MY DEATH??!" Alana said.

"No, silly, Jacques taking over. He's done such a good job so far."

"Motherrrrrrrr, that's not the point!" Alana said.

"What is the point?" Diana asked.

"There are two points. A) Don't kill people. Especially me people. B) I'm the queen. Not him. End of story." Alana said.

"Daughter. Alana. I carried you, I birthed you, I raised you.[6] I know you. I love you. Jacques was an excellent advisor to your father, and a good friend to me. He has done an admirable job these past few years ensuring peace and prosperity. Haven't the gods anointed him? He is, after all, older, more experienced, wiser, and in these unsettled times what we really need is a man who won't be blown about with every tuft of wind or news report from abroad. I remember when you had to wait weeks to hear from abroad, but nowadays with these telegrams machines you get information in an instant, the wires just buzz, buzz, buzz and off you go hearing about some new war to fight in some foreign soil.

"No, my daughter, the old ways are crumbling, and we need experience to guide us through these uncertain times. I love you, my daughter, but you are not Jacques." Diana looked at her intently, as though she had just spoken the truest words of love any human could have uttered.

Alana did not receive them as such, and in one of the only times I have on record, was speechless. She reached outside rage into that country beyond; where iron glows white hot and you are so indignant you're just stuck still, jaw dropped, mouth open, and stunned that another human could be so different.

Diana interpreted this silence as consent, and continued, "I have been uttering many prayers and offering sacrifices for our nation for these last many years, my daughter, and never have I received a sign of your anointing. I've watched the stars these many nights, and they told me you would be here tonight and we would be speaking, and that I would be telling you these words, but they do not say that Alana is to be queen."

"Do they say I should be alive? Because that's really the

---

[6] This is not strictly true, of course, especially after Titus' death, but Alana clearly thought it would be in poor taste and also a distraction from the main thrust of her point to argue that now.

issue we're dealing with. It just happens to be related to the fact that I will be queen." Alana pushed back into her chair, sensing futility.

Diana drew back in her chair and sat upright as her eyes got larger and she shook her head melodramatically as she said, "No, my daughter, they say that Jacques is our ruler. Leave well enough alone and let the experience and wisdom of an older man like Jacques be our King."

"Custodian," Alana corrected her and continued, "and I wasn't asking to be queen, I was asking to be alive. The queen thing will sort itself out independently."

"Sometimes our ambitions have to die in order for us to truly live," Diana said.

"In this case, you know this means my ambitions AND ME are dead right?" Alana said.

"Oh, stop being so melodramatic," came the reply.

There are moments in life when you will speak with someone who you consider to be reasonably intelligent. Maybe they'll have a similar background or be involved in a similar pursuit as you. And it will be a breath of fresh air in your life, and I recommend you take note, and get on your knees in gratitude after you find each and every kindred soul.

And then there will come a day when you speak to someone like Diana, and you uncover a chasm so deep, so wide, and so utterly bewildering that there is no hope of a possibility of bridging the gap.

Alana recognized this as one of those moments, and in a rare moment of wisdom, she closed her mouth, bowed her head and sipped her tea and did NOT say anything snarky about how she was going to go get a second opinion from an Oracle who might value her life just a tad bit more, and she and her mom left, on the surface, on reasonable terms, with the intractable mother-daughter conflict again buried beneath the surface.

Alana made her way back outside and set up a makeshift

camp with her soldiers to wait for the morning.

Later that night a couple of her men awoke to hear her in the distance, beating the bark out of a nearby tree with her bayonet, screaming half of all now-known profanities. She then proceeded to invent the other half. She was encyclopedic in her breadth and depth of invoking fecal imagery and sacred acts.

Needless to say, the morning found Alana tired and hoarse, but ready to get moving on. She once again ascended to the temple and made her way to the inner sanctum.

The cleaning ceremonies took most of the day: any visitor to the Oracle must be properly purified before she would be allowed her presence. Her disciples took her job seriously: The Oracle was the living embodiment of the Gods and spoke for them. Diana was sure to audibly huff disapprovingly wherever possible when she was involved with Alana, just to help remind her how she felt. You know how mothers are.

They started in the morning with the long walk across the grand courtyard. At every quarter hour Alana was allowed to take one step. There were some chantings about patience and long suffering in greeting the gods, but the lessons were lost on Alana in the hot sun. Then at noon she reached the statue of Athena, and was whisked away to the hall of alters, where a dozen alters lay ready to offer sacrifice to a pantheon of gods.

Alana made up her burnt offerings and was taken to a brass tub where she ceremonially washed her hands and her feet.

As the afternoon heat rose, a very weary Alana was finally ready to meet the Oracle.

With a sigh, Alana entered the final chamber in the back of the temple compound. A large circular temple, encircled by a white marble colonnade, and capped by a dome over fifty feet high. In the center burned a huge fire, and surrounding the entire chamber stood poles holding burning incense. That is to say, smoke was everywhere; some of it pleasantly smelling, and the rest the kind that sticks to you for ages after a campfire, though none of them would have recognized anything different, because they all pretty much smelled like campfire[7] all the time.

High priestesses of the most important goddesses stood encircled around the outer edges of the inner sanctum and hummed. The Oracle was seated on the ground, behind the fire, and pretended not to notice her entrance.

Her hair was the first thing Alana noticed: it was absolutely gorgeous. It was long and silvery white down to her waist and would have been longer still were it not twisted and braided every which way. The woman herself couldn't have been a day under sixty, but the hair was breathtaking. The Oracle wore a light toga woven from merino wool which seemed to float erratically above a bubbling volcanic lake.

The priestess of Athena challenged Alana as she entered, "Who enters the temple of the Oracle today?"

"I am Alana, daughter of Titus II, crown princess of all Atlas," Alana announced loudly to the hushed group. "I seek the wisdom of the gods."

"Then you shall have it." announced the priestess, and with that, the Oracle stood up from behind the fire, rounded it, and approached Alana and took her hand and bowed.

"Welcome, daughter of Titus II. Long have I foreseen and awaited your coming. You have seen the stars?" she asked.

"Yes, Oracle, I have observed their movements, and come with their blessing." Alana said.

"And you shall have mine as well." the Oracle replied. She picked up a crown of laurel leaves and placed it on her head. "What troubles the daughter of Titus II, and what wisdom does she seek?"

---

[7] And poop. Oh, the constant smell of poop they waded through back in those barbaric days before widespread indoor plumbing.

"There are forces that conspire against what the gods have ordained, and they seek the death of hers whose right it is to reign," Alana said to hushed gasps from around the temple. "There are none to stand up for the right." she continued. "I seek the counsel of the gods to know how to expunge the cancer that erodes our nation, our government, our people. I wish to crush the revolt in our midst and put an end to those who attack the ways of the gods."

The Oracle nodded deeply, "The old ways are crumbling," she said, "and great uncertainty rests upon us. Tell me daughter of Titus II, do you come to counsel the gods, or come to be instructed?"

Alana paused. In religious parlance pugilism she knew she could easily be beaten by the Oracle, so she went the safe route. "I come to be instructed" she reluctantly said.

The Oracle nodded again, "Because most who enter these chambers enter to instruct the heavens on their proper course, but I warn you that you must obey what you hear or you will be cursed two fold for your disobedience and arrogance. Olympus does not abide man's counsel," she said, and then with a smirk continued, "though sometimes it abides a woman's."

To be fair, Alana wasn't really expecting to be implicitly chastised when she came, and kind of just thought she'd get a response like, "yup, sounds cool," so she was super taken aback by this exchange, but I got to tell you, I don't have a lot of sympathy because seriously the Oracle claims to be speaking for deity, and you just don't mess around with a power that claims it can turn you into a tree.

Nonetheless, her experience the past evening had really put her in a good place for burying her bruised emotions very deeply, so Alana just smiled and nodded in reply until the Oracle did something else.

They say it took several minutes. It was probably awkward.

Eventually the Oracle put her arm around Alana's shoulder and led her to the other side of the fire, where a cauldron sat propped up in between three sticks. It was close enough to the fire that the water boiled from the heat. She reached into a bag around her neck and pulled out a handful of powder and threw it into the water which then exploded with a hiss. Smoke poured out from the top and wafted towards the dome above. She began half chanting half singing at the top of her lungs.[8]

"Hear us, oh gods, and send us thy messengers! Let us know of thy will and thy power! Let our words reach Olympus and let us receive of the matchless wisdom of its inhabitants! Oh, you who have cast out the Titans and have borne the travails of humanity, hear us and guide us! Here a child of Gaia seeks knowledge! As you have every other time, dispatch with your wisdom to me, guide me with your guidance, let me be your voice on earth!"

At this, the priestesses around the room chimed in unison, "As you have so many times before!"

The Oracle continued, "Bring us the wisdom of the ages and tell us your will!"

The priestesses again chimed in unison, "Tell us your will!"

The Oracle began speaking in what would then be referred to as tongues.[9] She moved and chanted and oohed and aahed. She sashayed her way across the temple floor, circling the fire and occasionally jolting as if she had been electrocuted, her eyes closed the entire time, her hair flowing in the breeze, swirling the smoke around, and breaking through clouds of incense every round. She danced effortlessly and beautifully, moving her body in ways Alana did not think were possible for

---

[8] This is the polite way of saying she was singing in a totally monotone voice. She probably thought it was melodic.

[9] And as I refer to it, gibberish.

an older woman.

Just when Alana was formulating an escape plan to get the heck out of dodge, starting to back away slowly, the Oracle abruptly stopped. The priestesses released doves which flew into the dome above, and the Oracle kicked the pot and dumped its full contents into the fire, putting it out immediately. This filled the entire room with a smoky steam to where it was impossible to even see your hand in front of your face. The Oracle fell down on the marble with a shout and remained motionless until the air in the room cleared out.

After a period of calm, a priestess came and raised her by the hand, and she led the Oracle and Alana into a small enclave in the back of the room, where the Oracle sat and stared just above Alana into the distance and began to speak again, this time in a very loud, very monotone, very robotic voice:

"Daughter of Titus the second, these are the words of the gods to you, sent to you from their dwellings on high in the holy lands above. You are to seek that which is lost, no matter how long or how far."

And with that, she slumped down and said no more.

Jacques usually woke up before sunrise, though today the rays from the sun chased him out of bed well after he would have started work on any other day. The last few days had been incredibly stressful, and he was up most of the night before receiving reports from abroad, and in discussions with the ambassador from Medea, whom he had called in to explain the actions of his nation. There were worrying developments along the southern border, and it was becoming increasingly clear that Medea was planning something. Something big.

He had seen this before. Years before the nations were wracked from within by waves of revolution fever and outbreak of civil war by forces demanding an end to the monarchy. The anarchic revolutions were quelled and resolved, but they were not so far distant as for the elder generation to remember the descent into violence and anarchy. Avoiding the worst was an ever-present concern on his mind.

He took care to sweep up the obsidian shards he'd been tinkering with as a hobby lately, wouldn't want anyone to walk in on those.

He lived in a small apartment a quick walk from Parliament. He felt it would have been needlessly confrontational to have moved into the palace, and since he had no family, no entourage, it suited him just fine to live simply. He didn't care about his spartan living arrangements, his lack of servants, and general absence of wealth because he had all the power he could ever want. Also, a part of him wanted to believe that he was egalitarian to his core, though I'm pretty sure everyone thinks they believe in giving everyone a fair shake, they just happen to also believe that they themselves should get a fairer shake.

Today, he hoped, would be a relief from the stress of the week as he walked through the bustling parliament square. He had no planned meetings in the morning, though plenty of legislation he was meeting with the prime minister about later that day. While every piece of my soul wishes to describe to you in detail the operations of the caretaker government of Jacques LePen (fascinating in its own right and deserving of a book), I must curtail my inner political scientist in the hopes of making this book readable, and merely comment to you that they considered themselves a temporary Parliamentary Republic, with Jacques playing the role of unelected head of state. Lawmaking was the realm of Parliament, and so he spent his considerable energy putting together a series of dominoes to redefine the entire state.

But that is a story for another time, and by that, I mean never, so please think kindly of me.

Jacques entered his dark office and made a beeline to his desk where he stood, thumbing through papers before he opened his shutters. Rays of light peeked through and into the room, and you could see the tiny dust particles floating in and out of the light.

"You used me," a voice said behind him.

Jacques didn't startle at all. He continued shuffling through his papers without a care in the world.

"Hello Rafael," he said, "nice of you to stop by. Are you here to provide some kind of actually useful service to your country?"

"How dare you," Rafael said, flustered. "I can't believe you would use me like that to kill Alana."

"I certainly have no idea what you're talking about," Jacques said, totally relaxed, barely paying attention to the conversation.

"You told me she was in danger in the palace," Rafael said, "so I told her to go to the barracks, which was your trap all along!"

"Oh, so you are the one who endangered the princess!" Jacques said, feigning surprise. "I'll have the inspectors visit you at once," he threatened.

"I'll inspect you myself!" Rafael said, and whipped out a small knife from under his long orange robes. "I can talk, you know," he said.

"But can you?" Jacques said, finally looking up from his paperwork. "You didn't even have the backbone to tell Alana."

"How do you know that?" Rafael said, taking a step forward, and moving the knife closer to Jacques.

"Oh Rafael, you sweet summer child, you truly are an idiot." Jacques said and he picked up the papers he just finished and tossed them into an outgoing bin on his desk and snapped his fingers.

From behind his desk two hulking men materialized from the large bookshelf. One was holding a shotgun waist high, pointed at Rafael's general direction. The other held up a huge .30-06 caliber rifle aiming directly at his head from point blank range. Rafael's eyes grew wide, and he immediately dropped the knife.

"I...was just trying to get your...attention," he stammered.

"And I yours," Jacques replied. "Titus tried that on me once too, and he never forgot the lesson. You impetuous rebel you. What kind of idiot do you take me for?" He motioned the guards forward: one picked up the knife carefully and put it in a bag, and the other punched Rafael in the gut. As he doubled over in pain, the guard hit him on the head, knocking him to the ground.

"Look Rafael," Jacques said, "I know you are young, and I can see you are frustrated, but you have to understand that threatening a government official is treason."

"Wait, wait, wait, wait. I am being treasonous??!" Rafael coughed from the ground. "Take a long look in the mirror buddy, you are the one trying to kill the crown princess? That's definitely a treasonous take on the law."

"When are you going to learn that I am the law," Jacques said as his voice dropped low and he narrowed his eyes at her. "I could have you executed tomorrow for this. Just like this!" he snapped again. "In fact," he said, "I could have you killed right now," he looked up to the guard leering over him, and the guard put the barrel of the shotgun into his head. "You dummies always make this so easy," Jacques said.

Rafael's eyes began to widen. This is not how he anticipated this turn of events. He wasn't going to kill the guy, just wanted to scare the little bureaucrat and get him to start talking shop. This...this was something else entirely.

"You wouldn't," he said, scowling at him. "They would find you out."

"I won't," Jacques said and waved the guard off, "but they wouldn't have."

The guard stood Rafael up and pulled an arm behind his back and twisted it up until he sweat from the pain.

"I couldn't kill a priest," Jacques said, chuckling. "It's bad luck you know. Even if the old ways are dying." He waved them out, and the guards took Rafael down into the depths of the cellars and locked him up.

"Apollo curse you all!" he screamed, and then fell down, crying.

CHAPTER 4

"Hold up!" the commander shouted at Alana as she approached the gate.

"What's going on up there?" she shouted back. It was getting late, and she was exhausted from the day-long affair at the Oracle.

"Just give it a second," the commander shouted back.

Alana stood back behind the gate and watched as an absolutely gigantic wooden horse was pushed through the gate and into the temple grounds.

"Do you think she's big enough?" Alana hollered out, laughing at the absurd spectacle of a dozen temple guards heaving and pushing the statue into the main courtyard.

"Just a few more feet," the commander yelled out to the women, to the sounds of frustrated moans. But with another heft the women had rolled the gigantic statue into the place of honor for the evening's festivities.

"It's Equisid tonight," the commander yelled to Alana.

"Equi-who?" Alana replied back, unable to hear over the din.

"You know, honoring Poseidon?" the commander shouted

back. "We can't forget anyone around here or we get in major trouble with the Olympians!"

"Ahhh, of course," Alana nodded, and walked out the gate into Delphi, still chuckling at the spectacle.

"Did you guys see that?" she said to her men, who were sprawled outside the gate, waiting for her.

"Did we ever? They've been trying to get it up here all day; it came in on the barge," one of the men pointed down to the Andaluvian.

"Well," Alana said as she looked up and judged the time. "Probably too late to get going, let's set up here and get going in the morning."

"Aye aye captain," the men replied, and went about preparing for the evening.

About that exact same time, Ethan ran quietly in the woods far in the deep western borderlands of Atlas. You could barely hear his feet touch the ground whenever he ran: he padded his way through the forest. Part of this was his youth and part of it his build; he was spry and light, and even standing still it appeared his entire body was taut as a bowstring.

He wasn't the best hunter in the world, not the best tracker, not the best shot, not the best outdoorsman, but if you were ever to try to create some sort of awesome competition where those skills were measured simultaneously, he'd definitely be in somewhere in the top ten. Part of this was his genetic advantage, part of it was growing up in a rural community in the mountains, but he always liked to say that it was mostly because he hated being hungry.

He spotted the deer just down the ridgeline and allowed himself to coast just a little bit. That deer was tiring. The meat from the buck would be his first large meal all winter, and the jerky would last him another month, along with whatever he could scavenge. This was his mealtime ticket out of winter.

He always relished the spring, not necessarily in the romantic way we all think about the return of blossoms and grass and barbecuing outside, but in the way that it meant coming out of the hunger of winter. He'd been out hunting four days now, tracking the buck for half a day, slowly gaining on it and wearing it down over the long distances he was so adept at covering. Long distance pursuit was his specialty.

The first stars came out and the moon began to rise. He paused to catch his bearings by looking up to follow them. His path had been circuitous as always, but it looked like he was only a day's journey back to his winter camp. A day's journey with a deer in tow that is! He doggedly picked back up his pursuit. His feet shuffled over the wet leaves from last fall, skimming over streams of meltwater, the only sound an occasional splash as he hit a puddle from the last rainfall. The landscape was brown and damp, prior to blossoming, in a general season in those mountains that I like to refer to as, "hideously ugly".

There were hundreds of poor settlers in the borderlands, all trying to eke out a living in an age of transformation. Ethan wasn't like them. While he was an excellent outdoorsman and obviously could take care of himself, apart from that there was nothing about him that would indicate he would lead a life special in any respects. Nothing, that is, except his mother.

Like so many before and since, Ethan inherited his significance.

"What was that?" one of the soldiers asked suddenly.

"What?" Alana asked as she looked up. She had been too deep in thought to notice anything as they sat around the fire eating a late dinner in the cold of the evening just outside the temple.

In the distance they heard a scream.

"That!" the soldier said, and dropping his dinner, picked up his rifle and ran to the gate.

Two uneasy temple guards challenged him as he approached.

"No men!" they shouted.

They all heard another scream from inside the temple.

"Oh, come on!" the soldier replied.

"Make way!" Alana shouted, running by the soldier and grabbing his rifle as she slipped past the nervous guards and into the courtyard. Loud voices were echoing around the granite walls.

Just as she entered, she watched the giant wooden horse erupt in a huge explosion, wrenching her backwards and throwing her on the ground.

The guards behind her were blown backwards as well past the gate and into the arms of the unsuspecting soldier, and they tumbled into a pile on the ground.

Alana moaned on the ground and rubbed her eyes, finding her eyebrows singed from the flames. She rolled over to see gigantic flames lapping 30 feet into the air. As her hearing came back, she could just make out rifle fire on the far end of the courtyard.

"Attack! Attack!" a guard shouted from a watch tower up above. "Shut the gates! Don't let them bring in their allies!"

One of the guards on the ground managed to extract herself from the confusion and scraped her way over to the gate, and pulling out her bayonet, cut the emergency rope. An iron gate slammed shut.

The other guard, left outside with the soldiers, looked at her companion and shrugged.

"Michaela I'm sorry! No way in or out now, fan out and watch for the escape!" the inside guard shouted. "Whoever it is, don't let them escape! Don't let them kidnap the Oracle!"

"On it!" Michaela shouted, and she began setting up Alana's men at positions around the giant wall.

Inside, Alana picked herself up and shook off the blast. She picked up her rifle and made her way carefully around the giant flames in the center of the courtyard, feeling the heat against her face.

"What in Hades is going on here?" she muttered as she walked.

Memories of his mother filled Ethan's thoughts as he followed the deer's tracks. Was she happy wherever she was? What happened to her? And most importantly, would she be proud of him? The last question loomed over him day and night, an unanswerable brick wall blocking his train of thought.

On this like many other hunts, as he pounded along he entered a state of calm meditation, his mind wandering through daydreams where he captained one of the newest steel-hulled coal-fired steamers, powering through deadly seas into undiscovered countries filled with all manner of monsters and demons, all of which were quickly dispatched through his own bravery, earning himself accolades that would be pinned on his chest by the Prime Minister himself at a grand ceremony in Parliament.

He, naturally, did not imagine much of his actual projected future: hunting, gathering, subsistence farming in poor soil, and then picking up the occasional odd job in between hewing lumber or coal mining. Really, in general he was just destined to be kind of screwed. Life is tough for an orphan refugee, even if he was an adult.

Ethan stopped without a sound and took a knee. He brought his rifle up, scoped his shot, and paused. He furrowed his dirt-smeared brow under his bright red hair shining through the layers of sweat and filth he acquired in the chase.

He watched as the deer ate and bounded off again.

"Maybe you are destined for Artemis," Ethan said, and put his rifle down and shrugged. He stayed there for what he said was an hour but was probably only a few moments before the presence of his mother descended upon him.

He was overcome with emotion as he felt her close by, could almost smell her, could almost hear her. The rest of the world stopped for a moment and he was wrapped in her love.

And in that moment, her green gem around his neck began to glow.

"What is going on?" He muttered. He'd never seen it do anything, not since he found it in his bed the night his mother died.

From the green gem erupted snaky tendrils of light that crept up his chest and face and wrapped around his head. The light exploded in his eyes and he fell into vision. His soul lifted up, and he found himself in his mother's embrace once again.

"Mother!" he shouted with joy.

Her soul encompassed him with love, and she paused time to commune with her son once more.

She drew back and nodded at Ethan, and said, "Follow me." She beckoned him with her hands and continued, "You are needed."

She walked away, but Ethan found himself stuck. He couldn't move to follow. "Wait!" He said, "I can't walk!"

But Jane just looked around and smiled and beckoned again.

He immediately dropped out of the vision and back into his body with a heavy gasp and a deep unsatisfied longing he couldn't shake.

But just as he filled with despair, he watched as the green gem sparked again and from it erupted a large dark circle with green glowing edges right in front of him.

"What is this..." he muttered, uncertain of what to do.

From his back he felt just the tiniest push towards the portal and a faint whisper.

"Ah," he said, "okay mom. I'll follow you."

And he stepped through.

Alana watched in horror as for the second time in her life

a green circle appeared in front of her, and from within the black center stepped out a young man.

"Oh no you don't, not here!" Alana shouted, and pulled an ink-black knife from her boot and pointed it menacingly at the man.

"Where did you get that?!" Ethan demanded.

"Where did you get that?!" Alana shouted back, pointing at the green mist circling back into the gem around his chest.

"Never mind that, you have my mother's runedagger!" Ethan whined, pointing at the knife.

"Your what?" Alana replied, confused. "Why don't you go back to the eternal pit from whence you came?"

"And why don't you stop threatening me crazy lady?" Ethan asked, and then looking to his right, he pointed at the giant burning horse. "And just what in the blazes is that?"

"I said, go back!" Alana shouted, "men aren't allowed in here!"

"Lady, I don't know where here is!" Ethan shouted in exasperation. "And stop threatening me with my mother's dagger!"

"Your mother?" Alana said, coming to her senses and looking at the blade. She remembered that fateful night many years previous.

In the distance they both heard shots fired.

Ethan dropped to the ground. "What is wrong with you people?"

Alana took a hard look at the man. He couldn't have been older than twenty, she thought, and even in the dark, she realized his skin was pale. He was a westerner; she was sure of it.

"You're far from home boy," she said, and then looking in the direction of the shots, then back at him, said, "oh come on, follow me."

And she jogged off towards the shots in the distance.

"You're going THAT way?" Ethan yelled at her. "You can

still hear right?" he shouted, "that's the direction of the explosions, you meant to go the other way!" he pointed generally behind.

But Alana kept on moving. Ethan looked around, and seeing no other viable options, picked up his rifle and followed her.

Zara slammed against the door again. Nothing. They had barricaded the other side. She pounded and pounded as panic filled her soul and she turned around to see the back wall.

The fires were growing.

Smoke filled her home and she was gripped by a splitting headache. She dropped down to the floor to try to catch a breath of air, but smoke was pouring through the house as a raging conflagration began to form behind her. Her home of dry wood and thatch was a tinderbox waiting to explode.

She clawed at life with shallow desperate breaths. This was not how it was supposed to end. This was not to be.

The windows were her only way out. She was going to have to jump through and smash open the shutters and hope they hadn't barricaded the other sides. This was not going to be pleasant.

But just as the fires began to rage and engulf the entire back wall, she watched in shock as a man calmly emerged from the flames and walked the few steps across the room to her. He burned with a yellow fire, the flames licking and surrounding him, and each step left a black imprint of a foot in the floor. Each breath brought her in and out of death.

The burning man dropped to a knee and touched his forehead with his index and middle finger, then brought those to her forehead. She felt a searing heat throughout her entire body, and her headache immediately died.

The burning man smiled and winked, and, as the flames walked their way up to him from behind, he whispered, "Go now."

He lifted her up by the hand and then he curled over into a ball. He paused to breathe in, and then expelled a huge breath out and roared the roar of a dam bursting: it was heard for miles around, and left ears ringing for a half hour. He unfurled and with a fury he exploded.

Zara was thrown backwards through a window and crashed through with the shutters bursting open and splintering from the force of the explosion. Shrapnel hit various federals outside, and Scipio was blown off his feet. Again. Zara landed in brush ten feet away. "Enough with the getting tossed around, eh?" she grumbled, and shaking herself off, she looked to see her home in ruins, a mushroom cloud of destruction overhead, and Medea's finest federal police blown onto their backs.

From her home a bright light streaked up and over her head and into the beyond, smoke being laid out behind the light as it flew, leading away from the police and into the desolation beyond the mountain.

That was her sign. She followed it and ran.

She now ran back up the path she had walked the night before through the forests of sunflowers glowing in the predawn darkness, lighting the way. Behind her she heard shouting as the federals picked themselves up and followed. She streaked up the path into a canyon pass darting up and over the rocks in the way, her grey cloak billowing out behind her.

Scipio dusted himself off and began shouting incomprehensible orders to the currently somewhat-deaf pursuing force, but eventually someone picked up on the general direction of ordering, and they began firing on her.

Zara dipped and bobbed, bouncing off every corner, and up and up into the canyon she went. Sunflowers exploded in shots on every side of her, laying down a carpet of glittering yellow petals on the path as a royal honor for her to walk. She ran up the canyon as it narrowed, with no escape from the shooting.

The federals formed a line behind her, and lifted their rifles to fire in unison, to end this chase. They steadied, aimed up the canyon to where Zara neared the pass, and...

From over the pass came the sun, its rays peeking over just as the fingers started to press on triggers. Its overwhelming light and heat seared their eyes. The federals screeched in pain and shaded their eyes to no avail; they could not see her in the sun. Zara paused at the top of the pass and allowed herself a moment of jubilation. She raised her arms in victory as she ran down the other side, the rising sun framing her heroic stance as she flew.

They stood no chance after that: the federal police were lowlanders, and Zara had lived in these mountains for years. They reached the pass with their lungs burning, gasping for air, and on the far side they saw her reaching the desolation.

The federals had read about the desolation and seen it on a map, but nothing could prepare them for the sight: they gasped as they looked upon it. Stretching out across the entire horizon as far as they could see in any direction there were hundreds of miles of flat salt desert. No plants, no water, no shade, nothing to protect you from the sun, and death as your only destiny.

Jaws dropped, and they watched as she reached the bottom of the mountain and sprinted into the barren beyond.

Scipio found them watching her an hour later when he made up the pass, coughing, heaving, burning, and occasionally puking his way as he climbed.

"So, she's off into the desolation eh?" he said.

They each nodded the nod of failure.

He cursed under his breath and weighed his options. They were not prepared for this. It was so crazy he didn't even consider the possibility.

"Well, just as well," Scipio gave a resigned sigh, "death is assured. Come now, fan out along the mountain range, and wait her out a week. If she doubles back, we'll see her long before she makes it back. And if she doesn't come this way, she'll be dead."

Each of the federals had presumed as much, and while a few went back for their supplies and equipment they had left behind, the rest dutifully began scoping out their watch posts for the next week.

Not that it mattered. Nobody passed through the desolation alone and unprepared and lived.

CHAPTER 5

Alana walked through the dark halls of the temple padding as quietly as she could with her rifle up and at the ready. Behind her Ethan nervously looked around, not quite sure what he was looking for, though he did notice one small detail.

"You have a limp?" he whispered.

"No, no, just hurt my foot," she answered.

"Looks painful," he replied.

"It is," she said.

The distant shots suddenly stopped. Alana looked back at Ethan and silently pointed down to the right on the next hallway. She was pretty sure they had come from down there. He nodded and gave her a shaky thumbs up and followed as she rounded the corner.

"At least he's quiet," she thought to herself.

A voice echoed out down the hallway and Alana froze.

Ethan tapped her on the shoulder. "What?" he mouthed.

The voice echoed again. "Diana!" it angrily demanded, "Open up!"

Diana was kneeling in prayer when she heard the

explosion. She picked herself up off her creaky knees and opened her door out into the temple grounds to see the giant pillar of fire from the courtyard reaching up into the heavens. She froze in her tracks, panicking, and not quite sure what to do. Hearing gunshots convinced her to close and lock the door.

She knelt to pray some more, that is, until the pounding on the other side.

"Diana!" the voice called out, "Diana, open up!" it demanded.

She blew out her lamp.

"We know you're in there, old woman!" the man erupted, then to another he said, "Break it in."

In quick succession four rifles shot into the locking mechanism, and she heard a giant thud against the door. Once, twice, and three times there was a push and a groan, and on the third, the solid oak door gave way and cracked into the room.

She wet herself at the sight of six large heavily armed men outside her door. One of them pushed through the door and grabbed her by the wrist and brought her out into the portico.

"Where is it?" the largest of the men demanded. He was easily six foot five, and muscularly built. He had short cropped hair, and a pale light in his eyes.

"Who are you?" Diana managed to say in her moment of fear.

"Don't you know me old woman?" the man said. "I am Tiberius. You knew my mother."

Diana furrowed her brow. She did not know this man.

"Never mind that," Tiberius said, and then from his pocket he pulled out a leather band laced with gold and silver thread reflecting in the dim light. At the end of the band there was a leather pouch.

Diana's heart sank. She knew that pouch.

"Where is it?" Tiberius demanded.

Alana could not make out what they were looking at. She nudged Ethan and pointed. He cupped his hand to her ear.

"The pouch has a cross, with some kind of snake around it," he whispered.

Alana gasped. "The cross!" she whispered.

They were huddled on the other side of the open portico; both looking through tiny gaps in the stonework to try and make out what was happening across the way.

Tiberius brought himself right up next to Diana and screamed down into her face. "I don't have the time for this lady, so either you're coming with me, or you're telling me, where is the cross!"

"How many?" Alana asked Ethan.

"I count four outside," Ethan whispered, "I think two went in to look for something."

"The cross," Alana said.

"Nobody knows what you're talking about," Ethan hissed. "Now let's get out of here!"

Tiberius held Diana up against the wall by her throat. "You're out of time," he said to Diana, "give it up or come along!"

She gargled as she tried to reply with her throat closed.

Alana saw her mother in extreme pain and couldn't stop herself. "Mother!" Alana screamed out from across the way.

Everyone immediately looked at her. In the darkness they could barely see the whites of her eyes as she pulled up her rifle to shoot.

"No!" Tiberius shouted at the men with him who aimed to fire back, "Go get her!"

Alana fired off a wild shot and bolted back the way she came. Three of the men gave chase. Ethan froze in the shadows, not knowing where to go or what to do, and the men went by, tunnel vision on Alana the whole way.

She ran back down the hallway towards the main courtyard, trying her best not to put too much weight on her injured foot. As she ran, her foot caught an errant stone and she toppled head over heels to the ground. "Pickled Persephone!" she screamed out as she hit the stone.

In a moment she was scrambling to get up, but one of the men crashed into her from behind, tackling her to the ground. They collapsed in a heap, but soon the others arrived, and they roughly took her back to Tiberius.

"So," Tiberius said, "Alana. We meet at last."

The men held her arms back as she looked up at Tiberius. "I don't even know who you are," she said, and she spat on him.

Michaela showed Alana's men the points around the wall where she thought the invaders might try to escape, for escape could be their only plan. Soldiers and guards from around town were mustering, and whoever it was in there would be ousted.

"How would I escape?" she thought. Alana's men lay stationed at strategic points like trees, or where the wall was a little lower, but she wanted to make sure every outcome had been anticipated.

And then it hit her. "The sewer!" she exclaimed and ran to the small grates on the low point on the wall.

"Well, which one of you has it," Tiberius asked. "Diana, you've got a minute before I shoot your daughter," he said, and pulled out a revolver and placed it against Alana's forehead.

"You coward," Alana spat out. "How dare you do this to royalty."

Tiberius practically exploded. "How dare you do THIS to royalty," he yelled, his face bursting red, and his hands shaking. Then, turning to Diana again, he said quietly, but with resolve, "Ten more seconds and this commoner will be dead. This is the last time I ask: where is the silver cross?"

Alana glanced in Ethan's direction. "Surely that coward

could help out here?" she thought. Her eyes grew wide and for the second time in her life, she began to beg the gods.

"He took it to his grave!" Diana whispered through Tiberius' gloved hand. "He had them take it to his grave."

Tiberius relaxed and smiled, pulling the revolver away from Alana and relaxing his hand from Diana's throat.

"That's it?" he said with glee. "Unguarded? Just out there," his smile grew and there was a new glint in his eye, "just out there for anyone to take?"

From across the way, Ethan saw Tiberius relax the revolver. "Well, it's now or never," he said.

Tiberius' eyes went wide. An explosion rang out from across the open patio, and the bullet flew straight through his thigh, then into the apartment behind him.

"GAAAHHH!" he screamed in pain and dropped his hands to apply pressure to the wounds.

Alana wasted no time, and as his head went down to look at his leg, she brought up her bad foot and kicked him straight in the face.

Both of them howled in pain at the same time. Tiberius fell backwards and onto the ground, Alana brought her bad foot down and steadied herself on her mother's shoulder.

Holding onto her mom, she looked at her in anger. "You never told me about the cross," she said.

She pulled on her shoulder, and started to hobble towards Ethan yelling, "Cover fire!" She dragged her mother along behind her as she hobbled her way.

Ethan fired at the invaders, keeping them from harming Alana or Diana: he was on the dark side of the small courtyard, practically invisible save for the muzzle flash; the invaders were lit up from Diana's room.

"Get them get them!" Tiberius yelled, frantically bandaging up his leg as best he could, and frantically waving at his men to make a move, but they were pinned down in the light.

"How did you miss him at that range??" Alana hissed at Ethan as they reached him.

"What do you mean how did I miss, I hit the guy!" Ethan protested.

"The legs don't count, hit him in the head!" Alana said.

"I'm not going to kill a stranger you homicidal maniac!" Ethan fired back. "I don't know him, let alone you!"

"Oh great, I'm stuck in a gunfight with some kind of priest!" Alana said.

Ethan went red with indignation. "You're the one in a temple!!"

Alana motioned back towards the way they came and started out. Ethan followed after firing a couple more shots.

They headed back towards the center of the temple, and Diana started running towards the grand courtyard and the burning horse.

"The gate is closed!" Alana called out. "No way out that way!"

Diana paused for a moment, then pointed towards the hall of alters. "We can get up to the wall this way, there might be a way down from up there!" and she guided them into the large open courtyard filled with altars. Whereas this afternoon it was lively and filled with sacrifices and activity, tonight it was pitch black and dead.

"This way!" Diana whispered and rushed ahead. Ethan followed her quickly, then looked back at Alana who was struggling to keep up.

"Why'd you kick him with your bad foot?" he said.

"Worth it," Alana whispered as she limped by.

Behind them they heard Tiberius. "Alana!" he shouted into the dark courtyard. "Stop!"

Michaela bent over and walked through the drainage pipes

underneath the temple. She had spent an unfortunate summer down here a few years back on maintenance duty and could pretty well navigate the system.

She headed towards the grand courtyard, but then heard the yell of a male voice. "Alana" she thought it said.

"I think that's coming from the hall of alters..." she mumbled and took a right turn and went towards the sounds.

All three of them dropped to the ground and hid by nearby alters.

Tiberius laughed, "I saw the limp, you can't get out of here," he said.

"I see you have one yourself!" Alana called out, and nodded her head at Ethan, who popped up and took a quick wild shot.

Tiberius didn't even flinch as the shot flew overhead. "I've got all of my men here, the game is up," he said. "You're coming with me."

Tiberius continued to walk forward with every word. Alana could hear his men making their way across the dark courtyard.

"I'm not going to let you touch my mother," Alana said, pulling out the black dagger from her boot.

"Oh, I don't need your mother," Tiberius said. "Just you this time."

Alana gritted her teeth.

From down below, Michaela triangulated the voices as best she could, slung her rifle over her shoulder, and climbed up the grimy rungs of one of the drains. She reached the grates and held them with her hands, trying to see where everyone was.

"Time's up!" Tiberius said. He had ducked down now, moving from altar to altar, to avoid any more wild shots from Alana's unpredictable bodyguard. He looked around the altar he had paused at for cover and caught a glimpse of one of them not too far away.

"If we can get her before the garrison gets here, this will be the biggest coup of the century..." he muttered.

Tiberius cupped his hands around his mouth and yelled out his final warning, "You're coming with us dead or alive!".

"Dead!" someone yelled into the fray. "She'll come but you'll be dead!" Before anyone could register what was happening, Michaela popped out on top of an altar from the drainage tunnels and immediately fired into the approaching men. With a lightning fast "pop, pop", she tagged one in the arm, and grazed the stomach of another before anyone could react.

"Down!" Tiberius shouted at his men.

"Up and in!" Michaela called out to Alana, Diana, and Ethan, who had taken up refuge behind that altar, the furthest from the entrance.

Alana wasted no time and practically dove into the open grate on top of the altar, using her considerable arm strength to let herself down into the drainage sewer below.

Michaela didn't even look at her or the other two, but kept her rifle up, and quickly panned around, waiting for someone to take a shot at her.

Ethan prodded Diana, and she was up and in quickly, then him, and lastly Michaela popped in behind and closed the grate.

It all happened in less than fifteen seconds. Tiberius couldn't believe it.

The men ran over to the altar and looked down into the blackness. "Should we follow?" they asked Tiberius.

He angrily shook his head. "It'd be a trap," he said, "get the ropes, let's take the back way out."

They escaped out the back way, oblivious to the dark figure standing on the wall, watching all.

CHAPTER 6

"Get up loser," Mateo barked at Rafael.

Rafael tried to open his eyes, but the harsh torchlight scorched his vision. "Matty?" He said groggily. "What time is it?" His head pounded, it felt like every muscle on his body was sore.

"For the last time, it's Mateo," Mateo replied flatly. "And there's no time for questions."[10] He held up a keychain full of keys and jangled them provocatively. "This is a jailbreak, gotta go, gotta go." He then opened the cage Rafael found himself in.

Rafael picked himself up off the ground and walked to the door and stopped as his mind started working again. "Wait, this isn't legal," he said, and held back. "I don't want to get into any more trouble."

"You can't get into any more trouble than you're already in dummy," Mateo replied. "Besides, this isn't about you, Alana is in trouble."

---

[10] There most certainly was, but people say that when they don't want to answer your questions.

"I mean, we all knew that already," he said as he stepped through the door hesitantly, "is there something new?" he asked.

"Just follow me, we've got to be quiet; I'll explain when we're outside. I just got word that she had a run in with some foreign soldiers, and we've got to find her before they do." Mateo replied.

Rafael sighed, and walked through the door.

"Don't they have soldiers for this sort of thing?" Rafael asked.

"None that we can trust," Mateo said, and put his finger to his mouth, and led him out and into the cold early morning darkness.

The sun beat down like the devil, frying anything that dared move below its harsh rays. All she could see in any direction was sand and rock.

"I really should have brought some water..." Zara said as she looked longingly into the desolate blue sky, then back down to the vast desolation that stretched before her.

As she looked out, she swore she saw a bird flying ahead of her, further into the desert.

"Well my friend, I hope you know something I don't," she said, and made her way after the bird as best she could.

"Where are you going?" Mateo shouted out above the din and thanked the stars that he managed to catch her in time.

Alana looked up. Mateo could just barely see her in the crowded station, the westernmost terminus of the railway, the last stop before the great western wilderness. He looked around her and saw a few soldiers with her, and what appeared to be a...westerner? His lighter skin was sure to stand out in any crowd those days.

"The question is where are you going, Matty?" Alana asked. "Don't you have important parliamentary business to attend to?"

"Not when my old friend is getting shot at again," he said.

"Didn't stop you the last time," Alana said, as she went back to her inventory.

They had lined up piles of supplies in a corner of the station that she had telegraphed ahead to order as she made her way here on the fastest trains she could get. Alana was a little short on currency, but her mother was happy to fund the escapade to feel some semblance of control over her daughter's life once again, even if she did stay in Delphi.

"We tried to help you, you know," and Mateo turned and pointed at Rafael, looking none too worse for the wear, shaved, pale, and dirty.

"Rafael!" Alana called out and ran to him and looked him over. "Are you with him now?" she asked, looking at Mateo.

"I am now," Rafael nodded.

"You okay?" Alana asked.

"I have been better, it's a long story." he said.

"Well," Alana replied, "it's going to be a long ride," and looking up at Mateo she said, "you can come, but you cross me once, and I will leave you to die out there," she said.

"Aye aye captain," Mateo replied. "Now who's leading this circus?" he asked.

Alana pointed at Ethan, who nodded back at them.

"I got us a wayfinder," she said, and then directing herself at all of her companions she continued, "he knows the way; he went to the burial grounds as a child."

Ethan nodded but said nothing.

"You all better be fit to race," Alana said. "We have got to get there before this Tiberius fellow does or we are in deep trouble."

"What is this we're discussing?" Rafael piped up. "What are we going to do?"

"Find the silver cross," Alana said. "And fast."

I could spend pages describing the joys of spring in the mountains: the hope of the sun, the retreat of the snow, and the extra spring in your step after trudging through a long dark lonely winter. Every movement is easier when the threat of that cold blackness is gone, and your heart sings with bliss. Ethan practically bounced from step to step. This was the season he lived his life for.

Though all of that was lost to the eyes of the uninitiated, those city-dwellers unaccustomed to joyful returns of pleasant living in the mountains. And so, while Ethan could only see hope and wonder as they traveled, to the rest all they recalled was that it was forested and wet.

They headed southwest on informal paths through the foothills along the mountains, frequently losing the path and then finding it again, though it didn't matter: with the mountains to your right you were pretty much guaranteed to hit the old western road eventually. They traveled through gorgeous aspen forests with the new leaves shimmering in the late spring sun, slowly fading into dry lands of scrub oak and granite boulders. The horses carried their gear, leaving them free to walk unburdened.

They passed the occasional settler with a wave, walked by a few farmers out planting, but overall it was a quiet, empty, pristine backcountry.

To those who have gone on long excursions in the wilderness, nothing I say here could possibly equate to the serene beauty and depth of experience you will encounter. To those of you who haven't, the description will be impossible to decipher and bore you to tears. It is enough to say that the wilderness holds the last temples on earth, and you will find them to be more than adequate at reinvigorating your sense of purpose in life.

"Tell me again, genius, why we're headed south?" Mateo said late in the second day of travel. Among all of them he found the monotony of walking the most grueling and yearned for the days when he could kick back in his office, ignore his meetings, and read the latest news releases and speculate on who was trying to outmaneuver who. I don't want to say the rest were dumb, but they definitely had different standards in the level of intellectual stimulation they demanded on a daily basis. Regardless, everyone felt a sense of wasted effort when they walked south, and their destination was to the north.

"Well, my brilliant friend," Ethan replied, "how are you on skis?"

"Wait, we're trekking through snow? I didn't pack for snow, we have to change routes," Mateo demanded.

"Ha ha, well I've done you the honor of foreseeing that difficulty, and we are skipping the whole, 'walk over a snowed-in pass and try not to die from hypothermia' bit." Ethan said. "And besides if we went north, you'd miss all of the beautiful scenery. Who doesn't like some beautiful scenery?" Ethan said as he waved his hand across the dry landscape. They had moved into a desolate section of land, with leafless scrub oak and other barren deciduous plant life dotting the way.

"Who indeed," Mateo replied.

"And there are even better things up ahead," Ethan said.

Rafael piped in. "Could it be another tree?" said Rafael. "Be still my beating heart."

"There are heathens in our midst who are immune to the beauties of a nice long walk!" Ethan called out. "Alana, who are these companions of yours?"

"Not hikers, I'll tell you that!" she replied. The complaining was starting to annoy her.

"Who are you calling heathens?" Rafael said. "I am a priest!"

"Well, I'll be darned." Ethan said. "But I don't believe you. Because if you were a priest, you'd already recognize this!" Ethan pointed far ahead, and in the fading light of dusk they saw an ancient stone well.

"Is that what I think it is?" Rafael asked.

"You betcha," Ethan replied.

Alana was the first to arrive and moved her hands along the lichen-covered stones. "What well is this?" she said. This was of ancient construction. Black lines swept across the ground nearby scarring the landscape, and the well was ringed by barren pomegranate trees.

"They call it Cora's well," Ethan said. "There's not a lot of water inside, but it never runs dry" and he lowered a bucket on a rope and pulled up a small scoop of cold glassy water and took a drink. Delicious.

After a quick dinner, they bed down nearby and slept a sleep that you could only dream of sleeping. It was a deep, dark, peaceful sleep which is easy to obtain if you just walked sixteen hours. Exhaustion really is the key to sleeping easy.

All slept easy save Alana that is. She awoke in the early hours of the morning in the cold and dark. She hadn't been able to sleep through the night ever since her encounter with the assassin and the dark figure, and whenever she did wake up at that time of night for the rest of her life, while she would never readily admit it, she could almost swear she saw dark figures watching.

Just like tonight. But this time, it was there on the horizon, and it was coming for her.

The moon had long set, and the stars shone bright in the sky.

Alana kept her eyes on the figure as it approached in the dark from the direction of Atlas, eerily floating over the ground and up the rise where they had camped.

Slowly, ever so slowly, Alana inched her hand towards her pillow. "Fool me once..." she thought.

The figure arrived at the camp and eyed Mateo briefly, then searched through the faces, looking for someone.

It hovered over every face it saw for a long moment,

drawing in and reading their soul, then moving onto the next. Alana held her hand under her pillow and closed her eyes as it hovered over to her.

She felt the same infinite darkness she had felt the other day and shuttered as an icy cold invisible hand reached down to feel her soul. She could sense its glee as it discovered its success.

Alana opened her eyes and stared into the abyss of the creature right above her. It shook with surprise and quickly moved to draw out her soul, but Alana moved first. Like a flash of lightning, she pulled out the black dagger she held with her hand under her pillow and drove it with all of her force into the side of the head of the dark figure above her. It landed with a satisfying thud.

Her arm shook with electricity as the figure writhed in shock and pain. Finally, it let out an unholy shriek and she felt it collapse in on itself.

"Go to Hades!" she grunted and jumped up wielding the knife, spinning around looking for other figures, ready to face anything.

"What are you doing?" Ethan asked as he rubbed his eyes and looked up.

Alana stood poised in attack pose with her knife drawn, hopping from direction to direction, ready to face any other demonic attackers.

"Alana?" Rafael asked. "You losing it?"

Slowly Alana realized they were once again alone. There was nobody else out there, but everyone was awake and staring at her as she apparently challenged the trees to a fight.

"You okay?" The soldiers asked.

"Heh," Alana replied, panting heavily, "bad dream I guess." And she sat back down on her bed.

"Some dream!" Mateo said. "I hope you never dream about me okay?"

The group laughed, and tried to get cozy to fall back asleep, but within a few minutes they all heard a low moan.

"What was that?" Ethan asked.

From the direction of the well they heard a low moaning. It was as if the entire earth was crying.

"Shhh," Alana replied, looking every which way, trying to find whatever dark figure might be approaching.

They heard a dripping, and in the starlight they saw small tears of dew fell from every branch and stem, and a general wake was heard from every side.

Then it stopped.

The stars shone bright in the sky.

Ethan looked back up.

The stars shone brighter in the sky.

And brighter.

And brighter, as if pulsing with a gleeful energy.

From the well a light sprung, shining out into the beyond, and a faint deep sound of wailing was heard. And from the well, a bright woman appeared. Light emanated from her whole being. From far away a green wave swept across the landscape towards the well, and from the wave appeared another woman. She embraced the lit woman, and they held each other for a minute, crying tears of joy that fell to the ground and blossomed into orange poppies. The wind blew in the smells of harvest time: wheat, apples, squash, a cornucopia of smells lay over the group, and the two women walked past them talking in hushed, excited tones, their muted laughter echoing across the hills.

They watched the women disappear into the fields beyond and life crept out over the rolling hills.

Ethan looked over at Mateo. "Told you so," and he fell back asleep.

The next morning was awash in greenery and life, as if spring had come suddenly to the hills. The pomegranate trees blossomed by the well. They talked little, and none but Rafael dared voice what they had witnessed.

"Did she not just come from Hades?" he said.

"I believe so," said Ethan.

"So...can we not use the same route?" Rafael asked.

And this is why you always want to find lazy people to help you do things, because they will always figure out the easiest way to do them.

"I'm afraid that path is for Persephone alone," Ethan said. "At least, that's what they say. We mortals have to go through the gates." and with that they departed for another day of walking.

To everyone's relief, they finally stopped their southern progress that morning and before they knew it, they had merged with the old western road.

And what a road! What terrible times it has seen! It was more of a path in their time, a disused series of wagon ruts stretching out as far as you could see in either direction through the grass in the rolling foothills. They followed the historic route the rest of the day, until in the evening they spotted a stone altar in the distance, which Ethan again promptly pointed out.

"And here is site number two!" he said to Mateo, "You'll, no doubt, want to see this."

Alana's heart jumped just a bit. "I think I've been here before..." she said.

They arrived at the altar just as the sun sunk beneath the horizon. On the base sat a stone on which was inscribed:

Long Live The Glorious Dead

Rafael traced the words with his hands, and Alana slowly walked around the altar in reverence. "Cairn Loire" she whispered. The group stood in awed silence. This marked the western border of Atlas, and the site of the last great battle on the continent, a clash of civilizations that each of them had heard about since their youth. They retired from the altar several paces to give it the respect it deserved, started a fire, and Alana spent the evening re-telling the story they all knew so well.[11]

"The treacherous westerners from Ariens," she began, "sought to conquer the continent. They knew they had no chance of defeating the united five nations, so they lie in wait for their opportunity to destroy us."

Ethan bristled at this characterization of his people, but he'd learned to not argue about the factors leading up to the war. History is, after all, written by the victors.

"They came from across the seas to destroy all in their path, and while they built up their fortress at Ariens, waited for us to make a mistake," she continued.

"They got their chance during the civil wars. Seeing my great uncle King Leo distracted by the uprisings in the borderlands along Elara and Medea, they massed their armies and sent them against us along the old western road. They never for a moment considered this would be their undoing."

She paused and let the fire crackle as she looked intently around the crew.

Ethan rolled his eyes melodramatically. "And how was it our undoing," Ethan said blandly, trying to end his misery.

Alana continued, "Well, westerner," she said with just a hint of accusation, "I'm glad you asked—they massed their armies and set out along the old western road, but a traitor rose among them, someone with a conscience, who ran for five days and five nights,[12] they say sped along by Hermes

---

[11] There was nothing she liked, after all, more than telling a good story, even if it had already been heard.

[12] We're pretty sure there was a horse involved, but those of the five nations love to tell this with a more superhuman element.

himself, and collapsed at Leo's feet to confess the sins of their people and the coming attack through their gasping breaths.

"I have no doubt you're all familiar with the legend, but maybe you don't know this; I learned of this detail from my father who was Leo's nephew and fought in this very battle. Leo made sacrifice to Apollo and begged for his help, and from Apollo he received a message: that he would be delivered from destruction if he only took his captains, his leaders, his right-hand men. These were the pure in heart, the ones who could be trusted under any condition. Every other man was dismissed.

"Leo took his leaders and laid ambush for the westerners here at Cairn Loire. They numbered perhaps a hundred but lay in wait for the ten thousand that were commanded by Aaron, the evil prince of the west.

"Leo hid his men and approached by himself, unarmed save for a little silver cross he had received from his grandmother as a token of love.

"'You shall go no further!' Leo commanded the opposing forces. It was him alone against an army that stretched back along the path as far as eye could see.

"They paid him no heed and moved to strike, but Leo shouted and held up the silver cross as high as he could. It exploded with light, blinding everyone in sight. The heavens rained down arrows from Apollo and destroyed the army as Leo was consumed in the light.

"The army was defeated and fled the field, and Leo collapsed from the exertion, with his captains coming out of hiding to carry him. There were many other battles and events, but this was the end of the westerners as a threat to our peoples."

She ended with a tone of finality and the fire slowly burned out under the great sacrificial altar of Cairn Loire, erected by Leo after the battle to give thanks to Apollo.

It took Ethan longer than the rest to fall asleep under that alter of victory over his people. Some of them, like himself, had found ways to integrate in the five nations, but most were scattered in tribes across the wild lands. He often wondered where he belonged; he felt like an outsider no matter where he went.

Before he could fall asleep, though, the green gem quietly awoke and reached out again. Its tendrils wrapped around him and he fell into a deep vision. A giant desolate plain stretched out as far as he could see in every direction. Suddenly a huge statue of a severe man appeared before him and reached into the sky. He strained to look up to see its full height, and when he brought his gaze back to earth an old woman appeared in front of him. Her eyes looked straight through him, and she said, "Come!"

He stumbled back from the surprise, and fell down, but did not land. He fell and fell and fell, seeing images of wars and battles, of smoke creeping down the Andaluvian, and of a dark figure waiting for him in the distance. Just as he landed back into his body out of the vision, he saw a faint glimpse of a golden gun and groups of men chasing him.

It took him some time to find sleep as his mind raced to find answers.

Zara looked across the flat rocky landscape as far as she could in any direction. There was absolutely nothing out here. It was as barren and dry as a bone. She had been walking for a day and a half with only the slightest rest here and there, desperately looking for something, anything to sustain her.

And there was nothing.

The birds she had followed seemed to have disappeared into the ground, eaten up by the unforgiving desolation.

Her head pounded. She stumbled on a rock and fell to her knees, looking out over the severe nothingness.

"This must be it," she said. "Here in Apollo's lands I die."

In front of her she saw a bird appear from the ground and

fly into the air.

"That's odd," she muttered, and slowly picked herself back up and walked forward.

Up ahead there was a gash in the ground, like someone had cut through the rock with a knife. You'd never see it unless you were up close. She approached the edge and looked down into a grotto that opened up below the gash into a beautiful colorful bowl.

"Water!" she screamed and let herself into the tiny grotto. It was just big enough to stand in. Water dripped along the edges of the sandstone bowl into the wet sandy ground below. Moss of different colors grew all around, and a blanket of dandelions spread out along the sandy bottom like a carpet.

Zara greedily eyed the water dripping off the walls. "God bless you," she whispered, and sipped and sipped as fast as she could, quenching her enormous thirst.

She then moved onto the dandelions, carefully pulling them out by the roots, washing off the sand, and eating plants whole.

Moving down and out of the grotto, she found a protected sandy spot, and slept like she had never slept before, fat and happy.

Ethan woke up and saw the partial moon overhead and the sky filled to capacity with stars. It's hard for us to picture the scenes you could regularly witness overhead for most people in this time period, with our epidemic of light pollution, but nights were spectacular shows of joy and wonder.

Joy and wonder any OTHER night that is. Tonight, though, Ethan woke up in a mild panic. He could feel his stomach sinking into his feet, and he broke out in a cold sweat. Something was very, very wrong, and the vision from earlier played through his head again and again. Was that his future?

He lay there, heart racing, for what felt like an hour, but was really probably only a few minutes. His breathing got faster and faster, shallower and shallower, his stomach turned over and over, and he tried to control the panic as it boiled over. For a moment it seemed as if the moon was slowly crashing into the earth, crushing everything underneath it, and he tried to escape into any spare pocket. He had no idea what was going on. This had never happened before.

He finally decided to do something about it, but just as he sat up, he heard a sound.

It was like a distant thunder rolling over the hills. His panic rose to where he couldn't bear to be on the ground anymore; he sprang up and tried to see anything out in the dark night, anything at all.

Alana, a light sleeper under the best of conditions, was instantly awake at his movement. "What are you doing?" she said.

Before he could reply, there were shouts and the sound grew louder.

"Horses," she said.

In the distance came a cry, "Death comes!"

In an instant the horses were almost on top of them. They could see riders from almost every direction, rifles raising.

"To the ravine!" Alana shouted, and in a moment the soldiers were up and armed. It was a beautiful ballet, with clanging pans and spare firewood flung in every which direction. Mateo and Rafael were totally disoriented, attempting to find anything with which to defend themselves; Mateo ended up with revolver, and Rafael, in a moment he would never live down, carried out one of the pans disturbed in the scrum.

Out of habit, not from any impending sense of danger, the group had chosen a mildly defensible position next to a deep ravine, and each flung themselves over the edge, rifles out and ready to fire into the fog of war. Alana and her men were largely from the artillery corps, of course, so you'd never wish to encounter them from a distance of several hundred yards being armed with even a mortar piece, but they could still do some serious damage with rifles to an untrained rabble.

The raiders seemed to pause for a moment just out of rifle range. Clearly the speed of organization had deterred them. Did they expect a professional resistance? In any event, there were a couple dozen of them, and they could count Alana's men; separated from their horses, likely with little ammunition as they scrambled to the ravine. The raiders had pretty good odds.

They kicked their horses forward, sped faster, and opened fire. These were prairie raiders; they grew up on horses preying on unsuspecting travelers. They could hit a man from a hundred yards at full gallop.

An exposed man in the daylight that is. Only one shot landed: one of the artillerymen was hit in the arm and quickly bandaged himself.

"Open fire!" Alana shouted, and they rained lead on their attackers. A few fell immediately on the first volley, tumbling from their horses into the tall grass screaming profanities. The rest broke off the charge and galloped out of range.

They came on again, this time spread out, huddled close to their horses to present a smaller profile, but still Alana and her men added casualties. Rafael watched from behind his pan as the men and horses were picked off. Ethan could practically see in the dark, and he scored hit after hit.

Appropriately dissuaded, the raiders gave up and dismounted. They took prone positions in the tall grass, some of them returning fire in the dark, the rest advancing forward under the cover of the foliage.

They exchanged volleys; a raider occasionally raising to a knee and getting a shot off, with Alana and her men returning fire. They could hear them inching closer in the grass, slithering slowly closer, always closer in the darkness.

"Let's surrender!" Mateo angrily hissed at Alana. "You want us to get slaughtered? Let me pull out a white cloth and go talk to them."

Alana shook her head. "You're going to surrender to the people who were trying to kill us in our sleep?" she said with incredulity. "I mean don't let me stop you, but also I hope you don't get killed in the crossfire. Excuse me for not jumping at the chance to give them a clear shot."

Mateo clutched his handkerchief with white knuckles. "Maybe they'd get you, but not me," he grumbled.

But Alana wasn't listening. The raiders were still hidden in the grass but crawling closer. "Fix bayonets," she whispered to her nearest commander, and he whispered the command down the line.

Each of the soldiers knew this was going to be a gruesome end. Ethan looked down the ravine behind them. Certainly not a good place to get caught on the run, as they could shoot him effortlessly from the ridgeline. But maybe if he made it to the other side? He could double back in the night and reach a horse and escape? At minimum he could then bring back a battalion on a manhunt and avenge their death.

Oh, and he wouldn't be dead, that was generally his primary motivation. And the primary motivation of everyone around him, except there wasn't really any chance of avoiding that at this point. Outnumbered and up against a ravine, they were done for.

The grass started moving just ahead. Death was upon them. The vision from last night flashed before Ethan's eyes again. Death came.

But in all the exchange of fire and panic, nobody noticed the figure slowly, laboriously approaching from the far eastern horizon. It came up along the edge of the ravine, perpendicular to the field of battle. Had anyone looked, they would have seen it: slowly tromping along, heaving a heavy object.

The raiders reached the edges of the tall grass along the ravine. The glint of their barrels shined out into the moonlight.

Alana and the defenders dug their toes into the loose scree on the side of the ravine and held their rifles ready to fire a single shot, then thrust forward with bayonets. And of course, poor Rafael held a large pan above his head in the darkness, ready to cook breakfast that came his way. Right before the final blow fell, the dark figure walked to the edge of the scene.

"Burn in the eternal fire you treasonous weasels," he said, and Ethan saw him heft a gigantic gun to his side.

And the world exploded.

CHAPTER 7

Jacques walked into the dark room projecting an air of refined elegance. He was dressed in his finest casual suit, cravat neatly tucked in, and a flower daintily hanging on his chest. He was a man of the old school, no occasion too dire to come well dressed.

"I'm afraid we haven't met," Jacques said as he looked down his nose disapprovingly at Tiberius. He took off one of his gloves and made a faint showing of acknowledgement of the dirty crew, waving his glove with all the disinterest he could show.

"I bet you are," Tiberius replied. He lifted himself up off his bed to stand as best he could and face Jacques.

"I see you have met the finest of our hospitality," Jacques said with a smirk as he pointed down at his bandaged leg.

"I can't wait to report back to Scipio how our alliance is treated," Tiberius snarled.

"It occurred to me that this was all the doing of your superiors," Jacques said with disdain, and stepped forward closer to Tiberius, and looked up into his eyes. He refused to be intimidated by these thugs. "I'm sure the true intelligence behind this operation will be more forthcoming with me than you have."

Tiberius grumbled. "Scipio has indicated that he welcomes you at any time to discuss this matter. He," and wanting to reaffirm his importance he added, "and I have been dissatisfied with the way you've handled the royal affair."

"As if either of you are capable of anything but the most self-destructive of work. I had to personally intervene to keep you alive," Jacques scoffed.

"You weren't needed," Tiberius snapped back, "and besides, your days of keeping people alive are over."

"So, you've come to kill her yourself?" Jacques gave his best pompous laugh. "No, I am in no need of assistance, this duty I can take care of myself. Relay that to Scipio when you make it back to Medea."

Tiberius shook his head. "You can tell him yourself," he said. "We do not intend to return to Medea at this time."

"You're going to follow her?" Jacques asked, breaking character for a brief moment, showing his surprise.

"Not follow, but we have a shared destination," Tiberius replied.

"I'm telling you, killing her would be an act of war," Jacques said. "I have my own man on the job, I need no help from foreign usurpers."

Tiberius snarled. "When I have the cross, let's talk more about who is usurping what."

Jacques laughed again. "You mean Titus' little toy?" Jacques leaned forward and held Tiberius' shoulder to laugh some more.

"No touching," Tiberius said, and stepped back.

Jacques rubbed the fake tears from his fake laugh. "It doesn't exist you idiot! It never has, it never will."

Tiberius narrowed his eyes and practically breathed rage at Jacques. "Then why do I have this?" He held out the empty leather case inscribed with the image of the cross.

Jacques shook his head as he continued to huff. "What a pouch?" He laughed. "It's empty isn't it? It always was, always will be." He relaxed and brought himself back up into his professional posture and continued, "Leo that old dog played the entire kingdom for a dunce when he hoisted some worthless scrap over his head and proclaimed miraculous power.

"Can you imagine how he must have laughed at night thinking how he was able to cling onto his power through an invented artefact from the gods? The tokens, the gods, all of them, they never existed!

"They were beliefs of our fathers, fairy tales from superstitious peasants passed down from people who didn't have a grasp of science, of human nature, of power. They were fools, all of them, content to live under tyrannical monarchs for generations.

"But the old ways are crumbling," Jacques said ominously, then paced back and forth as he continued his rant, "I've been through the holy sites, I've been through the holy lands, and I'll tell you what doesn't exist: them. They're not there. There are no gods dwelling on Olympus. There are no magical apparitions of omnipotent beings. There are no special powers, no special tokens. There is only one power, and that is my power, our power, the power of our people, which will be made greater as we band together." Jacques stopped himself from getting too worked up and composed himself by adjusting his tie.

Even Tiberius, sceptic as he was, flinched a bit when Jacques talked about desecrating the holy lands by traveling them. No mortal was allowed near Olympus, and by convention, most of the peaks north of Delphi. He shook his head: he could never bring himself to do the same, to walk in the realm of the gods. A small piece of us always holds on to what our mothers teach us in our first learnings, and our internal compass will always shy away from violating those sacred lessons, even when we have long discarded the vestiges of belief.

"The old ways are crumbling, you have that right," Tiberius replied. "And you will crumble with them."

"You have so much to learn, boy," Jacques replied. "More's the pity you'll never grow old enough to learn it." He turned on his heel abruptly and went to leave.

"Is that a threat?" Tiberius yelled.

"It's the truth," Jacques called out over his shoulder. "Please be gone by nightfall, Atlas can be dangerous you know."

"Scipio will hear of it!" Tiberius shouted back.

"I'll tell him myself," Jacques said.

Well the world didn't really explode. That was mainly Ethan panicking. But can you blame him? In his defense, everyone else thought they were dead too.

The dark figure hefted up a large rotary gun, a beast of a machine, the latest and greatest of technology, usually operated while mounted by a crew of men. But this giant man with amazing strength held it as best he could and sprayed dozens upon dozens of bullets up and down the line of raiders, cutting them down just as they approached their moment of triumph.

Ethan had never even heard of such a device. It was a brass monster with twelve individual barrels and fed by a giant line of bullets in a belt which spun up with a roar and gleamed out the starlight like a disco ball as it rapidly spun and threw its death into the grass.

It fired in quick succession; aiming wasn't strictly a necessity beyond ensuring he pointed it in the general direction. The raiders had conveniently lined up in their approach, and so it was only a moment, but in that moment, Ethan heard more explosions than he had heard in his entire life. Every shot seemed to stop the earth, and he watched them in succession, bending the air, shooting off shockwaves, blowing into their would-be assassins.

The world exploded for a moment. And after that moment the shooting stopped, and the grass no longer moved. Alana lay slack jawed in awe. Rafael slowly lay his pan down. Mateo breathed out relief as he put away his handkerchief and put his hand back on his gun. One of the soldiers let out a sigh of relief that sounded something like, "Holy sh…"

The man disengaged the rotary gun, then lumbered up to the rather shocked group of people. For a few tense moments were unsure if they should shoot or thank him, but they determined they would get no further than the riders by shooting.

The barrels still spinning, white smoke flinging into the air, he walked straight up to the ravine's edge, the toes of his steel-tipped boots inches away from where their chins sat moments before. He was dressed in a long thick dark cloak which fluttered in the slight breeze, the smell of gun smoke thick in the air. Glints appeared from beneath the cloak, but they didn't notice much. They were all too distracted by his otherworldly head. It was totally covered by a dark hood which appeared to absorb all light, and in the darkness of that night, made it impossible to see any features on his face. It was like staring into a black hole.

For a fleeting moment, Rafael wondered if this was Hades himself.

The figure looked them up and down, clearly unimpressed.

"Screw those mutinous mercenaries." he said, motioning to the bodies around. "This is my land. You call me Etienne."

Nobody moved or said a word. Alana watched the brass barrels slowly come to a stop with her jaw wide open.

"Well?" he said.

Ethan was the first to reply. "You got it, Etienne," he said. Etienne shook his head and laughed. "Get up here and explain yourselves," he said, and with that he turned and walked over to the glowing embers of their fire and set down his machine of death.

Cold pink tendrils snaked across the sky overhead, as far far away in the East, beyond Atlas, beyond Elara, beyond the Eastern sea with its islands and foreign lands, Apollo mounted his chariot and began to pull the sun up into the sky. Flocks of birds, alien to these lands for the winter, gathered from their resting perches and formed overhead on their northward migration.

The morning fire cackled as a group of bleary-eyed travelers chatted.

"So, you're from Atlas, eh?" Etienne said, slowly staring at each one. "Don't get many from the five nations around these parts. Not anymore anyway."

Awkward silence was all he got in reply until Alana mumbled out a "Yes," still a little dumbfounded by the evening's events.

"Who's leading you on this crazy expedition?" he said, stirring the fire with a stick.

"I'm their guide," Ethan offered.

"Of course you are, son. I figured that they'd need to get a westerner to walk them around these parts, even if you did just come strolling out of the womb. Nobody from the five nations can tie their shoes around here without getting one of us to help. Tell me, what tribe are you?" Etienne asked.

"He's of no tribe," Alana interjected. "We're all citizens of Atlas. We have no loyalties elsewhere." and she narrowed her gaze on Ethan, daring him to contradict her.

"Well this is a riddle," Etienne said, "ho ho ho," he laughed, "what could this possibly mean? By the gods I don't think the Sphinx herself could come up with a deeper mystery. Here we have some soldiers of Atlas,"

"How did you figure we're soldiers?" Alana indignantly

interrupted.

"Soldiers of Atlas," Etienne forcefully continued, looking straight at Alana, "their government-issued rifles clearly marking them to any outsider with at least half a brain, and anyone without half a brain would have noticed their defense formation, clearly we have some professionals out here."

He raised his eyebrows and tilted his head as if to taunt Alana and continued.

"Minus the priest with the pan that is," he chuckled as Rafael gamely bowed. "We have some soldiers of Atlas, a priest of Apollo, and," looking at Mateo, "someone who clearly is neither." Etienne pointed at Ethan and continued, "and here we have a westerner who isn't a westerner leading them somewhere west. North perhaps? Who knows, either way, somewhere where they are not welcome.

"And furthermore, to add to the mystery, we have to my right," he motioned over to the gully, "a dozen or so Carpathian mercenaries by the looks of them, who were clearly making a beeline for you and you alone." Alana looked up in surprise at the mention of Carpathians and he continued. "Yes, what a strange group indeed."

He left that hanging in the continuing awkward silence, far off songbirds welcoming the day with brilliant tones, and the cold pink stripes overhead warming up to deep yellows and golds. The sun appeared huge on the horizon, and gradually shrunk as it made its way above.

Alana shrugged. What the heck. If a Carpathian warlord knew she was out and about, what harm could it do her to reveal her plans to this crazy stranger. She was already a dead woman walking at that point.

"We are headed to the North," she finally said.

"Of course you are," Etienne said.

"We are on our way to the gates of Hades," she said.

"Ahhh, of COURSE you are," Etienne said.

"I wish to pay my respects to some men buried at the

gates," she said.

"So many great men buried there, many royalty, many kings..." he said, suggestively.

"And that is all," Alana said, "we go to pay our respects and then return, we did not know that the western paths were closed, and that the western tribes no longer ensured the safety that travelers enjoy in the five nations."

"Ah well princess," Etienne smiled, pleased again at himself for his intuition, "you may know that we have fallen on hard times. Happens to the best of us."

Alana ignored his provocation and continued, "we'll be on our way this morning. I do not carry anything of value, but can we perform any task to repay your kindness?"

"Ah, thank you, but my hospitality comes with a very specific cost: escort. I cannot let you proceed through my lands without proper protection. You said it yourself, we cannot guarantee safe passage to minors," Etienne pointed at Ethan smiling, "and their compatriots. Allow me to protect you through the western tribal lands." Etienne said.

"No," Alana replied quickly.

"This isn't a suggestion, I'm afraid," Etienne said.

Alana pursed her lips and weighed the offer.

"I have two horses, one for me, one for my gear, including," and he patted the gun beside him, "this here rotary gun, the latest design and all the rage among those in the know, which you may find yourself in need of in the future. Come now, you cannot resist, you know I am right. I am your only chance of survival in these lands."

Alana paused. She had not expected to encounter resistance; Titus II had been carried this way on the way to burial without incident. There are various settlements, some permanent, some roving along the way, and no shortage of good people, farmers, ranchers, what have you, but the evil of the night was unsettling.

Rafael stood and walked to Alana in the circle and

whispered in her ear.

"It would seem wise, old friend," he said. "There is something afoot in these lands."

Now, a normal person might stop at this point and re-evaluate her life choices. Maybe she'd start by looking back a few weeks and thinking hey, this is getting increasingly harder, maybe fate is trying to tell me something? You know, I could instead just wait a month and then cross to the North via some safe passes up above Fort Hall, or you know, go find a boat or something to take me there, and not risk everyone's lives further.

But much like a frog that is slowly boiled in water who stays in the pot, this was largely a theoretical dilemma in her head because frogs don't stay still in pots you dummies, and Alana doesn't reconsider her life choices, she makes things happen.

She stood. "Thank you, Etienne," she said. "We would be honored to accept your continued hospitality. We accept your protection, and I offer you mine: I will be your brother in arms, I will fight with the fury of Athena herself, I will die by your side. I do not fear the kingdom of the dead, and I do not fear any man who can send me there. Your protection is gladly accepted to ensure our success in the eyes of the gods, but I do not accept out of fear."

Etienne stood, his black robe billowing out as he moved, and underneath, the muted sounds of metal plating. He pulled his hood back, showing his face for the first time. His hair fell down his head in soft white curls, his face covered in white scruffy whiskers. Alana looked up and saw the face of an old man with deep blue eyes sunk into his head above hollow cheeks. She recoiled just a bit at the sight; he carried the look of a man who knew pain like a brother.

"So," he said, and his voice cracked a little bit. "This is it. This is it." He grinned from ear to ear. "This is it. This is the answer to the riddle." He stretched his hand out and they shook. "Neither you nor I, Alana of Atlas. There is nothing more I can fear. You shall have my protection, a gift many have sought, but only you receive."

Ethan stood up, "I hate to stop this little romance," he said, "but daylight's a burning, and I don't want to stick around to see if any of their buddies decide to come looking for them." He pointed along the mountains to the north. "Thataway my friends!"

CHAPTER 8

Zara stayed in her grotto for a few days, resting, drinking, and eating. But as the supply of dandelions visibly diminished, and the taste of the moss grew dull, it was time to move on again. She packed up all the food she could and headed out as the sun set.

She followed the gash in the ground that night. It eventually widened out into a narrow canyon with steep rocky walls and a sandy bottom.

She never saw water out in the open, but the sand in the middle of the canyon was always wet, and if she dug into it a few feet the water would pool up enough to get a few sips.

On the morning of the third day of walking, she looked up on the canyon walls, admiring the beauty around here and saw something.

Someone was watching her.

It stood still as a statue high above her, staring down at Zara in the middle of the canyon.

Zara froze. It was too far away to make out who it was, or where it was from.

The figure looked down at her, then disappeared beyond

the canyon wall.

Zara's heart raced and she scanned the canyon, then started running down the canyon to find a way to get out. "How did they find me?" she demanded.

She had to get out of the canyon before whoever it was came back, she would be a sitting duck trapped in the narrow space. Zara found a rockslide down canyon on the opposite side from where she had seen the person and scrambled up to the flat desolation above. She looked across the top of the canyon and couldn't see anyone. "Where could they be?" she wondered.

She looked all around her, and gasped. There was a gigantic statue of two feet, broken off at the ankles. The feet themselves must have been twenty feet long, making the original statue hundreds of feet high?

"Who are you?" she exclaimed.

She walked to the base of the statue to see the sandaled feet up closer, and found a giant word inscribed along the base.

"Ozymandias" it read.

"Strange," she said. "Never heard of him..." Zara looked up at the giant foot from the base; she could barely reach the bottom of the toe from where she was at. "This must have been enormous," she muttered.

She walked aimlessly around the side of the base, totally enthralled. She turned a corner and saw a small gap in the stone, just big enough to duck into. "Is that an entrance?" she wondered, and cautiously stepped closer. She could see an abrupt darkness at the gap, but it there almost appeared to be a faint blue glow emanating from within.

Suddenly she felt a tap on her shoulder.

"Hello?" an old voice asked.

Zara flipped around to see an ancient woman with heavy wrinkles looking up at her from underneath her thin brown shawl.

"Oh, hello Zara," the woman said, "nice of you to come by. I've been waiting."

"Your mom was Jane," Rafael said to Ethan as they climbed loose scree on a series of endless ascents and descents in the rocky western foothills as they wound their way north.

"IS Jane," Ethan replied.

"Sorry," Rafael replied. "I heard so much about her, the priests were always enthralled by her theatrics."

"Thanks," Ethan replied. "She was the absolute best. Always was up for a laugh, ready to talk, whatever you were up for. She was a great mom."

Rafael nodded. "She sounds lovely," he said.

After a small pause, Rafael continued, "So what exactly is a bearer in your culture," he asked. "I've long wondered, and as I've never really met a westerner, I've never gotten a satisfactory answer. The priests I work with claimed you were a myth to some extent, even a supernatural being, though it was never clear what exactly you did."

"First of all, I'm not really a bearer?" Ethan said. "That was really just my mom. Second, to be a bearer really just meant being a glorified gravedigger. You perform the last rites for those who pass on, and shepherd them to Hades."

"But you get to go to crowning and ceremonies and stuff, though? It's not totally without merit." Mateo chimed in from the rear.

Ethan continued, "Oh yeah, I guess you get to hover over the crowning to serve as a reminder to the king..."

At this point Alana coughed loudly.

"...ahem, or QUEEN," Ethan continued, "of her mortality. Do not attempt to overreach, lest death find you unready and you are dispatched with malice by the gods to some tortuous lower kingdom to suffer for your pride."

Some of the soldiers, infamously short on displays of emotion, had visible smiles at this point. They had really taken a liking to their guide. Alana was cold as ice as usual, and Etienne drew nearer to hear, though without drawing notice.

Noticing the others were smiling, and always one to capitalize on attention, Ethan continued, "But who wants to be Debbie downer about death all the time anyway, amirite? So you get a fancy title that makes you sound better than the dude who gets up into his elbows in entrails all the time, and you get to play grim reaper whenever anyone needs a good scaring, but otherwise it's kind of a drag."

They had reached the top of the hill and panted, looking back over their progress. The sky was a deep grey overhead, with overhanging clouds as far as one could see in any direction, covering the tops of the mountains to the east.

"But the runes," Etienne spoke. Everyone, including nerves-of-steel Alana, jumped. They hadn't noticed him taking interest in the conversation, and he had said almost nothing on the trek. Ethan turned to look at him.

"The runes" Etienne repeated. "You know Vallhallian, the runic inscriptions." Etienne said. "That significance is not lost on you, is it?"

"...Yes, the runes...," Ethan replied cautiously. "I know them. I write them. But it's just a funerary script. Here's the deal: we cart up the old dead dude to the gates of Hades, dump 'em, pile up some of them black rocks, and inscribe the story of their life, and our wishes for them in the afterlife, and boom badda bing, they are proclaimed dead and head off to their rebirth in the many realms of the dead."

Etienne scoffed. He said no more, though a few of the soldiers heard him muttering under his breath the rest of the day, "just a funerary script what an..." and they claim to have not heard the remainder.

"You don't really cart them though," Rafael continued, "I saw your mom when I was a boy, and she had some kind of stone, a wayfarer I think they called it? She could transport things with it."

"A wayfinder," Ethan said. "And yeah, she could do some wild stuff with that thing," he said. "But I have no idea how it works." Ethan touched the gem around his neck. "I honestly think she's still around sometimes because it seems to still listen to her somehow."

"Hm," Rafael said, and shrugged.

Ethan would never tell me everything that he saw in the wayfinder, though believe me I tried. I asked him how it came to speak to him, to 'reach out to him' as he would put it, and he said it really awoke that day he met Alana, and slowly it reached out more and more. He said that sometimes the visions were relevant to his life, but most of the time he'd catch glimpses of other people, other lives. He had to learn how to filter out relevance from everything he saw.

The next evening found them further north, approaching canyon country. Millennia of rain had carved out deep canyons in the western mountains, turning into deep, wide ravines in the foothills they clung to as they walked. They stayed as close to the mountains as they could, not daring to take to the road along the open plains nearer the coast, as there were various settlements and nomadic groups crisscrossing the prairie, and while there were many, many western tribes in those days, there was at least one they could not afford to meet again.

"We stop here," Alana called out as they reached the bottom of a ravine. There was a small clearing near the river, in an otherwise hostile world of brambles and branches choking the way.

Etienne looked around the ravine with pursed lips. His eyebrows furrowed.

"What's wrong old man?" Alana called out, "Is this too safe of an encampment? There's no way for anyone to spot our fire down here."

Etienne looked up and down the ravine a few times and

spoke, "I know this place."

"This is far from your lands, old man, we are well north of your home," she said.

Etienne shook his head, "It's been ages, but I know this place. We would do well to continue on...the difficulty I had here was dire," he said. "I was a young man then, and the ravine has been resculpted by flood many times since I was here, but I believe this was the place..." he trailed off in thought.

A crack of thunder pealed out in the distance, and with comedic timing, the entire sky opened up in a thunderous rain. The group took cover underneath the trees and undergrowth as the sky lit up in lightning and thunder and occasional hail.

"It looks like you're outvoted!" Alana shouted, "we'll stay here tonight, I'll take first watch. Shelter as well as you can, it's tough to sleep soaking!" Alana shouted to the men. She smiled and sat back to watch the sky. She loved the rain.

Etienne shrugged his shoulders as a very scared Rafael and Ethan looked at him with questioning eyes. "I lived through it once," he said and winked, "and I'll do it again. I've got no fear of anything this life can do to me anymore. Maybe you won't make it, but that appears to be a risk she's willing to take," Etienne smiled and lumbered off with his horses to bed down.

The showers didn't last long, but it was enough to get everything wet enough to make it hard to sleep. By the time the last person could get themselves to sleep, exhaustion overtook them all, and they slept like rocks, again, until the early witching hours of the morning.

Rafael was first to stir. It was pitch black: the clouds overhead blocked all light, and down in the ravine it felt as though a crushing darkness enveloped his entire body and prevented him from even the slightest movement. It was as if the air in his chest was being squeezed out of his body slowly, like a deflating hot air balloon, but he had no will or desire to breathe in and fill it up. He felt his entire body go limp like a rag doll, and he was overcome with despair.

The rest experienced the same, each, one by one, waking and succumbing to hopelessness.

And then they came.

Ethan heard them first.

Initially the sound was a distant rustling, then as it drew nearer, they could pick out distinct steps. It sounded as though a half dozen people were making their way through the thickets. Ethan went to scream, but the darkness entered and filled his mouth and lungs, clinging to his vocal cords, refusing him, and he lay frozen in terror. Crunch, crunch, shuffle crunch, the steps drew closer.

For a moment he could hear nothing, then a huge black horn exploded in his ears, which was followed by total silence. And in the silence, a harsh whisper.

"Yoooouuuu are nothing," the whisper slowly slithered into Ethan's ears. It sounded breathy and grating, like his ears were being rubbed with rocks by a dying snake.

"Even your mother knew you were nothing," it whispered again. And then many whisperings.

"She left you for a reason, she was glad to leave you, glad to be rid of you, just like your grandmother. Why do you think she sent you away? Why do you think they all leave you eventually? Your grandmother wanted to empty her home of a nothing, a worthless grandson who is nothing. She knew you had nothing, you were nothing, and so here you are with the other nothings. She knew and your mother knew. And your father too! Why do you think they all leave? You offer these Atlassians your assistance, and yet you know you are worthless. You have guided them to their death! You have guided them into your own death. Sssssoon you will fail, and your total complete mediocre insignificance will be lost to the world forever. Nobody who has ever known you has ever stayed with you, and nobody ever will."

The air was fully out of him now; he was totally deflated in every sense of the word, wishing to struggle, but he couldn't do anything except listen to the whisperings as they came upon him, filling up the entire ravine, and crushing him under its weight.

"Your grandmother will die, you know," it whispered. "She's dying because of you. You couldn't help her, you were worthless to her, and now she dies from your inadequacy. What a shame that she is stuck with you alone among all of the relatives she could have; she would have rather had anyone else in the world to care for her, anyone else that she would never have sent away. She was cursed by the gods to have a weak grandson who was worthlesssss."[13]

It's hard to say how long this went on, some felt hours, some say minutes. But each member of the crew was assaulted.

In Rafael's case, he didn't hear any whispers. He passed out of time and space and he was taken to a room in a foreign building. On the wall was projected a series of scenes from his life.

"I told you you were stupid," his mother shouted at him after meeting with a teacher. "Why can't you be more like your brother? Can't you see how well he has done in school? He's going to head the Treasury someday with a mind like that, and you can barely divide two numbers. He had mastered these subjects you struggle with years before you did, and here we are, your father and I, spending all sorts of money on a lazy dumb kid."

The scene shifted.

"What are you doing here?" she said. "Your chores aren't going to get done sitting here in the tree staring into the sky. How did you get to be so lazy? You didn't learn it from your father or I, or anyone else in our family. You're the laziest kid

---

[13] They said more, but he could never bring himself to tell me what.

I've ever seen. The Bakers down the street, do you see Annabelle stopping to watch the sky? I can't even look Mrs. Baker in the face anymore when I see her because she always loves to talk about how her children are such hard workers, and boy oh boy what does Rafael do up in that tree all day long? Your father is away right now working all day long all summer so that you can engorge your fat gut with the fruits of his labors, and the way that you thank him is by sitting around on your lazy butt? How can you even climb that tree with that tub of lard around your waist? Get down here right now and stop being such a slob. Ick. How I had you as a child I will never know. If I hadn't birthed you myself, I would never believe it."

There were many scenes like this, but the last one he saw was much shorter. All he heard was, "A priest? Just as I suspected. Too fat and stupid to get a real job. I always knew you'd be the failure of the family. I have to go."

Each individual was tormented in their own way for what seemed like hours. In those hours everyone had their darkest fears confirmed, their own worthlessness and insignificance proved. Slowly but surely each member gave himself (or herself) up. What was life if it was meaningless? Why take one more breath away from a world with a deeper meaning you could never be a part of? Everyone gave themselves up to death, the supposed deserved state for their worthlessness.

And suddenly in that darkest night a light shone out in the black. From behind the trees a broad piercing white beacon came shining through the undergrowth, cutting through the whispers, driving out the shades, and giving their eyes a pinprick of hope to focus on. Shadows moved this way and that as the light slowly hobbled and moved through the ravine. The traveler's eyes were blinded by its resplendent incandescence as it drew near. The whispers grew more shrill and fierce, and as the ravine lightened, they could see themselves surrounded by dark figures, animated inkblots in nature. With a final crash, Etienne came pounding out through the briars holding a terrifically bright sword.

"Be gone witches, servants of the eternal pit!" Etienne shouted, "I hold the fire of Ariens, the star-sword of the west! You have no power here!"

In the bright light their dark figures were revealed, and Alana could see the shapes of the Furies: coal black beings with dark wings and bloodshot eyes. In their hands they carried scourges and with each whipping the air rang out with a whisper of despair.

"You are nothing," they replied in unison. "You, of all people, are the biggest failure of them all."

"I have nothing to fear from you, foul demons," Etienne said, "and I will not answer to your baseless claims. You are servants of the pit, and you must obey the light of the heavens."

"Baseless they are not, Aaron," they whipped their scourges at him and flashes of dark screamed past. "Will you lead them to destruction as well?"

"Enough, you have had your warning! You are not fit to speak to such as us! You have no business with the noble on earth!" he shouted.

"You cannot be counted among the noble, oh homeless one, wanderer among the tribes. You have nothing to offer them except death, like all who follow you. Will you lead us all to destruction then?" The furies screeched with hate as they backed away from the sword.

"Enough! I will lead you to destruction as you request!" Etienne shouted, and sprang upon them, a tiger to his prey. His sword flashed out crashes of lightning as it rang, fierce songs of destruction being heaped upon their heads. He struck one in two, and she shrank and withered away into a puff of smoke with a vicious high-pitched scream. The others screamed and whipped their scourges, the darkness flashing through the air like bolts of black lightning, but the fire of

Ariens held them at bay. Etienne slowly beat them back, slashing and flashing his sword as he went, each stroke letting loose lightning and an ancient chorus of doom, sung by great men long since passed in tongues they could not recognize.

He reached the end of the clearing where Alana had stopped the night before, the Furies now keeping their distance from his sword as they hissed forth their hate, and he turned to the group, who had slowly regained enough strength to stand behind him. "What are you waiting for?" he whispered. "Get the hell out of here!" and he stepped into the undergrowth to chase off the demons.

Like a flash, the group scrambled to pick up whatever was most important and they were off. They passed by Etienne's animals and encampment not that much later, but in their panic, they had no thought for the absent member of their party. They ran past his things and his braying animals and headed out of the far side of the ravine. They ran like squirrels, like the scared children the Furies had taken them to be.

Each carried scars from that night for as long as they lived, and none could bring themselves to unveil to another the full terror and despair they felt the moment before Etienne appeared. Ethan would never tell me more than the first few minutes of his torture; the rest he couldn't even bring himself to speak, and he'd shudder and shut down into a low-grade anxiety attack if I ever asked. He left the demons behind but carried them with him.

They ran for hours to the north, incapable of talking, running with an animal fury, a primal horror taking over and pushing them forward, long past their point of exhaustion and ability to breathe. They ran towards the gates of hell to escape its jaws.

They collapsed the next day around noon, a shoddy band of pale terrified children. The sun beat down on them, but they lay where they collapsed, each panting and trying to come to terms with what they had just felt.

Later that afternoon Etienne found them. They were sprawled out on the ground, each trying to make some sense of the violation. Etienne roused them with some water, brought them all to sit together, and cooked a soup to help them recover.

They sat in silence, still processing the night's events. Alana could say nothing of the event, but Rafael eventually did.

"Tell me, great one," Rafael said to Etienne, "h...how did you come to save us? How could you move in the darkness? I was totally petrified. I..." he paused, "was sure that I was lost."

Etienne gave him a lopsided smile. "Well, Rafael, there's nothing they can tell me that I don't already know. Over many long years I've come to terms with what I have done and who I am, and they cannot say anything worse than what I've already heard, seen, and lived." He nodded his head and looked at the ground. "No, nothing worse than what I have lived."

They sat around, sipping soup and each too ashamed to speak of what had happened until Ethan finally piped up.

"Your sword," Ethan said, "where did you get that awesome sword?"

Etienne smiled, "My mother," was his brief reply.

Ethan looked down at the ground, "and the runes?"

Etienne's smile immediately disappeared. He looked up and stared at Ethan and said nothing. Alana cocked her head as she looked over. She hadn't noticed the runes inscribed on the sword.

"Who wrote those?" Ethan said, as he shyly kicked the dirt.

Etienne said nothing for a moment, but then replied equally as brief, "I think you know."

CHAPTER 9

Jacques' steamer slipped into Medea in darkness and tied up at port. Travel in those days was relatively slow along the Andaluvian; the train systems weren't yet connected, and the roads were middling at best, so the most reliable way to get anywhere was by boat.

Most reliable and most secretive. Jacques preferred to make these regular trips via boat for the same reason he avoided using the telegraph: if you were, say, on official business that required abject secrecy and involved various acts of questionable legality, you may decide to travel by private anonymous steamer.

The first and second cataracts did slow things down substantially as you had to go around and through a complicated series of locks and canals, but what was a man with taste and questionable morals to do except sleep his way down to Medea in private. He'd of course miss the incredible views where the Andaluvian meets the ocean, providing the stunning backdrop to the equally stunning port capital of Medea, but he'd seen it all before.

Jacques showed his papers to the federal police at the dock, storming through the various checkpoints across the city, and staring down the armed guards, daring them to question his freedom of movement. He was no ordinary citizen here who could be disappeared and tortured on a whim, he was the supreme ruler of Atlas.

He loved to think about his powers and privileges as he was waved on past the bunkers and guard towers, how HE was so important, but if he was honest, and he wasn't, but if he was, he'd have to admit that his special treatment was only due to Scipio's seal.

"Right through, right through!" a soldier waved, on seeing the document. Everyone knew what crossing Scipio meant, and nobody was willing to suffer the consequences.

Jacques strolled into the smokey hallways in the overbearing stone palace converted into the seat of the government of the military junta. Angry voices echoed through the halls, and while the record does not show this explicitly, I like to think that Jacques was super creeped out by the fact that there were people screaming in random cells sprinkled throughout the palace like chocolate chips in a cookie known for committing crimes against humanity.

Jacques was ushered down a series of steps and tunnels deep into the bowels of the ministry. Scipio didn't get to where he was by not being paranoid, and he had calculated every possible way of dispatching him. He knew exactly how easy it would be to shell the above-ground offices from the port, so he conducted all his business deep underground.

"I got your message, why are you here?" Scipio said without even looking up from his paperwork.

Jacques sat down with his characteristic elegance, dressed in his finest casual suit, cravat neatly tucked in, and a flower daintily hanging on his chest. As everyone I talked to always loved to repeat to me, Jacques was a man of the old school, no occasion too informal to come well dressed.

"Aaaarrggghhhh," a scream came from down the hall.

Probably.

"I need you to stop interfering with the plan," Jacques replied, not referring to the unsubstantiated screaming.

"Oh, am I interfering?" Scipio replied, furiously scribbling away at various notes on his desk, and shifting papers from one mountainous stack on the left side of his desk, to another equally mountainous stack on the right. I'm pretty sure he was just trying to intimidate Jacques with useless paper everywhere, but since he destroyed all his records, I'll never know. "I'm solving the problem YOU created, the problem that YOU are incapable of solving. The girl is my problem now," he said.

"That's your problem," Jacques said. "You're always so direct, always so easy to read. I can always tell it's a Scipio plan because it always lacks tact, imagination, and above all, inspiration."

"Arrgghhhhh" came another scream from the floor above. Probably.

"You've left me no choice now, have you Jacques?" Scipio put his papers down and looked directly at Jacques now. "Our agreement was for you to bring the girl here, and what did you do? You literally opened the door and asked her to go play wherever she wants. What good are my amazing plans when my counterpart can't follow the simplest part of the plan? Only a leader of Atlas would be so dumb, it's like they make you take stupid pills in order to run that ridiculous country. You wouldn't be a stump of a nation if there were a single intelligent person in the entire parliament!"

Jacques smiled. Now this was the Scipio he was expecting to meet.

"I had hoped," Jacques said as he regained a bit of his normal flair, now that the situational dynamics met his expectations, "to come to an arrangement with her. As you know, her father and I were close."

"An arrangement?!" Scipio yelled, and far down the

corridor another fictional scream echoed out in return. "An arrangement? You don't come to an arrangement with the daughter of Titus the second!" he continued yelling. "And you weren't close to him! Nobody was! That man was a monster! Totally unreasonable! Unquestionably the most insane ruler I've ever encountered." Scipio stood up and pulled down his collar to reveal a long snaking scar. "You know he gave me this, right?"

Jacques peered over in the dim light and shook his head, "I had no idea," he lied.

"The darn fool was drunk during a summit and got it into his head that he was being attacked. He came after me with a knife, and I just barely managed to keep him from getting it into my heart. I've never been so close to death in my life, and it was only because I didn't keep my guard up for one moment in time, one moment when everyone was relaxed and drinking, and suddenly a madman is trying to skewer me." Scipio sat down breathing heavily and attempted to relax. "No, you do not come to an arrangement with the progeny of that kind of monster. He was abrasive, petulant, headstrong, and while I consider him one of the worst tacticians I have ever faced, he had all of the luck in the world to keep anyone from outmaneuvering him in any situation."

"Maybe a little bit the hand of luck, maybe a little bit the hand of god," Jacques said. "Or the hand of Jacques...until his luck ran out of course."

Scipio raised his eyebrow, "Did it now. Did it now?" He glared at Jacques. "I am sure it was 'luck' running out. Regardless, a man with unholy luck has a child, and you take the chance at her being loose. No thank you. The girl is my problem now, and you know how I deal with my problems." Scipio said with a tone of finality.

"Yes, yes, with a total lack of imagination," Jacques said. "I figured you would send an assassin, but I did not expect you to have a spy embedded in army high command," he said as he slow clapped, "bravo my friend, bravo."

Scipio slightly bowed.

Jacques stopped suddenly and put his finger to his temple. "It's just such a pity that you showed your hand so blatantly, so obviously, may I say, so unoriginally, because you've just lost that asset," he said angrily.

Scipio grumbled but said nothing.

"It's like I said before. It's always so easy to spot a plan of Scipio's." Jacques continued. "And then to send in that madman butcher into the temple at Delphi was just egregiously stupid," he said. "You know I've already broadcast the rest of the nations what you've done. Nobody trusts you anymore, nobody."

"Nobody did trust me you idiot," Scipio said. "I've lost nothing, and I've gained the initiative. The other nations are useless, but the girl can't be allowed to escape."

"Our agreement still stands, she will be neutralized," Jacques said.

"Our agreement was she would be here now, not you!" Scipio snapped.

Jacques said nothing.

A knock came at the door. "Enter" Scipio barked, and an aide came in with a small piece of penciled paper.

"This just in sir," the aide said, and placed the paper on the desk.

"Thank you," Scipio replied, and scanned it over with a smile. He threw it on his desk in front of Jacques and waved his hand above the paper, "well, go ahead, read it now."

Jacques stood and took the paper and read:

"ONE DAY BEHIND AND GAINING"

Jacques furrowed his brow in frustration.

"Well?" Scipio said.

"I have my own people on the ground," Jacques said. "She will be neutralized."

"You're right, because she'll be sitting here next to me in a week," Scipio said, "that butcher you met is highly motivated to succeed."

"Ha!" Jacques said, standing and hitting the desk with his fist. "Alana will never come here. Your plans are checkered from top to bottom with failure. When you make her a martyr, your problems will triple!"

Fictional high-pitched screaming echoed throughout the building, and Jacques sat down with a flourish, unflappable again.

Scipio remained unconvinced. "Say what you want to make yourself feel better, old man," he said to Jacques. "But stay here as long as you like, and you can say hi yourself. This is too important to me."

"So important that you would subvert the entire command structure of the army of a sovereign nation to get her killed? So important you would conduct an assassination attempt across the borders of an allied nation?" Jacques said with venom.

"Step carefully, just imagine what else I could do," Scipio replied threateningly. "First Tiberius, and you never know what comes next."

Jacques looked at Scipio Barca quizzically. "Who is Tiberius?"

Scipio smiled.

Tiberius rode up to the rendezvous, wincing just the tiniest bit from the pain in his leg. It would heal soon enough, but still slowed him down a little.

"Ho there!" a Carpathian rider called out.

"Ho there!" Tiberius replied. The rest of his men rode up behind him, the horses gleaming with sweat from their long ride from Atlas.

"You say you found them?" he asked.

"A group of ours ran across them not far from here," the rider said, "but they were massacred" he said angrily. "We see now why Medea wants them dead, and we will help."

"Not dead," Tiberius replied, "I need the woman alive; the rest can die."

"It will be difficult for us to grant that wish," the rider replied.

"But you must!" Tiberius demanded. "She is too important to me."

The rider muttered, and his men behind him grumbled.

"Where are they now?" Tiberius asked, looking around the grey plains.

"We think they're riding hard to the north," the rider replied. "They must be trying to get to Titan through the eastern approach as the passes on the other side are snowed in."

"Can we catch them in time?" Tiberius asked.

"Definitely," the rider laughed, "we can take the roads, they must be hiding in the foothills." He said gesturing to the rolling hills to the east of them. "The eastern approach to Titan is well guarded by our brothers and just terrifically convoluted and exposed on the mountainside."

"Excellent," Tiberius said. "Lead us with extreme haste. We do not need rest."

"Okay!" the rider shouted, and then to his me he yelled, "Off!" and the horses pounded away to the north.

Ethan nodded awake before the others and wrapped his cloaks around him tightly as he shivered in the morning cold. He could see his breath here in the cold foothills, and a thin layer of frost lay spread out in the rolling hills. The sun was just starting to light the skies in the west behind the mountains and the dark blue glow of the sky above was slowly shifting to yellows and pinks.

A few feet away he saw Etienne huddled under his wraps, sitting on a log and staring intently into the western sky. He always asked for morning watch duty and was the only other awake.

Ethan slipped over to him in the silence. "What are you looking at?" he asked.

Etienne jumped a little from the surprise; he hadn't heard him coming. Quickly wiping his eyes, Etienne pointed up in the west and mumbled quietly, "The morning star," he said.

Ethan shrugged his shoulders as he looked at it, confused at whatever emotion Etienne was feeling. "Pretty," he said.

"Sure," Etienne said with finality, and stood up and started preparing breakfast.

They trudged up and down the foothills those days, staying as close to the mountains as they could to avoid contact with anyone else, occasionally spotting settlements or signs of life in the valleys below. Each of them carried a heavy heart, knowing their weakness, knowing their inferiority. Each wondered how Etienne had overcome the Furies.

What felt like weeks only took days, but you try walking under a constant grey sky and unending hills during the mosquito blooms of the foothills and marshlands, and it'll start to make sense as to why Rafael recorded in scrawling desperate handwriting that they walked for about fourteen more days than they actually did.

They began to see the wisdom of Etienne in maintaining almost a total covering of his body as they were each eaten alive by mosquitos. But the mosquitos brought out the lizards and rodents, and the lizards and rodents brought out the foxes and eagles, and balance would eventually be restored.

Eventually, that is, for now they were covered in bites and it sucked. But that wasn't the only negative.

Late one afternoon, when they were close to calling it quits, as they came over one of the endless hills thick with grass a harsh wind hit them, sucking the air out of their mouths and taking their breath away.

"There must be thousands of them!" Etienne exclaimed as he gasped for air.

Spread out in the valley before them they saw hundreds of tiny yellow dots as dusk overtook the northern skies. The wind practically blew them off their feet.

"Uhhhh, this is a problem," Mateo panicked.

"This is a problem..." Alana trailed off in thought.

"Get down you idiots!" Ethan shout-whispered behind them, and they dropped to the ground, and the soldiers led the animals behind the hill.

"Friends," Alana said, "we have a bit of a problem."

"I think I already said that," Mateo said in an escalating panic. "As did you."

The wind blew the thick dark green grass this way and that, as if angry gods dueled for which direction the tempest should come.

"Look," Rafael said, "I don't mean to be totally thick, but could maybe someone explain to me what we're seeing here? Forest fire? Large sacrificial burning? An exceptionally large gathering of stationary fireflies?"

Etienne spoke first, "It appears your Carpathian friends have not forgotten you..."

"And they brought some friends along with them..." said Alana forebodingly.

Mateo piped up in panic, "We are doomed we are doomed we are doomed," he said, "I say we give them Etienne and make it clear he did the killing, we were just innocent bystanders trying to rob graves like respectable citizens, and then we run like mad in the other direction," he gesticulated wildly in the opposite direction.

"Calm down you idiot," Etienne said, "you are one crazy son of a,"

"Wonderful woman," Rafael interjected, "his mother is a wonderful woman, as are all of our mothers."

"...wonderful woman," Etienne finished, then continued, "What you folks are seeing here is making history! What an honor you have to observe this! This is the first time it's happened in a generation, and you get a front row seat! How lucky!"

"Woohoo," Mateo moaned.

"I never thought I'd live to see the day. Boy do those tribes hate each other. I wonder how they got over that? Someone has been busy..." and Etienne trailed off.

"Wait, what am I looking at?" Ethan asked.

"The tribes of the west, long scattered and leaderless since the fall of Ariens, are gathering." Etienne pointed at the center of the mass, "those will be the Carpathians who we are anxious to avoid," and he pointed to several lines of light leading along roads to the center, "and those will be outer tribes coming together with them." Etienne stood, overpowered with emotion. "I never thought I'd live to see the day."

"Never thought you'd live to see the day, or never thought you'd live past the day?" Alana asked.

"The fall of Ariens broke them as a people, shattered the center of mass, and sent the remainder scattering in every direction. It's easy for you Atlassians to scoff, but this is momentous. They've never had enough gravity to return together again." Etienne held his hand of his heart in reverence.

"What are our options, guide and protector?" Alana asked. "Or is this momentous occasion cause for joy, mixed with minor annoyance at our imminent death?"

Mateo huffed and his thick chin quivered as he practically shouted in frustration, "At what point do we decide this is too much to do? The world has changed so much since your father was buried; the old ways are crumbling. How many armies are we going to need to beat in order to find this thing?"

"SHHHHH" Ethan elbowed him.

"Oh, back off you hick, those fires are over three miles away, they can't hear us from that far" Mateo said as he slapped his arm away with an arm roughly the size and jiggliness of a tuna fish.

The green gem suddenly reached out and enwrapped Ethan in vision. He paused and stared into nothingness.

Etienne looked at Ethan in panic. "What's going on, Ethan?" He said.

Ethan broke from his vision and pointed behind them "They're here," he said.

"Down!" Etienne screamed.

BLAM BLAM BLAM

Shots erupted from further down the hill.

"On your horses!" Etienne shouted.

"We are so screwed," Mateo said.

"Leave it all, but keep your rifles, for the love of the gods keep those!" Alana shouted.

"Follow me!" Etienne shouted. "I will keep my word to you, you are under my protection!"

They cut the loads from their horses, mounted, and rode the only direction they could: down the hill, from the frying pan, into the fires.

The pink and orange hues above settled into purples and blues, and then a star twinkled out in the night. Constellation after constellation appeared, and Alana looked heavenward as she rode in terror into the springing trap. "There is a way, there is a way, show me the way."

But even in her pleadings, seeds of anger and doubt sprouted. What use was her trip to the Oracle? The hundreds of sacrifices she had performed? The prayers to Hermes for safe travel and guidance? What's the point of observance if it doesn't translate into assistance? How does it matter that she followed the laws and ordinances exactly as prescribed, if she couldn't count on the gods to come to her aid when she needed them? Why was it that she was required to pay them notice at all times and every day, but they could pick and choose when to pay notice to her? As the trap sprung between the riders, she grew furious. Everything she had done; all of her work, was useless in the end. Nothing mattered, and the gods didn't care. If there were gods at all.

The riders that had found them had overtaken the top of the hill, and seeing their escape, sought to hem them in against the mountains. There would be no escape. Between Alana and the thousands of the united western tribes there stood no chance of freedom.

Well, not quite.

Ethan saw the mountains hemming them in and offered a frantic prayer to Hephaestus. As the horses sped down the hill, even in the dim light he began to see the outer encampments of westerners begin to mount and come to intercept them. "Please," he pleaded, "grant us passage"

What came next is hotly (pun intended) disputed, but by Ethan's and several others' accounts, high up on top of the steep snow-capped mountains to their right, a flaming figure emerged in the coming darkness, and struck an imposing facade against the increasingly-starry sky. He watched the ruckus below with mild amusement as sparks flapped off his heavy blacksmith's apron he wore in front.

Ethan looked up on the mountain with wonder. He pointed to the figure, the mountain, and the encampments. The figure surveyed the situation and assessed.

After a moment, the flaming figure drew from beside him an ancient hammer, carved with intensely intricate patterns burning white hot to a degree that it shone brighter than any star behind it in the sky. He lifted the hammer high up above his head with both arms, and then struck it against the mountain with an echoing boom.

The ground shook and the trees swayed beneath the escapees at the blast. High up, the tops of the mountains began quaking with a force never before seen on earth. The peaks cast their boulders to the ground, and the entire mountain range began to shake and move from head to toe. The fiery figure steadied himself with the hammer as the mountains shook, then disappeared from the peak. Moments later they heard the deep sound of bellows blowing from deep within the mountains and out into the plains. The mountains fully tore apart, forming a grand divide between them, with a hot blast of air from an oven blowing down out of the canyon as it ripped. Fires burned up and down the rent mountainside, the landscape now the very likeness of Hades itself, and short lava bursts exploded on either side of the canyon, draining from the peaks down to the valleys below, running rivers through the encampments, and momentarily scattering the united tribes.

The figure then appeared again further down on the mountainside and pointed to Ethan as they rode. He lifted the gigantic hammer up in the sky with one hand, and with some effort pointed up the canyon as lightning crackled and pointed up the canyon. And with that Hephaestus bowed his respects to Ethan, took his hammer, and once again dwelt inside the mountain.

"We're saved!" Ethan shouted around to the rest of the group. "To Titan we go!" Etienne, always flexible in his choice of plan, spurred his horse faster and yelled behind him, "Follow me if you wish to live!" His horse kicked up on its hind legs and roared a warhorse cry, and they sped up the newly formed canyon.

From in front and behind, thousands of riders cursed their gods in confusion at what just happened, and urged their horses onwards, but Alana and the rest were already well ahead of them at the mouth of the newly formed canyon. Up they sped behind Etienne along steep walls of burnt black rock. Some of the group began to slow as their horses tired as they were not suited for an extensive pursuit. Slowly the group spread out along the hot canyon trail. Alana, with the finest steed, took the lead, with others struggling to keep up. She was determined to make it out of the trap, and her indomitable will drove her faster than everyone.

And yet, even in the moment of deliverance Alana's anger at the gods simmered. A fine path to be had for sure, but her men were falling behind, and the pursuit was still hot...

Behind her a shot rang out in the canyon. A lucky shot to be sure, but it felled one of her men, and he was lost forever to the pursuing horde. And still they rode on.

With another shot, another was hit in the leg, blood trickling down onto the hot ground, hissing and throwing up steam as it splayed on the burning rocks along the path.

A third shot hit Mateo in the shoulder, and he fell with a high-pitched scream.

"Hold your ground!" Alana shouted to the others behind her, "Form a line! Covering fire!"

Quick as a flash her men reacted, off their horses and rifles up before they hit the ground in prone position firing. A fierce night battle commenced; the pursuers hemmed in the narrow canyon were unable to outflank the tiny band who were well concealed behind rocks in the canyon, and who exacted deadly revenge on any who approached Mateo in the open.

The westerners rained lead on the soldiers as best they could, and slowly advanced up the canyon towards Mateo, hopping from steaming boulder to steaming boulder. They were approaching him, and almost had reached him, but then up stood Etienne with fire in his belly as well as his mechanical gun.

Up whirred the clinking as the barrels started rotating, and then Ethan watched in shock as Etienne engaged the firing mechanism. The twelve barrels blast out bullets in rapid succession, and even as he braced against the kick, Etienne was slowly pushed backwards along the ground until he ran up against a granite boulder behind him that stabilized him.

The rocks and hills soil around Mateo exploded, and the westerners, some Carpathian, some others, were forced to retreat out of range. They were at an impasse, and Mateo was in the middle.

Alana swum in expletives like a fish in the ocean, and she cursed the day she allowed a desk jockey to come on the journey. She swore that anyone else would have had the dexterity to hang on and make it through, but now she was stuck dealing with his incompetence.

Between quick spurts of gunfire, which seemed like an eternity, she considered her options.

"We can leave him, right?" She whispered to no one in particular. "Look at that wound. They'll be able to patch him up. If we bring him along, we're all dead for sure."

Etienne looked at her in disbelief. "What did you just say?" he said.

"We cannot retrieve him, and every second we waste we bring judgement upon ourselves. We all chose to come, and there's nothing we can do." She said resolutely. "We must continue on the mission."

"The mission? The mission??!" Rafael said in exasperation. "What do you think this is?" And removing the decision from her hands, he spat out, "screw it," and he picked himself off the ground to return to his childhood friend, alone and bleeding in no man's lane. He owed him a deliverance after all.

"Rafa!" Alana called out. "What are you doing?"

The same childhood friend now despised him, ignored him, and looked down on him, but for a moment in time long ago they were friends, and Rafael would never forget it. He would die here and now, what difference would it make? Better to die a priest than live a cockroach.

He huddled over as low as he could get and ran this way and that to avoid the gunshots, quickly weaving his way to Mateo. Mateo moaned as Rafael approached, "what are you doing here?" he demanded.

Rafael smiled back. "Just a moment," he whispered.

From within his clothing he searched for his light sticks, the ones he had greeted Alana with at the bridge oh so many days ago. In all the excitement they had broken to pieces, but ever resourceful, Rafael pulled out a mashed handful of pieces and rubbed them together with his fingertips.

The westerners were thoroughly confused at this point, unsure if shooting Rafael would get them Alana, or scare the rest off. And so, they stopped and watched what unveiled before them. Rafael knelt in front of his friend and traced the amber arcs of flame with his fingertips in the darkness, drawing light on the canvas of the black night. The characters hung in the night air in strokes of fire, etched into the night with a chisel. He called out his incantations as he finished the charm. He called protection down upon Mateo with the ancient symbols he drew with his hands in the sky.

"You idiot!" Alana screamed in the silence, "you're drawing a target for yourself!" she screamed in fury.

Rafael was unfazed. He drew artful calligraphy and symbology, calling upon the powers of Apollo to save them. The westerners watched in entranced confusion, the soldiers and Ethan in admiration, Alana in frustration, and Etienne in joy. Who was this boy?

Alana screamed again, and Rafael heard her this time, and distracted, turned to face her, and the charm was broken. The westerners weren't sure what to do, but they were starting to feel this would not end well for them, so the shots rang out again, and this time Rafael fell, entrapping two of their party in no man's land, doubling the decision.

Ethan stood up to run to him. Alana shouted, "No, not you! I need you! You need to get me to the royal grounds! You have nothing to gain by going back!"

Ethan shook his head and replied, "I have nothing to lose either," and off he went.

He didn't make it more than a few moments before far

behind him, further up the canyon he heard deep booms which echoed down the canyon walls. He turned his head around as he sped along and looked up the canyon expecting to see another fiery apparition, but there was nothing but darkness. "Thunder?" he thought.

He flipped his head around and watched the fiery hell of the newly born canyon erupt in explosions in front of him.

You've no doubt been to firework shows celebrating whatever random assortment of holidays they fire them for in your country, dear reader, but only a select few have had the privilege of coming under heavy artillery bombardment. And by have had the privilege, I mean have suffered the misery and terror. I must admit, I have yet to experience this pleasure, and my sincerest condolences to those of you that have.

Next time you go see fireworks, get as close to the explosions as you possibly can. Feel the shockwave from the explosion pulse through your body. Smell the burning sulfur. And then admit that you have no idea what it could possibly be like to have those exploding in your face, not in the sky.

The shells from the bombardment erupted in the mouth of the canyon, spewing death and smoke in their path.

Alana saw the shelling down the canyon, then looked up the canyon and smiled. For an artilleryman like herself, this was the smell of freedom.

Hephaestus had opened up a direct path to Titan, and he must have caught the attention of the outer sentries on the old eastern approach. Ethan zig-zagged his way to Rafael, not taking any chances even if the Carpathians and their allies were under heavy bombardment and saw the last of the amber light fade out above Mateo. "They must have seen the signs," he whispered. "Rafael you old dog you."

Hope started to spring inside everyone once again. Titan! Land of the free! The great northern hope of the nations. Long neglected by its sister nations, it could yet be counted on in a pinch. Here and now Titan was proving to be their savior.

By the pale moonlight that illuminated the canyon, the outer sentries of Titan fired round after round into the mayhem calculating their distances from the last amber light. They wrought total confusion among the western tribes who had pursued Alana's company, and functionally stopped them dead in their tracks. In the darkness Ethan and company heard screeching round followed by screeching round, ending in the largest destructive power Ethan had ever seen. Yellows and reds and whites exploded and heaved black rock throughout the canyon entrance and screams and cries of men and beast alike were heard.

Everyone in Alana's group, now emboldened, followed Ethan and rushed forward to attend to the others. They bound them as best they could and hefted them onto horses like luggage. With that, they beat an orderly retreat up the canyon to the sounds of shelling.

The initial barrage only lasted a few minutes but sent enough of a message. From time to time as they climbed an occasional shell was fired from high above just to remind their erstwhile pursuers. Alana wasn't worth certain death to most of them. Not with Titan taking their side.

Several exhausting and miserable hours scrambling up a rocky path later, the group rounded a gigantic boulder in the path, and were challenged by several soldiers, rifles at the ready.

"Halt!" the first one said. "Please identify yourselves. Please note that if you so much as move you will die, and I will not feel even the least bit bad about it."

Alana, at the back, weary and trudging alongside as Mateo was draped across her horse, called out from the back and came forward.

"I am Alana, crown princess of Atlas, daughter of Titus II. These are my aides. We seek the protection of Titan." she said.

The sentry looked her up and down. She was covered in

mud, sweat, blood, and tears, panting from the high altitude, and clearly one step short of collapse.

"If you're the princess, I'd hate to see the subjects in your realm," he said. He looked back and saw his commander give a thumbs up. "You seek our protection? You've got it. Tell me these two aren't western spies though before you can pass."

"They are my guides," Alana said before Etienne could loudly object for his wounded pride. "They have protected me from the riders you so eloquently saved me from earlier."

The sentry looked them up and down and nodded. "Well, move along then, the Private here will take you the rest of the way." And a boy they had not seen standing next to him appeared to melt away from the boulder and motioned to follow.

"Thank you, Captain," Alana said, and bowed.

They walked past the small group of soldiers keeping watch over the long border ridgeline, their trenches, and their signal equipment. They ascended another painful half mile before the guide stopped them and looked back for several minutes, searching for someone who wasn't there. He motioned them to follow him off the path over several boulders, and into an overhang. He returned and brushed away their tracks as best he could.

Inside the overhang he removed some shrubs to expose a small, narrow entrance, just enough that a horse could squeeze through. They stumbled through into the blackness beyond.

They shuffled and bumped into each other as they left the moonlight for true honest-to-goodness, can't-see-your-hand-in-front-of-your-face pitch black. As they tried to catch their footing and mumbled their complaints, the Private finally spoke.

"This way to Titan" he said, and he lit a lamp. In front of them lay an enormous open natural auditorium, filled with glistening and glowing stones and gems of every type, stalactites, stalagmites, you name it. "It's not far if you go under the mountain," and he picked his way across the rocks strewn across the way, meandering towards one of countless passages. He was young and spry, and quickly darted ahead of the larger group.

"Do you think he knows where he's going?" Rafael whispered to Alana.

"I'm sure hoping," Alana replied back.

"I can hear you people!" the boy called back, his yell echoing through the caverns.

The group jumped to follow, scrambling through the cavern into the passage behind the guide.

Ethan stayed behind with Rafael and Mateo, doing his best to help them hobble their way to freedom. Alana eventually noticed their absence up front and wandered back to find them.

It was getting darker as the private with the lamp scampered off faster. He would notice the needs of others later in life, just not now.

"Hold up!" Alana called, her voice echoing into muddle through the caves.

The four of them tried to go faster to catch up with the group, but soon they found themselves in the pitch black, arms outstretched, feeling for the walls as they made their way forward.

"Could it get any worse than getting lost in a pitch-black cave?" Alana whined.

"We could be chained up?" Ethan said.

"Why would you even say that?" Alana asked, "don't jinx us."

"Hey! I'm supposed to be the superstitious one, not you!" Rafael huffed in pain.

Alana abruptly stopped.

"Bad news guys," she said.

"What?" they all said.

"There are two passages here; I have no idea which way they went." Alana said.

"Hello!" Alana called out, echoing down the way. "Hello!"

They waited a few tense minutes, and no reply.

"Curse that eager beaver private!" Mateo said as he gasped in pain.

Ethan tried listening as hard as he could, but there was nothing.

The group grew restless. The thought of being stuck here was not exciting to anyone, especially with the wounds that needed caring.

As the minutes ticked down, Ethan pulled out his mother's necklace. "Help me find the way," he said quietly. He wrapped his hand around the thick leather strands and felt the green gem underneath.

"Please mother," Ethan pleaded. "Please."

"What's that?" Alana asked.

From between Ethan's knuckles thin green wisps of light emerged and curled their way into the cave, casting eerie shadows on the walls.

"Shhhh," Ethan replied, and continued his silent pleas. "Please mother, please."

The green light sprang towards the passage on the right and laid out a ghostly trail up the path.

"That way," Ethan whispered to the group and began to follow.

Alana and the others followed in amazement as the green light shot from passageway to passageway leaving them a clear dimly lit trail.

It wasn't long until the green light lost its energy and started to fall flat on the ground and melt away, but as it did, another light took over: a dim starlight shone into the cave.

They followed the starlight out of a large entryway into a brisk evening on a mountainside facing Titan where they found their compatriots.

"Took you long enough!" they teased.

For the first time in weeks they were safe. They patched up Rafael and Mateo as best they could and bedded down under the brightest stars they had ever seen. Sleep came to them quickly.

CHAPTER 10

Alexander, staff sergeant and long-suffering aide to Tiberius found him the next morning, staring in anger at the cloudy haze hanging over the canyon entrance from the night before.

"Well that was unexpected," Alexander said.

Tiberius looked at him with fury in his eyes.

"Unexpected?! Unexpected! To say the least you Neanderthal! The Carpathians said the trail was winding steep and narrow, not a wide highway they could sweep on through! We had should have had them totally hemmed in! All we had to do was close our fist and they were ours. First the advance party is easily destroyed, and now after tracking them across miserable marshlands for miles we find them, only to have them slip away. I'll say it's unexpected." Tiberius ranted.

"Well, you can't really blame them for not predicting seismic activity" Alexander said. He was so much more capable of resigning himself to his fate than Tiberius ever would be.

"They knew there were volcanoes around here, they could have chosen another spot for the trap. And don't even get me started on the artillery. What do I need to do to get these savages to tell me that the canyon they choose to camp out by leads directly to Titan and practically has a get out of jail free card attached to it in the form of a brigade standing by to save any random passersby???!" Tiberius railed.

Alexander stayed much calmer, but also generally much less worried about accomplishing the mission at hand, as he knew he could always count on his commanding officer. And besides, it wasn't his honor on the line with Scipio. "In their defense, Tiberius, they just stopped killing each other a few months ago, so I'm just glad we didn't end up in a full-on shooting war last night." he said.

Tiberius pursed his lips. "Fair. Grade the savages on a curve. But still. How this was unforeseeable is beyond me." he said.

Alexander rolled his eyes. Tiberius was never reasonable. "Well, next move?" Alexander asked. "Follow?"

"Nah, that's suicide at this point. Even I can't invade a country with a few men and innumerable unreliable allies. Let's head down to port and send ahead for a friendly vessel. We know where they're going, we'll just get them a little later, and this time, I'll be shooting them myself instead of hoping that the incompetence brigade can get them." Tiberius said.

"K boss, you got it," Alexander said. "We'll be ready to head out in minutes."

"Thanks," Tiberius said, and went off to consult with his allies before leaving. "Vercingetorix you idiot," he mumbled under his breath. This was a misstep, for sure, but he still had plenty of time to reel Alana back in.

Titan in springtime is the most beautiful place in the entire cosmos. There are no humans or gods who don't agree with me.[14] Maybe you don't, and while I'm sure you've visited beautiful places before, nothing can compare.

Ethan woke up to a shock. Before him a beautiful green valley spread out surrounded by snow-capped mountains as far as the eye could see. In front of him lay a giant deep blue lake surrounded by what appeared to be every wildflower that had ever lived on the continent. Songbirds returned from their long winter absence and sang his name. The breeze tussled the lakefront and flowers, and, drenched with perfumes, nuzzled the party awake. If there is a heaven, it is springtime in Titan.

They were sore. Endless days of walking and riding, coaxing animals up and down difficult terrain, followed by a mad dash up a dark canyon had taken their toll. Nobody was free from wounds of some sort, and some of them had minor gunshot wounds, like Mateo, with a bullet in his shoulder and a nasty stench from his drenched, dried, and drenched again bandages. Rafael winced and moaned every time he moved: he had been hit in an arm, a leg, and a bullet had grazed (and likely broken) a rib as he fell.

That is to say, they were totally unprepared for the beauty into which they trespassed.

As Rafael blinked his eyes in the bright northern sun, he tried to make sense of where he was and what had happened. For a moment he was convinced this was death, but slowly the images rolled back in his mind: the riders, the fiery figure, the hasty escape, and the miraculous caves of the night before. Miles and miles an underground maze, filled with subterranean lakes, rivers, rock formations, all in the craziest shapes you'll ever see. He wondered what god had built it, or how such a hell could exist outside the realm of Hades, ruler of the underworld. "What tales I have to tell my fellow priests" he thought, and then coughed just a tiny bit of blood. "If I can

---

[14] Save those with allergies, who are exempted from this sweeping declaration.

get back to my fellow priests..."

The sentry from the night before smirked as the group stared down at his home. The flatlanders had no idea what wonders he guarded. He stood and swept his arm out dramatically across the valley. "Welcome to paradise," he said.

Ethan continued to stare in wonder at the beauty and was the only one who could voice a reply. "Welcome indeed," he said. A giant flock of pelicans drifted overhead and alighted on the water. For a sublime iota of time, they were indeed in paradise.

They made their way down the grassy slope to Titan, smallest of the five nations, and last to be settled. The capital city lay nestled by a lake, sprawling out to the mountains in the south, and settlements and factories spreading out along the rivers leading out of the valley to the north. Of the five nations it had the fewest connections to the other nations, as most direct routes were largely impassable in winter (though that was solved through extensive railroad tunneling later, this was still in the early days pre-connection). They had a bit of a chip on their shoulder, as they were usually left out of any serious matters, being so far away from everyone else, and largely an afterthought on any party invite list.

Alana had only ever met one resident of Titan, and he found them at the military barracks, where their injuries were being taken care of, and Mateo's utterly disgusting bandages were finally getting addressed by poor nurses who couldn't possibly have been getting paid enough.

"Welcome Alana, princess of Atlas!" Artur bowed at the entrance. "What a joy to see you again! I'm so happy to see you safe here in the high northern redoubts of the five nations. You are welcome here any time, we only ask that you not tell anyone else of our transcendent beauty or we'll be overrun by refugees fleeing the dreary monotony of the flatlands."

Alana smiled. "Thank you, my dear cousin. We are forever

indebted to you and your kindness," Alana said, attempting a small bow, obviously hindered by various aches and pains and uncontrolled swelling. It had been a rough couple of weeks.

Artur walked to Alana and gave her a hug, the rest of his entourage smartly shaking hands. Don't be confused by their greetings, no reasonable person on earth would have claimed them to be cousins, but these were royals, not normals. It's like those people who find their fifth cousins thrice removed and then claim to be super tight because of that shared great-great-great grandma, except everyone knows they're just being super weird. Artur and Alana were separated by some forgotten ancient common ancestor, not like the weird first cousin you dread seeing at a family reunion and then pretend like you're busy when they're in town.

No, they were incredibly distant relatives, but sure, you can call them cousins if you want to be strange about it.

Artur walked around the room acquainting himself with everyone, shaking hands, memorizing faces and stories.

"I thought we were dead for sure," said Ethan. "I had given up on any hope. Your men saved us," he said.

"No, no, no, not my men," said Artur, "I am but prince of Titan, and serve the queen myself. You'll have to give due credit to my mother, Queen Ophelia, and her generals. I am a lowly captain. I haven't served on the western lines for..." and at that he paused as his eye caught a glimpse of glistening metal under a dark cloak.

He pushed past some of Alana's soldiers and found Etienne standing in the back, elegant and imperial as always. Artur stood next to him and stared up into his dark countenance, scowling. Etienne removed his dark hood out of respect, and Artur pursed his lips at the sight of his sunken eyes and thick matted-down white hair.

"And how did you come to arrive here...westerner?" Artur asked, the vitriol practically visible in the air.

"I apologize for any intrusion, Captain," said Etienne, "but

I was leading this group through the western lands, and as we were attacked, had no other route to offer but an escape through Titan."

Artur looked him up and down. "You'll have seen the route through the caves then?" his voice was low and dangerous.

"Captain, I asked the sentry to bind my eyes, and my horse was led through by the others," Etienne said. "You may ask your man."

Artur looked over to the sentry who was nodding. "You let him in??!" Artur asked in disbelief. The sentry's nodding slowed down, and his eyes shot back and forth as he hesitantly replied, "Yes?"

Alana pushed through the group to intervene. "This man saved my life and has guided us to safety through a dangerous foreign land. We required his assistance, and he gave it freely. You may place any blame on me for any trespass."

Artur reigned in his emotions and looked at Alana. "Very well then, a friend of my cousin's is a friend of mine. However, I must ask that he depart as soon as possible. The rest of you may stay as long as you wish of course," and he glanced up at Etienne with fire in his eyes.

"Of course, captain, I shall be gone in moments." Etienne bowed.

Artur looked at him, "but you cannot return by the same way, it is a secret path, and it must be kept that way," he said.

"Of course, captain, I will retire to the north. You have nothing to fear." Etienne returned his hood and walked out of the room.

Ethan interjected. "But wait, you cannot go! We are in your debt!" he shouted.

Etienne turned to face them, and simply said, "I found you once, I will find you again." and with that he left.

Awkward silence settled in on the group for several minutes as the group went back to tending and nursing their injuries.

As Artur inched his way to the door, Alana caught his gaze. "Thank you, cousin. Your people have saved us." she said.

Artur waved off the thanks with his hands, "my pleasure," he said with hostile curtness. He moved outside the door and called in, "come to the palace when you are able," he said, and snapping his fingers to gather his entourage behind him, off he went.

"Come in, come in, welcome to Titan, welcome to Titan, splendid, splendid!" Queen Ophelia welcomed Alana into the great hall. Here was a woman who spoke with her entire body, arms waving wildly over her head as she motioned her in. Her skin was unnaturally unevenly lighter than most, due to years of splotchily applied creams of every scientific making. Ophelia was dressed head to toe in multiple layers of long, flowing, colorful gowns, and as she waved the fabric fluttered this way and that, giving her a look not too dissimilar to a jellyfish. Well, a very colorful and very royal jellyfish.

Alana stepped forward past the giant oak doors and walked down the center aisle. The building wasn't large by our standards, but it was solidly built, with rows of oak columns holding up the roof; the walls themselves stopped short and offered no support to the roof, presenting an opening to the outside all around the entire building, giving the roof the appearance of floating. Giant fires lined either side of the building as she walked down.

"Thank you, Queen Ophelia, long may you live, and we are grateful to be in your presence. Only through your graces have we survived. Long may Atlas owe you a debt of gratitude." Alana said in her usual elevated royal monotone voice. From behind her, the rest of her party shuffled through the doors, looking up in awe of the light streaming through from around the entire building.

Artur stepped forward from a corner to stand next to his mother. "For such stalwart allies, we offer you our deepest generosity," he said, and came forward to direct them to their seats from which they would address the queen.

Alana and her group sat down, as did Artur. Ophelia stood in her same pose, arms outstretched, fabric moving about in the draft, though she cocked her head to the side, and looked up and outside through the gaps above the walls. She stood like this for several moments in silence until Artur gave a discreet cough. She started a bit, and then sat down in her chair.

Ophelia began, again, every word emphasized with some movement of hand or face, "Splendid, splendid, now tell me how you came to arrive in Titan, please leave out no detail, leave no stone unturned, tell us all we wish to know about your journey. We have so few royal" her voice inflected with heavy emphasis on royal, "visitors at all, and never when the passes are snowed in."

Alana nodded her head, "of course, dear queen. I assembled this group to travel to the north..."

"Ohhh, the north, such a desolate wasteland it is!" Ophelia exclaimed.

"Dear queen, we live in the north," said Artur, "our guests understand it to be quite lovely here."

"But the north is full of those cursed black rocks and then there's talk of the Sphinx and the ocean, oh the ocean is dreary they say I've never seen it myself but it is full of dead people did you know my dears that on ocean voyages when someone dies they just throw them overboard and there they lie? Can you believe such an uncivilized practice takes place? You'd think they'd give them a nice coffin or bury them on land instead of acting like some savages, but my husband, god bless his soul, told me all about those ocean voyages and the dead people lying in the ocean, and the north is full of oceans and so I've no doubt it's full of dead people don't you think?" Ophelia never spoke in sentences, only paragraphs.

There was a brief silence as Alana tried to determine who

she was addressing, and decided it must be her, and so she replied, "I don't know that there is much voyaging going on in the north sea, so it cannot be full of the dead."

"Oh but you are mistaken my dear for any voyage in the north must by necessity throw their dead off into the ocean and so the ocean is full of dead people that is how it is and that is the most dreadful thing I can imagine, aside from those savage westerners on our borders, did you know they've been encroaching further and further into the mountains, and who knows when they're going to stop by and ask for a cup of tea what have you, but I've told my generals, and General Ariel tells me all the time he says 'don't you worry Ophelia, we have great defenses, my men build the best defenses' but how dreadful those westerners are they are getting closer and closer every year and bigger and bigger and we stay the same over here we don't know how much longer we can stand without open warfare with those cursed savages I hear they eat their dead, but I suppose that's fewer for them to throw into the ocean." Ophelia said.

Artur, red in the face, spoke up at this pause, and said, "Dear Alana, what my mother means to say is please continue and tell us how you managed to avoid the westerners on your journey."

Alana was thoroughly confused at this point, but she decided to soldier on.

"We encountered some westerners," she continued.

"Oh, how dreadful!" Ophelia exclaimed, raising a hand to her forehead and sighing.

"But we were able to escape them, thanks to your assistance, oh queen," Alana said.

"But of course of course my men are just the most wonderful soldiers I never have to go looking for one they always are ready to volunteer, 'please send me!' they shout, whenever I go out there are just dozens of boys ready to assist in the defense, and oh dearie me the women as well, such great help they are going to and fro, east and west north and south, but oh dear, did you say you're headed to the north?" Ophelia exclaimed in horror.

"We are indeed headed to the far north, to the gates of Hades," Alana said, looking at Artur with confusion but addressing the queen. "I wish to pay my respects to my father, as I did not have the opportunity to properly when he died."

Ophelia threw up her hands again and Alana cringed just a bit as she prepared for the assailment of words. "Splendid, splendid journey your father was a splendid man I never did meet him my husband did and my husband said what a splendid man except for that awful temper of his he once threw my husband out during a game of cards, so incensed he was that he was losing, and my husband he said that's what killed him you know that short temper and short fuse went right to his heart and if he'd have had a bit more patience he would have lived a long full life but then again my husband died early too and he never got angry at anyone but you can't help that I suppose." Ophelia said.

Alana pursed her lips and furrowed her brow. In any normal circumstance she would be challenging whoever said such things to a duel, but all did not seem right below that crown.

Artur was trying desperately to figure out how to save the latest outburst, and after a few moments of silence, before Alana could reply, he interjected, "and how can we help you on your way then, princess Alana?"

His mother practically jumped out of her seat, "but of course, my manners, you shall have a full royal accompaniment, we shall trumpet you out of the kingdom, my own carriage shall carry you forth, it will be the grandest procession we have ever seen! You can have all of the supplies you need, why spring has come and we'll be trading with our southern neighbors in no time, and those shipments from Medea due come loaded with the most amazing foods you've ever heard of, why I once ate oranges while it was snowing up here and I said how is such a thing possible but my son says we have a good relationship with them and it's all because of..."

Artur jumped in at this point, "because of our excellent mutual love in the five nations, we are just such a wonderful group of peoples with a shared heritage and shared language and shared culture, and we would just do anything for each other, like we will do for you. Well, you heard the queen, let me get back in touch with you soon with your arrangements, and you'll be on your way!"

And with that, he ushered them out of the hall into the blinding northern sun, all while Ophelia stood waving and undulating in the background shouting out, "splendid, splendid, splendid journey, come again soon but next time don't get anyone killed splendid, splendid, splendid journey!"

While they were meeting with Ophelia, queen of Titan, Etienne was doing his best to put as much distance between himself and Artur as possible. "Old hatreds die hard I guess," he said as he got off his horse and gave it a quick rest and a drink at one of the many pools along the route.

He looked back across the long plains and farmlands he had just traveled and saw in the distance two figures closing fast.

Just as he suspected, he was being tracked.

CHAPTER 11

Artur visited Alana once more. His initial friendliness had melted down into a very business-like tone.

"The quartermaster will provide you with whatever supplies you require," he said.

"Thank you," Alana said. "My men, I'd like them to stay here until the passes clear, then return to Atlas."

"I'm sorry," Artur said, "we have no capacity to house them here any longer. A day or two's journey from here to the east there is some open ground on the lower slopes they could camp at until they are ready to move, but I'm afraid that's all we're able to offer."

Alana looked at him with confusion, "There's literally nobody in this entire building, how are you space constrained?"

Artur's voice became colder. "We have no capacity to house them any longer." he said.

Alana brought herself to full standing height and inched nearer to Artur. "These men are shot up, exhausted, and your ALLIES may I remind you!" she exclaimed.

"Fine," said Artur, "in recognition of our allied state, you may remain here for one day longer, but then I'm afraid you must go."

Alana shook her head. "Well, if there is no more hospitality in Titan, they will go to Ithaca." she said.

"Great, Ithaca has plenty of room for traitors," he said.

"What are you getting at?" Alana asked.

He pointed at Mateo, "most people get shot through the back when they're running away, not through the front. Bullet exit wounds are easy to pinpoint," Artur said.

Mateo blushed. "I have no idea what you're talking about," he said.

"I'm sure you don't you moron." Artur hissed. He directed himself to Alana once again. "There's a mail delivery going out to Ithaca in a few days, they'll stop by for them." Artur said abruptly and with finality. "They'll stop by for them IN THE GROUNDS I just told you about. Travel safe, believe me, it was a joy to host you," he said, and walked off.

"What's his deal?" Mateo said huffily.

"I have no idea..." Alana trailed off. It wasn't clear at all what could have happened.

The two figures, now recognizable as soldiers from Titan, entered the thick wood they saw Etienne enter not long before. "We're close now, the tracks lead off this way," one said to the other. They dismounted and led their horses through a small clearing.

A few feet away there was a twitch, and a trip line swung up from the ground, tripping them both. They fell to the ground just as a hulking figure emerged from the earth as if the mud itself animated. Etienne arose from the ground, covered in dead leaves from last fall, and quick as a flash was on top of the soldiers, from his side a long sharp knife flashing. He drew first blood, stabbing one soldier deep in the thigh. The soldier screamed in agony and grabbed at his leg and rolled over to remove the knife. The other jumped on top of

Etienne, wrestling with him over and over on the ground.

Etienne carried the strength of many adventures and trials beat, but that doesn't necessarily translate into your core muscle power being able to overpower a highly trained soldier of Titan at the peak of his fitness, so Etienne was slowly overpowered. The soldier wrestled his way on top of Etienne, and with his hand grasped Etienne's throat and with great force pushed down, choking Etienne and driving his neck and head into the inches of soft spring mud and dead leaves.

As the mud reached past his ears, and he began to black out, Etienne wriggled a hand free, and with another small twitch, grasped the revolver at his side. Without the maneuverability to remove the weapon, and visibility obscured by mud, he aimed as best he could, and fired through the holster.

The shot exploded directly into the foot of the soldier on top of him at point blank range, and he immediately rolled off to the side groaning in agony and grasping at his now mangled foot. Etienne gasped for air and wiped the mud off his eyes enough to see the first soldier holding a long bloody knife, limping towards him as blood dribbled down his leg. With his good leg, the soldier launched the last few feet, knife outstretched, aiming to bury the knife in Etienne's chest.

The knife struck.

And glanced off some hidden armor underneath the mud and dark cloak Etienne wore, and it fell to the side as the soldier crashed into Etienne, injuring his hands and knocking his head on the hidden steel. Etienne pulled out his revolver, tossed it up, grabbed it by the barrel, and bludgeoned the soldier's head several times until he blacked out.

Etienne rose and steadied himself on a nearby tree as he panted heavily from the fight. He wiped away the mud from his face as best he could. "I'm getting too old for this," he said.

The one soldier was out cold for several hours. The other one, shot through the foot, was lying prone in the mud grasping frantically, scraping the ground with his fingernails, trying to escape by any means necessary. In an outright panic, he pulled himself along the ground by his fingertips as his foot burned with the pain of a thousand suns.

Etienne slowly walked over to the man. Etienne's neck was blood red, his blood vessels across his face stuck out everywhere, and he was covered in mud and dirt. He brought forward his revolver and aimed it at the soldier.

The soldier winced but said nothing. He had no hope.

Etienne lowered his weapon.

"Tell Artur that I will do as I said. I will depart to the north. He can trust me at my word, he always could." Etienne said. "I'll never return."

The soldier slowly opened his eyes and his heart skipped a beat. He was going to live? At the hands of one of the western monsters?

Etienne looked at the young man, shaking in fear in the mud, and could only see himself. "Young man," he said, "I am a son of Ares. Neither you, nor anybody Artur sends can possibly kill me. Save your strength for the battle that comes. Leave an old man be."

And with that he whistled and in a moment his horses arrived. Etienne hefted himself aloft, and looking back at the young soldier, he threw the revolver on the ground for him. "Take it," he said. "And pay it forward," and off he went to the north.

The young soldier breathed in the clear mountain air with a huge gasp and thanked the gods for his good luck. That afternoon a brief furious thunderstorm passed overhead, shaking the earth with its fury, and then leaving all calm and still. For the rest of his life, he counted that day as the best one he'd ever had. That day when he watched death descend like a thunderstorm, and then swiftly depart leaving the rest of his life in calm.

Alana and Mateo stared at Artur as he stomped away.

"Yeah, I have no idea what has gotten into him..." Alana said again. She had never experienced such reversals in people before, but she would later say it was one of the clearest signs of a duplicitous dealer, and someone you should avoid.

Alana turned away from Artur and back to the group. No need to bother with the feelings of others today. She had stuff to get done, and she was a doer.

"You all heard it yourself, we are no longer welcome in Titan." Alana said. Her men groaned and rolled their eyes. These northern divas. "And furthermore, you are no longer welcome with me."

At this there was a gasp or two, then silence and confusion, but Alana was deadly serious.

"We lost a man back on the trail, a man who was killed on my account. On account of my ignoring the obvious dangers of continuing. It wasn't his time, and it's my fault his number was called." Alana started. "I'm not making the same mistake twice. I don't care what lies ahead, this is my journey, and I will not endanger the lives of my friends any longer. It's too dangerous for you to continue." she said.

There were some murmurs, and Rafael blurted out, "but because we're your friends we need to see it through! We're stronger together."

Alana shook her head. "No Rafa, we are more visible together. We are a bigger target together. We have to spend more time foraging for water and food together. Everything is worse about traveling in a big group when you're trying to avoid detection. I originally thought there would be safety in numbers, but I see now that that is false. You must stop here, and I will continue without you."

Some muted discussion broke out among some of the soldiers, but they knew she was right. If she had traveled alone and kept off the roads, it is likely she never would have been spotted by anyone. There's just too much ground to cover in the open wilds.

"Well, we're off to Ithaca then?" Ethan said.

Alana shook her head.

"Uhhh," Ethan said, we all just overheard you telling Artur we're going to Ithaca."

"Sure," Alana said, "THEY are going to Ithaca. You're coming with me."

"Ahem, and excuse me if I misheard you, but you JUST said you didn't want to endanger your friends any longer." Ethan said.

Alana chuckled, "We're friends? You barely would lift a finger to save me from certain death when we met! I don't recall much friendship then?"

"How dare you!" Ethan erupted in faux indignation. "I saved your life! It's you who has spent this entire disaster of a vacation threatening my life!"

"I mean it's what most great friends do, yes. Sure, good friends might meet and shake hands, but every great friendship I've ever had has been rekindled with the introduction of a good death threat." Alana replied.

"That certainly does make us great friends," Ethan said, "judging by the numbers."

"Well, as a GREAT friend, then I must implore you to hold to your word and guide me the rest of the way," Alana said.

"Uhhhh, if it's too dangerous for them, I'm quite sure it's too dangerous for me. I was definitely the first one screaming like a little child at the first sight of danger I'm pretty sure. Really though, bringing me is just going to make it MORE dangerous, so as a friend I must insist you continue alone." Ethan said.

Alana shrugged. "Well, okay Ethan, whatever you want. But what would your mother say?"

Ethan pursed his lips and grunted. He had been bested. He cursed the day that he decided to tell her about what precipitated their first meeting.

"Fine," he said, "I'll be your darn guide, but don't blame me when we both die because some new foreign army out to kill us finds us by tracing my urine tracks as I wet my pants on our next escape."

Mateo, sitting on a nearby bed, poked his head out a bit and asked, "So what of us?"

Alana replied, "There's a route to Ithaca through the northern passes which must have just opened up; you'll be able to safely cross the mountains together with the mail delivery, and from there descend back down to Atlas. You'll be there in no time at all."

"Anything you'd have us report?" Rafael asked.

"Nothing in particular," she said.

"So, this is it?" Rafael asked.

"This is it for now," Alana corrected him. "I'll see you all very soon safe back at home."

The group got up and said their goodbyes, Mateo nursing his wounded shoulder, Rafael wincing with labored breathing, both dreading the long horse ride ahead of them. At least they had a few days to rest, and they wouldn't be chased by murderous zealots at the same time.

Rafael and Mateo walked out, and Alana nodded at her soldiers. She huddled with them briefly and whispered a few words, then wished them luck. They smiled and nodded and made their way out.

"What was that all about?" Ethan asked.

"Nothing Ethan, nothing to worry about! I'm just telling them how much I'll miss them, but not you! Not you, Ethan, I get to keep seeing you! How lucky for me! How lucky for you!" Alana said with a fake smile.

"Indeed," Ethan said, rolling his eyes, "how lucky of both of us.

Alana picked up a few bags and exchanged her sarcasm for a more down-to-business tone, "We leave in ten minutes, saddle up," she said.

Ethan followed her outside making faces and waving his arms and saying under his breath, "We leave in ten minutes to take our chances with a grisly death, come along oh ye whose life I do not value."

As they rode the main road northwards out of town, Ethan wasn't totally sure, but he could have sworn he could hear in the distance someone exclaiming with great glee, "splendid, splendid, splendid!"

They rode north the first day in silence. Ethan was still feigning outward indigence, but he was inwardly pleased. It took him a full day to realize that though, as his frustration from being strong armed into the journey at every step gave way to the sheer excitement and bliss of wanderlust.

Someone can spend their entire life within a short radius of their home and believe that every need they have ever had has been fulfilled, and falsely believe they are a homebody, destined to reside in their corner of the planet forever.

But let them smell the spring unfold in a foreign land, thunderstorms thrashing the earth to let loose the smells of life, and in the perfumes of unknown flowers they will catch the scents of their childhood home. We may have been civilized and we may have created stationary citadels from within which we proclaim our native allegiance to a land demarcated with fictional lines, but our earliest ancestors were travelers of the whole earth. Their blood runs in our veins, and when aroused, will awaken our most primeval yearning to go forth and discover.

As he looked out over the green valley stretching for miles and miles to the north, dotted with steaming geothermal springs, and framed by snow-capped mountains on either side, stretching off into the horizon, an ancient aching awoke in his soul, and beckoned him onwards. He never was again the same person. He could live in a place like anyone else, but stay somewhere too long, and the deep ache would pound harder and harder until he made his offering to our first parents and ventured out into the wilds.

That night as they stopped, Ethan finally spoke. "Let's do this thing. I will walk to the ends of the earth. We are going to finish it."

Alana smiled. "Now you're talking. Let's do this thing."

CHAPTER 12

"Who are you?" Zara asked the old woman. Her clothes and shoes were well worn, though functional. And even backlit by the setting sun, her eyes glowed a deep green, accentuated all the more by her snow-white hair.

"An old friend of your father's," the woman said.

"How do you know my father?" Zara asked.

"Oh Zara, I know a lot about a lot of things," the old woman said.

"How do you know me and I not you? How are you here?" Zara said. "I have so many questions."

"Of course, my dear, of course, but let's get back to shelter before we lose the sun," the woman said, pointing to the western skies. "What brings you over here my dear?" she asked.

Zara pointed at the black opening. "I thought I saw a glow," she said.

"Interesting," the old woman said curiously, "very interesting. Come along now," and she began to walk back towards the gully.

"Is there anyone else out here?" Zara asked. "You

haven't...seen anyone lately, have you?"

"Worried about your pursuers my dear?" the old woman asked. "No, no, no, you're quite safe with me, never you worry."

"Okay that's freaky," Zara said. "How do you know about everything?" She asked.

"Oh, I don't know everything, but I do see many things," the old woman said. "And I have been waiting here looking out for a long time. I wasn't sure if anyone would ever come, but here you are."

They made their way down a set of stairs that had been chiseled into the gully wall, made to be almost invisible, and across the gully that had led Zara this far, then up similar stairs on the opposite side. This set of stairs led up the wall but then cut up a small channel that fed into the gully, and then along a sandy path up to a cave in the smooth sandstone walls.

"Welcome to my home!" the old woman said. "It doesn't look like much, but the roof is solid, and I never worry about the wind."

Zara looked around at the small dwelling. It was so cozy here.

"Can I offer you some eggs?" the old woman asked. "And maybe something to drink?"

"That would be lovely!" Zara said. The old woman motioned her to follow and led her up the path a little bit more to an area enclosed by rock walls on three sides, and a pile of boulders with a narrow wooden gate on the fourth. Inside roamed a couple dozen hens and roosters.

The old woman picked up some eggs, then walked her back to the cave, where a small constant dripping of water like Zara had seen before was led by a stick to drip into a pot. The old woman cracked the eggs into a cup and mixed them into some water.

"I'm afraid there's not a lot of firewood to be had. When it gets hot tomorrow, we can bake in my oven up above, but for now everything is raw," The old woman said.

"Thank you," Zara said. "I was expecting to find no one here, and glad to have anything to eat," she said and downed the eggs. "How did you find this place?" she asked.

"I came here off and on for years before I moved out," the old woman said. "It was always a great place to do some thinking. But then I had a falling out with someone I love, and my safety became uncertain, and I felt it was wisest to come out here permanently."

"Wait a minute," Zara said as it dawned on her.

The old woman sighed.

"You're Marie, aren't you!" Zara said. "The wayfinder! How foolish of me to not see that immediately."

The old woman made a small bow. "At your service, my dear," she said.

"Ethan," Alana said, "what happens to us when we die?"

Two days had passed since they had parted from their friends at Titan. They walked north through an increasingly sparsely inhabited landscape, factories and farms slowly petering out as they went further and further away from the capital city. The snow level on the mountains on either side of the narrowing valley dropped lower and lower the further they walked, and while it got colder as well, they had some solace in the numerous hot springs that dotted the valley, marking themselves for miles by the steam spraying off of the surface high into the air like welcoming smoke signals.

"Well, for one," Ethan said, "your heart stops, and all of your bodily fluids drain down to the lowest point of your body, discoloring your corpse. Your muscles spasm and stiffen, and..."

"No, what happens to us when we die?" Alana said in a far-off voice. She had been silent in thought all afternoon.

Ethan thought for a moment, feeling the breeze brush him through the hilly grasslands, wondering where to begin and how far to go.

"They say your soul separates from the body," Ethan said. "Your body is left behind, but your soul separates and becomes disoriented. It wanders the earth alone."

Alana listened as she stared into the distance. "So they say, but why do we wander?"

"My people believed the eyes are the window to the soul, and its windows to the world. Without them, it cannot see. You wander without sight of the world. They say there's nothing but the sounds and smells to guide you." Ethan said, and shuddered at the thought. "But some say that cannot be, that the soul is luminescent, and can see through the darkest of things that this world can conjure. But with this sight, you also see your own failings in life, and your entire true life is laid bare before you. It is too much for most to abide, and so there is a period of mourning, where you must come to terms with your own death. Some cannot accept it, and they persist, attempting to reach out to right wrongs that they created in life, or somehow mend their broken ways and rescue their legacy, but that ends in futility. The dead cannot change the land of the living. The gods forbid it."

They passed in between a series of steaming ponds, hopping over the warm streams that connect them.

"How long do they wander that are mourning?" Alana asked.

"There is no set time," Ethan said. "The question really is how long will it take you to accept your own death and move on? Nobody can say."

"How long will it take you to accept it?" Alana said.

"I don't know. How could I know? My mother was ordained to help others accept, but I don't know how long it took her," Ethan said as he felt the gem she gave him, "or if she ever could accept it."

"It will take me a long time to accept it," Alana said. "A very long time. I have so much to do here, I cannot imagine doing it all in a lifetime." Alana paused occasionally in each phrase, enveloped in thought. "A very long time."

"So it is for many. My people ordained bearers of the dead ages ago to help guide them to their rest," Ethan offered. "My mother took them to the edge of the world, guiding their souls to her Valhalla, sending them on boats or biers or whatever their family demanded if necessary, but she always brought them to their rest. She guided many to their rest and peace before she found her own." Ethan said.

"But what peace can exist beyond this?" Alana said. She pointed at the thick puffy clouds being blown at a brisk pace high above, and the pine trees along the edges of the mountains, and puffs of steam from hot springs near and far. "How can I find peace outside of life itself? There is no peace in darkness," she said. "There is no hope in death."

Ethan shook his head. "This is but the beginning. There is yet much to come beyond this. There are many lives and many kingdoms ahead of us. Our journey is just beginning." Ethan said.

"So they said," Alana said. "So they say. But I am not queen of those kingdoms in the beyond. If they are there, they are ruled by unknown gods and demons. This is my realm. This is my peace."

They rode in silence after that, as the clouds overhead slowly churned from puffy white into dark black storm clouds. It was going to be a rough night. Alana slowly pulled back from the brink of a slow burning anxiety attack she was hiding.

"What of my man? Back on the trail. We lost my man, the soldier. What is happening to him?" Alana asked.

"My guess is he's more disoriented than most. Stuck as a stranger in a strange land. It'll take him a long time to find his way," Ethan said. "This is why most prefer to die at home. The transition is easier when you're in familiar surroundings."

Alana had a rare wave of guilt sweep over her. "I just...there was nothing I could think to do at the time but leave him behind. It has taken over my thoughts these days, and I am," she paused and censored herself, pulling back from exposing her feelings to their full extent, "I am concerned for his soul. Is there nothing we can do for him?" Alana said.

"Well, there is one ritual we could try. My mother did it once. She said she had only used it a handful of times, but it's the only thing I know about." Ethan said.

"What will it do?" Alana asked.

"We will attempt to conjure a messenger to find him," he said. "What messenger, I do not know. There are many gods in this realm, and many are disguised when they interact with man and do not allow us to know their true nature. All I know is there is a messenger who might help. There is but one way to call him." Ethan said.

"Well, I can't think of anything creepier," Alana said. "I'd probably rather go back the way we came and find him myself than seance our way into some being of questionable intentions and integrity."

"Going back does have the unfortunate consequence of certain death for ourselves," Ethan reminded her.

"Good point," Alana said. "Can we start up the seance? It seems so wrong to leave a soul a stranger in a strange land. Even if this does sound imminently creepy."

"I was really hoping you'd opt for some other word choice, but sure, creepy is fine with me. Let's stop up at that next spring, I'll need some water." Ethan said, and his stomach dropped as he watched lightning in the far distance start inching closer. If he was honest, he wasn't quite sure he wanted to tinker with deathly things any more than necessary, especially when a large storm that threatened to also strike him with lightning at the same time was approaching. "What's wrong with me going to Ithaca?" he thought. "Those other guys get all the luck. I hope they get haunted by the undead or something, just to serve them right for getting the easy route."

They veered off road for a bit to get to a better position at the spring. The grey sky overhead grew darker, and soon rain was trickling down as the storm drew nearer and nearer.

They reached the spring, and Ethan quickly dug a shallow trough around a hastily built altar as distant thunder turned to lightning overhead. He filled it as best he could with the hot spring water. The thick grove of trees surrounding the spring offered some protection from the storm raging overhead, which was made all the more surreal by the heavy steam that blew off the spring into the trees around, giving the entire area over to what appeared to be dense fog. Dark shapes writhed and shifted everywhere they looked as the breeze played with the steam. The fog surrounding them lit up with white flashes with every lightning strike.

Ethan pulled a pigeon they had caught earlier that day. Before the rain started coming down in sheets, he managed to start up a fire on the altar and placed the pigeon on top. It immediately began to char, and the burning feathers produced a putrid scent that wafted through with the rest of the steam.

Alana sat through all of this, her back against a tree. She hugged her legs and while she pointed her head in Ethan's general direction, her eyes stared off, unfocused into the distance. She had never seen anyone die before, and in her unfocused dreary gaze, she kept looking back to see the soldier, her soldier, fall to the ground in the dark, lifeless. She wrapped a large coat around herself and pulled it tight as she shivered with the passing breezes.

Ethan looked at her with a bit of fire in his eyes, annoyed that she had contributed nothing to her little pit stop, but he was too afraid of upsetting her to say anything, so he just resented her silently like usual. He stoked the fire with the full amount of dry underbrush he could find in the storm, and with the steam and the rain and the smoke swirling all around them in the tight thicket of trees surrounding the small bubbling spring, flashing white with every strike of lightning, he knelt down in front of the fire, and shaking just a bit from the cold, he raised his arms high and chanted.

Alana couldn't pick out what he was saying. It was as though his mouth suddenly filled with rocks, and he spoke a thick halting language with severe tones. Gusts of wind blew through and cleared out the smoke and steam just a little bit here and there, but for the most part Ethan knelt in an alien landscape, chanting as he knelt, shivering in front of a rapidly disappearing bird being consumed by fire.

This didn't last that long before he stopped. Ethan lowered his arms, and his head sunk down.

"What?" Alana said after a moment. "Did it work? What happens next?"

"I, uh, I'm not sure," Ethan said.

"Didn't your mother say?" Alana said.

"Wellllll, I was really little when we did this, you know, so it's not totally clear what happens next," Ethan said. "I kind of expected to find out as we did it."

"This is the first time you've done this?" Alana asked.

"Technically, yes. First time I've done this, though I was present that one time as a child." Ethan said.

"Does this count?" Alana asked.

"Unclear," Ethan said.

"We don't actually know." Alana said. She relaxed just a bit as her own internal tension eased.

"Correct, we don't actually know." Ethan said.

"What would you suggest?" Alana asked. "You are the expert, and you can guide the dead." It might have been just Ethan's own eyes, but he swore she bowed her head just a little at this statement. "Or we can stay here and embrace the rain," she concluded. Part of her was hoping to stay in the rain and hope the tears of the gods could wash away her guilt, if even just a little.

"I'm not sure, but let me think," Ethan said. "I'm just trying to help here. I haven't lost anyone...for a long time that is. This stuff isn't science, you know? It's not like you fill out form A parts 1, 2, and 3 and suddenly some long-absent god shows up and says, 'you know what, I'm going to give you the time of day because you made sure to dot your I's and cross your T's!' No, it's more like, oh here's this thing that worked once, why don't you try it again sometime and good luck to you." Ethan said.

"What happened the last time?" Alana asked.

"It rained then too..." Ethan said, his voice trailing off as he choked up just a tad. "We stood here at the altar and talked about him until the rain stopped and the fire stopped, and the earth became still again." Ethan said. "It was...I can't really explain it. It was like communing directly with their soul."

"That sounds lovely," Alana said, and she stood and walked to the fire. It was quickly burning down to charcoals, the rain smothering any remaining heat as the drops hit the hot coals and hissed as they extinguished the fire.

She stood at the makeshift altar with Ethan as they watched the fire die in the rain. The rain pounded down, and soon Alana's hair was matted down, and water was streaming down her face, though not all of it from the heavens.

"I am sorry," Alana finally said, "my greed and impatience brought this upon you. I have no other excuse. There is nothing I can say but sorry. I will find your parents and give them my meaningless apologies, and any friends you have I will make amends for as best I can, but the truth is there is nothing that can be done.

"I do not mourn your death, nor your passage into the unknown realms where you will be coated with everlasting honor. But I mourn your separation. I only hope that you can find your way off this earth into the beyond, and that your future reunion with family and friends can numb the temporary sting you and they feel now. May the remaining wanderers in loneliness and sorrow find peace in the future."

At this point Alana and Ethan knelt, and he began to chant

again. The fire was completely out at this point, and the ashes were giving off smoke as the rain beat down on it. They were both thoroughly drenched as the rain fell in torrential sheets. Ethan's words took on a low chanting melody, and he raised his voice louder and louder above the din, and there they knelt, both crying; Alana for the soldier, Ethan for his mother, both bathed in steam and smoke, lightning crashing all around with loud roars. For a small moment, Alana's heart opened, and she was touched with peace. It wasn't much, like taking a gulp of water on a hot sunny day, but enough to get her through for the moment.

From Ethan's necklace small wisps of green began to curl outwards and upwards.

Another gust of wind blew through the fog, and they saw movement up ahead in the flash of lightning. Thunder rang out loud and clear, and the wind died down for a moment, but up ahead a shadow formed in the steam and smoke. The wisps of fog curled up and around, various demons summoning in their eyes and unholy figures appearing and disappearing as the smoke curled around the trees in the wind. They could taste the electricity in the air from the lightning as their hearts raced faster and faster as some unknown spirit apparated in the smoke.

A dark figure slowly took form in the smoke and steam and glided towards them.

Ethan's heart sank into his stomach. "What is that thing?" He whispered.

Alana pulled out a black dagger from her boot. "Not again," she said, as she positioned herself to spring and attack.

"Again??" Ethan said in panic.

As the figure neared the spring and took on a more distinct shape, it paused, and then with great feeling it shouted,

"Booo!"

Both Ethan and Alana screamed high-pitched bloody murder.

Etienne pulled off his hood and revealed his face totally consumed in a smile. He began laughing uproariously, drowning out any thunder.

"You should have seen your faces! Ethan, you're as white as a sheet, it looks like you either saw or are a ghost!" Etienne gasped for air as his chest heaved with laughter. "And Alana, I mean you're always expressionless, but boy oh boy did the life drain right out of your eyes when I came through."

He laughed and laughed some more as he skipped over the stones of the spring to meet them.

Alana wiped the rain and, uh, definitely not tears off her face and with uncharacteristic humility, she smiled. "Nice to see you, Etienne."

He was still chuckling as he gave her and Ethan hugs. "I told you I'd find you, but I didn't realize that you'd come find me." Etienne said.

Ethan's heart was slowly coming back into line, and he managed to eke out a question, "How do you figure?" he said.

Etienne laughed, "I'm camped right over here," he said. "I thought maybe some choir of Titans had come and found me and planned to sing me out of the kingdom, but lo and behold, it's you. Come over here, let's dry you both up." Etienne said, and motioned for them to follow as he skipped back over the spring.

Alana and Ethan looked at each other, shrugged, got their horses, and followed along. It didn't feel good to be laughed at after such a sacred experience, but also, it was really, really, really good to have someone around who was super good in a fight.

The storm quickly passed by, and from the ashes in the altar, a bird emerged and, dusting itself off, flew off to the southeast on a mission.

CHAPTER 13

Far to the west of Alana and her crew, Tiberius sailed around the cape of Estellian on the Queen Anne. Alexander found him on the aft deck, expelling his dinner off the ship in heavy seas. While he was a marine, the whole marine part of the marine job was the least pleasant for a landlubber like himself. Captain Nelson and his crew took immense pleasure in this, because, and this will surprise you, a man like Tiberius who was intensely dedicated to successfully completing a mission as quickly as possible in the exact manner he desired was an unimaginably huge pain in the neck to host onboard.

Their allies, the Carpathians, had failed him, which was still gnawing at him. "Those incompetent savages," Tiberius thought. Scipio was wrong to rely on any tribes, but that was a conversation for another day. The western tribes were weak allies, he thought, and they would bring them ruin.

Alexander brought him some water. "I'm glad to see this, commander." Alexander said, watching Tiberius recover. "We were beginning to wonder if there was anything human about you."

Tiberius reserved his few smiles for the moments when

absurd compliments were being delivered by inferiors, and this was no exception. He awkwardly and possibly forcibly grinned.

"There isn't," he grunted. "At least don't get too used to it. That demon Poseidon may hate me, but there are no gods on land that would defy me. We will be back to normal soon enough."

The sky shook with a sudden outburst of lightning, hail began to pummel the ship, and they scrambled below deck.

"No gods on land, but possibly some above it?" Alexander teased.

Tiberius reverted to his usual stone face. "They can try, but they will fail, like all others," he said with solemnity.

Nothing would stop him from the great prize, his birthright. Nothing.

Alana, Ethan, and Etienne slipped out of the realm of Titan without further incident. They passed through the borders undetected; the northern desolate reaches were far less guarded than the other passes. There was just a sleepy little garrison bored to tears in the daily monotony of guarding an almost meaningless border, not watching that hard for any traffic leaving the kingdom. It was all just as well; Artur had long abandoned any hope of extinguishing Etienne.

They dropped down a narrow canyon with a very faint and disused trail, picking their way down a rocky stream which eventually disappeared into a black sandy wash. They exited the short canyon and the kingdom of Titan and entered the great northern wasteland; If there ever was a country of death, this was it.

It was one of the most beautiful landscapes that Ethan had ever beheld. For miles every direction there was an immense plain of sharp black obsidian rock, broken up into pieces and spread throughout the land. The sky seemed to hang lower here on the northern edges of the earth, with a thick cloud cover menacingly hovering directly above. Wisps of fog blew through the distance like shades. Harsh winds picked up and blew tiny sands of obsidian into their eyes. It was a beautiful, hostile place.

They quickly found out that this was NOT a place you wanted to travel through on foot. Firstly, ouch, those rocks are sharp. Secondly, there was nothing of sustenance out there. Nothing really grows there except moss and lichen, and while I haven't done an exhaustive calorie count of what they brought vs. what they consumed, they probably had to resort to hunting rats or something absurd. They were much too prideful to admit that in any writing, but it just doesn't add up.

"Remember the hot springs?" Ethan said as they trudged along the featureless landscape. "Maybe we could get some more hot springs out here? They were so nice and..." Ethan shivered and his teeth chattered, "t-t-t-toasty warm."

As he said this a bank of fog practically dropped on top of them. Usually he'd consider fog a minor inconvenience, but this fog had a serious grudge against people. It was a thick blanket of water, practically dripping with water. Ethan felt as if he could put out his hand and wring it dry. It quickly soaked through their clothes and was sure to up the misery coefficient to eleven.

"Mother of pearl," Ethan said. "Where are those hot springs when you need them?"

Etienne pulled his cloak around him tighter. "I'd give my left arm to get another soak back in those. I had no idea they were so nice, or I would have conquered Titan a long time ago." he said.

"Stop your complaining, you whiners," Alana said as she pretended to not be a solid block of ice.

"You're just saying that because you refused to get in," Ethan said. "Your loss. I think if I can survive this little excursion, I'm going to apply for refugee status in Titan. I know exactly what I'd write on the application. 'Dear sir or madam, I am a climate refugee. My body requires to be in your hot springs all day long. Please accept me, I will bring lots of cake. Love, Ethan'."

Etienne chortled and Alana rolled her eyes.

"You knew we'd be coming this way; this is your own fault. Prepare better next time," Alana said.

"I mean, I knew we'd be about a hundred miles to the west of here on the western roads, not running for our lives from crazy people as we sneak out of Titan like thieves, sure." Ethan replied. "And, you may recall, we had a moment where we dropped everything, so all of my gear is being worn by some tribal warrior right now. I hope he likes my silk underwear, that was my only pair."

Alana looked at him with one eyebrow raised, and said with disbelief, "Your only pair of silk underwear?"

Ethan looked at her with raised eyebrows, "My only pair of underwear," he said.

Just then they heard some rocks topple in the distance. Just a few small rocks really, but it definitely wasn't caused by them.

They strained their eyes and ears to see or hear anything and stopped their horses. Suddenly they were acutely aware of being watched from all sides. Something was clearly out there.

The three dismounted and stared off into the distance. Another footstep.

Etienne whispered to them both, "Well, you're all welcome for staying around."

Alana elbowed him to stay silent.

Ethan looked at him indignantly and said, "What do you mean you're welcome? I'm here against my will."

Alana elbowed him.

Another footstep.

"They said she had moved up here, but I didn't believe

them..." Etienne whispered as the sounds drew nearer.

"What do you mean she?" Alana hissed. "And when were you planning on mentioning this to me?"

"You know, I didn't want to worry anyone unnecessarily," Etienne said.

"Who's w-w-w-worrried?" Ethan asked.

"Worry no, but endangering us is okay?" Alana asked.

Etienne elbowed her to stay silent. "Shhhh" he whispered.

A faint golden light appeared in the fog and bobbed ever so slightly as it moved. It drew nearer and brighter. They watched as a lion slowly emerged into view, a pale golden light emanating from its body.

A lion, except the addition of some wings, of course. And this lion, well, this lion was super creepy since it had the head of a woman, with long golden hair and super angry eyes.

"The Sphinx??!!" Ethan exclaimed, "you didn't mention we'd be dealing with the freaking Sphinx?" he growled. "I'd rather take my chances with the armies of bloodthirsty cannibals waiting for us back over the mountains," he said.

The woman opened her mouth and the sound of rushing waters came out, followed by a piercing dagger of a voice. "Whoooo daresssss passss?" she said.

Etienne pushed Ethan and Alana back. "I got this," he whispered.

"Who dares challenge us?" Etienne shouted. "We are entitled to walk these lands, they are free and open to all," he said. "The gods gave you a city, and yet you abandon it to torment travelers," Etienne said.

"Thissss is my city," she snarled. "These are my lands now."

"Your claim is invalid," Etienne said, "your city destroyed, you must remain there, you have no right to challenge anyone on this path. Depart now, oh great evil."

"These are the dying lands," the Sphinx replied, and she roared up her two hind legs, baring claws that were at least six inches long and sharp as knives. "No mortal may tread. You are forbidden here," she said as she inched nearer.

Etienne drew his sword and paced back and forth. It began to glow with a pale white light. "Stand back, beast, we tread where we desire, the earth is for mortals, and we command you leave us be." Etienne said.

The Sphinx dropped back down on all fours and squinted to see the sword, and then laughed. She backed up and began to pace around the group as Etienne held the sword out pointed towards her, and she roared with laughter.

"Aaron, is that you? I never thought I'd see you again," she said. "Are you coming to finish what you started? So many of your people came through here," she said mockingly, "so many came through cursing you, and yet here you are to finish the job. Why the wait? Perhaps you dread your unhappy reunion?" she said and laughed again. "I'd be more than happy to arrange an introduction for you; you're so close to Hades already! Or do you come to lead even more to their deaths? Was a nation not enough?" she said, the cynicism practically dripping off her tongue as she spoke. "Oh, great Aaron, prince of the west, with no one left to command, you travel all the way to the dying lands to command me. My laughable prince, you are a long way from home, and you have no power here," she said. "It is you who have no power here."

"Foul beast," Etienne said, "it is I who can engineer the introductions. I cannot be defeated, least of all by you. Give up now and leave us in peace. I hold a power that is older than you." The fog reverberated with every word he spoke like the string of a bass, the mists visibly echoing the sound waves out.

"The so-called star sword?" the Sphinx cackled. "Don't make me laugh. I long ago discovered your secrets old man. You have no power here."

"You left out the part about the Sphinx?" Ethan said, infuriated. "You didn't think it was worthwhile to say, 'hey Ethan, guess what, there's like this mythical creature and it has claws that will penetrate your entire skull and go out the other side and hey maybe you want to call in sick or something?'"

"And who's she calling Aaron?" Alana asked, as the three of them stood back to back to back, watching the Sphinx slowly circle nearer.

Etienne ignored them. "This man is a bearer, he carries the green gem, you cannot harm him!" Etienne exclaimed, and grasped at Ethan's neck to draw out his mother's gemstone. "You know he has passage through these lands, the gods forbid you interfere."

"Uh, what about me?" Alana said.

"What about you?" Etienne whispered.

"Ahhh, the Eye of Rhea," she purred, "interesting...but ultimately unsatisfactory" she said. "No, Aaron, conducting mortals is violation enough. You all three will perish." the Sphinx said. "Unless, of course, you can answer the riddle."

"I was wondering when we'd get to that part." Ethan said, "and also wondering when we were going to get to the, 'hey Ethan, you're going to be tracked by a demigod so you potentially want to run away and hide in a hot spring the rest of your life'"

"Will you shut up already about the hot springs?" Alana growled.

"So be it witch," Etienne called out.

"Excuse me??" Alana shouted.

"Not you witch, that witch!" Etienne said, then turning to the Sphinx again, "Give us the riddle!"

The Sphinx stopped and her fiery red eyes stared into Etienne.

"What is whitewashed but is never clean?" the Sphinx said.

Etienne held out his sword at the ready at eye level, tracing her every step.

"What is whitewashed but is never clean?" the Sphinx

shouted again.

Etienne held his sword with his right hand and placed his left on the fastener of his cloak.

"What is whitewashed but is never clean?" the Sphinx demanded. "Answer now!"

"Your ugly teeth" Etienne said through his own gritted teeth.

"Wrong!" the Sphinx shouted, "The entrance to hell!"

And with that, she roared and leapt for Etienne. Before she was off the ground, Etienne ripped off his customary dark robe, and underneath his drab exterior shone the uniform of a vaunted cavalry officer of old. He wore a silver breastplate, polished to a mirror. Underneath he had heavy colorful garments, with various ribbons splayed out representing numerous battles and campaigns he had waged. His trousers were once white, though yellowed now with age. It was as if a museum set piece had stepped forward from a different era. Onto his head he pulled on an equally splendiferous cavalry helmet, plumes of colorful feathers splaying outward, his long white locks of hair flowed out of it and spread out across his armor. He hoisted the star sword with thick leather gloves and brought it forward to meet the beast. It flashed lightning as it sang.

He stepped to the side and took a knee to dodge the Sphinx, at the same time slashing the paw of the Sphinx as she sailed over him. She landed hard on the other side, blood draining out of her paw, and roaring ever louder.

"I am Aaron, prince of Ariens!" Etienne shouted as he stood up with effort. "I am a son of Ares, I hold the fire of Ariens, the star-sword of the West! A thousand generations we have ruled the western tribes, and I am the last prince of all!" Etienne shouted, and brought the sword up again, which glowed with a cool white light. "You cannot beat me! I have tamed the lightning of the gods, and with it I am made exempt from death!"

Ethan watched the runes light up and down Etienne's blade and glow with a golden fire as he spoke. He saw the words now in full light, and read them once again:

To never know defeat
To never taste death
Until you defend your enemy
With your last breath

The Sphinx roared back, and in an ancient tongue conjured up a defense which she spat out hissing the magical curse. She jumped again at Etienne, this time her claws glowing with pale blue electricity, and as Etienne brought the sword up, its lightning crashed against her claws and broke in two in an enormous explosion that sent the both of them sprawling. The top half of the sword shattered, leaving the hilt and bottom half in Etienne's hand, the sword breaking such that the bottom half pointed out like a thin needle at its furthest tip. And yet, still it read:

To never know defeat
To never taste death

The Sphinx collected herself, then pounced on top of Etienne as he struggled to rise, pinning his hands down underneath her two forward paws, and again roared the sound of a thousand waves crashing in the surf directly into his face. She quickly brought up one paw and slashed his face with her claws, marking his cheek with deep gouges. She then brought her claws down to his neck and went to stab him, but her paw stopped.

She pushed and pushed against some invisible force, but could not bring her paw down, her claws against his neck, unable to go any further. She grunted and strained but could not kill him.

"What is this magic?" she said as she strained against the invisible power.

Etienne held his chin high as he maneuvered as best he could to avoid the claws and escape her grasp, and he replied, "It is as I said. I cannot be killed, beast. Your claim here is forfeit. You have been weighed in the balance and have been found wanting. Your life is discarded, and your soul thrown to the wind." And with his left arm, he grasped the sword laying on his right side and pulled it under his body as he lay pinned, and with a jerk, he pushed the upper broken needle tip into her throat, and from then into her skull.

She died in silence; a thousand years of fear instilled into the heart of humanity gone with nary a whimper. Her wings dissolved and her entire body reverted to nothing but a dead lion which slumped lifelessly on Etienne.

Etienne rolled the lion's corpse over his body and lay on the ground panting as Alana and Ethan tended to his wounds.

I will say that there is a significant amount of controversy surrounding the various accounts of this battle, and many who will immediately discard as laughable any story involving a mythical creature, but I can report to you here what I believe and what Ethan swore to his dying day.

Etienne, prince of Ariens, and son of Apollo, killed the Sphinx and saved his friends.

CHAPTER 14

After a time of panting and rest, Etienne then slowly stood with a struggle and sang. By tradition, this is the time of the first singing of the Arensong, that great lament of the fall of Ariens.

The song itself is haunting and beautiful, and Etienne's voice started raspy and deep as he gained his breath and strength. In the twilight of that dying land, he stood and held his head low and mourned his people. The sky wept in agony, and the black volcanic rock that had been broken up in sharp gashes throughout the land melted in sorrow. The sharp cracks joined together that day to create smooth black rock plains ever after.

By the end of the song, Etienne was standing and with every stanza the fog itself would push further back, edging away from the pain, until he had cleared their path for a hundred miles in any direction. The sun hid itself and the sky poured rain with no clouds overhead. The entire earth wept for Ariens.

My personal favorite stanza is the last. There are a few different flavors of the Arensong you can find today, but all of them end with this:

> To never know defeat
> To never taste death
> But Ariens that vaunted gem
> Has drawn its last breath

"Aaron?" Alana said when he had finished. "You are Aaron of Ariens? The evil prince of the west?"

Ethan was beginning to breathe again at this point and became aware that he was soaked in sweat. At least, he hoped that was sweat.

"Aaron the prince?" Ethan said. He crossed his legs and casually held his hands in front of his crotch. "The general of the great war? That Aaron?"

Etienne stared off into the distance, part here, but part in another world. "Yes," he said after a pause. "I am that Aaron."

Alana looked at him in amazement, and circled around, looking his armor and uniform up and down. "How can that be?" she said. "Didn't you die like years ago?"

"Do westerners all live this long?" Ethan said. "Do we all get to live this long? I have got to seriously reconsider my level of panic with regards to my lack of future investment," he said.

Etienne shook his head. "No, I hate to burst your bubble, but this is a single-use ticket," Etienne said. "Unfortunately, I am cursed to live." he tapped his fingers on the shard of his sword that was still left.

Ethan took the sword and traced the runes with his fingers. "To never know defeat. To never taste death." He hefted the sword and tried its balance as he swung it carefully around. "Whatever happened to sticks and stones will break my bones but words will never hurt me? This seems pretty benign? Like I write stuff down all the time and it doesn't happen." Ethan said.

"I thought the same," Etienne said. "And yet, here we are."

Ethan paused as he pointed the sword off into the distance and considered the viability of tattooing something on his arm along the lines of 'power to fly and turn anything into a cake'. Etienne wondered if he could get Ethan to write something about power to turn anything into a soft bed.

"Cursed to live?" Alana interrupted their thoughts. "I think you have that wrong. Cursed to die, yes, I understand. I am cursed to die, but to live? What a joy! What goodness from the gods! To think: what great deeds could a man accomplish with such a life? What kingdoms and honors could you have as your own with an endless life? How big of a kingdom could you amass?" Alana was dumbstruck with the possibilities. It was truly the very root of her wildest dreams.

Etienne spat on the ground. "What goodness indeed!" he said. "I cannot be killed, Alana princess of Atlas! But that doesn't mean that the people I love will live as well. Here these many times I have saved and guided you, confident that I would escape to live another day. Think of all those who I have guided in the past. They are gone. Everyone is gone. I watched my lover die. My family died. My entire nation died, and my people scattered into the squabbling western tribes. And yet, here am I, walking the earth in sadness like a shadow. I am dead in all but name.

"I am damned, and there is no glory for the damned, my young friends, there is none. And what glory can I have? What power does one man have against a nation? What can a single person do? I watched my people destroyed and scattered and could do nothing. I could never be killed, but I could be captured! I could be imprisoned. I could be tortured. I could have judgements much worse than death passed upon me. And so when you met with the Furies in the gully and they tormented your souls, when they spoke to you of your secret failings and they tempted you with death, they could not do any worse than that which I have passed through already. I have been torched by the most raging of furnaces and cannot be touched by their hate. I laughed at their flimsy attempts. How far they were from what I have passed through already.

"I have been captured many times, but every time I escaped my captors, I fought, I slept on my sword and gun every night and broke my way out of a never-ending nightmare. I have lived through hell on earth. I have walked a path that you cannot possibly bear, and so no, Alana, princess of the five nations, it is not joy, it is hell. No Alana, princess, no, there is no glory in damnation. Life is a gift while you live it, but step beyond its bounds and this earth becomes your prison, your hell, your greatest nightmare. I have nothing left. All I have is in the endless beyond from which I am barred."

Alana, very uncharacteristically, had nothing to say in return, and sat in continued shock at his revelation. She, naturally, did not agree with him on any point, and believed him to be inferior to her in every way, which is why he had gotten himself into such negative situations in the past and had ended up like this. She was convinced that she would have done everything a zillion times better, but alas, that is what everyone thinks of the experiences they observe everyone else go through, and so you just have to excuse her, I guess.

"So, walk me through the whole Aaron/Etienne thing?" Ethan said, attempting to interject before Alana could say something insulting.

Etienne sheathed his broken sword, gathered his things, and motioned for them to continue walking. "I will go with you a spot further, but this is where I leave you two for your journey. I have but one more thing to do for you, but for that I must leave. However, since I'm sure you've heard some ridiculous over-propagandized version of the great war between Ariens and Atlas, I'll give you my take on it."

"Can't wait," Alana said sarcastically.

And with that, they began walking again, leading their weary horses.

"I am Aaron, son of King Aren, king of all the Western

lands, Lord of Ariens. My name is cursed in my lands, and so I call myself Etienne. My people come from a land far to the west, and many generations ago sailed to Ariens and built a new home. We went from success to success, incorporating outsiders into our nation, making treaties with various peoples and tribes, and building up a large nation.

"We developed and cultivated these wild lands, growing huge bounties of food and making incredible advances in engineering and the sciences. The other kingdoms just looked on our wealth and power with envy.

"Leo of Atlas was the worst offender. We knew he intended to destroy us as soon as he consolidated his power among the five nations. We were saved by the anarchic revolutions that wracked his nations. Leo always suspected us of having fomented the discord and revolutions among his people, and while we definitely didn't foment any of the discord and revolutions, we also definitely did foment the discord and revolutions." Etienne winked to Alana as she gasped in horror and said, "Sorry, not sorry," and continued.

"We knew we were next on his list of 'nations to conquer and subdue', so we plotted our attack. However," and at this point Etienne looked at Ethan, "we were betrayed."

"A young woman, a bearer of the dead, discovered our plan. She objected to it on principle, and raved about it to all she could, 'Offensive wars are unjustifiable', or some other such idealism, but we ignored her and struck east with every soldier we could, and off we went for King and country. This was the only chance we'd ever get to settle the score before the cards were no longer in our favor. It was our only chance of survival.

"She ran. I'm not quite sure how she did it really? She could have taken a horse I suppose, but she later claimed to have run the entire way. She found Leo out campaigning in the field and alerted him to our treachery.

"Leo immediately came, in his trickery bringing

contingents of the armies of all of the five nations out to bear and lay a trap in our path.

"Oh Ariens, oh Ariens, oh diamond of the West. Oh diadem of diadems, oh Ariens oh Ariens. There does not pass a day when I do not mourn them. My entire soul aches for my nation, my people, my family. We have ceased to exist, and I led them to their destruction. You cannot know my pain. Nobody can know my pain.

"We were so close; victory was in my hands and I held it like sand on the seashore as it slipped away the harder I grasped. Leo united the five nations against us and brought an army we couldn't match. In addition, he made an unholy bargain with the god of thunder, and the day we met in battle he rained down lightning on us, cackling with fury.

"We were routed, and I awoke on the battlefield the next day, having been knocked unconscious in heavy hand-to-hand fighting. All around me I saw the doom of my people. In the dark fog of that dreary morning the same bearer who betrayed us found me among the dead. She revived me from among the corpses, tended to my wounds, and in a final act of vengeance, left me with an insult and a curse, which she burned into my sword as a reminder. To never know defeat. To never know death.

"She left me to my fate, and I have wandered these many years aimless, and unable to follow my people into the great beyond. These many years I have spent in mourning, attempting to do what I can for my fallen people, but it has been of no use. My burden has been too great for me to bear, and I have no heart left to feel.

"And yet," Etienne said as he paused and surveyed the route in front of them, "I think my time is come. I think I know the answer to this riddle."

Alana and Ethan were largely silent during his confession. It's kind of awkward to pester someone with questions after they just described to you a mystical curse that has led to decades of emotional pain, and also happens to be the sworn enemy of your nation, but hey, there are probably more awkward situations. I mean, not many?

Far to the north they saw a dark wall of clouds blocking the entire sky. Etienne pointed that way. "Make your way to the sea," he said, "which you'll find with the clouds. Once you reach it, trace your way west until you find a way across to the place of burial. Here I must leave you. You are safe now, and this is as much time as I can spare. I have a lot to do."

Ethan gave him a hug, Alana an awkward handshake. They exchanged pleasantries and goodbyes, and Etienne turned to head south by a different path. Before he left, he wished them luck and said, "You will see me again, sooner than you think. I do not envy what you now must do, but it is what must be done. I gotta tell you, it's so nice to be old, and not have to go through all the crap that you have to when you're younger. What a joy to know I don't have to do that stuff anymore."

Alana rolled her eyes. "Thanks for the vote of confidence," she said.

"You're welcome," Etienne said, "and you and your people are welcome for germ theory. Enjoy not knowing anyone who died of dysentery. You're welcome."

He left, and Ethan paused and watched him until he disappeared over the next smooth hill, and he quietly whispered under his breath, "please don't leave me alone with her."

"What was that?" Alana asked.

"Please tell me you have a plan," Ethan coughed. "I think it's about time you tell me what exactly you plan to do when we get to this absurdly-placed burial ground. And maybe let's try telling me beforehand what you expect before dumping it on me last second."

Alana looked at him in all seriousness. "We're going to dig the old dude up of course," she said. "What did you think we were going to do? Dad is coming back up and he'd better have that silver cross somewhere on him or I am going to be pissssssed."

Now it was Ethan's turn to roll his eyes. "Great. Just great. Why are all of your plans so terrible?" he said.

"I think the word you're looking for is thorough, why are all of your plans so thorough," Alana said, "and the answer is because I'm a freaking princess and I get stuff done."

And with that they set off to the north, towards the dark, dark wall of clouds in the distance, covering the entire sky.

The Queen Anne was totally still. On the plus side, everyone's seasickness had faded away (or they at least claimed it was gone), on the minus side, they weren't going anywhere.

Oh, that, and they couldn't see a thing.

The entire ship was fogged in with the darkest, most evil fog you've ever seen. You couldn't see to the top of the smokestack above, and you certainly couldn't see any land. It's not usually a situation you want to be in, because it's kind of hard to know where you are on a featureless sea, which is only a problem if you're on a ship navigating treacherous waters filled with rocky islands at every turn. The nautical charts weren't totally up to par either, so everyone was on edge.

Especially Tiberius.

He'd been on plenty of boats in plenty of seas en route to way more dangerous missions than this. By comparison, this was probably the least stressful of any task he had taken to. Possibly the most annoying, as tracking down a woman across hundreds of miles was one of the more difficult tasks he'd attempted, but super doable.

No, he was on edge because this was his chance to finally right a historic wrong. A Great Wrong. A Great Historic Wrong if you will.

Tiberius thought that fate had brought him to Scipio's

attention, or that his performance as a newly-enlisted soldier had invited attention of the upper echelons of leadership. The reality is that the upper echelons don't care about developing talent of the faceless teeming grunts on the lowest levels, they care about nurturing loyalty among their star performers, and by star performer I mean well performing officers of the upper noble class.

No, Scipio found Tiberius because he was looking for him.

Or, more appropriately, Scipio was looking for Tiberius' mother.

Tiberius was a nobody in Medea. Son of a widowed woman, struggling to eke out a living in a crappy town on the edge of the nation, but there was one small thing that set him apart from the hundreds of recruits that passed through the doors of The Naval College, and that small thing was the woman who bore him.

Scipio found Tiberius and tickled his ambition. He unearthed his bruised pride. He let loose a thousand dreams of 'what could have been' and gave Tiberius the opportunities to rise in the ranks and found ways to promote him over others. Tiberius went to his deathbed firmly believing these promotions were just results of his actions: his perfectionism, his vision, his control shining through in every operation, lighting the way for his ascending star.

He prided himself in his impeccable, stellar performance, and his unprecedented ascendance through the ranks. His birthright demanded as much. If Tiberius, son of the forgotten royalty, dedicated himself to a task, it would be accomplished. He was totally blind to anything except his successes.

His men were in awe of him, and there were rumors of his unmatched potential throughout every branch of the armed services.

But then...

Not every task he had been given was completed to satisfaction. Skirmishes were won, but at great loss. Mistakes were made, mistakes that would never be made by a career officer. His crucial role in battles was usually that of a carefully engineered figurehead. Alexander, son of a strong ally of Scipio, was always in the background, scheming and engineering.

There's nobody who could question the dedication of Tiberius to his task, and his unparalleled arrogance, but there was a growing number of officers who recognized a carefully engineered progression when they saw one. Somebody up above was looking out for Tiberius they whispered, but only fewer knew who.

And why.

In truth, Tiberius was unbearable to all who didn't fall within his reality-distortion field. And even those who didn't count themselves as the lucky few who were totally under his spell, victory is a seductive temptress. It's easier to overlook qualities you absolutely hate in others if you think the bearer brings in the results.

And he did, to some degree. But he didn't, to another.

Scipio held his hand on the scale to tip the results in the way he wanted, and by stroking the ambition and appetite of a bruised ego with something to prove, a man whose love for his mother blinded him to the traits she so desperately wanted him to emulate, and by engineering situations where Tiberius could reconfirm to himself his own divine selection, Scipio created exactly what he needed. He had himself a bona fide, dyed-in-the-wool extremist.

Tiberius was wrapped in the black fog, losing all sight of any lights on the boat as it enveloped him and lifted him up. He thought of his mother, spending her life on the run, sacrificing everything she could to stay alive, and his blood boiled at the thought of those who had done that to her.

They had no right!

He was practically giddy with excitement. All the long years of waiting and daydreaming of the moments that were to come, and it was all converging on one tiny shard of rock in the North Sea. Soon he would vindicate his mother, justify his birthright, and he would show the gods what it meant to have his will imposed upon them. Nothing could stop him. He was totally sure of it.

The lights flickered behind him, breaking his concentration and bringing him back to reality. The fog was lifting. They'd be on their way again soon. He was going to win. Finally.

The boat started to pick up steam and chug forward, and one by one the stars lit in the endless expanse above, and Tiberius embraced the dark smiling.

CHAPTER 15

Ethan woke up soaking, wedged in between two mossy rocks. It was pouring rain yet again.

"Seriously, how much rain does this place need?" he muttered, still half asleep. "What a miserable pond we've discovered."

From the moonlight, he could see the dark fog had started to clear out to the north. Further on the cliffs dropped down into the ocean. His feet were covered in bruises and scratches, and in a much stranger world would have won a competition for his most goblin-like feature. They were ready to be done covering endless miles each day for sure. They and he were looking forward to a rest.

And at the same time, he was confused. The journey made less and less sense as they got closer and he put real thought into what was about to happen. What exactly did Alana hope to achieve by bringing back the silver cross?

The object itself was shrouded in mysticism. Given by the gods to man as a token of power? Forged by man to channel their power? Or just imbued with fictional powers by overreaching storytellers? It was all unclear.

Every breeze cut through to his heart and pointed to the single overriding question of this entire journey. Why?

And why do I care if she's queen?

The answer, of course, was that he didn't.

He tried to roll over and sleep a little bit more before the sun rose.

Zara slept on the sandy cave floor Marie had offered her. They had talked a little more into the evening, but when the sun set, they decided to continue the conversation in the morning.

Zara couldn't believe she had met Marie! The significance of her being here and alive was not lost on Zara, and she awoke in the dark of night with her mind racing. She stood and walked outside so as to not disturb Marie too much, and she walked down the path towards the gully. Looking up to observe her stars, Zara's gaze stopped at Ozymandias in the distance.

"There's no doubt," she thought, "that is a glow."

She heard steps behind her, and up walked Marie.

"I'm so sorry for waking you, I just couldn't sleep!" Zara apologized.

"Oh, don't worry my dear, I get plenty of rest out here," Marie said. Then, pointing at Ozymandias, she looked at Zara, "you see the glow?" Marie asked.

"Of course," Zara said. "A pale blue glow."

Marie looked at the statue and shrugged. "Your father said it glowed too," she said. "It's why I came so far away." Marie kept looking at the statue intently. "I could never see it."

Zara raised her eyebrow. "Who sees the glow?" she asked.

"Beats me," Marie said. "But now I know of two."

"Well, one," Zara said.

Marie patted her shoulder, "I'm sorry," she said. "I'm sorry."

If Alana had been honest with herself, and there's no record that she was, I'm sure she entertained equally confused thoughts. Did she actually believe the silver cross held power? What relevance does an ancient artefact have in a modern world? Did it hold incredible destructive power? So does the artillery. Does it allow you to move your thoughts instantaneously to another? Go pull up a telegraph. Will it heal you from harm? Find yourself a good doctor. Will it conduct you from one side of the country to another? Hop on a train. There are no powers reserved for the divine.

The powers reserved by the gods were already appropriated by man. Prometheus might have done us all a solid by stealing fire and giving it to mortals, but we don't have a casting call out for other traitorous gods. We're not begging Athena to steal us the secrets of precision artillery strikes, nor Hermes to grant us the secrets behind engines with increased horsepower. Prometheus stole us fire, but we took the rest ourselves.

Even if the old stories are true of the silver cross: the burning fire, the targeted destruction, the wrath of god laid bare on man, what power can that possibly have over a million-man army supported by tens of millions of shells? What use is the power of the old world, even if it can be found and wielded? What can the old gods conjure up in opposition to the great power of man as she harnesses science and technology? What priest or shaman can stop an army?

We have obviated the old needs of groveling to ever-more absent gods.

You can't hold back the waves, and you can't...actually you can hold back the waves with artificial barricades and a lot of engineering. You can stop the Andaluvian in her course. You can change the world in a very physical sense. The old ways are crumbling.

And yet, our primeval demons still lurk beneath the surface. We have eradicated the darkness everywhere but within us.

No, Alana wasn't overthinking everything like Ethan because she woke in a cold sweat from her latest nightmare; nightmares that had grown more and more frequent over the past month. This time she saw her father far off ahead of them on the path, wandering among the smooth black plains. She walked, then ran to meet him. He stood at the bottom of a small hill, trying to continue up the trail, but he had no shoes. Every time he attempted to ascend the hill, the rocks under his feet would break up, rendering sharp blades under his feet. The old king would cry out in pain and slide back down the loose rocks to the bottom of the hill.

"Father!" Alana called as she reached him, "let me help you!"

He looked around and around but could not see her. "Leave me be, demons of the deep!" he cried, and shook his head and once again attempted to summit the path, this time scrambling on all fours, gouging his feet and hands in the process, and slipping back down to the bottom of the hill.

Alana cried and cried, and called to him again, but this just infuriated him more as he spun round and round looking for the sound. He called out ancient curses on his tormentors. Alana noticed his feet and hands quickly healed, and he once again set up the side of the hill, and once again came down drenched in sweat from the pain.

He swore at the gods and at man and tried again and again.

Alana awoke in a cold sweat as the rain tumbled down and the rocks she slept on opened up and cut into her back and legs.

Later that morning she saw the hill from her dream, and at the bottom she saw piles and piles of fresh loose scree.

No, Alana wasn't overthinking the significance of the silver cross like Ethan. He spent his day in the hypothetical; what was the role of the gods, what did the silver cross mean, why would it exist today in the first place, but for Alana the questions were all deeply practical.

The silver cross only mattered because it mattered. The gods only mattered because they mattered. There was no power on heaven or earth that she lusted after, but the power to rule as queen, and if the silver cross gave her that, that was enough. Fire and brimstone could wait. There was no other reason for the silver cross but to have the silver cross.

As they crossed the top of the hill, she heard something fall down the hill, sliding on sharp rocks and the voice of her father cursing in the wind as he shook his fist once again.

While there are those who have experienced deep searing losses of loved ones who then rely on the hope of the divine as their saving grace and eventual reunion, Alana entertained no such thoughts. The gods that built this world must be long gone, because nothing good could possibly have created such pain.

"You must forgive me for asking this again, guide," Alana said with a hint of bitterness, "and of course I do not mean to question your competence in any way, but this 'path' you claim to have been following all this way, does it exist?"

"What do you mean, does it exist??" Ethan said with indignation.

"I mean in the literal is it physically possible to see, or are we yet again chasing the shadows?" Alana replied.

They had reached the tall, black northern cliffs overlooking the North Sea and were picking their way along the cliff's edge on their way towards the west. There was no sign of a break in the cliffs for miles in any direction, and the black sand beach below was probably over three hundred feet down. An unrelenting surf pounded the sand, with kelp, wood, and all manner of seashells strewn out below.

"You know, you're right Alana," Ethan replied, "I think I was mistaken. We probably need to head that way," he said as he pointed back vaguely in the direction he last remembered being warm, "for a few hundred miles. At least." He paused to look back at her, "I know of an amazing blacksmith back in Fort Hall, I bet we could make you a new silver cross, a better silver cross!" He knew better than to insult someone with so much proficiency with a weapon and so little temper, but she couldn't kill her guide. Yet, at least. He cocked his head and gave her his winningest smile to deflect her fury as best he could.

But she hadn't heard him. She looked far off to the sea. "What's that?" she said and pointed to the horizon. Through twists of fog tall white cliffs shone out as if floating on the ocean.

"That's it!" Ethan said, as the words from the Sphinx came back to him. "What is whitewashed but never clean?" he muttered under his breath. "The entrance to hell." he announced.

Alana's entire body smiled, and a sigh of relief exhaled from her whole soul. It was so close.

Though...

"Uh, how are we supposed to get over there?" Alana asked. "I had a very different impression of just how far away from land this quote unquote island was supposed to be".

"Well that depends, how good are you at swimming?" Ethan asked.

The butt of a rifle swiftly connected with his own.

"Okay, okay, I get it, you can't swim. That's fine, you can stay here, I'll take care of it," he said as he dodged another swipe of the rifle.

He kept dancing as Alana chased after him saying, "peasant, I swear to you if you led me all this way for nothing, I will see you work the stone quarries for the rest of your days."

"No more swimming jokes, got it!?" he yelled back as he ran dodging her blows.

"You miserable dung sweep, how do we get across?" Alana yelled as he pranced out of reach.

"Princess, princess, don't you worry!" Ethan said, "I'll take care of it. Now look right over here, there's a way down the cliff."

Up ahead a road swept in from the southwest with deep wagon ruts marking the path. The ruts had cut into the stone itself. This road had been used for quite some time.

"This is our original path," Ethan said, "before the entire Western world decided to try and kill us. Or you, really, I'm just an innocent bystander." Alana appeared to be ready to raise her weapon, so he cut to the quick, "I sure was hoping we would find the road, or that would have made an awkward trip." he pointed to the right where the path seemed to fall off the cliff, "an awkward trip...and fall.".

Alana and he walked over to the cliff where the path seemed to disappear and looked over the edge.

"And that," Ethan said as they looked down, "would be the dark staircase."

There weren't stairs per se, but some poor soul had cut in a very narrow path down the cliff face, descending all the way down to the beach. Alana peered over the edge and her stomach dropped just a bit. She wasn't sure she would trust her life to such a sketchy path.

"But I insist, royalty first," Ethan said with glee. "Peasants must follow!"

Alana finally gave him the smallest of fake smiles and led her very skittish horse down the cliffside.

The entire path carves out a balance between a sheer drop down to the black sand beach on one side, and a smooth black cliff face on the other. The trickiest parts are the switchbacks, as you try to narrowly squeeze your way around tight corners without dying.

They made it down faster than it seemed, and on the beach took in their surroundings. Kelp, driftwood, decent number of seagulls, you name it.

"Uh, this sure looks like a nice place to visit, but it's missing the part where we get to the burial grounds," Alana said, "and the part where you magically whisk us across the water."

"Sure ain't," Ethan said, and he pointed down the beach. The fierce waves were kicking up mists of water high into the sky, and far down the beach through the mists and kelp and whatever else, an old man visibly supporting every one of his steps with his cane hobbled their way.

It was as if an old pile of thick gnarled rope had animated into a man. With each step he appeared to creak as the knots quietly moaned. The ocean breeze blew his long white hair out behind him, and the mist collected into small creeks and drizzled down the deep leathery curves of his face. With one arm he steadied each step with a cane, and with the other held tight a thin grey shawl which wrapped around his tiny thin frame.

Alana and Ethan stood mesmerized at the sight of him and watched as he slowly approached. He drew up to them, closer than what you'd consider comfortable, and said nothing as he looked them both up and down.

"I am Kharon," he said.

Alana opened her mouth, but Kharon held his finger to his mouth and silenced her. He then looked up into her eyes, searching inside as he gazed. He looked and looked, mumbling as his eyes darted around in hers.

"Alana," he said, "They said you would come now, but I never quite believed it. I've heard so much about you, and yet I know so little."

Kharon turned and looked into Ethan's eyes. He looked but a moment. "Ethan. Such a joy to see you again. You've grown so much. You are always welcome in my home." He embraced him as he continued, "your mother had so much to say about you. But that is a story for another day."

"Th...thank you?" Ethan replied. The whole interaction was turning out to be a lot more intimate than either of them expected. Alana wondered if uninvited soul-searching breached any royal protocols.

"Follow me home, we'll wait until high tide to make the passage," he said. "No use standing around out here when we could be sitting in a cramp damp cave." and he turned and began walking towards the cliffs, chuckling at himself. "In any event, you'll want to rest after your journey. And I'll want to hear the whole of it." he called back.

They shuffled after him on the black sand beach, the coarse grains crunching under every step. In a sheltered inlet they passed an ancient rowboat, every square inch of it inside and out intricately carved with foreign symbols and intense pictographs, with two large barely legible words which read:

"Abandon Hope"

And with that, they were led into Kharon's cave.

In the words of a salesperson, they might describe the cave as "cozy" or "well-loved". In the words of Ethan, it was "appropriately sized for a mouse" and "covered in junk". It turns out you don't get to be a super old lonely hermit without turning into something of a hoarder. There were all sorts of bits of flotsam and jetsam covering every corner: a whole collection of glass bottles of every color, and weathered shards of glass of every make and description. Naturally, the entire potpourri spilled out of the cave into the surrounding sand. It was a mess.

A small fire burned near the front, and on that Kharon made them some kelp tea, which is the kind of tea you serve to your worst enemies and unwelcome house guests, and can only be swallowed if Kharon is looking right at you when you drink it, and otherwise is quickly spit onto the sand of the floor of the cave, which was definitely wet from the surf already. Yeah, it was definitely the surf.

There was no furniture or other semblance of a home, just

some rocks which Kharon uncovered by sweeping his cane around in erratic stabbing motions. Once cleared, the three of them sat down for a chat.

"Well?" Kharon said as they uncomfortably balanced on stones and tried to pour excess disgusting tea onto the ground without him noticing, "tell me everything. And excuse my manners; it's not often that I receive visitors," he said as he took a sip and gave them a wide-eyed side glance, "of the living type."

Alana had recovered from the shock of having her soul read by a stranger. "You'll have to excuse me Kharon, as I'm not adequately familiar with your work," she said. "My guide, Ethan," and with this she swung her knee out to knock his just as he moved to surreptitiously pour a little tea out, causing him to spill it on his legs, "neglected to mention how exactly we'd be making the, uh, passage over to the royal burial ground."

Kharon chuckled. "Well, first of all, there aren't any royals, and I wouldn't really call them grounds."

Alana furrowed her brow. "But there are kings buried there. Great kings. Great kings from great kingdoms. My kings." she said.

Kharon shook his head, "They once thought themselves kings, perhaps, thought themselves royal, but where are they now? Where is the royal road to Hades? No, there are men and women buried there same as you and me."

Alana opened her mouth to object, and Kharon talked over her, "fine, same as Ethan and me. Either way, my point stands. Where they are there is but one king, and none of them are it. Dust to dust and from star to star, we all start the same, and we all end the same. There are no royalty among us."

Alana had very serious objections to philosophical discussions in general, largely because she knew philosophers and there's nobody more likely to drive you crazy than a philosopher, so she wisely decided to retreat and avoid the metaphysics behind his statements.

"The grounds, I am here to visit the grounds." she said.

"Rocks, really," Kharon replied, and took a sip to hide his enormous smile.

"The rocks," Alana said robotically, "the rocks. I just want to find my father among them. Now how exactly," Alana smacked Ethan's knee, preventing him from gaining tea relief yet again, "are you involved in this? I owe the great ki...MEN," she caught herself before Kharon could interject, "men, I owe the great men..."

"and women!" Kharon interjected with glee.

"AND WOMEN a debt of gratitude for their great deeds and I wish to pay my respects." she finished, wide-eyed and red faced."

"And how would you know of these deeds?" Kharon asked. "Who has told you? Did you read their own writings? Where they exalt themselves for how they were able to lift themselves out of humble royal circumstances..."

"But there's no royalty among us!" Alana exclaimed with glee.

Kharon rolled his eyes. "Lift themselves out of humble privileged circumstances" he said, giving her the stink eye, "to manage to rule a kingdom bequeathed upon them through sheer luck, and not due to any actual capabilities? Have you paid them your taxes, eating a little less through the winter so that their horses could be clothed in silk? Have you slaved away in the burning sun building their pompous memorials while they slept on furs and grew fat on the fruit of your fields? If these are great works, then yes, yes, they have done great works." Kharon said as he raised his voice and finished his tea.

Alana's blood boiled as you can imagine, but direct insults to her and her family were getting a little bit easier for her to emotionally manage.[15]

"And suppose they are old man? And suppose I have?" Alana replied. "Perhaps you could have done better? Maybe you'd make sure to burn down the palace and live in a tent when you lead the people? Some of us are born extraordinary, and we have a duty to the ordinary, a duty to help affect the greater good. Some may lose so that all may gain. Who's to say how the calculus balances out? Who's to say what was right or wrong? How can you know unless you have walked in their shoes and seen their challenges?" Alana declared.

"Do you not know who I am?" Kharon said with a knife-edged voice.

"...and your part in this? I think I'm missing that bit," Alana said through gritted teeth.

"Ethan, you didn't tell her?" Kharon asked. "What's all that about?"

Ethan raised his eyebrows and looked back at him with a nod, "uh, don't you see how much fun this is? Do you think I'd throw the chance of this encounter away?"

"Wait, wait, wait, how do you even know this guy?" Alana asked. "Could someone please explain to me what is going on, ideally before I get onto a boat with two crazy people." she said.

"This," it was Ethan's turn to smack Alana's knee, "VERY KIND gentleman who is definitely not crazy is our only option for reaching the royal non-royal burial grounds non-grounds." Ethan said. "Unless you're up for a fifty-mile trek to the west where we might be able to scrounge up a fisherman with a boat and hope he's not superstitious."

"I am Kharon," Kharon said.

"We've established that," Alana interrupted.

[15] I think some of that can be attributed to the fact that Ethan had spent the better part of the last week calling her the daughter of King Timid the Second. So there's that.

Kharon ignored her. "I am Kharon, and I ferry the dead across the Styx and onto the gates of Hades. I have been ordained by the gods to this task and have performed my labors for many generations. There is but one type of person I carry across, and it is not a living one." he said.

"Ahhhh," Alana said as it clicked in her head. "I thought that was more of a spiritual duty, and not necessarily a physical one." she said.

"It is both," Kharon said. "I am the only conduit between dead and living. All who die pass through my care."

Alana quickly shifted from indignant frustration to immense curiosity. Some may call her borderline bipolar in this phase of her life, but they didn't bother themselves with labels so much back then. "But how do they find you?" she said.

"Every soul of the departed is left to wander the earth. Some are in agony, being untimely ripped from their mortal tenure, others are swept clear with peace. I call to them here, guide them here from all corners of the earth with my voice. I attend to each of them, hear their stories, walk in their shoes if you will," he gave Alana a knowing glance, "and then send them on their way to the hereafter. I am the last stop for all souls on earth." Kharon said.

"And what a stop it is!" Kharon continued. "Some tell me their deepest secrets, their darkest confessions, tales of which would keep you up at night in agony. I hear it all and hold the burden of all of the dark terrible things of humanity. Some escape their karmic reward on earth, but for those who do evil, dark clouds gather on the other side of the Styx, and their justice is always served with vengeance.

"Some tell me of their fondest loves, their husbands, their wives, their children. Moments spent in tall green grass in spring. Dances in a moonlit autumn. Births, marriages, reunions. Their happiness buoys us across the water, and on the other side the gates can barely contain the shrieks of joy.

Their time with me is short, and they lean over the bow, stretch their eyes as far as they'll go, and look forward to their final and most happy reunions.

"The joy I have seen surpasses all description. There is no happier thing in all of the world but the long-awaited reunion of family." Kharon looked out to the churning sea. "There is no happier thing..." he trailed off.

"But you'll take us?" Ethan asked.

"You, yes. And since you accompany him, you too," Kharon said as he looked at Alana. "But only for your mother's sake, and," he paused and looked at him, "for your grandmother's sake."

"Has she been here?" Ethan asked.

"Not recently, if that's what you mean." Kharon said, and Ethan sighed with relief. Maybe there was still a chance.

Ethan gave up any pretense of drinking tea at this point, and casually tossed the kelp water out the door when Kharon looked down. It was defensibly terrible sure, but you don't tell that to a freaking hermit who you need to throw you a bone.

The sound of the splash jostled Kharon out of his thoughts. "But, as a formality, will you show me the stone? It is your passage." he said.

Ethan pulled at the dark leather banded necklace hanging around his neck and popped out the ancient kite-shaped deep emerald gem. It caught the light of the fire for a moment and seemed to hold the fire inside for a moment, and then emit and blast it ever stronger into the cave, bathing them all in a dark green light.

"The eye of Rhea. More beautiful every time I see it," Kharon said as he sat entranced in its gaze. "More beautiful every time."

"They eye of what?" Ethan asked. His mother had always refused to tell Ethan anything about it, always replying to his questions that he was far too young, and she would tell him when he was older. "How does it work?" he inquired intently.

"That, my young friend, is not within my realm of expertise. Your grandmother always said it was a deep longing cut into reality. But if you'll allow an old man his rest," and he looked out the cave, "I need to prepare for the passage. Please tell me when the surf reaches the boat." He shuffled the two outside, and he lay down on the floor of the cave for a rest, because dealing with those smelly kids was exhausting, and have you ever been an old person? As Ethan would say later in life, "being old is tiring and we sleep a lot."

Ethan and Alana exited the cave, and Kharon was snoring almost instantaneously. The harsh waves crashed on the black sands and inched slowly up the incline towards the boat.

Ethan sat and watched the water and wondered what kind of person his grandmother was. It had been years since he had seen or heard of her.

CHAPTER 16

Jacques knocked on the door. He didn't have to wait long for an answer.

"Whatever you want, you'll be more successful if you come around back," called out a voice.

"Well, I've finally found her," he thought, "Lack of decorum? Check. Absence of decency? Check. No question about it. This is her." He stepped around the tiny shack and there was Marie, out chopping wood in the clearing behind her house in the immense forest. Her hair was long and threaded in beautiful blonde braids, with grey hair slowly colonizing its way through the whole bunch.

"Oh Jackie, what a pleasure to see you," Marie said without even looking up as she thumped another block of wood. "And by pleasure, I mean be grateful my shotgun is inside."

"Marie, you know I am distraught, it was a terrible tragedy." Jacques said. "But I have no idea what could have precipitated such mindless violence.

"Terrible tragedy yadda, yadda, yadda, I don't believe the hogwash you sent me: my daughter was killed by demons from the underworld? Not a chance, not my Jane, she was too good," Marie said, giving him the stink eye. "Unless you are finally admitting to me your true form."

Jacques chuckled. "You've never lost your charm, now have you?" he said. "Though you do seem to be prone to losing things; contact with your daughter, wars, you know, the small stuff."

Marie huffed. "I thought I smelled a rat around here watching me," she said. "It's none of your business when I talk to my daughter."

"Oh, my dear Marie," Jacques said, "on the contrary, it is absolutely my business to carefully watch all enemies of the state."

"I don't know what you're talking about," Marie said. "And if you're watching me and Jane so well, how can you not find those responsible for her death? Or does your lack of trust in me translate into lack of ambition in tracking?"

"Oh, I assure you all is being done to track your daughter, and," Jacques paused for a moment, "your grandson."

"You leave Ethan out of this!" Marie demanded as she thumped another block of wood and rested the axe on the chopping block. "He is of no interest to you."

"To the contrary, Marie," Jacques said, "I find that rebelliousness runs in your family. It would be a shame if he were found and needed to be questioned about his family history."

"What kind of family history?" Marie asked angrily. "You know all about my history."

"You're not trustworthy," Jacques replied. "That was Leo's greatest mistake. You betrayed your people to help him and he could never believe that you had different motives, but I can see that you're one who always looks out for yourself."

"We always ascribe our own faults to others," Marie snapped back. "We can only see in others what we see first in ourselves."

"And is that what drew you to Leo? Your gullibility?"

Jacques replied.

"What do you want Jacques," Marie asked. "Did you come all the way here to argue and threaten an old woman?"

"You stole it, didn't you?" Jacques said. "Titus never had it, the carrier is empty," Jacques pulled out an empty leather case engraved with the silver cross.

"Ah ha! Your true purpose revealed!" Marie exclaimed.

Jacques rolled his eyes, then he lowered his eyes and glared silently.

"I didn't steal anything," Marie said dismissively, "especially no mythical item like the silver cross.

"I've seen it Marie," Jacques said. "You know I have."

"Well that makes one of us," Marie said. "I don't have it."

Jacques took a long look in her green eyes. "You see more than you say bearer," he said, "I'm glad Titus expelled you, you can never be trusted."

"You just can't trust someone who knows more than you," Marie said, "and that is your greatest mistake. You surround yourself with fools because you can't trust wisdom you don't have yourself."

Jacques guffawed. "Trust a fool to spout nonsense," he said. "This comes from the woman who made the worst decision in history."

"I have history to answer to, and it will judge me kindly," Marie said.

"But I will write that history!" Jacques said.

Marie stood up and glared into his eyes, "but I have seen the future, and I know what will be written."

"So, she gave the wayfinder back to you," Jacques said. "I should have guessed as much."

"I don't need a wayfinder," Marie said. "I have learned its magic."

Jacques sighed. "Well, then my proposition should be simple for you," he said. "Titus was our king, and you know the custom: the king to rest in the royal burial grounds, to be borne hence by a bearer of the dead. It has been this way across countless kings and kingdoms."

"Well, it's got to end sometime, because us bearers aren't going to last many more countless kings if we keep getting countlessly knocked off," Marie said with another thwack.

"Titus will be the last king." Jacques said with finality. "This ends here. The old ways are dying."

"As is your sense, young man," Marie replied. "Does his daughter know about this?" Marie stopped chopping and looked expectantly at him.

Jacques said nothing.

"Well Jackie?" she needled. "Does his daughter know this? Or his cousin?"

Jacques winced and then replied, "Only those who must know do know. Which now includes you." he said.

"It sounds like you've got bigger fish to fry, Jacques. Why come out here? Why get me? You can dump him off in the nearest unmarked grave you want." Marie asked.

Jacques, with his characteristic charm and grace replied, "I'm afraid the monarchy has outlived its usefulness."

"I am shocked, shocked to hear you say that," Marie interjected. "Nobody could have predicted this."

Jacques ignored her, "The monarchy has outlived its usefulness. You know that. I know that. Most of the government knows that. But,"

"But that mob of people who are waiting to string you up by your thumbs don't know that? Oh Jackie, you always were such a coward," Marie said.

"It will take time for the rest of the kingdom to understand," he said. "And besides, Titus was a friend of mine, Marie. I take care of my friends." Jacques said.

"Indeed, you do," Marie said, "by killing them and stealing their thrones. Helluva way to build friendships. Reminds me why we remain enemies."

"Regardless of your personal opinions of the matter,"

211

Jacques said, tensing his voice just enough to remind Marie of the threats that stood behind it, "I expect you to fulfill your duty. We must pay our respects."

"And what respect this is." Marie observed. "Please never respect me."

"I never have," Jacques said obligingly.

"But what am I getting out of this," she asked. "Don't tell me you're going to let me read my own mail now!"

"Your grandson," Jacques said. "I will permit him to live."

"How gracious of you," Marie replied.

"I am, if nothing, a magnanimous and kind ruler," he said.

Marie shook her head. "Don't touch my grandson," she said. "Don't you dare let any harm come to him. You will not let things get out of hand with him like you did my daughter. You must swear to protect him." she said.

"I swear it," Jacques said.

"No no, I know how you work Jacques, and I know you can never be trusted, but I have no choice: I know that, and you know that. Today he's just a kid who lost his mother, but you owe me for this, and you'll repay him."

Jacque bowed, and said, "I always repay my debts."

Marie rolled her eyes, "I know. Favors are your currency of choice. You keep him out of your line of fire, you keep him out of the capital, and I keep my mouth shut and bury your problems."

She was right, favors were his favorite form of currency, the only moral compass he had. "I agree," he said, "I agree. He will have my protection."

"Then I will take Titus and bury him in the royal grounds." Marie replied.

Jacques bowed deeply, "always a pleasure doing business with you," he said.

"The displeasure is all mine I assure you," Marie replied.

She put away her axe, tidied up her home for a minute, then stood at the door and took one last deep breath and looked around. She knew how this worked. This was the last time she'd ever see her home. She'd need to escape again, but this time to a much further and desolate locale. Jacques may need her to dispose of Titus, but he was going to get a two for one deal here.

They would burn her home to the ground to rake the ashes clean looking for the silver cross. But she, and she alone, knew they would not find it.

It wasn't long before the sea climbed its way up to high tide, and Alana fetched Kharon from his cave. She touched his shoulder and like striking lightning, he immediately jumped up from full on deep sleep and was instantly on his way. Ethan was much slower to engage, watching the waves come in and out, in and out.

They entered the boat, and Alana noticed on the other side the inscription:

"All Ye Who Enter Here"

Again, the entire boat was covered in the most intricate carvings she had ever seen in her life. Alana and Ethan sat in the back, and Kharon pushed the boat out into the surf until he was up to his waist in the ocean, then pulled himself into the boat and made his way to the front, legs dripping wet. Facing them, he took the oars with unmatched skill, and rowed them out to sea. Where he grasped the oars, grooves had formed to his hands over the many, many years of pulling.

Each stroke was as powerful as if ten men were drawing the boat. His tiny frame hid more brawn than they could have possibly imagined. His arms were practically bursting out of his skin, as his muscles and sinews showed through in dramatic fashion. They would later say the old dude was ripped, as well he should be after doing this for literal ages.

But perhaps more impressively, he never once looked behind him to orient himself towards his destination. Looking towards the rear and watching behind was all he needed to perfectly predict his path. He had done this enough that the past was all he needed to see the future.

"You know it's not here, right?" Kharon said as the sound of the surf faded in the distance. He was calm and composed as he spoke, and you'd never guess that he was exerting such force on the water.

"Why is everyone intent on stopping me?" Alana despaired. "I know. I know. It's mythical, it doesn't exist, it's not actually powerful, it won't be here. I get it. Stop. But I need to see for myself. I must see."

"I'm not trying to stop you," Kharon said with a half-smile. "Note how I'm actively not stopping you. But I feel I should at least prepare you for what is to come."

"How can you know of what is to come? I have learned one thing in all of my years of walking my path alone, and that is that nobody can know what is to come." Alana said.

"I definitely predicted total failure for us, let's just make sure that's on the record," Ethan interjected.

They both ignored him, and Kharon replied, "I know everyone's story," Kharon said. "I have heard them all. There is nothing new under the sun. And what you seek cannot be here. You have a much longer path to walk, I am afraid. This is but the first step."

Alana was pretty darn sick of older dudes telling her what to think, and her annoyance was compounded by the fact that she was stuck in a rowboat, and there's really nothing you can do to get away from your fellow passengers. Except look off the side and watch the seas and hope they lose interest, which she did.

"And what steps follow?" Ethan asked, his curiosity clearly piqued. Also, they probably had another hour to go, and why not bug Alana for another hour?

Kharon replied: "A woman spurned of her throne by a shadowy power, enticed to leave her claim while she seeks unneeded legitimacy? There but remains a crisis to befall the kingdom and the victory is complete: she will be smeared for her absence, claiming that she cared not for her people in their moment of need. A beginner could write this plot it's so simple. That which you seek cannot possibly be here because the powers would never allow it! They would have recovered it themselves were it that easy. This is your first mistake, but it will not be your last.

"Do not despair, though. In youth we take action with no wisdom and stumble from mistake to mistake, and in old age we have enough wisdom to prevent us from taking action, and so we are left to die with only our wisdom, and no success." Kharon said.

The rowboat moved forward one masterful stroke at a time. Up and down, to and fro, Kharon held a steady line and inched closer and closer to the looming white cliffs.

"But do not let me dissuade you from your quest! An old man like me takes no chances because he sees the failure present in each one. We are beset by the demons of indecision and inaction, and so the young reap all the rewards." Kharon continued, largely talking to himself and rambling at this point,[16] but what did he care, he was an old man. Ain't got nobody to impress.

"But," he added as an afterthought, "even if you do fail, you learn wisdom. And really, that is all that you can take with you beyond the gates," Kharon said, and he flicked his head backward to point at the looming cliffs, growing larger and larger with each stroke. "It's all anyone can take." he said.

Ethan started to see a thin black line tracing the cliffs from top to bottom. Was it an entrance? It was as thin as a knife in the distance. The cliffs themselves must have been a thousand feet high. It was totally otherworldly.

The seas tossed the boat up and down, but Kharon

---

[16] Pro tip: if the other person in the conversation hasn't spoken more than a word or two at a time in the last five minutes, you are definitely rambling.

powered through at a totally constant rhythm. Up and down, to and fro, Kharon rowed, Kharon kept the beat like a drum. Up and down, to and fro. He had seen life so many times, he didn't need to look to know where it was going.

Which is a real shame because the sight was breathtaking.

Massive white cliffs that appeared to touch the clouds above towered over them in the distance and drew nearer with every stroke. Back and forth. Up and down. To and fro.

In the center of the cliffs ran a narrow slit down the entirety of the cliff face in a perfect vertical line. It was an entrance.

They neared the tiny channel cut in the cliffside which held a narrow inlet of water, roughly fifteen feet across. They entered the channel and were immediately thrust into another world: the ocean calmed, and the sun was gone. While they could see a bright sky high above them in the channel, barely any light reached the surface, and it took them several minutes before their eyes adjusted enough to see the wonders before them.

The entire cliff face on either side of the channel was covered in intricate carvings as far as they could see in any direction. The pure white stone had been chiseled into a bas relief epic storyline as had never before or since been created on this earth.

Alana and Ethan were utterly speechless and overwhelmed with awe. They drank in the scene with reverence and adoration. The only sound was the lapping of the channel water against the cliff, and the occasional scuff of an oar on a side of the cliff face.

Some of the stories they could pick out: there were scenes depicting the founding of the great cities of old; Knossos, Persepolis, Alexandria. Alana scouted out the sacking of Troy high up above. They saw the birth of Gaia, the fall of the Titans, and the rise of Zeus. Ethan pointed out the death of Medusa, and the escape of the Argonauts. Their jaws dropped lower and lower as a humongous tapestry of life unfolded before their eyes. There were epic battles long since lost to history, great warriors, legendary journeys, and weaving its way throughout, passionate love.

"Behold," said Kharon, finally interrupting the silence, "the book of life."

"It's...incredible," Alana said. Her eyes darted back and forth between the walls, picking out what she could in the dim light, and reaching her hand out to try and touch a wall just to feel what a wonder of the world felt like. Though honestly, she'd get plenty of that later. "Did you do this?" Alana asked.

Kharon smiled. "You are the first among the living to behold it," he said. "And yes, I did. Thank you. I'd say that doing this has kept me sane, but I don't think it's intellectually honest to make that claim of myself."

"Where are all of these stories from?" Ethan asked as he practically cricked his neck staring upwards and all around. "How do you know this?

"I told you. I accompany all to the gates of Hades. I am the repository of the entire story of mankind, and this is the book wherein I write it down. The deeds of all men are known to these walls, and eventually, to the gods in their judgement. This is the book of life." Kharon said again. "Here are written their deeds, and on the black cliffs on the other side of the gates are written the judgements of all men."

Ethan would never really be able to tell quite how long they rowed. He was overwhelmed with amazement by the sheer intricacy. Uncountable stories carved into limitless walls, and not a single mistake visible, nor even the slightest sign of wear: it was as smooth as if the rock had been formed that way from the beginning of the earth. They could have rowed for years, or it could have been minutes, he would never be able to tell.

Eventually they reached a smooth cliff wall again at the end of the passage, and Kharon smiled and winked. "There are still a few more stories left to tell," he said.

At the far end of the passage the cliff walls dropped and opened up into a smooth white stone bowl cavern, with white steps carved into the side of the smooth bowl leading up and out into the island itself. Kharon tied up the boat, and the three of them ascended out of the book of life and into the gates of Hades.

In the near distance, short black cliffs shot up from a scruffy plain. Small mounds of slate dotted the landscape in every direction, with spotty short grass growing among the slate heaps, and on every mound, a small rectangular jet-black rock inscribed with runes.

Kharon pointed to a break in the cliffs that was just visible and said, "The entrance to Hades. You are forbidden from entering unless you desire to stay."

He turned to walk back down the steps and Alana stopped him.

"Wait, master," she said, "do we not lack your instruction?" she said.

"I have nothing left to offer you," Kharon said. "I have foreseen all that is to come, and I have naught to do but wait. And besides, Marie never told me where she buried anybody. But Ethan can read the inscriptions I presume. Otherwise..."

"Otherwise?" Alana asked.

"Otherwise he was right, this was a really dumb idea." Kharon said.

"I can read, I can read, hold your darn horses," Ethan said, and he began to go from mound to mound, searching for the hallowed resting place of Titus II, king of all Atlas, son of Titus I. Kharon wandered off back in the direction of the boat.

It is not known when the tradition of burying royalty at the gates of Hades began. Ethan figured it had been a pretty long time when he stopped recognizing Kings' and queens' names. He figured it had been an obscenely long time when he stopped recognizing the names of the kingdoms. This was an ancient tradition.

Which was unfortunate, because it was going to take a long time to find the right one.

They had not expected this volume of graves, because burials of this nature had largely stopped at that point, with the exception of Titus II. The old ways were changing, and fewer and fewer held true to the ancient religion. And well, there were fewer and fewer royals all the time. They had severely underestimated how many royals had gone before them.

Light began to quickly fade, and they had to give up for the night. They scrounged for some mushrooms among the brush, combined with the meagre rations they had left, set a fire, and settled down on the rocky ground for an uncomfortable night to try and get some sleep.

After an hour or so of hazily half sleeping, Alana was overtaken by a sense of panic. Anxiety gripped her chest like an icy cold hand and paralyzed her heart with fear. The fire had burned down to embers, and the wind picked up, blowing tiny glowing orbs out and up into the wind. The sky was inky black. She could see no stars.

As the smoke of the fire drifted slowly upwards, it began to take shape. A dark figure apparated in front of Alana from the smoke. Her eyes went wide and she fumbled for her knife as she waited for the figure to strike.

But it did not.

It stared at her and waited calmly as she fumbled, and as she fumbled, she realized it was motionless. It stared right through her soul. Alana stopped moving and looked up at it.

From within its cloak a black bony hand extended and beckoned she follow. The wind picked up and the glowing embers from the fire encircled and surrounded the figure and blew off up into the sky. It again beckoned, and she paused for a moment and considered. It again beckoned. Alana shrugged, put on her boots, and followed.[17]

They approached the black cliffside that Kharon had pointed out the day before. It was impossible to see clearly in the overwhelming blackness of the night, but she could hear its looming presence. The dark slit that she had seen from afar wasn't nearly wide enough for a human, but as the figure approached, the cliff widened up and enveloped the figure and it disappeared. She paused for a moment at the wall, wondering what to do, until in the dark she could barely make out the bony hand reaching back out from the slit, ever beckoning she continue. She took a deep breath, stepped forward, and the sheer black rock opened up and enveloped her. And she fell.

In the blackness it was impossible for her to tell which way she fell. Was she up? Was she down? Did she move forward? Alana lost all sense of time and direction, and the emptiness slowly expanded and expanded and bore down upon her until she could no longer hear wind whistling in her ears. For a time, she was lost for breath. She fell outside of time and space. Just as she began to lose hope and give herself up, lost to the eternities, she caught sight of a dark deep red glow which grew and grew and grew.

Suddenly, she hit the ground.

Her feet stumbled onto a dark path in a subterranean chamber dimly lit in red. She fell to the ground on her hands and knees, panting for air. The dark figure stood directly in front of her, and its robes brushed against her head as she gasped for oxygen, finally breathing in warm air. She looked up from where she had stumbled gasping for air, and up above the bony hand again extended and beckoned.

They walked along the dark path in the earth, and the

---

[17] As one does, I suppose? I'd really recommend that you, dear reader, ask a few more questions before just walking off with a demon from the underworld, but what do I know.

feeling of emptiness slowly fell away. Her senses returned one by one, but the last to return was sound. Far off in the distance she felt a pounding arise.

Each step drew them closer to the pound, pound, pounding resonating deep within the earth, and eventually they came to a large open chamber where the sound shook her entire body with every stroke. A river of lava flowed across the bottom of the chamber many hundreds of feet down, and steam exploded upwards from its depths. A stone bridge ran across the river and on the other side she saw humongous black gates guarded by terrible figures encased in black armor holding long axes at their sides. A huge line of souls stood outside the gates, awaiting judgement.

The figure walked ahead a few paces, turned around, and...

"I know, I know, you're going to beckon to follow you, I get it, just throw me a freaking bone and calm down," Alana said, "I'm coming along just as fast as I can." And she stepped forward and followed across the bridge.

The dark figure walked up to the other side of the bridge, passing by the entire line with obvious confidence and waved a dark hand. The armored guards snarled but drew back their axes and bellowed out a call. The pounding stopped for a moment, and in the silence the gates melted away.

They walked past those in the line, some expecting great happiness, others consigned to their fate. One familiar face caught Alana's eye and gave the briefest of smiles.

"Thanks", he mouthed. Alana didn't have the sense to react then, but relief flooded her for a fading moment. He had found his way.

They moved forward past the guards, and on the ground Alana saw inscribed in the stone the words of millions who had walked here before. "Abandon hope, all ye who enter here."

They passed into the beyond, down one of several paths

into a dark tunnel. They descended quite far, Alana trying not to slip as she followed the figure that appeared to have no respect for gravity, and eventually bottomed out. The path wound up a short incline and opened back up into a cavern.

Alana gasped. The chamber was huge, it seemed to be as tall as the earth itself. Hundreds of paths wandered off in a maze-like configuration. Directly in front of her she saw towering walls with thousands of cells, glowing red bars blocking the way, and behind them fog and steam blew out from the chambers beyond. Above the incessant and thundering beating, she could hear screams of pain or shouts of anger. The smoke shook with each beat as the entire world seemed to draw its power from the rhythm.

They took a path that led them into the wall, up and down again fully enclosed inside the earth, this way and that, occasionally opening up into larger passageways where they would cross bridges over a cool blue flowing river of souls, music rising up from the current, and laughter echoing through the halls.

They turned down a path and came to a dead end. At the end of the path deep red bars glowed blocking the way, and beyond the bars Alana could see a shroud of fog and smoke lay shaking in the beat. The figure stood, raised its arm and pointed ahead into the chamber, then bowed its head in respect and stepped back to allow Alana to pass.

She walked up to the pulsing dark red gate and stopped. She could feel a slow heat coming off the gate. Alana looked through the bars and only saw the pulsing fog behind. She turned back to look at the figure, and it flicked its finger at the gate, motioning her forward. Alana shrugged her shoulders, took a deep breath, and stepped forward into the red gate.

She passed right through as if it didn't exist at all. She felt only a tiny bit of warmth as she crossed the threshold, and then found herself stepping blindly through the haze. After a few paces the cloud lifted, and she found herself in a dimly lit chamber. At the far side sat her father, Titus II, king of Atlas, defender of the five nations. He sat with his head in his hands, dressed head to toe in his ceremonial uniform.

"Daddy!" she squealed and ran to him. "Daddy, daddy, daddy!" she exclaimed.

Titus wearily lifted up his head and looked at this shrieking fan, barely registering this bundle of excitement and joy practically delirious in front of him. He gave her half a smile, and said, "Why hello," nodded with a bit of a jolt, and dropped his head back into his hands.

"Daddy?" Alana said. She furrowed her brow and dropped to a knee by his side. "It's me, Alana. It's been so long. I haven't seen you since I was just a girl. Where have you been? What are you doing?" she said. "What happened?"

Titus kicked his feet out and leaned back against the chamber wall, his hands behind his head. "Of course, Alana. Miss me much?" he said. "You always were a little on the needy side, I could have predicted this is what you'd be like after all these years. I've just been waiting around here for a while, being 'rehabilitated' by these monsters." he said as he laughed. "As if I were in need of 'rehabilitation'", he scoffed, pounding a fist against the wall. "This place is a joke run by anti-monarchist peasants! They don't know what's good for them, what I can give them, what incalculable benefits my leadership could provide them, and so here I sit day after day waiting for people who get it, my supporters, those poor excuses for failures, to release me."

"Are you being punished daddy?" Alana asked. "Can I get you out of here? Is that why I was brought here?"

"You?" Titus said. "I doubt it. You couldn't shoot a cow from ten yards, and you most definitely don't know your way around here. No, I'm stuck waiting for someone who gets it to come and figure this place out and let me free," Titus said.

"Daddy, I was ten, and the gun practically weighed more than I did, anyone would miss," Alana said.

"I didn't hear those excuses from anyone else. You were always the only one who felt the need to excuse poor performance. There's no excuse for poor performance. No wonder they hate the monarchy down here, look at what you're going to do to it," Titus said. "All the more reason for me to get out of here and back to Atlas. Can you get a message to Jacques? Now he knows a thing or two about serving royalty, he can make stuff happen! Prince of a man, I hope he's excited to get his king back!" Titus said.

"Daddy, I don't think you're going back," Alana said hesitantly. "I don't think anyone goes back."

"It's because of Zara isn't it!" Titus said. "I knew she'd be trouble in the end, I knew she was watching and waiting for the right moment to strike." Titus stood up and with him Alana stood as well. He grabbed at her coat with her hands and drew his face next to hers, "This is why you needed to be diligent! I need constant diligence! How have you missed the signs! I knew Zara would be back but nobody was ever smart enough to find her, and I kept telling them you need to be diligent and you can find her, but nobody was ever diligent, I am surrounded by idiots, idiots all the time, do you know what it's like to rule over idiots! The only person I could talk to my entire life was Jacques, he was the only one who would ever understand, you need to go find him and tell him that I am here and he needs to come get me before Zara unleashes her plan! She's been lying in wait for the right moment and now with nothing but weakness in her path she must sense her opportunity!"

Titus paced back and forth, shaking with frustration, and muttering to himself. Alana began to cry.

"What are you still doing here? Crying? We never show weakness," Titus scolded her. "You never understood that." he said.

Alana wiped her tears and replied, "I can be strong daddy," she said. "I can be strong."

"Good," Titus said. "Now stop delaying and go get Jacques."

"But daddy," Alana said, "he's trying to kill me. I came here to get the silver cross to fight back."

"Kill you?" Titus said in bewilderment, "The silver cross?" Titus stopped in his tracks, cocked his head and looked at her, then repeated himself. "The silver cross? You came here for the silver cross?"

"Yes, Jacques told me he thought maybe you still had it. I'm here to find your gra...find you and look for it," she said.

Titus looked at her with unfiltered scorn. "Jacques knows I don't have the silver cross!" he thundered. "Does it look like I have the silver cross?" he said. "Do you see a silver cross on me? No! I'm covered in rags and surrounded by idiots," he said, and he paced again, muttering louder to himself.

"But if you don't have the silver cross," Alana asked, "where is it?"

"Where do you think it is?" he shouted. "Zara has it! She stole it from Leo! Unless you want to tell me like all the other weaklings that it was her right to have? But it was not! It was not her right! She didn't deserve the throne! Only the best can ascend, and she was not the best. I was the best, and my father and mother saw that as well as anyone and they made sure that Leo that old fake couldn't keep it away from me." Titus was breathing heavily, having worked himself up the most he had been in years. "But they never did find that silver cross, and I know Zara has been waiting for the right time to spring her trap." Titus walked to the side of the chamber where the roof was lower, and he stretched out onto his toes and banged his hand on the ceiling and yelled upward, "But you didn't deserve it or the throne, you were weak, and I was the true heir! You were weak!" he screamed as he banged his fist again and again.

Alana's eyes filled with tears and she backed away slowly from Titus. To her immeasurable relief, through the fog by the entrance she saw a dark hand extend...and beckon. A whisper came from beyond. "It is time," it hissed.

"Oh, now you speak," she muttered.

Titus snapped his head and glared at the hand. "Off you go," he said to Alana out of the corner of his mouth, without taking his eyes off the beckoning hand. "Get Jacques, tell him to come here. I'll fix this mess you've gotten us into," he said. "And tell Zara that I'll find her. She can flaunt her temporary success in the realms above all she wants, but I will be the ultimate victor. It is my right."

"But daddy, Jacques wants me dead," Alana said.

"Stop being absurd," Titus said. "Now go. Do something right for once."

Alana nodded her head, and unable to speak through her tears she gave a quick wave and walked into the fog and into the gate.

Outside she found the dark figure lording over her menacingly. Alana wiped her tears away as best she could and tried to retrace her steps. The dark figure moved into her way. She went to the right, and the dark figure blocked her again. To the left, the same.

It held out its black bony hand and pointed her to an empty cell.

She looked at it, confused.

It directed her to the cell again.

She shook her head.

It let out an unholy screech and pointed her towards the cell.

Alana's tears stopped, and she looked at this dark figure closely. This did not seem right. She tried to push through, to return back up to the surface, but a blast of cold air shocked her and threw her on the ground.

The figure screeched and pointed.

"No!" Alana shouted, "I'm not staying!"

The figure blasted her with a freezing wind, pushing her

back towards the cell, screeching as it went.

She dug into the stone ground as best she could, but she was getting pushed back. It was only a matter of time before it would get her into the cell.

"I've seen you before..." she whispered, and then held up her hands, "enough!" she yelled. "You win!"

The creature stopped and lifted its hidden hooded head and coughed up a scratchy laugh. It again pointed its bony figure towards the cell.

Alana smiled, and reached into her boot and pulled out her pitch black runedagger. It seemed to suck in all the light around it.

The figure didn't notice it at first, but then did a double take.

"You can burn in hell!" Alana shouted, and dove at the creature with the black knife, burying it in its face, whereupon it let out an unholy roar like the rushing of waters, and it disappeared.

Alana ran back through the caves, twisting and turning her way through the dungeons. Dark figures began to follow, slowly at first, but then faster, just one, then dozens. They cracked and cackled their way behind her, and she ran faster and faster, practically jumping out of the giant gates, down the bridge, and looking quickly behind her to see a hoard of dark, threw herself into the paths beyond, and when those melted away, jumped into the abyss on the far side.

She immediately fell once again outside of time and space and woke on the black rocks outside the gates. The fire was out, Ethan was stirring,[18] and she was covered in sweat and crying. A harsh sun began to rise in the distance in a dark red sky.

Alana bit her coat and cried like she had never cried before.

---

[18] It took Ethan a long time to get Alana to tell him what happened. As far as he or I know, she never told anyone else.

Zara walked up to the base of Ozymandias in the dark of the morning, just before first light. From the entrance she saw the day before, she could see a faint glowing of light.

Marie stood behind her and shooed her in. "Go ahead my dear," she said. "I saved it for you."

Zara nodded, and stooped down to get into the passage. There was a short staircase down and at the bottom of the staircase was an old oak door. The cracks all around the door emanated with a pale ice blue light. Zara took a deep breath and stepped down the stairs.

She had never before wanted the silver cross. Each step was a weight as she drew nearer and nearer. Never before did she consider she would be asked to carry it, for she would never ask for it. And yet, its gravity drew her in with each step closer.

She unlatched the door and opened a small room. There were dusty artefacts strewn about, all bathed in what was now a clear ice blue light coming from the corner. Zara walked over, reached up, and pulled down a small bundle off of a small shelf that circled the room near the ceiling.

It was wrapped in soft cloth, and Zara peeled off the layers to reveal its breathtaking beauty.

It was solid with a very satisfying heft, but only about the size of her hand. The cross itself was clean and straight, but the serpent surrounding it eating its own tail was stunning; it was full of intricate detail that appeared to go on and on the closer you look.

Zara held it close to her chest, closed her eyes, and breathed in.

So much time on the run, running away from people who wanted this. And now she had it.

She closed the door and walked back up the steps into the sunrise and found Marie gleaming. "Your father would be so proud of you," she said.

"Thank you," Zara said. "Thank you. I wish I could see him again."

They walked back slowly to Marie's home.

"Why did you take it?" Zara asked as she felt the silver cross again. "You never tried to use it."

Marie bowed her head. "I was waiting for you to ask," she said. "My people had an old saying, 'A star will fall to Ariens and will raise up a peacemaker.' I once thought that I could fulfill that promise and bring peace to our nations." Marie sighed. "I was wrong of course. I instead brought war, and that war did not bring peace, only more wars."

"I'm sorry," Zara said. "You didn't deserve what happened to you."

"What matters most is you do what you think is right," Marie replied. "It doesn't matter so much what people say, just that you did your best. I did my best, and while things didn't play out quite the way I had hoped, I think everything will end up all right."

They reached the bottom of the gully and Marie stopped. "Follow this downhill another five days to the ocean. There's a little wild food here and there, and you've apparently already learned you can dig for water. When you reach the coast there's a little cove where you'll find a ship that can take you where you need to go."

Zara looked at her in amazement. "I still have no idea how you do that," she said.

"I told you, I am a wayfinder," Marie replied, "I can see many things."

"Thank you," Zara said, and gave her a hug.

Marie slipped a necklace into her hands. "I made this once long ago, but I think you should take it."

Zara held it up to look at it. It was a smooth leather band holding a polished piece of brass with strange markings on them.

"What is it?" Zara asked. "What does it mean?"

"It sounds better in my mother tongue, but it means To Make the Peace." Marie replied. "Something to help you."

"Thanks," Zara said, and put it on.

"Good luck," Marie said, and Zara turned to leave.

"One last thing!" Marie called out.

"Yes?" Zara said as she turned around.

"Tell my grandson to come!" Marie replied.

"Who's your grandson?" Zara asked.

"You'll see!" Marie called.

"Remind me?" Ethan intreated her.

Alana recited her family line. "My father, Titus II, was king of Atlas. His father, Titus I married my grandmother, Hera, sister to King Leo. Leo was without child, and the throne passed from him to my father Titus II on his death."

Ethan furrowed his brow. "I thought that's what you had said before."

"What's wrong?" Alana said.

Ethan kept reading.

"What's wrong??" Alana begged.

"It's just...this is the grave of Leo." Ethan said. And somewhere deep inside of her, Alana knew what was coming next.

Ethan continued, "It lists his ridiculous titles, but then ends and says he is survived by his...his daughter."

Alana's heart sank. "A daughter??" she asked.

"Yeah..." Ethan said.

"I had...I had never heard of a daughter. Nobody ever spoke of one," she said, and they looked at each other quizzically. "Does it...does it give a name?" She asked hesitantly.

"Zara," Ethan said.

"Zara, of course," Alana mumbled.

And time stopped again for Alana as she pondered the ramifications. "If she's the daughter, where does that leave me?" she asked under her breath.

From down by the water they heard shouting. Alana and Ethan raced back to the boat, and when they arrived, they saw Kharon on the steps, blocking the way with his staff. In front of him, down the steps stood a company of foreign marines trying to push past him onto the island. Alana knew them immediately. These men were from Medea. Several small boats of theirs floated in the white stone bowl cavern.

Poor Ethan couldn't read obscure symbology on uniforms, so he had to pick it up by context.

"This land is hallowed," they could hear Kharon saying. "You are forbidden from entry."

The standoff slowly escalated as the men pushed their way up the steps, and Kharon backed up to the top of the cavern. "Make way," they shouted, and "This is your final warning" and other such melodramatic language. Finally, one of them grabbed for Kharon's staff, and Kharon swept it out from him, and then cracked his head with it, sending the man dropping like a stone fifty feet into the cavern below. Quick as a flash, a gun was drawn, and before they could blink a shot rang out in the cavern, and Kharon fell backwards, shot in the gut.

Ethan rushed forward and caught him before he hit the ground. He held him in his lap as the life drained out of him. The marines from Medea ascended the stairs, taking no notice of Ethan, but quickly surrounding Alana, disarming her, and keeping her at gunpoint.

Ethan stared into the eyes of a man who had befriended his family for generations feeling helpless in every way. He stroked the white hair out of his face and tried to make him as comfortable as possible. Kharon made a small sound, and Ethan moved his ear closer to hear.

"I foresaw it," Kharon said, and smiled.

He died on the doorway he had escorted so many to find, and as he died, a million stories died with him. They have been forever lost to the beyond, and we are the poorer for it.

The largest of the group approached Alana.

"I am Tiberius," he said.

She stared at him blankly and said nothing.

"I am Tiberius," he said.

She widened her eyes and glared at him, "And? Your point is? I have made your acquaintance, and I don't know why you followed me all the way up here, but as you can see," she gestured wildly around the dark graves, "I don't really have anything to offer you, so please leave me alone!" she shrieked.

"The only son of Zara," he continued.

Alana's jaw dropped. "Ah then, well why didn't you say so," Alana said. She calmed down really quickly.

"I've waited my entire life for this moment," Tiberius said and grinned from ear to ear.

Alana looked up at him. "I have waited the last ten seconds for this moment," she said.

Tiberius gloated as he ignored her and continued, "you banished and hunted my mother,"

"Ahem, my FATHER banished and hunted," she interrupted.

Tiberius glared, "banished and hunted my mother," he continued, "and now the chickens come home to roost!" he exclaimed. "Alana, daughter of Titus II, crown princess of Atlas, you are nothing! Meet Tiberius, the lonely wanderer, cast off from Atlas, raised in exile and poverty, distant from the throne I am owed, and here returned to claim what is rightfully mine and to punish you for your insolence!" he exclaimed.

Alana nodded her head, "Okay, nice to meet you Tiberius, the lonely wanderer, cast off from Atl..."

At this point, he had had enough, and Tiberius had her tied up and gagged.

"Welcome to hell," he said.

As befits royalty, Kharon was laid to rest at the gates of Hades.

Ethan lay Kharon down among the graves of the royals at the gates of Hades, crying many bitter tears over his passing. Ethan and Alana were then rowed back out past the book of life on their way to the Queen Anne, Kharon's boat sadly forever marooned without its owner. Through his tears Ethan looked at the cliff walls containing the book of life. To his amazement, the smooth section from the day before had been filled in. The work of a true master now fully adorned the cliff walls from cavern to sea, not an inch left undone.

He looked up and down the new section and recognized many figures and scenes, but the one that stuck out to him the most was down near the water line: a boat with intricate carvings was rowed by a wiry old man, and in the back sat a man and a woman, each peering off the edge in wonder.

CHAPTER 17

In the far southeast, the federal police of Medea still camped at the mountain's edge, watching for any sign of life coming out of the desolation, too afraid of Scipio's wrath should their premature departure bring failure to their ultimate cause. The sun baked them all day long as they watched the mirages in the distance: huge lakes of water formed and disappeared in their eyes. At night they shivered as the cold winds whipped up salty sandstorms and they covered their eyes as the shotgun of mother nature peppered them with debris and slapped them away. They waited a week, two weeks, three weeks even, to make sure they were thorough.

But nothing emerged from the endless white salt flats of death.

Nothing to them, that is.

Long after any human should have perished, and far, far away from where any human should have been able to reach, on the southeastern shores of the continent a ship of vagabonds sailed into desolate natural harbor on the southern ocean on the far side of the desolation to wait out a squall. On its dilapidated sides, sides that had seen more adventure than any other ship in any fleet, grey and peeling words wrote out the name, "The Argo."

One of the sailors spotted a grey heap of cloth near the water's edge. "Ahoy down there!" he yelled to a companion. "Take a look!"

The captain and a couple sailors took a small boat out and rowed to the cloth. As they approached, it stirred. The captain cupped his hands and called back, "It's still alive!" and hopping off the boat to prod it with his foot, he called again, "Prepare food!"

The sailors lifted the heap of a body into the boat, and in no time at all they were back on board.

They lifted the body to the deck and laid her out. There was Zara. Skinny, parched and famished, moaning and in pain, but alive.

The sailors couldn't get much out of her that first day, though they'd learn more over the coming days as they nursed her back to health on the ship's continuing journey. However, she never did make it clear to anyone how she managed to cross the desolation and live.

For that day, at least, there was just a faint gurgle when the captain asked her, in total incredulity, "Where did you come from?"

And in quiet slurs all she could muster was, "god's country."

It wasn't the worst day of her life, I think? But certainly not the best.

It had been a bit of a whirlwind over the past twenty-four hours for Alana, so one could forgive her for collapsing onto the floor of the ship's brig, functionally catatonic.

The only way one might notice she was still alive was by the streaming tears dripping sideways out of her eyes on the floor as she lay on the aged wood panels, staring off into oblivion as the ship lurched forward under steam power, shouts from the sailors echoing up above. They had left Ethan and her down below, safely locked up in the lower deck for Alana to cry out her eyes and Ethan to hug his knees in the corner and again revisit all of his previous decisions in life, trying to make sense of why he found himself, yet again, in a precarious situation that WAS NOT HIS FAULT he screamed inside.

The brig below deck was dark, dank, cramped, and utterly disgusting. The ceiling was too low to stand, so lying in a heap crying was probably just as good as any other option on the table, and realistically there were no other options on the table. Ethan started crying for this reason alone.

He had spent the entirety of Tiberius' speech with an utterly puzzled and confused look on his face. "Where exactly did I go wrong?" he tried to pinpoint exactly when he should have taken a different path. At one moment, he was on an archeological expedition of some spiritual significance, communing with his mother and an old family friend, and the next he was getting prodded around a graveyard by bayonet as Tiberius recounted all of the wrongs done to him by Atlas. Which, he was none too fast to point out, he was barely a citizen of, but that just seemed to make him madder, so Ethan did what he could and found the grave of Titus II.

One moment it seemed like he was on a fun adventure, and the next he was being implicated in high treason and his best possible option appeared to be a short hanging instead of a long one.

Oh wait, it seemed that way because it was, in fact, that way.[19]

Alana was utterly crushed. People she loved, people she

---

[19] I mean, except for the whole treason charge, that's ridiculous. Ethan was a bit emotional at this point, so you can excuse the dramatics to some extent.

idolized, people who were her direct progenitors were criminals. Her father knew Zara! Her father was a fraud! Her father!

Her father! The love of her life! How she idolized him as a child. He was such a hard worker, so dedicated to his duties, and here he was, involved in treason of the highest affair, robbing his cousin of the throne, and installing himself. And worst of all, to hunt Zara down! No wonder Tiberius was dragging Alana off to certain death. Had their positions been reversed, she would have been even the quicker to come to a harsh judgement.

And there her father was, all his life, a usurper. A fake. A fraud.

It made her sick.

He was so melodramatic with his ethics, always moralizing on the actions of others, hanging his uprightness over his wife's head, obsessing over his own perfection. He was "chosen by the gods!" he'd said, and he'd preach to anyone in earshot, and often force entire rooms full of people to stand around and hear of right and wrong, and how they had performed the latter, and he on the former.

He considered his integrity to be above reproach, and made it clear that everyone knew it, and Alana could wretch just thinking about it.

As a child, she took it at face value that her father was the morally upstanding righteous king of a fallen nation. It was once great and strong, ruling far and wide, but became weak through the moral decay of its people. It had been her mission in life to continue his work, to be a shining beacon of uprightness to the common folk, the unchosen, the plain, the mortals.

Come to find out, his obsession merely papered over his own weakness. He knew what he was, and nothing would ever change that.

She had idolized, honored, and loved him for virtues he

never possessed. Her shaman was nothing more than a sham. And looking back, she was embarrassed that it took her until now to see his harshness, his veniality, his own naked self-promotion not as characteristics meant to show her the way, but what they were: his own insecurities out on full display for anyone who could see through the sham.

And, it occurred to her, many did. Many must have seen through it. Her thoughts went back to her return to Atlas, and she realized that through one side of their mouth the justices and ministers were praising her, but out the other they knew of the darkness of her father. She was just sick to her stomach. Who else knew that she was nothing? Who knew and said nothing?

"Maybe if I had just gotten a map for her at Titan, she could have made that last bit alone," Ethan puzzled to himself in the corner. "Yeah, I think I probably could have been a little bit more convincing. Maybe if I tried to stand a little taller? I think tall people get a little more respect."

What are your morals when you find out that nobody else possesses them? That you are the only one not in on the joke?

She felt betrayed. She felt taken advantage of. She felt stupid. She had been duped along with everyone else, and here was this man, this royal, this son of the gods who claimed to be so much, but it turns out he was just as studied as Alana, just as focused, but focused on his own image, how he appeared to be, and that is why he was so royal.

How can you reconcile the behavior of a whole life when you discover the lie?

It didn't help that Tiberius had the body of the great Titus II exhumed and burned right then and there, "no longer worthy," he said, "of resting here among the noble." Ethan was prodded around the graveyard until he pointed to the right grave, and the men of Medea made short work of the memorial. They unearthed the casket, and as much as she wanted to look away, Alana's eyes were transfixed on her father's face when they opened the casket.

There he was. Just as she remembered him.

The embalming had done its work, and that along with the cold of the northern ground had left Titus frozen in time. He was much smaller than she remembered, much more weaselly in appearance. His now-pale face was scrunched up in a look of eternal self-righteous indignation, just as he had spent his life. Trace amounts of loose black obsidian tracked along the bottom of the casket.

Tiberius stood lording over Titus for several minutes. Taking in every last detail in a cathartic meditation. This was the great moment of his victory. His mother's tormentor at last at his feet as he had always dreamed. He closed his eyes and threw his head back and basked in the harsh northern sun above. He had won.

And, on the same fire that had warmed Alana and Ethan the night before, Tiberius had Titus burned to ashes, not fit to be buried next to the ancestors of Tiberius. He had the impostor's tomb destroyed, inscriptions scratched out, and took his ashes himself to dump into the sea.

...but not before Alana noticed that his men carefully combed through them. They meticulously sifted through every piece of ash that they exhumed and burned.

Looking for the cross of course. They hadn't found it yet.

"Could I have stayed home?" Ethan thought to himself. "Why did I even walk through that stupid portal? I could have been free as a bird with a significantly longer life expectation, and instead all I've done for weeks is have people try to kill me. Or at minimum I could have wised up and disappeared at some point along the journey, really any point, along the trip..." Ethan shook his fist. "I could be back at home chomping down on some nice deer jerky right this freaking minute" he thought.

"He won't find it," Alana mumbled. The trail was cold. Somehow, through it all, the silver cross was lost. Nobody had it. Not her, not Titus, not Jacques, not Tiberius.

And they all wanted it.

She seethed in rage at Jacques. If it weren't for his treason to begin with, she never would have ended up on this absurd quest. Somehow, he must have known that she would end up here; he was always one step ahead.

Above all, Jacques knew people, and he knew the young are so easy to be persuaded to give up so much for so little. The world is bright and new and there are great conquests that are just within their reach if they but stretch a little...

Which is an illusion. The old are lost to adventure; they've pushed their entire lives and all they have is a tiny slice of the world. Herculean efforts yield tiny results, and so they find ways to justify their acceptance of the status quo each passing day.

Alana would never know that Jacques was so certain the silver cross was gone forever, because he had spent decades trying to find it himself.

And so how fitting that the object that was almost his undoing is the undoing of his last enemy.

Or so Jacques thought.

The silver cross, though, was now so far from Alana's concerns. It was not hers to have. The primary concerns of her entire life until this moment were totally irrelevant.

The only question now was this: should she live, what would she do now?

The Argo slipped into the dark harbor of Medea in silence. Tattered vagabonds lined the decks and looked out at civilization for the first time in a long time. Each one had a glint of freedom in his eyes, and every one of them couldn't help but smile. Finally.

Except Zara.

She watched the lights on the shore with increasing anxiety. It was nice that these sailors had picked her up and saved her from certain death, sure. But taking her directly to the capital seemed a bit like a step backwards. There wasn't much to do: the ship was going that way, and she long had a policy of avoiding sharing any information about herself with anyone, in large part to avoid things like what just happened to her. She had been chased her whole life, and once, just once, she let her secret be known to one person, one person who she loved more than anything, and look what it led to.

The Argo creaked into the harbor and anchored just outside the bright new docks and struck an immediate contrast: ancient, peeling paint, name barely visible, with an unholy rattling that would cause you to either lose your hearing or your sanity, and a tattered and exhausted crew who possessed neither.

"We'll anchor here and dock in the morning," the captain said as he passed by Zara. "It's a little too dark for my liking to tie up now, but you have my word we'll deposit you onshore in good condition in the morning to make your way back into civilization." He wasn't quite sure what to make of this mysterious passenger, but knowing full well what being marooned felt like, he couldn't allow another soul to suffer that way. He was glad to help bring her to what he thought was a safer place.

"Thanks," Zara said, "you have been so kind to me, and I have no way to repay you," she said.

"Kindness has a way of coming around," the captain said, "I have a feeling like you are owed this from some past life."

Zara smiled faintly as she buried her dread and anxiety at the thought of having to escape the heart of Medea. "Perhaps," she said, "perhaps it is finally my turn."

"So, do you want to talk about this cousin of yours?" Ethan said after a few days. How many? It's hard to say when you're stuck below deck and your only knowledge of the passage of time is the delivery of your food, and the periodic removal of the bucket placed in there for your...expulsions. By that metric, it had been three buckets since they were placed in the brig, and Ethan wasn't sure how many buckets he could last before finally—gasp—soiling himself in front of her. Conditions were already unbearable, and that last indignity would be the final straw for him. It's hard to die of embarrassment, but he was sure as heck going to try.

"How so?" Alana creaked, the first time she had spoken since two and a half buckets ago. She at least stopped crying a quarter bucket ago, and sat in the corner of the cell, staring blankly outward. She hadn't touched any food, and Ethan occasionally put water up to her mouth so she'd last a little longer. It's not clear if he did that out of kindness, or because he was afraid of what smells may come when she had shuffled off this mortal coil.

"Remind me how your family tree misses a cousin?" he said.

"I don't know," she said. "Dad never said anything about a cousin. Everyone said Leo died childless. End of story, move on with your life, accept the fact that the line of succession runs through his sister, who gave birth to my father. Done-zo, that's it." she said.

"You don't have family reunions?" he said.

"Look, my grandpa didn't sit us all around the fire and talk about how he conspired to steal the throne for his son, if that's what you mean? I mean, I guess I could have guessed that that was his intent because of the dark cloud that followed him everywhere he we...OH WAIT, I'm sorry that a tiny child didn't piece it all together for you. I'll be sure to flag that for her next time so that while she's picking daisies outside the palace that she pays attention to the fact that her father's cousin somehow disappeared. I'm sure she'll go put on her best checkered hat and pull out a magnifying glass and then give up and go throw a tea party."

"Sorry, I don't mean to pry, I'd just kind of like to attach some sort of meaning to my life, given that it appears to be headed to end in a way I never expected." Ethan said. Alana nodded knowingly in the corner.

Ethan continued, "I figured I'd at least have the dignity to have enough space to curl up in the fetal position in my final hours, but I'm afraid if I tried that I'd end up with bucket number four on me, and I tell you what, after what they've been feeding us, you DO NOT want bucket number four on you." Ethan said as he shook his head wide-eyed. "I mean, at minimum, it would have been nice to have been old enough to grow a beard before getting sentenced to death. The wanted posters would have looked so much cooler." he said.

Alana managed a meager smile. "I'll see what I can get them to do next time," she said.

"I mean, you could always try to get me out of this right? Just tell him I'm some dumb kid that got wrapped up with the wrong crowd and I'd like to go home now?" Ethan said. "I can put on a pouty face if that helps."

"Definitely," Alana said, "and how nice I wouldn't even have to lie about the dumb kid part!"

It was Ethan's turn for a meager smile. "Anything for you, my liege," he said.

"Eh, you're going to have to stop saying that," Alana said.

"Sorry, force of habit," Ethan said. "Besides, that gorilla isn't going to get my allegiance just any dumb way. I'm no easy sell, no sirree. I require being kidnapped and having my life repeatedly threatened in order to pledge allegiance to a monarch. Just showing up with a family tree and a silver cross isn't enough for me, no sir."

"I mean, we've got the kidnapping nailed down, so don't get too excited." Alana warned. "But I should tell you, don't hold your breath on the silver cross," Alana said.

"I don't get it," Ethan said. "What's the deal? Are there no more silversmiths in your kingdom? Just uh ring up one of ye olde servants and voila! New silver cross. Better than the old one, and more fashionable."

Alana smiled. "I'm sure they all wish it'd be that easy. But then there's the whole magical-power-of-the-gods thing," she said. "It's hard to conjure that kind of believable story right on up."

"Nothing a few sacrifices couldn't help along, amirite? Grease someone's palms a little bit and you're golden." Ethan said.

Alana began to cheer up in spite of herself. "You? Sacrifice?" she said. "The gods wouldn't listen if you sat on an altar for a month. They'd be all like, 'new number who dis?'"[20]

"Which is so different from the answers you are getting?" Ethan teased.

"You're right," Alana said, suddenly serious. "You're right."

And for the first time in a quarter bucket, she began to cry again, and Ethan shut up and stared off, feeling guilty for ruining the mood.

My dad always insisted on including all the bits about the buckets and his colon whenever he told this part of the story; it was so embarrassing to me whenever he'd have people over and get to this part, but dad could never resist a good potty joke. In his honor, I've included those as well. I sometimes wonder if he held onto his childish humor because he was forced to grow up so fast.

He carried emotional scars from the imprisonment, the death threats, the trauma. The worst parts he never talked about, but I knew they were there under the surface because some nights I'd hear him wake up screaming about being chained or trapped or drowning, and my mother would always soothe him and calm him down, patiently helping dad

---

[20] I have taken some liberties with the dialog, so just laugh at the anachronisms and keep on moving ahead and don't write me angry letters.

come to terms emotionally with what he experienced.

Every time he told the full story, the language would get more outlandish, the banter and jokes would get dialed up, and his own suffering would be diminished. I've tried to focus on the entertaining aspects just like he always did, but I am also just so proud of him for all that he could do under such difficult circumstances.

CHAPTER 18

The sun rose over a muggy harbor in Medea, and all around factories cranked to life and began adding anew to the dense orange-ish smog that clung to the small waves around the harbor, the tinted light slowly fading in with the rising sun. Zara took to the deck and watched as The Argo hoisted anchor and made its way to the docks. A few of the disengaged sailors found her near the bow, and said their goodbyes, making a few small charitable donations for the woman with nothing.

They navigated to the main docks, Zara prepared to disembark as quickly as possible and fade into the gathering crowds on land as work spun up for the day. She was pretty sure she could melt away into the countryside, hopefully Scipio hadn't raised any alarms.

As they drew nearer though, Zara noticed they were approaching a strange ship at dock. It had familiar markings, and it took her longer than she'd care to admit to notice it flew a different flag.

The flag of Atlas.

In the tinted light up lumbered two men along the docks: a short stubby disheveled man, walking beside a tall elegant fellow, gentility and grace personified. It had been some time since she had seen the latter, but she knew the former immediately.

Scipio Barca let his eyes wander to the incoming ships and noted the woman in grey.

"It can't be," he muttered as he squinted.

Alerted to his interest, Jacques LePen followed Scipio's gaze to see...

"Zara?" Jacques said with shock. "Here?"

Scipio flung his head to Jacques as Jacques casually turned to him. "How do you know..." they both demanded simultaneously, and then, "she's mine."

In an instant, Jacques sprung to his ship, calling out to his captain as he flew down the dock to prepare the engine and alert the guard.

Scipio ran one way, then back on the dock. The Queen Anne was usually nearby...and he realized he had sent her away. The nearest ship was...he ran this way and back, totally unable to decide what to do in his panic. Everything was just too far away for him to do anything to stop what he was watching.

Zara broke into a panicked cold sweat. She couldn't have gone this far just to trip at the finish line! She bolted to the other side of the ship, the far side away from Jacques and Scipio, hoping to use the bulk of this tattered ship to screen her movements. She quickly gauged her distance to shore. If she jumped now, dropping the twenty feet to the water, she would only have a swim of one or two hundred yards on the far side, and then freedom. With tunnel vision in full force, she lifted her leg up and over the bar, balanced on the far side...

And felt a hard-grizzled hand grab her ankles and hold her steady. "Have you ever even been on a ship before miss?" the captain asked as he held her. "You jump from here and you'll get sucked right into the screw underneath. No ma'am, we don't treat our guests like that here on The Argo, or as you'd have it, here under The Argo. We don't like attracting the sharks, you see the crew is afraid of them."

Zara's eyes grew wide, and she gestured wildly to the port side of the ship where Jacques was bringing up steam and preparing to engage. "They're after me," she said. "I need to get out of here. Now." Zara said.

"Step right this way, miss, we're not known for our generosity for nothing," the captain said. "Nobody mistreats our guests." A sailor jumped up and brought her down, linking arms with her as they followed the captain back to the bridge.

Jacques' river steamer had brought up power and moved in to block the Argo from entering the docks. Scipio had the attention of a port employee, and soon various soldiers began filtering into the docks, rifles held at the ready. Messages were dispatched further afield for naval support.

Jacques signaled The Argo, and through a megaphone addressed them. "Halt!" he shouted above the din, "you are carrying an internationally-wanted criminal who must return with me to Atlas!"

Scipio went apoplectic on the docks. "This is sovereign territory!" he shouted, "You can't conduct policing operations on sovereign territory you idiot!"

Jacques looked back and shrugged his shoulders. "International waters" he mouthed.

Scipio blew his top, and with red veins protruding out every inch of his neck and forehead he screamed about continental shelves and international treaties and obligations, but Jacques just calmly shook his head and pointed to his ears. "Can't hear you," he mouthed again.

"Boy oh boy have you been holding out on us little lady," the captain of The Argo said to Zara, and then to his men, "I don't think we're welcome here anymore," he yelled. "Let's try another port," he said, and ordered the ship hard to port, and it began to turn to sea.

Jacques signaled once again and shouted through his

megaphone, but as The Argo turned, the Captain looked at him and shrugged his shoulders. "Can't hear you," he mouthed.

"Send a shot across the bow," Jacques yelled. His boat wasn't made for combat, but it could easily take on a shabby wreck like what was before him. The sailors brought up the main pair of defensive guns, a pair of four inchers on a swivel mount, and they shot at almost point-blank range as the Argo turned, splashing just ahead in the water.

"Oh no you didn't," the captain of the Argo muttered.

Jacques signaled the ship again. "Prepare to be boarded," he yelled in a heated anger, and he fired again, this time just taking a piece out of the bow, wood spraying everywhere as a small little bite of the Argo exposed up front. "When will these stupid freighter captains learn," Jacques muttered.

"OH NO YOU DIDN'T," the captain of the Argo shouted. The sailors looked at him for guidance and he looked around the docks and under his breath he said, "Oh screw it," and then shouted, "Bring 'em up and lay it on!"

The Argo cut the engine and sat on the water apparently on command for Jacques, and he smiled, totally pleased with himself. This was going to be easier than he thought. He was so used to people chickening out at the slightest threat of force.

He was slightly confused by all the activity aboard The Argo, though. The sailors threw off pieces of canvas lying haphazardly around the deck, and then with the creaking of a thousand screaming banshees, metal on metal was heard grating as the sailors pulled and pushed the levers and cranks. They hoisted up on the main deck, near the bow, and on the aft, three sets of nine-inch guns, mounted and manned.

Zara's jaw dropped. "Wait, you've been holding out on me! You didn't tell me you were a gun runner!" she shouted.

The Captain shrugged. "You never asked," he said.

"I have to ask?" Zara said in shock.

The Captain ignored her. "Fire!" he yelled.

Jacques had just enough time to soil his pants as he

watched the giant guns emerge from below decks before his very eyes and loom over him like a giant steel hammer. All six barrels swiveled and pointed right at him. He lost his usual decorum and jumped off the ship as it exploded.

Scipio blinked and rubbed his eyes. One minute ago, the yacht was right...there right? And now Jacques' ship was...gone?

Splinters exploded everywhere and the ship swamped. The several survivors, including Jacques, swam for the docks a short distance away.

"We'd better get the heck out of here," the captain said.

This time it was Scipio's turn to demand they stay. "Halt this instant!" he shouted at the top of his lungs, but the Argo began steaming away.

The Argo was going to have none of it. From the docks in desperation Scipio shouted, "Fire!"

The soldiers on the dock began, from a distance, peppering them with rifle fire. No bullets met their mark, but it was enough to annoy the captain yet again.

"Just shut them up for a minute," the captain said to his fire officer, and with a, "yes sir," the docks lifted up and melted away under exploding shells. Scipio ran for cover as the shells fell, lifting up wooden planks like piano keys and generally blowing everything to pieces as beautiful newly painted shrapnel flew in the air and rained down into the harbor like hail.

The crew of the Argo cheered.

Jacques reached an outcropping of debris and hauled himself up. Facing the Argo, he pulled out five obsidian rings put them on the fingers on his right hand. Holding up his right hand towards the Argo, and supporting with his left, he began screaming ancient incantations.

"Just what do we have here?" The captain asked his first mate.

"A nut job?" He replied.

Jacques screamed and immediately from his fingertips a black portal exploded. A single dark figure emerged from the portal and, hovering over the water, approached The Argo. Jacques screamed and screamed, and from the portal emerged another figure, then another. Jacques screeched one last curse at the top of his lungs, his veins bulging out of his neck, and with pure hatred willed the portal to remain open. Four more figures emerged before he collapsed in pain.

Pointing to Zara, Jacques addressed the figures. "Take her!" He shouted.

The captain's jaw dropped.

"I take it back," he said to Zara, "that is exactly how we treat guests, please feel free to jump off the boat next time."

Zara nodded, "Next time you should let me go!"

"There ain't goin to be a next time," the captain shouted, "for either of us!" Then to the crew he yelled: "To the sea, to the sea!"

The crew desperately tried to make steam and get out of there, but the figures were on top of them.

They came up on deck, all seven of them, surrounding Zara and closing in fast.

From her chest, a blue light flashed.

Zara knew what to do. She stared into the abyss, the dark cold nothingness that the figures came for, the soul-suckers, and she pulled out the silver cross.

The figures didn't react at all, they joined arms and bowed their hooded heads and chanted.

Zara lifted the silver cross above her head and screamed back at them. "I am Leo's daughter! I am the heir to the silver cross! You have no power to take me!" And she screamed into the abyss.

From far above Apollo heard her screams, and answered his talisman, and sent down his power.

Silver bolts from above struck down with a crash, smashing into the figures and obliterating them instantly.

Zara stayed on the deck holding the cross, screaming curses into the empty space the shades had possessed, curses of what she would do to them if they should ever approach her again. She then ran to the stern of the ship and shouted out curses at the boats being manned to board them, and again from above giant booms erupted and the bolts smashed into any attackers.

Zara gave out a final scream and collapsed in exhaustion.

The crew of the Argo stood motionless, shocked at what they had just witnessed. The captain was the first to move.

"I said to the sea! To the sea! Let's get her out of here! We gotta get this witch away from these people!" The captain shouted, and slowly motion returned to the ship and they found a way to start moving again.

Jacques witnessed the silver cross and cursed the day. His worst fears were being realized. Scipio looked at Jacques and shook his head. He didn't know that the snake had become a necromancer. This was going to make things even more difficult. He smashed his hand into the rubble. First Zara, then the cross, then Jacques. His absolute worst-case scenario was playing out in front of his eyes.

The Argo picked up steam and headed out to the open sea.

But on the horizon, two battleships appeared. Scipio's messages had gotten through to the outer ships.

From miles away they began to fire, and the whistling shells flew overhead, splashing harmlessly in the outer harbor after overshooting.

"Uh oh," the captain said.

White puffs of smoke went up again and again from the battleships in the distance.

"Hey witch, got any more of that magic?" the captain hollered at Zara.

Zara moaned and remained catatonic on the deck.

"We are in trooooouuuuuble," the captain said, and the screaming whistling shells came down closer.

The captained turned to the crew he shouted out his

orders. "Flip around!" he yelled, "back to the docks!"

"To the docks?" his pilot screamed. "We just left the docks you idiot!"

"Get as close as you can!" the captain shouted.

"Closer??!" came the incredulous reply, "why in the world do we want to get closer?"

"The battleships can't target us at that range, they'll hit the docks. Swing us right on by as close as you can, we're headed upriver to Atlas!" the captain yelled.

Now it was his first mate who spoke up as the ship turned and steamed back to the docks, whistling shells just missing them as they steamed. "Atlas? We can't go to Atlas!" he screamed, "we just tried to kill their prime minister!" he shouted above the whistling.

"That was the prime minister?" the captain asked.

"Yes!" the first mate yelled.

"Who knew?" the captain said sheepishly.

"We all did!" the first mate yelled, gesturing wildly around at the crew.

"Well, it's either Atlas or hell, take your pick." the captain said.

"I don't think this is an either/or situation," said the first mate. "At this rate it's going to be Atlas AND hell."

"Either way, I'd recommend you duck, we're coming into range." the captain said nonchalantly, and they hit the deck as the rifles from the shore came into play.

Scipio was still running back and forth trying to figure a way to stop this unmitigated disaster, but it was of no use. The Argo steamed past the docks, shelling the city as it went, and continued upriver. The battleships had to stop as the river was too shallow for the bigger ships, and they all watched as the Ago slipped upstream along the Andaluvian.

"We'll get them further up," Scipio said, and he raced back to his office to begin sending messages.

"The wayfinder," Alana said to Ethan.

"What about it?" he replied.

"I never told you I've seen it before," she said.

Her tears had dried somewhat, and in the calm of their imprisonment, she could open up.

"Where?" Ethan said, "my mom had it with her your whole life."

"Your mom opened a portal in front of me when I was a girl," she said, "the night my father died."

"You mean the night my mother died??" he replied.

"Yeah." she said.

"What happened?" he asked. "They never could tell me much."

She described her night: the strange voice, wandering the palace, and Jane appearing from midair to running off to her parent's room.

"I didn't see much, it all happened so fast, but there was an accident, and she died," Alana continued, and described the details: the guards in panic, her mother in hysterics, her father stiff as a board.

Alana reached down to her thigh and pulled out a dark blade. "She carried this," she said, "and I picked it up and never told anyone."

Seth looked it over. "The runedagger," he said. "Made from the stone from the dark gates. They say it can defeat demons."

"I know," she said.

They sat in silence for a few moments.

"But the wayfinder," Alana said, "can you use it? Can you create a portal?"

Ethan shook his head, "I have no idea how to use this thing. They never told me how it works!"

Alana looked at him. "Our lives might depend on you trying."

Ethan nodded. "It's reached out to me a few times, but I

can't figure out how to create a portal, I can only see visions."

He held the necklace close and concentrated as he felt the gem through the leather straps holding it in place. He brought his mind into the stone and called to the heart of the gem. "Please," he said. "Please."

The gem began to glow and shine its green light into the brig.

"Yes!" Alana exclaimed.

"Please," Ethan called out into the beyond.

"Oh my sweet mercy, what is that smell?" a guard appeared out of nowhere, climbing down the stairs, stomping over and loomed over the prisoners in the brig of the Queen Anne.

"Uh, if you fed me any better, you'd be more pleasantly surprised by my bucket," Ethan replied, quickly tucking the necklace back into his shirt.

Alana began to moan to distract the guards and held her knees in close, staring into nothingness. "Nobody has seen the horrors I've seen!" she moaned, "the bucketed horrors!" she moaned.

"What was that?" the guard said.

"The bucketed horrors!" Alana called.

"No, no, no, I saw something, you wait here," he ran above deck for a moment and was back with Tiberius.

Tiberius took one step into the brig and moaned.

"I can't do this, the smell is atrocious," Tiberius said as he held his nose. He looked back at his men and said, "bring them above deck, this is intolerable." A large man opened the door and before Ethan could kick the bucket over onto him, he had picked them both up, and was rudely jolting them in the general direction of the stairs above deck.

They could barely hobble the few flights up, their sore legs knocking together after the buckets spent in confinement, and the man behind them occasionally pushing didn't help. They emerged like groundhogs into a grey netherworld.

"Fog," Alana said to Ethan, noticing his disorientation.

This wasn't your normal, "oh slow down and be careful" fog, this was a thick blanket that clung to you. The mists swirled right in front of your eyes, making and unmaking thousands of patterns. You couldn't even see the ocean off the sides of the boat through the haze. They were totally encased in a cloud.

Tiberius cornered them in the foredeck, away from the others and began.

"Where is the silver cross," he said.

"I told you, I have no idea you idiot," Alana replied.

Tiberius shot her a look of fire. "Not you, usurper." And he swiveled back and stared into Ethan's eyes and pointed. "Him".

"What does he have to do with any of this?" Alana asked in anger. "He's a nothing, a nobody, an insignificant..."

"...thaaaank you..." Ethan piped up.

"A commoner. He has nothing to do with anything. Save your avarice for me, you ungainly monkey," Alana said, full of righteous indignation.

"I think he's had you fooled this entire time, you imbecile," Tiberius said, staring Ethan down, not even giving Alana a glance. "He knows more than he lays claim to..."

"Uh, I think you've gotten me mistaken with someone else. Let's start with your first mistake, thinking I have anything to do with Atlas at all. Bzzzt, wrong answer. The correct answer is that I was brought on this little side adventure against my will, and I continue to be brought against my will, which I would love if anyone around here would consider my will in these situations." Ethan said.

"You have a will?" Alana asked. "What was all of that talk about needing to re-examine your end of life planning?"

"You know what I mean!" Ethan said in exasperation.

Tiberius approached Ethan, staring him down like a creeper. "What's that you carry around your neck, nobody?"

he said. "Why was it glowing down there?"

"What's left of a shirt. And it was my favorite too." Ethan said. "And I am naturally radiant!"

Tiberius tugged at the necklace and pulled through the leather straps to expose his grandmother's gem: the eye of Rhea. It shone green through the fog, mesmerizing the entire crew.

"Interesting," he said. "Very interesting."

A strong breeze immediately slammed against them, so hard it shook them off balance, and Ethan fell, being held up only by Tiberius grasping at the gem, which shot off rays of green into the mists.

From far behind them they heard frantic screams, "Sound off! Sound off!" Tiberius dropped the gem and whipped around to see the ship in disarray. He ran back to the aft deck to find the captain ordering anchor dropped.

"What are you doing?" Tiberius demanded. "We're to move at speed! You can't stop us here now!"

"Stop us? I'm stopping me. You feel free to go on right ahead," the captain said as he pointed in front of the ship. The breeze had blown off the fog, and straight ahead stood a jagged black cliff, a thousand feet high. The sea began to bubble, and waves hammered the boat from behind, pushing it towards certain doom.

Tiberius was infuriated. "Scilia?" he screamed. "Scilia?" and again. "How did you get us out here?" he demanded to know.

The captain shrugged. "We've been in this here fog for a couple days now, landie. We can't see through fog; the ship drifted enough to bring us here."

Tiberius was infuriated. "You've delayed us long enough with your refusal to steam ahead in the fog, and now we're stuck behind Scilia! This has got to put us behind another day!" he screamed.

The captain did not care a single bit about Tiberius and his obnoxious whining. The grizzled veteran just looked straight ahead and said, "Aye. Unless you care to thread the Grinder and get us all killed instead of just your wee little lonesome."

Tiberius looked ahead into the cliff and saw the break. Two islands make up Scilia: the one on the north presenting a cliff, and the one on the south an island with a lower profile. There's some story behind a giant smashing one or not the other or some other such nonsense, but let's focus on the fact that in between them there is a narrow channel.

Appropriately referred to as the Grinder.

Tiberius saw the break and immediately calmed down. "Well okay, that sounds reasonable, why yes. It'll cut off a day, right? We won't have to go around all of the outer shallows." he said.

"Landie, I think you misheard me. That way is certain death." the captain said with an offhanded laugh. "Only folks I know who do that are drunk or suicidal."

"But you can make it..." Tiberius half-asked, half declared.

"Aye, but only while just unbelievably drunk," the captain said.

Tiberius stood firm on the deck. "We're going through the Grinder," he declared.

"Nae we ain't," the captain said, with not a note of worry in his voice. "We're goin' to weigh anchor right here and wait out this squall a safe way away, an' live to hear your eternal complaining on the far side."

Tiberius pulled out his gun and aimed it at the Captain.

"We're going through the Grinder," he said.

The captain paid him no heed and kept about his business, ignoring the gun at his temple.

"We're going through the Grinder," Tiberius said more deeply.

"Go right ahead, I'll give you a lifeboat, you'll make it further out there than you will with me," the captain said, nerves as cold as steel.

"I've got a boat right here," Tiberius said, and pulled from his coat an order, signed by Scipio. "I have the right to command this vessel under any circumstances. Read it up right here, you squid sucker." Tiberius said. He held the order up high and yelled for the rest of the crew to hear, "I captain this boat now," he yelled, gesticulating at the order with his pistol. "I captain this boat now!" he said.

"Who yer goin to captain?" the captain said with a smile. "Ain't nobody here that'll work for you." The whole ship had stopped to watch this duel by now, and the sailors were quietly smiling, brimming with overconfidence. The marines watched with bated breath.

Tiberius called out to his marines, "Let's see them, boys!" he called, and each marine pulled a gun on the nearest sailor. Tiberius pulled his gun away from the captain's temple and shot the first mate in the thigh. "I'll captain who I want to captain, captain." he said.

The first mate dropped to the ground in agony, bleeding on deck, and a sailor rushed to assist, but Tiberius shifted his gun to the sailor, then dropped to shoot right below his feet. The sailor stopped, and the first mate writhed in agony.

"I captain this boat now!" Tiberius yelled.

"It's a ship you landie," the captain said quietly. "This here is a ship, and you don't belong on it."

Tiberius pointed his pistol around the boat and issued orders. "Remove the first mate, take him below to treat him," he called. "You there," he called to his men, "remove the captain from the deck, take him below to the deck."

The marines grabbed the captain by both sides and marched him up front to take him to the brig. They passed by Ethan as they got to the stairs below.

"Sorry about the bucket," Ethan said. The captain looked at him, totally confused, and Ethan just shrugged his shoulders. "It was probably her," he said, pointing at Alana.

As they took the captain down, Tiberius yelled out to the

259

sailors, "We're going through the Grinder, raise anchor, and set sail that way," he shouted.

The captain broke his otherwise permanently calm demeanor and became visibly infuriated upon hearing this, and shouted, "But you can't captain a boat you imbecile! You'll get us all killed! And worse, you'll destroy my ship!"

"Who can steer her?" Tiberius called out. "Because this is my boat."

"Ship!" The captain growled as he looked back with extreme reluctance and scanned the sailors.

"Who can steer her?" Tiberius called as he stepped up menacingly to the wheel, daring the captain to try him.

"The night pilot," the captain said, as the marines pushed his head below, and off to the brig he went.

"Bring me the night pilot!" Tiberius shouted, and slowly the sailors began to reluctantly move and prepare the ship.

A few minutes later a petite sailor was brought to Tiberius, looking around totally dazed. Was this a dream? It seemed more likely than reality.

Alana squinted on the far side of the deck.

She watched the night pilot move and rub his eyes, hearing the strain of keeping his voice artificially low, catching sight of his high cheekbones and fluid movements, and while she wasn't the only one on deck to realize this, she was the only one to verbalize.

Alana said, "Is that a..."

"Super small dude, you bet it is." Ethan replied, interrupting.

"No," Alana said, "that looks like a..."

"Really, really tiny man. Yeah, I get it." Ethan said nonchalantly staring off into the mists. At this point, he figured his chances of survival hovered around zero point zero zero one percent. Tiberius appeared determined to kill him one way or another; in this new dimensionality of horror, it appeared that they'd die together via drowning.

"No, that's a girl!" Alana shout-whispered at Ethan as various marines and sailors heard the noise and looked over to give her dirty looks.

"Whatever," Ethan said. He didn't care. Girl or no girl, he was dead.

But Alana was right. When it came to the night pilot, he was a she.

The night pilot kept up her disguise through her entire career, mostly through always being the night pilot, but also because extreme competence married to zero social outreach put her into a class of people that didn't need a gender. They just needed respect. And respect she had.

A squall was forming, blowing the fog away and creating whitecaps. The night pilot resolved to do the impossible, convinced that she, and only she, could make it the possible. This could be her finest hour.

"What'll you have, captain," the night pilot asked as she yawned and rubbed her eyes. She had finished piloting the ship just a few hours previous and was usually sound asleep at this hour.

"We're going through that," Tiberius declared with assumed authority, pointing to the passage between the islands.

"Running the Grinder, eh?" the night pilot said with hidden excitement at the challenge. "Feelin' a little suicidal, are we?" she said. "Or maybe a little drunk?"

"That's what he just said," Tiberius said as, he motioned below deck with his gun.

"Well, hold onto your butts, and don't shoot anyone you whiney peasant," she said, and started shouting indecipherable language to the sailors on board. Hearing someone with competence take charge was infectious, and the sailors were soon scrambling aboard the ship, getting ready for the challenge. She had a reputation on board, and every sailor to a man was filled with relief. If anyone could get them through this, the night pilot could.

"I want you to take the ship right through there, then..." Tiberius started.

The night pilot put up her hand to quiet him, straining a little bit on her tiptoes to reach his pursed lips with her finger. "You want to live landie, you shut up. This isn't my first rodeo. Just get out of here and let me work."

Tiberius, stunned to hear the authority in her voice, drew confidence that he was going to get the results he wanted. He put away his gun and retreated back to watch the show.

And what a show it was.

The night pilot instructed men to sound off and read the depths continuously. One on the right, one on the left. She placed spotters around the deck to watch the sides of the ship. And she stood at the stern, piloting the ship, calling out orders to the engine room below. It was a constant bedlam of shouting as depths and distances were shouted from man to man, and the night pilot heard it all, and moved the wheel with power.

The ship approached the passage slowly. "Ten fathoms!" screamed from the left. "Twelve fathoms" screamed from the right. "One hundred yards," shouted a spotter in the front. The night pilot smiled, and adrenaline coursed through her body. This was going to be fun.

"This is definitely not going to be any fun," Ethan muttered from his position in the foredeck.

Waves battered from all sides, and the challenge lay before them. On the left, a high jagged cliff marked the path of the passage, with huge menacing rocks strewn irregularly at sea level, ready to destroy any approaching ship. On the right, tidal pools previously below sea level were filling up in the storm, the strong currents pushing the boat to crash into the rocks around the pools. And everywhere churning, water always churning.

Sail to the left and you lose the ship on the cliffs. Sail to the right and you founder the ship in the tidal pools. All while a squall picked up, churning up flotsam and jetsam, thrashing the passage, and making a general mess of things.

The Grinder was a mile long. One mile through the two islands of Scilia.

"Hard forward," the night pilot shouted to the engine room, and she lay her entire body on the wheel, tensed and ready to spring.

"Fifty yards" came the shout from the right. "Fifty yards" came the shout from the left. "Five fathoms," came the simultaneous shouts.

The sea crashed up against the back of the boat, pushing it into the cliff, and with a heave, the night pilot yanked the wheel to the right, and for a moment they sat parallel to the cliffs, "five yards" shouted in panic from the left, and in a moment the engine pushed them out of danger and into the channel. "Hard reverse," she yelled into the engine room, and in an instant the huge ship was righted, and she sprung again upon the wheel and shouted the engine orders, and in a moment they were sailing into the channel with shouts of, "ten yards", "eight yards", "twelve yards" echoing off the cliffs, with shouts of "five fathoms", "six fathoms" intermingled.

All through the channel the night pilot shouted her orders, reversing, pushing forward, the screw propeller whining and humming under the water as it strained under the conflicting orders. As the ship would draw near to the cliff, the men sounding on the left became more panicked, and with quick twitches and heaves, and near constant shouting of orders to the engine room, the night pilot brought them through the channel inch by inch, yard by yard.

The cliffs loomed overhead on the left, dark jagged spires looking down in disgust on the ship, reaching with their rocky tendrils as best they could. On the right, churning tidal depths swirled with entering water, and tugged and tugged to bring the ship in to meet the other lost inhabitants in the Grinder.

And still, they came.

At the front of the boat, Ethan, white as a sheet, collapsed shaking in fear after the first few near misses. He huddled against the rail, put his head between his legs, and for the second time in not nearly enough time, prayed to whatever gods would listen.

Alana stood stoically on the bow, facing down her demise. She watched as they passed the wreckage of several ships on both sides: fools who had attempted this passage before. Ethan was having a panic attack, but she was still dead inside, and accepted whatever the fates had in store for her. Her emotions had not recovered for her to feel fear.

The night pilot was in a trance. Numbers were shouted all around, and as her view was blocked again and again through the mists of fog, her mind was a hotbed of geometry, as she figured angles and velocities, and called out her orders and threw herself against the wheel.

Tiberius watched the results of his decision with mingled terror and glee. "What have I wrought?" he whispered as he watched the ship career nearly-sideways from a current. And yet through his fear, giddiness of his own power over others sapped his judgement, and he basked in self-invented glory.

Lightning fell from the sky like rain all around. Winds blew the trees on the land around them, and as the ship came against the last turn in the Grinder, and the last squeeze of the passage lay in front, every man lost his nerve at the sight of the challenge in front of them. A narrow passage, with no more than a couple yards on either side, and shallow churning waves lay ahead. Beyond that, grey uncertainty, highlighted with flashes of death.

Every man lost his nerve, but not the woman.

No longer even attempting to artificially lower her voice, the night pilot called out commands at the top of her high-pitched voice. "Hard reverse", "ballast to center", and she lay upon the wheel like a fury, playing it like a guitar. She strummed it every which way, and in the shallows righted the ship forward. She called out confidence to her sailors with every holler, slowly filling them up with resolve and steadiness. And with the thunder fighting against her every word she talked that entire ship of men forward through the last pass and out into the open sea, a clear route in the sea lay ahead. Nothing to delay Tiberius now.

For a moment all was silent, and then a cheer went out. Sailors and marines alike came one by one and patted her on the back and sung her praises in the rolling seas.

"Competent work," Tiberius said as he passed her with a nod. He always gave short nods to people to make them feel like he was especially important.

"Go screw yourself landie," she said in reply, and began plotting a course forward.

At that moment, far ahead, the sea rose up in opposition. From the grey mists and churning whitecaps, a figure appeared ahead of them. A grand presence swept the sea clean in front of them, and from the oceans a trident sprang, hundreds of strands of lightning hitting it and shooting forth, and with its full power it swept out a wave. Poseidon himself threw his disgust at them, and a wave one hundred feet high came churning out, racing along the seafloor to break them.

Quick as a flash, the night pilot screamed out her orders, and in an instant they were climbing the giant wave, she calling forth more power from the engine, and for one last moment she held back certain doom with the power of her voice. They climbed the wave at an angle, on one side able to touch the sea, and on the other looking down a perilous drop to the waves. She drew forth strength from the crew and roared out power.

Against all belief the ship powered up that rogue wave and made it to the top. The ship arched along the wave, stood for a moment high up in the ocean, the propeller screw whining away furiously as it spun out of the water and into the air, and as lightning crashed all around them, the ship sank down the other side of the wave, speeding towards the depths.

They hit the bottom of the other side, buckets of water splashing over the bow and sweeping the ship.

The water spilled off, the bilge pumps roared, and the crew shouted for joy. They had lived. They all had lived. The Queen Anne had defeated the Grinder.

After their celebrations calmed down Tiberius was the first to realize that while no sailors or marines were lost overboard, there were two people who did find their way off the ship.

Alana and Ethan plunged into the depths of blackness, tossed out like feathers in a hurricane.

In the fading light, the captain of The Argo hauled himself up to the highest perch he could get on the smokestacks and looked out upriver. Lower downriver, the Andaluvian cut out a giant fertile valley; the breadbasket of Medea. Higher up, though, it cut a deep narrow channel in rocky cliffs. He called it Hell's Canyon, but that was a name from another era. The river made a huge bend up ahead, carving out the commanding cliff face on which the fortress of Cairn stood.

"How are we going to get out of this one?" the first mate asked when the captain came back down.

"I don't think we're going to," the captain replied, and he pointed along the riverbanks up and down Hell's Canyon, and in the twilight they could just make out dozens upon dozens of camouflaged boats along the bank.

"Oh boy we are screwed," the first mate said, and then squinting through a pair of binoculars, "all of this just for us? This seems like it would take a little more planning."

"It does, doesn't it?" the captain said suspiciously.

"Do you think...?" the first mate asked.

"Definitely." the captain said.

As she emerged from her trance, Zara couldn't figure out what they were talking about, but the gravity of their hushed tones was enough to deter questions from any of the bystanders.

"Well, how about we pull a peacock?" the first mate asked.

"Hmmmm...a peacock," the captain said as he stroked his chin. "Do you think it'll work?"

"Do you have a better idea?" the first mate asked. "I think our options are to die in a fire here or die in a fire back there," he said motioning downriver to the inevitable fleet that awaited them.

"Well, you don't have to tell me twice," the captain said. "Peacock it is." He shouted to the rest of the crew, "get your feathers ready!"

"We're saved!" Ethan shouted as he coughed up seawater.

Alana bobbed next to him in the churning ocean and screamed, "We're dead you idiot!"

They couldn't see anything. The waves obscured their views in any direction, and they had lost sight of the ship immediately upon getting tossed.

There was nothing for them to do but give up.

Ethan almost sprang out of the ocean with joy. "Are you kidding me?! We're off that ship of death! We're saved! The gods have saved us!" he yelled.

"You imbecile, look at us! We're doomed! We have nothing!" she screamed. She was furious at his everlasting stupidity and optimism. How could he not see? There was nothing but darkness for them.

"Nah," Ethan shouted in near ecstasy, "just you see, the gods will save us, just like they did the last time."

"What are you talking about?" Alana shouted.

"You know, when Hephaestus came and made us our own canyon!" Ethan said. "How could you forget that! It was amazing! And Poseidon just threw us off that boat! We are looking so good right now I can't believe it."

Alana shook with rage. "Are you mad? That was a wave!

There was no Poseidon! And we are drowning in the middle of the ocean!"

"You didn't see him?" Ethan said. "It was so cool, he just hopped right out of the ocean and took one look at Tiberius and was like, 'not today sucker' and he spat us right out of that boat and into the water. What luck!" With his adrenaline, Ethan had the strength of ten men, and tread water like he was walking on it.

Alana laughed at him. "You little country mouse, that was a cloud and a wave. Have you never seen clouds where you come from? That's what they look like."

"Whatever princess," Ethan replied, "but remember Hephaestus, that was amazing!"

"There was no Hephaestus you child," Alana screamed. "Nothing. We haven't seen a single god on this entire quest!" she yelled in frustrated despair. "Nothing! There has been nothing! This entire affair has been worthless. A waste of time. A failure. We haven't been helped by anyone or anything!"

"Uh please don't tell me you also are going to deny the amazing Persephone thing we saw? On like our third night she returned from that well and spring blew over the ground? That was astounding! I have just been blown away by how near we are to the gods. I never had any idea. I assumed they were distant uncaring beings, and here I find them on every corner waiting to throw us a bone!" Ethan refused to give in to Alana's despair, and every word bounced with glee.

"WE'RE STILL GOING TO DIE IN THIS OCEAN!" Alana heaved. "No amount of childish imagination is going to save us," she shouted. "WE ARE ALL ALONE!"

"Eh, just you wait," Ethan said. "I'll be having this argument with you onshore in no time."

And like manna from heaven, from the waves appeared some flotsam: a weathered old tree trunk floating in the waves. Ethan grasped onto it with both arms and held tight.

"What did I tell you?" he laughed. "This is amazing."

Alana swam his direction shouting, "That was a coincidence!"

Ethan gave her a saccharine grin. "Amazing!"

The tree sank under their weight, and Alana looked to him in triumph. They would die after all.

But alas, the waves brought them an empty barrel. Ethan swam and retrieved it.

"STILL A COINCIDENCE," she shouted.

Ethan just shook his head. "Alana," he said, "it's just like my mom used to say: you can never lose hope, only surrender it. It's time to stop giving up."

Alana said nothing. The lightning cracked and the wind howled, but with their last strength they lashed the two together and their little raft held together. Far off on the waves Ethan saw a trident give a final salute, and the waves shifted, pushing them away from Scilia and toward the mainland.

"OKAY I ADMIT THAT LOOKED AWFULLY SUSPICIOUS BUT I STILL SAY COINCIDENCE", Alana fumed while Ethan rejoiced.

Far away, the night pilot smiled. All of the sailors smiled. Tiberius was storming around angry once again, his true lack of power showing through again. He could never have the complete control that he so desperately wanted.

CHAPTER 19

"What exactly is a peacock?" Zara said groggily as the ship built up power.

"It's kind of a cross between a chicken and a piñata," the captain said.

"That's not what I meant." Zara said.

"Right, you probably have never seen a piñata," the captain said, and proceeded to ignore her. In the early flat light of the morning they set off north to run the gamut.

The sailors manned the guns, bringing out and installing various miscellaneous weapons all over the deck until the ship bristled like a hedgehog.

"Full speed ahead!" the captain yelled. "Don't stop until we're on the bottom or on the other side!"

And with a tremendous lurch the ship jumped forward.

From either shore, smaller ships hidden away began to fire as the Argo came into range. The sailors on the Argo took whatever cover they could as they waited for the signal. As more and more ships came into range the firing became more intense, though largely inaccurate. The pilot had been through this kind of rodeo before, and Zara held on tight as he jolted the ship from one side to the other, randomly pausing, speeding up, bobbing and dipping as he went, much like she would imagine a pea...

"Let's show 'em our tail!" the captain yelled, and almost instantly every gun on the ship began firing. Explosive shells rang out and into the sides of the canyon, ripping up the embankment, burning up the camouflage installments, but on top of that several guns fired smokescreens of every color. The river was soon choked in reds, purples, greens, and blues as smoke hid them from the shoreline.

"Behold the peacock!" the captain shouted at her with a huge grin on his face. This was always his favorite maneuver.

They dipped and bobbed, leaned and churned, and took on the occasional shell: the foredeck burned, the smoke stacks had holes blown through, and the bilge pumps pushed as hard as they could to keep them afloat with the pounding, and the Argo slipped through the hidden armada, and around the river bend.

Suddenly, Zara gasped as she saw the great fortress of Cairn looming high overhead on the clifftops, the immense hostile fortress looking down on them with its huge guns and impenetrable defenses.

"Atlas..." Zara said wistfully.

"You know the place?" the captain asked.

"You might say I own the place," she replied. Right then as they looked up, the guns far ahead started to swivel into position. Zara felt panic boiling over yet again, "Uh, wait a minute wait a minute wait a minute," she said.

"I thought for sure they wouldn't try to kill us this time..." the captain said.

"THIS time?" Zara yelled. "There was another time??"

"Lightning doesn't strike the same place twice, right?" he said as he barked orders around.

"You mean lightning already struck here ONCE?" Zara hollered with a mix of amazement and unbelief.

"Ah, nothing to it," the captain said.

"Nothing to it??" Zara shouted.

"I thought you owned the place?" the captain said and winked.

Zara saw smoke puff out far above them and an unholy whine buzzed louder and louder. She dove on the deck and covered her head.

SPLASH. A huge round just missed them, sending up a wave enough to shake the boat from side to side.

"It's like I said," the captain said, still standing on deck, totally unfazed, "lightning doesn't strike the same place twice."

Zara looked up at him and replied sharply, "There is no physical law that prevents lightning from striking the same place twice!"

"And they've not gotten any more accurate since the last time we came by," the captain said cheerily.

"I think you're the bravest person I've ever met," Zara said as she stood.

"Likewise, princess of Atlas," the captain said with a bow. "Welcome home."

Zara wasn't sure what to say, but had her lines handed to her as more puffs of smoke blew out up above. "I have a bad feeling about this."

"Surely one ship can still get through," said the captain, "they have always been so bad about their artillery here," he said.

The hidden armada from Medea held back behind the last bend, knowing the cost that an incursion would exact on their tremendous numbers, but the Argo churned forward, haltingly jolting from side to side on its way up the bend and around the guns.

They pressed on, the booms of the guns hundreds of feet above echoing down Hell's Canyon. The shells kicked up enough smoke and spray that Zara was sure that it had started to rain.

"Almost there!" shouted the captain. He turned around to catch his last glimpse of the fort and smiled a toothy grin. It looked like they were going to make it out of range after all.

But as they reached the far end of the range from the fort above, the long-distance guns fired one last salvo, one last desperate shot, perfectly timed, which smashed into the rear of the Argo.

The back of the ship lifted up in the water from the explosion, and everyone fell to the ground and slid towards the bow. The stern stood up above the water for a moment as if held by a god in the sky, and then smashed back down into the river. The gunners above cheered. Victory!

The Argo, for not the first time in its life, was disabled. The entire stern was chewed up into bits, with no real chance of self-propulsion, it foundered in the river. Holding onto the deck at midship, Zara came to, ears ringing, and the black mist of the explosion clearing. The ship was slowly pushed against the far bank by the current and there it rest.

"Well boys," yelled the captain, "time for plan B!"

Zara shook her head. She'd never met people so immune to setbacks. "Is nothing ever a problem for you?" she asked.

"We've been through much, much worse," he said. "But I'm afraid this is where we must part company; they'll be down to collect you shortly, and we must be off before they collect us as well."

Zara shook his hand and bowed her head. "Thank you, captain. Thank you. You've saved my life and my freedom. I could never repay you."

"Just one question before you go," he said. "We've all been dying to know."

"Of course, anything," Zara replied.

"Anything?" the captain asked.

"Well, almost anything," she said with a smile.

"I reckoned as much," the captain said, and continued,

"what in the blazes is that thing you pulled out of a hat back there?" He pointed at the cross hanging around her neck. "I've been all around the world, but I've never seen that."

Zara scooped up some loose odds and ends that would be simple to trade for a horse and supplies to last for a short journey, until she could get her feet back under herself.

"Miss?" the captain asked, and Zara zoned back into him. "How did you get through?"

Zara looked at him and confessed, "Have you not heard of the silver cross?"

The captain looked on and said, "The silver cross?" He thought for a moment. "You mean King Leo's thing?" He asked in confusion. "I thought that was a myth!"

"Then so am I," she said.

And with a shrug, they left. She followed the others on a rough path the thousand feet up the far bank, and then stopped. Zara looked up and down the Andaluvian, pondering what to do next. She looked back to Atlas and Medea and shook her head. She had had enough of the five nations, getting expelled at the drop of a hat. She turned her eyes to the west and walked towards the grand empty expanse of freedom.

Under a bright southern sun, a forest dipped and bobbed.

Sahil climbed to the top of a tree and surveyed. Hundreds of trees were bouncing in the waves coming in from the storm offshore, but all the rigging was holding.

He stood in the far southwest beyond the five nations, where for hundreds of years his people, a small nation of farmers, built a forest in the ocean. Far out to the sea Sahil could see the retreating storm clouds over the rocky spires of the Grinder, and every year he and his people lashed floating planters together on the edge of the ocean, filled with pioneering trees, drawing closer and closer with every tree. The roots split through the box and burrowed down through the ocean into the ground below, providing an anchor for the land to come. Onto this land his people moved and moved on to reclaim more of the ocean. While others fought for land, they built it.

He wasn't quite sure what they would do when they finally built their kingdom out to Scilia, but someone knew and that someone said it was going to be awesome. For Sahil's part, he was learning the trade, surveying these most distant trees, bobbing in the ocean, roots still reaching for the seafloor.

A huge wave crashed against the vast plantations. Sahil watched as the entire forest's edge, filled with the most recent trees, lifted up as the wave passed underneath them. The forest itself became a wave, green treetops lifting up into the sky and crashing back down. Each planter was lashed together well, though he did see a few lines break and noted where he'd need to make repairs later, but everything largely held.

The wave fizzled out quickly, as the larger older trees were anchored solidly in the seafloor, and he saw as the deep canals they had left behind in neat rows heaved beyond their bounds and water spilled out onto the forest floor.

Back beyond the edges of the ocean he surveyed the immense forest his people had created, pushing far inland. Miles and miles of land built for and by them.

And in front of them, miles to go before they slept.

Sahil climbed from tree to tree, inspecting the lashings, fixing what he could. Luckily, the worst of the squall had missed the forest, but more waves were now coming and stressing the system, and any breakages had to be repaired quickly, or other trees would be put at risk. He worked quickly on the outer edge, bounced and tossed here and there, but made quick work of any weak points.

He stopped for a moment to admire the storm as it blew out to sea. Then he paused and his heart stopped. There was a ship.

"Ugh," he muttered. "Not again."

The ship was bearing straight for him.

"How did they even find me?" he said out loud. How could they even see him? He looked around and around. How was this even possible.

"They have no business here," he said. He was enraged and climbed down his tree as fast as he could. He'd need to alert the others if they were going to do anything about this, and the others were a far run away.

But when he reached the bottom, he noticed something else.

The makeshift raft had held, and Alana and Ethan rolled up against the outer planters. The currents were kind enough to deposit them back on the mainland after the short storm. Ethan looked up and down the coast in this makeshift land factory. "What in the world is this?" he said.

Alana was overcome with amazement. "Trees...in the middle of the ocean," she said. "What kind of world is this?" She pulled herself onto the nearest box and helped Ethan up next to her.

They sat on a box bobbing on the edge of a vast ocean, lashed together in a forest, and for a moment Ethan wondered if he was actually wrong, and that they had, in fact, died. Their confusion was interrupted by Ethan pointing out to sea. There was a black dot on the horizon. And it was headed their way.

"Ho! You there!" Sahil shouted. "Are you okay?"

Alana and Ethan scanned the trees and saw nothing. A lithe man dropped out of a tree onto a nearby box. He was short, tan, and probably in his mid-thirties. A large machete hung at his side, and he carried several lengths of rope wrapped around his bare chest.

"Who are you?" Alana shouted back at him. "And what is this?"

"You are in Thebe," the stranger said. "I am Sahil, a farmer here, and this," he said gesturing either way along the coast, "is my field."

"Thebe exists?" Ethan asked. He thought it more fairy tale than real, so this came as a real surprise to him. He and Alana both knew it from maps and various stories but had no idea the grandeur of what to expect.

"Ha," Sahil said. "You're not the first to ask me that," he said. "And maybe not the last? In either event, our hospitality is extended to survivors of shipwrecks, but..." he pointed off to the approaching ship. "I take it your friends are here to collect you? Allow me to direct you back on board," he said as he ushered them to the edge of the box they stood bobbing on.

"Oh, they're here to collect us all right," Ethan said. "Now let's say, and this is a purely hypothetical example, what if we don't wish to be collected?"

Sahil smiled. "You too? Follow me, my friends."

Far off a cannon sounded.

"Run!" Alana shouted.

The shell ripped through the trees above them and exploded as it hit a trunk just beyond, sending up a huge fireball and splattering shrapnel in the ocean and blowing holes in the swaying leaves.

Sahil popped his head back up after diving under the nearest trunk. He squinted at the ship, then back at Alana and Ethan who were huddled down under some roots. "Who are you??" he exclaimed in shock. "Who are you?"

Before they could answer the report from a cannon sounded again. The ship was closing in.

"Well I guess it's going to be one of THOSE days," Sahil said, and hopped off the floating box into the water. "Follow me!" Alana and Ethan dove into the water to follow.

Shells exploded in huge fireballs in the trees above them. Smoke poured out of the forest into the immaculately clear sky above. "Down" Sahil shouted to their bobbing heads as the next shell whistled overhead, and they dove deep underwater

277

and saw shrapnel spray into the ocean tracing lines of bubbles, the shrapnel slowing and sinking into the depths beyond. Some of the bits bounced harmlessly off their submerged bodies. They slunk between the floating rafts of trees, slowly making their way through the ocean as the forest burned above. Sunlight began to shine into the shade through the holes being peppered into the leaves above.

"Down!" Sahil shouted, and another shell sprayed above. They came up to see a small fire starting on the outer rim. "You Zeussian nightmare you," Sahil said. He watched in horror as years of painstaking work went up in an inky smoke. He coughed as he shook with rage. "They are going to pay...down!" he shouted, and down they went.

The Queen Anne reached the edge of the forest and stopped. The Thebens had left a few ocean channels open for navigation by their smaller boats, and the Queen Anne stopped right in front of one. Sahil peeked around a raft and tapped Alana on the shoulder and pointed back. "What are they doing?" he said. From the deck came a volley of rifle shot, and they ducked back under the water, swimming their way to firmer ground where the rafts had knit together firm ground through the passage of time. There they could hope to run their way to safety.

"What are you waiting for?!" Tiberius screamed into the night pilot's face from inches away as he gesticulated wildly in the direction of the canal. "Go on in! It's wide open! They're escaping!" The entire ship stopped to watch this latest in a series of showdowns with Tiberius.

"Sir, I'm afraid it's too shallow for our ship sir!" the night pilot hollered back up into his face as she once again stood on her tiptoes. "We've run aground! It's much too shallow, much too shallow sir!"

Tiberius was red in the face with frustration. "You lie," he hissed. "I heard the soundings myself, we're just fi..."

278

The night pilot called out orders to the engine room, and they heard the boilers fire up and the screw whine below. The Queen Anne inched forward begrudgingly, shaking as she went.

The night pilot stared up at Tiberius with a look of total innocence. "Sorry sir, but if we go any further, we won't be coming back out ever. You can hear from the shaking that we're flat out stuck. Need to wait for the tides to escape this stretch."

Tiberius grunted "Am I always to be surrounded by incompetence?" he shouted. As he struggled to form words, the night pilot gave them to him.

"Sir, probably sir, but you can use the small boats to pursue sir, they'll have a much easier time getting further!" she hollered back, with a barely-perceptible amount of spittle hitting Tiberius in the face as he stood peering over her.

"Of course," he thought. "The boats." He felt a giant relief. He was so proud of himself for coming up with another solution to this never-ending sequence of problems.

"Marines, to the boats!" he shouted, and within minutes every marine was in one of the three smaller boats, rowing their way down the grand canal as the Queen Anne loomed behind them, stuck at the entrance.

Tiberius stood on the stern of one of the smaller boats as his men rowed and yelled back to the night pilot. "What are you waiting for? Shell the forest! Burn every last inch of this criminal hideaway!" he shouted.

From on deck the night pilot shouted, "aye aye sir!" and lifted up her right hand to reveal a huge knife which she used to salute Tiberius. She bent back over for a moment and Tiberius heard a snap.

"What was that?" he mumbled.

And with a small splash the rope holding the anchor fell into the sea, and the ship was freed. It lurched backward out of the channel and with horror Tiberius watched as the entire crew let out a "hooray!" and the captain emerged from the depths onto the deck, half a bucket after his untimely departure. The night pilot gave him a huge enthusiastic salute and shouted in Tiberius' direction, "The bridge is yours, sir!"

With a hearty laugh and a quick salute to his crew, the captain quickly gave his orders, heed to starboard, forward ho, and, "get the heck out of dodge!"

Tiberius watched in horror as The Queen Anne slowly turned to leave. "Captain! Captain! You can't leave us here!" he demanded with indignation.

"Nay, it's a fate befitting a mutineer," the captain hollered back. "All hail the captain of Thebes!" he hollered, and the sailors behind him shouted at the tops of their lungs, "All hail the captain of Thebes!"

"But I have orders!" Tiberius shouted in desperation.

"I've taken your orders and wiped my butt with them and thrown them into a bucket," the captain yelled. "We're off and not a moment too soon. We'll see you in the court martial." With the entire crew giving a one-finger salute, the Queen Anne put in full power, and steamed off.

Sahil stopped to look back again. "What are they doing?" he exclaimed. "What in the name of Hades are they doing?" he said. This day was getting weirder and weirder. The fire lay smoldering at the edge of the forest, the distance between the floating rafts hindering much progress of the conflagration, and through the smoke he watched as the ship that just lay waste to his work turned around and left.

He looked back at Alana. "What kind of bipolar people do you have after you?" he said. "This doesn't make any sense."

Alana's mind was slowly coming back after many buckets and days of total capitulation. "There's no way they just gave up..." she said.

"That's what I'm saying," Sahil said as he looked back.

Ethan heard a splash and he pointed to the canal. "They

didn't," he said. And through the smoke and leaves they saw three boats moving up the canal. A figure on the boats pointed through the mists right at them.

"Ugh. Run. Again." Sahil said. And the rifle shots rang out.

They had gotten back into the cover of the trees when Sahil called out. He pointed down a line of trees. "Go that way, really fast. When you hit the path, hang a right, then a left, then, oh it doesn't matter. Just run. I'll find you. You two will leave a trail a blind man could follow." And he disappeared into the forest to the right before they could argue with him.

Ethan reached out forlornly, "but wait..." he said quietly. He looked back at Alana and shrugged. A shot rang out from a few hundred yards away.

And so off they ran deeper into Thebes.

Tiberius and his men, having given up on any hope of return to the ship, dedicated themselves to finding the fugitives. They spotted them far up the canal and heaved against the oars to reach land up ahead. Dusk began to fall on the forest.

Sahil grabbed his machete between his teeth. "Oh no they didn't," he muttered through clenched teeth. "You don't come back into my forest and destroy my trees and get away with it," and spying a hole in the ground, dove into the ocean below.

The last boat in line sprung a leak.

The marines looked down to see a huge geyser sinking their boat almost instantaneously. The four of them began to bail, but there was no use. It almost immediately swamped them in the middle of the channel. "Hey!" they called out to the others in front. Tiberius and the others turned to see four of them treading water.

Then three.

Then two.

Ten feet away a marine gasped as he came up to the surface. "There's something in here!" he shouted. "My leg!" he screamed, and in the fading light the others could see his blood staining the water. The others pulled him to the swamped boat and exposed a large clean gash along his leg. At that moment the second marine gasped as he came up next, screaming. "Sharks!" he yelled in panic. The other boats turned around to collect them and found the same: large clean gashes along their legs, and the marines babbling about being dragged underwater and attacked by a huge shark.

On the edge of the canal, Sahil came out of the water in the cover of a root system, machete back in his teeth, breathing heavily. "That oughta slow them down," he muttered with a smile. He listened to their screams of "sharks!", and watched as they slowly circled the boats, monitoring the water below, scanning for sharks. Sahil patted his machete affectionately. "Thank you, my little shark. Thank you," he said.

A mile away Alana and Ethan were totally stopped in the dark. They had lost the path, found it, then lost it again, and had just retraced their steps back onto the path before any hope of finding their way was lost with the last bit of light. On the path behind them they heard a light padding, and they hid off to the side until they saw Sahil emerge from the darkness.

"Sahil!" Ethan exclaimed, and stood up to embrace him. Sahil was soaking wet and panting from his run. Ethan pulled back from his jubilant (and unwanted) hug and pointed down. "You're missing a shoe," he said.

Sahil looked down and found he was down to just one shoe. "Eh, wouldn't be the first time," he said. And with a smile, he lifted up his machete in one hand and a chunk of wood in the other. "They just don't make boats like they used to," Sahil said.

Ethan smiled. "Thank you, you wonderful man. Thank

you. I will never forget this kindness."

Sahil brushed the glowing praise off. "I have no idea who you people are, but your enemies will not, in fact, be collecting you. Allow me to welcome you to Thebes. Right this way." Sahil said as he melted into the forest, and Ethan and Alana ran to catch up.

"Thanks," Alana said as they ran. "Thanks."

CHAPTER 20

"Come in my sweet boy Etienne. How I've missed you," a warm voice responded from the other side of the door. Reluctantly, Etienne entered.

"Are you still calling me that?" he said coolly as he walked in the room.

"Of course, my Etienne, my morning star, my son," his mother replied.

She was sitting at her desk when he entered, and she stood to greet him, walking over to him as though she were wafting across a totally undisturbed lily-strewn pond. Etienne was frustrated for being called away from his business by her demands, but that anger was tempered by the sheer beauty she embodied. His mother never walked anywhere: she moved with an enchanted waltz as though she only sailed through glass seas of life, and never once indicated any evidence of disturbance.

She hugged him and put her hands on his shoulders and looked up into his eyes. "My Etienne," she said as she smiled.

"Aaron," he corrected her.

She rolled her eyes. "I am your mother, and you are my

Etienne. Your father can call you what he wants, but you always carried the joy of my father deep in your bones, and you honor him by holding his name." She curtsied and bowed her head and brushed away his remaining cool demeanor as she half sang, "And besides, Aaron is such a serious name for such a serious man. You are my little boy. You are always my Etienne."

Etienne (or Aaron, depending on your preference I suppose) wondered at the time if she just couldn't read his emotions when he was angry, for she so often appeared oblivious to his annoyance.[21]

"You called for me?" he said, duly humbled by her sublime motherly love. "I'm due in planning in a few moments, but you said it was urgent."

"Of course," his mother replied. "My sweet, sweet son, I have a great burden to ask of you, and I know you will be loath to receive it. But please, for your mother's sake, listen."

"As you wish, mother," Etienne said, as he toyed with his pocket watch. He was under a considerable amount of stress, and every second counted for him that day. He hadn't slept more than a few hours all week.

"My Etienne," she said warmly, "my dearest, I have been sorely tormented by the route you are choosing to take, and I think you are in the gravest of errors. You cannot go through with this assault." his mother let her words hang in the air like icicles during a silent snowfall.

Etienne opened his mouth to object, but she put her fingers on his lips to silence him.

"This is against your nature, against what we believe, against the reasons we left behind what we did, and against what is right and good. Don't let your ambition cloud your judgement, listen to me. You cannot do this. You must stop." She spoke with calmness and decision, yet her warmth and

---

[21] He later, of course, realized that she could, like all mothers can.

love never ceased to reach out to him in look and tone.

Etienne felt frustration rise to the surface. If there was anything he hated, it was being contradicted.

"Is this why you interrupt me, to echo the words of weakness plaguing the kingdom?" he said, "to entreat me to follow the path of your father, the appeaser?"

"Peacemaker, my Etienne," she corrected him with a sigh.

"Security is peace, mother. For far too long we've seen the arms of the Five Nations grow longer and longer, and they ache to come and take what we have! What I do now I do for the good of our people, the good of you." Etienne said.

"But what do you gain by sacrificing your soul?" she asked. "What are we if we are not the ideals we hold?"

"We won't be around to have ideals if we don't attack now. The Five Nations haven't united to come and crush us not due to lack of desire, but due to lack of opportunity! Our spies in the east have fomented open rebellion in their lands, and now we can strike! If not now, then never. If not now, we will find their armies bearing down upon us, and what will we do when they crush our people? The cliffs will not protect us from such a foe. They will envelop our valley from side to side like the locusts of the west, and there will be no peace for us, no ideals, just death and destruction." Etienne had pulled away and was flapping his arms about as he predicted apocalyptic despair. "No, mother, what I do, I do for you. We are no match for their combined power, but we can match them in courage, in surprise, in viciousness, and that is what I intend to lead with."

"This is not who you are," his mother said. "You know this. You are my little Etienne, the boy who bathed me in kisses and hugs. You are channeling this viciousness from others, but it is not your own," she said as she fought back her tears.

"I am your son," Etienne replied, "and I need to protect you, and all of us."

As his spirit fell away from hers, she tried one last gamble. "You have heard the bearer speak of this doom as well, my son? You know of their ability for prophecy?" she tried.

"The little girl? Marie? She's a tiny child! She has yet much to learn about the world. For one who knows nothing of life to tell us of death? I cannot accept her words seriously," he scoffed.

His mother fought back the tears as she saw her son escape from her grasp. He was once her little Etienne, but now she had to accept him for what he was: his own man.

"But, my Etienne, will you not do it for me then? Throw down your sword, make peace with our enemies, speak meekness to power as my father before, and draw down the destructor from his perch?" she drew nearer to him and held his hand for one last time. "For me Etienne? For me?"

Etienne shook his head. "Mother. Eva. I'm sorry, but I do what I do for you and all Ariens. There is no other way." As far gone as he was down his path, he would yet recall for the rest of his days the pin prick in his heart at this moment. His last chance to change. And yet he gave in nothing.

Eva sighed and resigned herself to what the fates had allotted. "There are many paths, my morning star, and you will find me waiting for you at the end of all of them. Come," she said, as she drew him to hug him the last time, "erase the distance between us. I may not be the advisor you desire, but my love for you will find you across your battlefields, across kingdoms, and across time. My love binds you to me forever, and you will never find yourself outside of it. You will be my morning star long after all on earth has passed." She took him in her arms and Etienne finally relaxed. For a moment he allowed his love to surface, and he felt at home and peace like you can only ever know in the arms of your loving mother.

But he was gone the next morning.

Etienne awoke in tears covered in a cold sweat. A deep red sun was setting in the far west, dipping beneath the ocean, and he groaned in the gall of bitterness, weeping angrily and smashing the ground with his weary fists. He knelt on the hillside and doubled over in pain. The regret never left him. He could not find rest from his pain, no matter how far he went.

He had collapsed in exhaustion after days of hard riding after leaving Alana and Ethan. Even having blacked out and sleeping the dreamless sleep of the dead his old nightmares had found a way to surface.

He untied his horses, loaded them up again, and set off once again southward down the coastal trail. He was not an unfamiliar sight in those lands, and while his friends were marked for death in their travels, none would harass him, the fallen prince of Ariens.

He was mad at himself doubly so for missing the mustering outside of Titan: how had the tribes united and begun amassing? He had missed the signs leading up to that, and had no idea what was going on, but sadly, he had no time for that. Decades of life with nothing going on and no point to existence, and now at the end he was racing and fighting for every second. The irony was not lost on him.

Etienne ignored passersby, took any shortcuts he could, and tried to go as fast as the horses could handle. He only had time for one thing, and one thing only, and that was tracking down Vercingetorix and stopping the war. There was only pain for his people on that path.

The moon was waning. There wasn't much time before a new moon would rise, so there wasn't much light on the trail as he rode, but it was a clear trail, rolling along beaches or sandy hills, so very little by way of obstacles to be worried of. The stars were his guide as he rode, and as morning approached his morning star shone especially warm and bright. Just for him. The very distant warmth fell on his cold tears.

"Mom, we have to move again?!" Tiberius whined as his

mother gathered up the few possessions they had.

"I'm sorry Tiberius, but this is the last time, I promise," Zara said in the most patient way possible in her hurried state.

"But whyyy," he whined.

"You know Ty," Zara said, "I just thought we'd get better weather for you if we went further south! You'll love it down in Medea, you'll never be cold again!" She raced around the room picking up the last couple items they'd carry.

"Mom, I know when you're lying to me. It's because the bad guys are coming again isn't it?" Tiberius questioned.

Zara cursed the day that he became old enough to see through her thinly veiled attempts to reduce his anxiety, but immediately acquiesced. "Yes, our friend just came by to warn us," she said. "But also, the weather; the weather is so much nicer," she said with a mischievous smile.

"But they're in Atlas! We're in Ithaca! Can't they just leave us alone up here? We never did anything to hurt them!" Tiberius said. He was a teenager, and the whiniest he'd ever be. I mean, better than the murduriest he'd ever be, but still not like the most enjoyable child to be around. Nevertheless, his mom never showed any signs of annoyance with him. She had deep bags under her eyes, and she was skinny as a rail, working whatever odd jobs she could get, and while Tiberius never went hungry, she had more than one night a month where she'd beat back the hunger pangs with generous helpings of tea.

On the face of it, it wasn't a great life, but Zara never saw it that way. She could only ever see the joy of being with her son. For her, it was always the best possible world. A great life for two people who loved each other.

"I'm sorry Ty, but you're right." Zara said as she came over to him and held his hands. "You're absolutely right. I thought we were done with the drama, but there's a new person who is looking around for us. But I promise, this is the last time they can reach us. There's a place far in the south where they will never find us again. I promise. We will be so far away we'll never be in danger again. We'll be safe always." Zara kissed his forehead.

"You promise?" Tiberius asked.

"Cross my heart," Zara said as she drew a big X over her chest. "Let's go Ty, I'll tell you all about it on the way," and she held his hand and whisked him outside and down the dark road, their meagre belongings in a threadbare bag thrown over her shoulder.

They walked down the street in cold brisk air. Nobody here, or anywhere else they had lived for that matter knew who she was. All the better, because Atlas was after her. Again.

Zara's mere existence called into question Titus II's legitimacy as king, and so he had made it his personal mission to ensure her constant harassment wherever she went, and if possible, her and her son's death.

Luckily, this kind of mission was impossible to engage in with large efforts or he feared his own illegitimacy would be uncovered, so Zara managed to stay a step ahead his entire life. She relied on a few key loyalists, the kindness of strangers, the will of the gods, and the biggest factor: the total ineptitude of her pursuers. And in the end, she outlasted him.

She thought the death of Titus II would bring the end of the harassment, but apparently Jacques had caught wind of her as well, and so here they were, again getting pushed around by forces they couldn't control. Forces that wanted them to disappear solely for their fact of their mere existence, and not due to any ambitious designs on ruling. Zara had long ago given up any desires for that. She just wanted to live.

They hurried down the cobblestone streets toward the river in the dark as homes put out their lamps for the night one by one along their route. A logging boat was headed out soon, and she had been promised two spots for stowaways, no questions asked.

"But why Medea?" Tiberius whined as he walked just a

little bit slower than his mother would like. "We don't know anybody there. We don't even know anybody from there. I won't have any friends!" he said.

"Shhhhh," my dearest, she said. "I am your friend. The gods are your friends. We will find friends, don't you worry. We can get friends anywhere, but Medea is the only place where we'll be safe," she said, and peeped with glee when she saw the boat in the distance. "We're going to make it!" she said.

She had tried to stay close to familiar territory and people for her son's sake, but this last run-in had convinced her. She lived her entire life on the run, and she couldn't let that be her son's life as well. They had to move as far away from the arm of Atlassian politics as was possible, and so she pulled out a map and drew a circle around a settlement on the dusty edge of the world, and that was going to be the end of it. Her son would grow up safe, and while he would never be a king like her father, he would be alive. She had long ago given up any dreams of grandeur. Now as for him, she could only hope.

They nodded to the boatman and stowed away in the back. They'd have a few days of misery headed down the Andaluvian surrounded by logs and whatever was living in them, but they'd finally be safe! She dreamt of the life she'd give her son: staying up late to watch the fireflies, growing peppers in their garden, and huddling inside to snuggle during thunderstorms. She was so, so tired, worn through with life to translucence, but she beamed with happiness as she held her son. Her son. How she loved him.

They snuggled in, and as Zara looked back, she saw flames reaching up into the heavens. They had left just in time.

Zara never had anything else she could really love with her whole soul in her entire life. Her husband left her from the stress (or the attractiveness of the other woman, but that's neither here nor there), her crown was denied her, and she had no hopes of a life with anything approaching normalcy, but she did have one thing, one thing that made life worth living and beautiful, and that thing was falling asleep in her arms to the sway of the boat on the river. She had no dreams for herself, but for her son she imagined the world.

It took them a few weeks to make it to that dusty outpost in the south. It was chaotic and dirty and rowdy and uncertain, but it was definitely one thing for them in the years up ahead: safe.

CHAPTER 21

Tiberius awoke to a bright day of crushing humidity and the low din of insects. Every part of his body was sore, and it appeared that every exposed piece of skin had been bitten by mosquitos several hundred times.

"What a miserable place Thebes is," he thought. "No wonder everyone tries to get out of here."

Alexander walked over to where Tiberius was lying and tried to wipe away the veritable faucet of sweat showering off his brow. "What now, sir?" he asked.

Tiberius' head ached with a dull pain as he recalled the fruitless night following featureless paths in this watery maze, eventually collapsing with exhaustion shortly before dawn. He had two boats with some supplies, a dozen or so patched up marines, and no idea where Alana might be.

And things were going to get worse for him soon.

"We can't stay here," he said. "The Thebens will be on their way, and I have no doubt they'll be...unhappy to see me." Tiberius said.

"Unhappy sir?" Alexander asked.

"No reason," Tiberius said, remembering the last time he had come to Thebes.

He stood up and stretched. Everything hurt. What a miserable day.

"Where is Alana?" Tiberius thought out loud. He was desperate to find her and return to Medea to collect his honor with Scipio.

"The question is, where will she be," Alexander offered.

Tiberius nodded his head. "You're right," and as he patted him on the back both of them winced with the pain. Sleeping in a root-infested mosquito hellhole was not a recipe for morning happiness. "There's only one place she could be headed," he said.

"Do you think we can cut her off?" Alexander asked.

"We're the only ones who could," Tiberius said with a smile. "Let's get moving!" he shouted. "Back into the boats, we're rowing north!" he shouted.

Alexander nodded. He figured as much. "Up to Ariens?" he asked.

"I think that's the fastest way to catch up, we can avoid this swamp terror maze and make up ground on the open road," Titus replied. "We can make the great western road by nightfall and head inland."

"But can we make it in time? It seems like a stretch," Alexander said, doubtful.

"Nothing a forced night march can't solve!" Tiberius said demonically as he patted him on the back.

Alexander made his way around to the anxious men and convinced them of the merits of the plan. They didn't have enough supplies to last long, but with a push of speed they'd make it out of this with a big win.

The men quickly shook off their aches and pains and steeled themselves for a very long slog. While they complained and murmured in low tones amongst themselves, they were all secretly glad. A long march was a singular task they could understand and could dominate. The alternative, slinking around a mosquito maze and attempting to avoid international incidents seemed so much less appealing.

Sahil set a fast pace through the increasingly dense forest on a "path" that seemed obvious to a Theben, but to an outsider appeared to be senseless undergrowth, just like every other direction you could see. The channels of water faded away as they worked their way inland, and roots grew thicker and thicker underneath until Alana and Ethan could no longer tell where the original boundary between ocean and land once stood, and to be honest, neither could Sahil. That information had long been lost with time. A visitor from an era deep in the past wouldn't recognize any of the land they were traveling through, but then again, that is true for so many parts of the earth.

They were occasionally hailed by farmers as they half ran, half walked the meandering paths, and after a quick word of warning they'd be off, and the farmer would head in the opposite direction.

"Where are they off to?" Alana said as she watched another one bound off into the distance behind them.

"They're off to make sure our guests don't get too friendly," Sahil said.

"Them and what army?" Ethan asked.

"That is the army," Sahil replied.

"That's the army?" Alana said with incredulity. "You must not see a lot of action out here? I'm pretty sure our local police force could successfully invade your entire country at this rate..."

"I'd love to see them try," Sahil said. "Do you see your friends behind us? If one Theben...Theber...Citizen of Thebe can stop a dozen—remember what I did yesterday—imagine what a dozen of us can do," Sahil said.

"Does it help that this is a mosquito-swarmed hellscape?" Alana asked.

Sahil shrugged, "It helps that this is a mosquito-swarmed hellscape," he said. The heat was totally oppressive, squeezing them from every side, made worse by the constant "nnnzzzzz" of mosquitos in their ears.

"The trees are nice," Ethan offered, attempting to say something nice about the host country saving them from certain death.

"Will they kill them?" Alana asked.

"The trees?", asked Ethan, confused.

"No, you idiot, the marines after us," Alana said.

Sahil laughed, "no, no, no, what are you talking about? We are civilized here! I mean, they'll casually suggest that they repay us for the years of backbreaking work that they just destroyed, and they may casually suggest that in a way that includes forced labor, who's to say," Sahil said.

"Forced labor? I really doubt you'll get any such thing out of Tiberius," Alana said.

Sahil stopped dead in his tracks. "Tiberius? That's your friend?" he asked.

Alana almost ran into him from behind before she could stop herself. "You've really got to stop calling him a friend. Not a friend, definitely not a friend, did you see what he was doing? But yeah, he was the one back there."

"Okay, I take it back, you're right, probably kill them, definitely." Sahil said, and off he ran again. "Tiberius," he mumbled. "You could have told me it was Tiberius before, would have saved me a lot of trouble..." he sputtered as he ran.

Alana and Ethan were soaked through with sweat and constantly batting away bugs who were suicidally attacking them.

"Do you think he knows him?" Ethan asked, and then heard Sahil again up ahead:

"Tiberius, she says, son of a... could have said why yes this is Tiberius, don't bother being a humanitarian." Sahil grumbled. "Next time tell me who is trying to apprehend you!" he hollered over his shoulder.

"You got it," Alana called out, panting as she jogged behind him. "The very next time I am running for my life from someone and end up in an ocean and land on your little tree stump, for sure I will tell you who is trying to kill me."

"Thank you!" Sahil called back.

They ran through the ferns and swatted off spider webs and mosquitos and strained gnats out their mouths whenever they were foolish enough to open their mouth when running. And every so often up ahead they'd hear a series of curses followed by, "Tiberius she says. NOW she tells me."

That night they rested in Sahil's family home. Like other homes in Thebes, it was built over a hundred feet up a gigantic tree and required an absolutely terrifying climb up a series of jimmy-rigged stairs: infrequently placed planks coming out of the tree's trunk, supplemented by whatever branches happened to have grown in a helpful place. Ethan did okay going up, though Alana did grit her teeth in absolute panic the further up they went. One slip on a wet branch and she would be...she tried not to think about it.

The home, though spartan, was placed above a good portion of the forest canopy, giving them miles and miles of views over forest they would never forget.

There they ate fruits neither Alana nor Ethan had seen either before or since; beautiful citrus bowls, stone fruit of every variety, roots and fungi from the bases of the trees, alongside a deep dark cider. It was a totally restorative meal, relieving them from their many days of suffering. They were led to hammocks made from strong cords woven from tree bark, and very securely fastened to upper branches, but which still hung precariously high over the ground. The residents of Thebe were perfectly safe from any intruder while they slept, if you could get over the fact that if any of the supports broke you would almost immediately die.

It was only the desperate exhaustion that eventually persuaded Ethan to overcome his fear, and much later, Alana. Before they slept, though, they watched the most beautiful sunset on earth, with the sun drooping below the very distant ocean. The stars came out in force, covering the entire sky with light. The stars glow stronger by the ocean, and it seemed as though one could look at any blank patch of sky, and if you focused hard enough, you could see thousands of galaxies pop into view in the far distance. Some of the stars shone a little brighter on our tiny crew, sending their deepest thoughts and hopes their way.

CHAPTER 22

"What are you doing?!" Etienne slammed his fist down. "This is madness!"

Vercingetorix laughed. "Little man," he said, "why are you bothering me like the gnats to the horses? This is not your concern. You know nothing of victory, only how to lose."

"I know all about walking my people into a trap," Etienne said. "And you are repeating our greatest mistake."

Vercingetorix laughed again. "What would you have us do, little man; oh high prince of losing? Ride the prairies and wait for the five nations to unite again and push us from our land back into the western seas? We are not welcome on these lands; your fathers made sure of that."

Etienne shook his head. "We are a great people, but our greatness is when we unite to build up our lands. Retake Ariens," he said gesturing to the west, "occupy our former capital. Build up our cities once again and re-light the star foundries and we can build more than what the gods could imagine!"

"There are no gods, just men," Vercingetorix spat out, "we are all that's left here, after our gods forsook us, again, thanks to you. And I have found a way for us to do what you could not! I united the scattered western tribes! We act as one nation again, not powerless squabbling children. And now I have acquired a secret power to destroy the five nations, and when they are beaten, we will occupy their cities and their foundries. We will reap where we did not sow, gather where we did not scatter seed."

Vercingetorix was shorter than Etienne, but he brought himself to standing and looked down at Etienne as he sat at his table. His long dark beard was speckled with grey strands, and his brow was wrinkled from permanently glaring at people. "I will lead our people—my people," he corrected himself, "to restore our greatness, and it is my deepest desire that you live to see it all done without and even in spite of you."

Etienne stood, towering over Vercingetorix, and quickly bowed. "And it is my deepest sadness that you are throwing away another generation of MY people."

"We learn from the best," Vercingetorix retorted.

Etienne cursed and turned and left. He went back to his small camp he had made at the edge of the mass of united tribes. He felt powerless as the tide of events swept him up and along.

"So, wait, tell me where we are going?" Ethan said as the three of them walked deeper into a more crowded forest. "Can we go back to me being the guide? It's so much nicer being the one who can push everyone around. At bare minimum, I really wish you'd go to the trouble of telling me where we were headed."[22]

Sahil rolled his eyes. "Well, guide," he said, "we're headed to the Elders. They want to have a chat before we send you on your merry way."

"Is this like an optional thing? It sounds non-optional, or,

---

[22] They had. Twice. He had ignored them and totally zoned out.

as you may say, forced." Ethan whined in the back.

"Oh, it's optional all right," Alana said, "and I have optioned that we are going to do it."

It was Ethan's turn to roll his eyes. "I figured you were going to say that," he grumbled. "But I tell you, when I'm the guide again, I'll double your mileage out of spite."

"I hate to tell you this, but your guiding days are over," Alana said. "Not like they ever began in the first place, Mr. 'all I did was follow a trail.' Let's just get out of here and get home."

"Righto my liege," Ethan said, and then to Sahil, "so who are these elders again?"

Sahil thought for a moment, trying to think of the right way to reply, phrasing his words very carefully. "They are our leaders?" he said. "Yeah, they are our leaders."

"You sound very convinced of this," Alana said.

"Well we don't really have a system of government that you would be familiar to you. These elders are the closest we come; they call themselves advisors. They say they are here to dispense with their infinite wisdom and serve as intermediaries with the gods." Sahil said.

"Wait, if they serve as the only intermediaries with the gods, and you don't have a system of government, doesn't that kind of make them dictators?" Alana asked. She was beginning to understand how the mind of a Thebe works.

"Ummmm," Sahil said, trying to decide how to answer.

"So, people around here worship the ground they walk on?" Ethan asked, sparing him the need to answer.

"Kind of?" Sahil replied. "In theory, all of Thebes reveres the elders and goes to them for counsel...in practice, it is a little more complicated." Sahil said.

"Complicated?" Alana prodded.

"I think you'll understand when we get there," Sahil said, trying to put an end to it.

What Sahil failed to explain was that Thebes was the most

advanced society on earth in the practice of selective hearing.

The Elders said a lot of things, and if they said something you agreed with, great awesome, that was the truth and it was something you'd be sure to tell all your friends when you met them, and try and convince them of your diligence and dedication to the elders.

If they said something you disagreed with, you wouldn't even hear it, your brain would totally filter it out and you'd be incapable of even knowing that they said something contrary to what you believe. In fact, you'd be convinced that they said something you agreed with.

There were plenty of cases where the elders, in conversation, would say something to the effect of, "it would be unwise to plant an orchard there," and the recipient would return home and describe how the elders referred to the wisdom of planting something that wasn't an orchard, and then bend over backwards to redefine what they were doing to not be an orchard ("it's really only sixty or so trees, and a real orchard is more like seventy plus") and then go ahead and do what they were planning on the whole time.

It didn't really function as a system of government, but there's not really evidence to suggest that the elders cared; there weren't really any systems of compliance built into the basis of government, just a few dudes in trees dispensing with advice.[23]

Sahil brought them to the center of Thebes: six ginormous trees planted in a full circle around a huge clearing. Alana looked up the trees several hundred feet to see tiny homes built around each of the trees and connected with rope bridges and tried to beat back a dizzying fear of heights.

Up they went. They ascended the typical litigation-friendly method of climbing in Thebes: small pegs tapped into the

---

[23] Which is the finest form of government on earth according to my Libertarian friends.

trunk, circling up, up, up, occasionally supplemented by the odd branch.

"What is the mortality rate here?" Alana asked as she slipped and clung for dear life onto the trunk with both hands, a few leaves disturbed by her feet falling forty feet below.

"Say what?" Sahil said, high above her.

"Never mind," she grunted as Ethan gave her a hand, avoiding imminent death, and up and away they went.

At the top Ethan escorted them into a small sitting room in the largest of the six dwellings. It would barely do to fit the nine of them, but all was well as the elders tended to speak quietly anyway.

After the three of them were seated, six ashen-faced elders entered the room solemnly. They dressed in long robes that trailed behind them, causing not one, but two to trip up on the extreme amount of clothing. They came in one by one, all with shoulder-length white hair wrapped up in hipster man-buns, each claiming at minimum one hundred and fifty years of life and near-constant communion with the gods, but I'd wager none of them were a day over sixty. None had beards, though a few had a day's worth of white whisker growth on their thin faces.

With great dramatic fanfare exhibited by each individual ancient one, they flared their arms about and slowly sat on the ground in a semicircle around their guests. Ethan was totally incapable of understanding their incomprehensible multisyllabic names, and since it doesn't really matter to you, we're going to stick with his convention and refer to them by number, one through six, left to right.

Elder one, throwing his arms up in the air and flicking his fingers about above his head, said, "Welcome to Madrera, center of Thebe and spiritual home."

Elder two followed with, "We are the Wise Six, direct descendants of Daphne, keepers of Madrera and overseers of the eternal tree."

303

"What wisdom do you seek?" said Elder three.

Sahil looked a little embarrassed as he coughed and said, "Oh, uh, great wise ones, these foreigners came into my care after escaping from violent captors."

At this point Elder six whipped out a very fully baked chicken from underneath his robe in a quick movement which he clearly thought was imperceptible to everyone else, but which caused such a stir that Sahil stopped and everyone looked at him. Elder six peered off into the trees through the windows for a moment, acting as though he did not notice everyone else staring, and as slowly as he could, brought up a leg of chicken to his lips and took a bite.

Sahil, eyeing Elder six with a raised eyebrow, continued, "After escaping from violent captors..."

Elder one interrupted, "But what has become of the captors? What number of people need we muster to repel them? How are they armed? How shall we go about feeding them and what manner of food shall we prepare when we have banded them together against such a threat?!" he raised his voice.

In the corner, Elder six started in on the breast. Chomp chomp, mouth open widely as he chewed, still looking outside as he moved the chicken up and down, still firmly believing that by moving the food up slowly nobody would notice him.

Sahil raised his voice over the chewing, "Their purposes have been thwarted, oh ancient one," he said, "and they are not to be found."

Elder four piped up at this point, in an almost incomprehensibly loud monotone, "SURELY TO BE PUNISHED BY THE GODS FOR THEIR INFRACTIONS LIKE ALL OTHER SINNERS BOUND FOR HADESSSSSSS," he said and bowed his head and continued to mumble a much quieter chant.

Sahil recoiled a bit in shock from having someone yell into his ears, but eventually replied, "most, uh, definitely, your honoredness."

Elder one became slightly agitated and said, "why do you spend our time here then if the threat is gone?" He shouted out the door to an absent assistant, "please inform the people they no longer need to band together against such a threat!"

Sahil looked over at Alana, silently pleading that someone else would start talking, but he kept going after she gave him the 'not my circus, not my monkeys' look. "You requested their presence yesterday, oh superannuated one," Sahil said.

Elder one threw out his hands in front of him in frustration, "BESIDES that, of course, why do you bring them here?" he said.

"I, uh, I" Sahil stuttered, and for a brief moment all they could hear was Elder six licking each one of his fingers individually and slowly throwing chicken bones out the window as surreptitiously as possible.

Ethan was enjoying this immensely, but he'd never met an awkward situation he didn't desperately want to be a part of, so he dove straight in. "Great Thebens," he said in his most deep melodic voice as Sahil threw his head back and sighed with relief as the focus shifted, "keepers of the uh...turning tree, uh the eternity trees and uh lovers of Daphne and commoners with the gods and all that, Alana and I are travelers from Atlas, and uh we left our homes looking for...for...uh answers as to deep secrets of the gods," he added a hint of vibrato to every one of his long syllables as best he could.

Elder four piped up again in his deliriously high monotone, "WELL WE THE WISE ONES WE HOLD ALL THE ANSWERS."

Elder six, slowly from underneath his robe, unveiled a four foot long loaf of bread which he brought out inch by inch, staring off into space, pretending like it didn't exist until his entire arm was swung out to the side at which point he eyed it out of the corner of his eye, then swept it back behind his back, and held it there with one hand, the other hand occasionally reaching behind his back to drag off another piece. Chomp chomp.

Elder two nodded his head solemnly and said, "True wisdom can never be given, only earned by those who are worthy to earn it through their own efforts and striving."

And Elder three chimed in to state, "and only we can give you true wisdom as the wise ones."

Elder five had been nodding his head the entire time, going deeper and deeper with every bow. He was seated directly opposite Alana, and she just figured it was some kind of deep cleaning religious ritual. At this point his nodding stopped, his head hung low, and from within his cavernous chest arose a chortling snore. The other elders totally ignored him.

Elder one tried to get back on track by asserting his leadership and said, "We have seen many foreigners and sent them great visions of understanding for their quests."[24]

Elder four agreed, "And they have acknowledged how we have given them such great wisdom. Even great scientists have come to us and later told us how we helped them understand the laws of nature through our communion with the gods and with nature, as special keepers of the eternal tree."[25]

Ethan was having the time of his life. "We sought a great power of the gods, a great power that has been lost," he said.

Elder one quickly replied, "Great power can never be given, only earned by those who are worthy to earn it through their own efforts and striving."

"And only we can give you true power as the wise ones,"

---

[24] There is no record of any other foreigner ever speaking to this man.

[25] There is no record of any scientist ever speaking to this man. There was once a sham scientist from Thebe who claimed to understand how to manufacture gold from tree roots, and it's generally believed that's who Elder four was referring to at this point.

Elder two reaffirmed.

Ethan asked, "And pray tell great masters, how can we acquire this great power? For we sought the Silver Cross."

Elder six finished his bread at this point, and next brought out a bowl of soup. Alana looked at him in shock. "How much more do you have down there?" she whispered in disgust, but Elder six ignored her, and the rest didn't hear her over the snores of Elder five.

Elder two replied to Ethan, "You must earn it through your efforts."

And Elder one agreed, "We can give you the secrets to great power."

Ethan looked back and forth at both of them, and said, "and what might be the way to obtain it?" he said.

Elder two looked at him in annoyance, "through your efforts," he said.

"We once gave great power," Elder three said, "to a visitor who came seeking a way to help his orchard grow, and we gave him great power through giving him great power. The strongest among our people have marveled at the great power we have given."[26]

Elder five began snoring so loudly the leaves growing on the roof of the dwelling began shaking. Elder six stood up at this point and walked out without saying a word. He left the soup bowl behind, and stepped over everyone awkwardly, his robe getting pulled over Sahil's head as he walked out.

Ethan decided to further mess with them. "I see, oh geriatric ones," he said, "for we have observed great power on our quest. I witnessed Hephaestus move a mountain," he said.

Elder one looked at him in shock, "Blasphemy," he said.

Ethan continued, "and I watched an immortal slay the

---

[26] This claim is obviously harder for me to refute, so I'll let it stand due to lack of data, not my belief in it of course. "Marveled" is such a slippery word, it can mean so much.

Sphinx," he said matter-of-factly.

"Impossible!" cried Elder two.

"And," he said with the coup-de-grace, "she," he said pointing to Alana, "she entered Hades as a mortal."

"IT CANNOT BE," shouted our favorite monotone, Elder four.

Elder six came back in extremely slowly. In both hands he balanced two enormous cakes, topped with strawberries which tumbled out and spilled on everyone as he picked his way carefully through the crowd of people. Again, when he sat down he played invisible, slowly staring out the window, and without looking, brought up chunk after chunk to his mouth with his left hand. Chomp chomp.

Elder five snored on.

Alana had had enough. She stood up and made her way out, "that was a dream you imposter, and you have no right to share it," she said.

Ethan looked up, "but it's the truth!" he insisted.

"Ethan, you sweet little child," she said angrily, "how little you know. I had a bad dream. People have bad dreams all the time. And the Sphinx? That was a snow leopard. You've never seen one, I know, and they are so scary wary for wittle boys, but it's no sphinx," she said.

"What are you talking about?" Ethan said, "it spoke to us."

"In your wildest imagination, sure." Alana said. "But not in reality, no. And we've been through the rest," she said as she ripped him apart. "There was no Persephone, there was no Poseidon. Give it a rest. Stop trying to impart divine meaning to every moment of our life together. Stop looking for something that isn't there. There's no meaning to any of this. To me, to you, to these comical fools," she said motioning at the elders, "to any of it. Get it? Nothing. No meaning. No meaning to any of this. Just some people fumbling around an incomprehensible universe!" she yelled.

She walked out of the room and then turned back as her

anger bubbled over just the slightest bit more. "You are nothing," she shouted. "I am nothing. We are nothing. There is nothing." And she was off.

Elder six had stopped eating (finally) and sat with his frosting-covered mouth agape. The others looked out with wide eyes as she left, then back at Ethan and Sahil, then back out at her.

Elder one was the first to speak, "Well she is definitely not earning power through her efforts!" he puffed.

Elder two stood up and brushed strawberries off his robes, "Indeed she is not!" he said.

"I CONCUR WITH THE ELDERS," loudly monotoned Elder four.

The awake elders stood and left one by one, with Elder six mumbling something to himself about where he could find lunch. Sahil and Ethan were left with Elder five, who was calmly dozing as his snoring lightened.

Ethan's face was burning bright red from Alana's invective, but he leaned over and touched the old man, waking him. "Great one," he said humbly, "your friends have left, I think we're done here."

Elder five looked up and gave them both a huge smile, the bottomless well of love inside him reaching into their souls to lift them both up. He looked at Sahil and spoke warmly, "Why don't you help this young man back home," he said to Sahil. "He could use a friend."

And with that he stood up and left as well.

Sahil clasped his hand on Ethan's shoulder. "Okay," he said, "let's get you home."

CHAPTER 23

Thanks to a favorable current, they reached Ariens even before Tiberius expected.

"Finally, something goes my way," he complained.

The city itself lay in ruins before them. Immediately behind the city the eastern cliffs beyond lit up and glowed in the beautiful deep red sunset.

"No wonder they called it The Jewel of the West," Alexander said under his breath.

Lit up by the setting sun, ruined sandstone buildings radiated with a deep luminescent orange. Before its fall, deep sandstone buildings lined neatly planned streets spotted with beautiful gardens, tidy squares, and miles of well-kept farmland stretching out to the south beyond thick battlements covered in bright flags waving every success of the kingdom far and wide. But today the farms were ruined. Salt had been plowed deep into every inch of fertile ground by a vindictive enemy, and what topsoil that hadn't been blown away sat in salt-stained clumps. Everywhere in the city sandstone blocks lay crushed in the streets. The trained eye could still sort of make out and describe each individual building, but they were sad remnants of a glorious past, their roofs missing, walls crumbling, and moss and ivy crawling up their surfaces.

In other words, it was the perfect picture of despair.

They rowed into the ruined harbor and quickly unloaded and made their way through the city to the far cliffs. They walked through the brick streets, trying hard to move fast, but also astounded by the beauty of a once-great city.

"Grandpa," Tiberius muttered under his breath as he surveyed the ruins and destruction, "how did you do this?"

The four great cardinal cathedrals stood as skeletons, their once-renowned stained-glass windows shattered, and roof beams blackened from the fires lay rotting in the open air. The streets were overgrown with long grass, and sand lay covering every surface touched by the wind. The city was slowly retreating back into the earth, eroding away more and more every year. The grand palace stood in the center of the city, totally unrecognizable for what it once was except the great center court visible from afar, large blocks strewn about haphazardly.

In one corner, at the base of an empty, dark, burned away hollow lay the only recognizably tended place in the entire city. Flowers from every corner of the continent grew in neat rows surrounding a small pile of white stones. From among them rose a plain headstone.

"What does it say?" Tiberius asked Alexander.

Alexander directed one of the men to run over and check, and he called back:

"It just says Eva!"

"Strange," Tiberius replied, "it looks like it's been tended to, but nobody has lived here for years..." He looked twice, but then they continued on to the east.

The main road lay south through the city walls, but there were a few small paths through the defenseless eastern plains. There were no defenses on this approach because none were needed: the large cliffs formed a crescent moon around the north and east sides of Ariens, preventing any direct assault in strength. Large waterfalls cascaded off the northern edges into the valley below, made larger from the spring runoff of the mountains in the distance. At first glance it appeared impregnable to any outsider.

There was, however, a way through it.

Over the ages, small cuts were chiseled in the sheer cliffside to form hand or footholds. They were irregularly shaped and meandered in dizzying puzzles for anyone attempting to climb. Make the wrong move and you'd end up in impossible positions on an exposed cliffside.

"Should we wait until morning?" Alexander asked Tiberius. "This seems perilous to climb in the dark."

"Didn't stop my grandpa, not going to stop us," Tiberius said, and he started climbing.

"We could go around south!" Alexander called. "It wouldn't take long!"

"Any delay is a delay too long!" Tiberius shouted down.

Everyone knew how this would end, but they were all stuck waiting for Tiberius to reach the inevitable conclusion.

"Hey," they all heard a few minutes later shouted down, "can you see where the next position is?" Tiberius called.

"It's too dark!" Alexander called back.

"Are you blind?" Tiberius shouted down, "the sun barely set!"

"You're at least fifty feet up," Alexander called, "we can't see a thing that far away."

"I'm surrounded by morons," Tiberius spoke as he tried to figure out how to contort himself to make it to another hold at least ten feet away.

"I said we can't see but we can hear!" Alexander called back.

"I'm glad!" Tiberius shouted.

Thirty minutes later Tiberius came down off the wall in a foul mood. "Stop sleeping, you lazy drunks," he said, "if you were all half competent, we'd have been able to take the shortcut, but instead we'll night march around the long way,"

"We expected nothing less," Alexander replied, and grumbling quietly, the men stood up and followed Tiberius to the south.

Zara made her way up the next hill on her way west. The great western road stretched out into the distance as the sun went down. After escaping the wreck of The Argo she meandered here and there, trading what she had scrounged for a horse and some supplies. Uncertain at first what to do with her newfound freedom, she eventually decided to head west. She couldn't see the end from the beginning, but she did think that taking the silver cross to the last place she knew it was used might give her some insight.

Surveying the darkening landscape ahead she saw dozens upon dozens of fires being lit to the northwest.

"What is going on here?" she muttered. "The world must be turning upside down. There hasn't been a group this large out here since dad was here."

And to the southwest she saw one tiny light flickering on the moors.

"Rest!" Tiberius commanded. The marines collapsed from exhaustion, panting as they lay on the ground. Tiberius bent over and rest his hands on his knees and heaved huge breaths trying to recover. What a day!

Alexander rolled over on the ground and looked up at Tiberius. "How much more of this can we take?" he moaned. "Please just kill me now."

The rest of the marines moaned in compliance.

"Oh, come on men," Tiberius stopped to breathe, "what's wrong with," pant, pant, "a compulsory 24-hour march?" He sat down and put his head between his knees before he dry-heaved the nothingness in his stomach. "It sounds like you're," deep breaths, "getting soft."

They were making such great time down the great western road! In between his heavy breathing, Tiberius was elated. They had covered way more ground than he thought possible, and they had a chance of getting Alana before she made it back to Atlas.

"All we gotta do now," Tiberius said, breathing a little shallower and less desperate and gesturing wildly to the east, "is keep on heading east on this road and cut them off."

"So you're saying the only thing that stops us from success is total, constant, abject misery?" Alexander asked.

"Exactly," Tiberius replied between pants, "total, constant, abject misery," issuing one of his extremely rare smiles. Misery always made him smile. It was his oldest friend.

"Nothing to it," Alexander said.

The sun sank deep below the ocean far in the west, and the marines broke out the last bit of food they had scavenged.

"Wait, what's that?" one of the men said. He pointed off to the northeast.

Tiberius squinted in the fading light and almost jumped. "Sal-freaking-vation, my friends. Salvation."

Tiberius stood up and gesticulated wildly to the north. "The Carpathians!" he shouted in glee. "The Carpathians! They're actually on schedule! They're on the move! This hasn't happened in generations! I can't believe they actually did something right!"

Tiberius went around grasping the hands of each one of his men and helping them up.

"One last sprint, men, and when we catch up with them we'll have horses and food and water and all of the best hospitality our savage allies have at their disposal. We're saved! Let's give it one last run on the home stretch, and we'll never have to run again!" he demanded with exuberance.

It was hard to say no to someone with so much joy, though that was probably the case because there was a promise of food at the end of the misery. So off they ran into the night, abandoning the road they worked so hard to reach in order to link up with their fellow bringers of death.

Alana was in no mood to speak to anyone that night, but Ethan couldn't resist. When they made their camp on the moors at the edge of the forest he spoke up.

"What is your problem?!" Ethan finally said. "We were guests up there you crazy person. How do you yell at a bunch of old dudes? Sahil risked his live saving us, we were guests of honor, and you just rip that all up so you can get mad? Get a grip princess!"

"And worse," Sahil jumped in, sensing his opportunity, "you destroyed my chance of getting them to give me some advice on how to snag a mate. Serious party foul girl, serious party foul," he said.

Alana stewed for a moment, then replied, "Your wise men are a bunch of wise a..."

"Wise AND wonderful men!" Ethan cut her off and chimed in. "A bunch of wise AND wonderful men, I was telling Alana this myself he said to Sahil. We are ever so grateful that you brought us to them! Thank you, thank you for giving us that shot," he said as he shot Alana a dirty look, "and also saving us from getting shot."

Alana rolled her eyes. "Okay, okay, you're right. Thank you Sahil. Thank you for trying to help us," she offered begrudgingly. "I'm sorry that I ruined your moment to ask them on strategies for landing a woman," she said.

Sahil crinkled his nose and looked at her in confusion. "Who said anything about women?"

Alana ignored him. "I'm sorry, you're right. I'm sorry. I won't do it again."

Sahil, with greater confusion, looked at her. "Who said anything about again?"

The next morning a deep fog had gloomily settled in over the moors.

"Ah well this is familiar," Ethan said with faux cheer. "I'm looking forward to another day of shapeless horrors trying to kill me."

"I got news for you kid," Sahil said, "the horrors that are going to kill us are very shapely," and he eyed Alana.

"We should make Cairn Loire by afternoon," Alana said. "At least, if we can see it in this fog. Let's try to make the road and then get the heck out of this misery. I've got a totally destroyed life to get back to. Those shards of my dreams aren't going to sweep themselves up on their own," she said, and they were off.

"Tell me, Sahil," Ethan said as they began what they believed to be their last day's journey together, "what's it like to farm trees?" he asked.

"Well," Sahil stumbled for words, "it was always my fondest tree...m," he said, glancing at Alana.

"Very funny," she said.

"Excuse me, my fondest dream." Sahil said. "Here's what it's like," he said in a hushed excited voice. "You wake up. You look around. You make meticulous plans on how exactly you are going to plan out the next section of forest. What trees should go where. How to plan the roads. Everything needs to be just right, because you only get one shot, and then you live with those decisions for all time. No pressure. So, you just painstakingly plan this to the minute detail. And then..."

He let his words hang in the air with excitement. "You eat breakfast and spend the rest of the day watching the leaves grow."

Ethan laughed. "Well that sounds just utterly riveting."

"Let me tell you," Sahil said. "You don't know what excitement is until you've spent a week watching bark."

"Someone has to do it, I guess?" Ethan said.

"Do they?" Alana asked. "Can't you just say hey we're

good? Done with the whole tree thing? Let's just be cool with stuff for now, and let's build something else."

"And give up our entire way of life?" Sahil said in mock horror. "Okay, fine, what else do you have for us?" he asked.

"You could..." Alana thought, "travel the world?"

"Done that," Sahil said.

"Wait what?" Alana asked.

"Next suggestion," Sahil said curtly.

"You could..." Alana thought and thought.

"This is my point," Sahil said. "What else is there? We are descendants of Daphne, naiad of Olympus. That lustful terror Apollo pursued after her, wishing to force himself upon her, and she resisted and fled. They ran from the top of Olympus to the last edge of the world, where the earth meets the sea. There she stopped on the edge of the world, gazing out into Scilia in the distance, unable to move further for the ocean in the way.

"Up Apollo came in his lusting fury, and Daphne stepped into the waters and she was there transformed into a Laurel tree, saved at the last moment from her terror. And from her our first parents were born; we planted the six trees surrounding Daphne, the same six you stood in yesterday with our Elders. Daphne has long since passed out of this earth and into the beyond, but her shadow remains on that spot, where we place a crown of laurel leaves in her honor and remembrance."

"That's beautiful," Alana said.

"So, you have built out a land around her to dwell yourselves in her presence?" Ethan asked.

"We plant for food, for space, for shade, for shelter, all of the above," Sahil replied, "but primarily we plant so that if Daphne ever need run again, if her place on Olympus is made unsafe and she is forced to escape the terrors of the others, she will always have a safe space among us. She will have a great forest of family to hide her, and one day, the distant Scilia will not mock her as unreachable when she stands helpless on the shores," Sahil said.

And after a pause to let that sink in, Sahil continued, "What else would you have us do?" Sahil asked Alana. "We already do that which is most important to us."

And through the fog they saw a figure on horseback approach.

CHAPTER 24

Riders approached his group at breakneck pace in the early dawn. These were no trained soldiers, they were mere marauders who had been summoned and grouped together for the first time in an age, but they rode with rifles at the ready to kill the group of foreigners trespassing in their lands.

The riders rode circling them, marveling at their disheveled quarry. What could these people be?

"Who are you, and what is your business here?" the lead rider shouted as they came to a stop and leveled their rifles at the men.

"You are welcome allies indeed," Tiberius called out, panting heavily and again trying to catch his breath. The rest of his men stood exhausted, ready to drop if touched by a feather. They were dead men walking at the end of this death march.

"I'm Tiberius, Master Sergeant in the 15th Marines, Medea."

"Tiberius, eh?" the lead spat. "You're a long way from home," he said. "What brings you here?"

"Still chasing those Atlassians you bumped into," he

replied.

"Chasing them? Still? You folks know how to ride a horse right? It'd save you a load of trouble. You might even be able to speak when you find them," the lead said, to the laughter of the rest of the riders.

Tiberius ignored him. "Can you lead us to Vercingetorix?" he said.

"I mean I lead you there, but I doubt you'll be able to make it there yourselves," he said, again to uproarious laughter.

In another life, Tiberius would've had his rifle on the man's throat at this point, but he was tired after all, and realistically he had no way of threatening mounted cavalry while at a point of total exhaustion. Also, he was pretty sure they would kill him and his group to a man if he misbehaved in the slightest. So, he was forced to stay calm.

"Just me," he said. "The rest can wait for assistance. But please, any food you have; we haven't eaten a full meal in two days,"

"Right-o, pedestrians," the lead called. "You, off your horse," he called to a rider, and they gave the horse to Tiberius. "Follow me," he said. "The rest of you take care of this motley crew," and with that he rode off, Tiberius close behind.

"Answer me this riddle," the woman on horseback said. "What does a Theben, a westerner, and an Atlassian do crossing the moors in the morning?" She laughed, looking down at them. "And unarmed as well! You must have nothing to lose."

Alana looked up at the woman and saw something she had never observed before: a face filled with love. She bowed and replied, "Indeed, we lost almost all we carried, but escaped with our lives. We are headed home from a great quest."

"Great quests leave you with great treasures do they not?" the woman said, "otherwise they are great follies."

"No, we acquired great treasure, but it was in knowledge," Alana replied. "So, while the quest was undertaken in folly, it was fulfilled in triumph."

"So, you return empty handed?" the woman said.

"So, we return empty handed, but better equipped," Alana replied.

"Can I offer you anything on your return?" the woman asked.

"We appreciate the kind offer, but would never take away from someone as wise as yourself," Alana said, then, glancing at the woman's saddlebag, she continued, "though I would be much obliged to know by what power your saddlebag glows with such light."

The woman's eyes widened.

Ethan muttered quietly, but not too quietly, "What are you talking about?"

Alana didn't reply. In the fog they heard horses approaching from behind them on the road. "Run!" she yelled, and the three of them scattered as the woman on the horse stayed put, confused, and seconds later horses had surrounded all four of them, and riders were prodding Alana, Ethan, and Sahil back to the road at gunpoint.

"I'm sorry," Alana said to the woman, "I'm sorry you're getting the thick of it."

The woman had no time to reply before she heard a familiar voice shout out.

"That's them! That's them!" Tiberius came riding into view. And as quick as he appeared, he stopped dead in his tracks. "Mother?!" he said, looking at the woman.

"Mother!?" Alana said in shock.

"Tiberius!" Zara replied with unbridled joy. "I have such great news!" she called.

"Thanks!" Tiberius said, "and hold on." He put up a hand and directed his attention back to Alana.

"You will never be able to escape me, usurper!" he shouted

way too loudly given the distance between them. "Tie them up!" he yelled at the riders, pointing at Alana, Ethan, and Sahil. A couple of riders reluctantly jumped off their horses and tied their hands behind their backs.

Tiberius hopped off his horse and walked up to Alana. "You thought you were so impressive, you thought you were just the most amazing queen escaping like you did," he shouted in her face. He pushed her to her knees, stepped back, and kicked her in the face. "That's for Delphi!" he screamed in rage.

Alana fell backwards on the ground without even as much as a whimper. She struggled to raise herself with her hands tied. As everyone watched in silence, she sat up, then worked her knees around, and planted her face in the dirt, then pulled herself back up to kneeling. They all saw the grit in her face. It was covered in dirt, and her nose bled into it mixing into an unholy concoction. But she kept determined eye contact on Tiberius as she rose back to standing, saying nothing the whole time.

Tiberius sneered. "It's just like Scipio said, you think you are so tough, but you are nothing but a usurper," he said. He pointed at his mother. "My mother was hunted by agents of Atlas for years!" he said, practically shaking with rage, "She spent her entire life running and hiding, and you people just took her throne and tried to kill her for it."

He spat on Alana and punched her in the gut.

Alana doubled over in pain, again saying nothing, but she raised her blood-strewn face to look directly at Zara. "I'm sorry," she said to Zara calmly and deeply. "I had no idea. They tried to kill me too."

Zara put both hands over her mouth and said nothing.

"Let's get them back to camp," Tiberius said. Riders picked them up and put them over the saddles and rode off roughly with them.

Tiberius calmed and spoke with a bright voice as he

directed himself at Zara once again. "Now tell me mother, what was the great news?"

Zara could barely speak through the shock, but she managed to squeak out a response, "The hummingbirds," she said, "they came back."

Tiberius shook his head. "That's great mom," he said, "now what in the world are you doing out here?"

Zara looked at him and said, "I could ask you the same question."

The riders carried them flopped over their horses like saddlebags into camp, then they were marched through the various encampments to the center. Their hands remained tied behind their backs, and they tripped and tumbled a few times on the uneven ground, but eventually made it to a large tent with several angry-looking soldiers standing around it.

"I think we've made it to the inner sanctum," Ethan whispered.

"What shall we do now we've gained their trust?" Sahil replied.

"Shut up," Alana whispered.

A rider kicked at their knees from behind, and all three of them knelt on the grassy plain.

A large bearded man emerged from the tent and looked down at the three of them.

"You're awfully small for causing me so much trouble," he said.

"And you're awfully big for being so small a man," Alana replied coolly.

Vercingetorix laughed. "I like her!" he shouted at his men standing by. "She is not afraid like the rest of them," he said, "no wonder Tiberius is afraid of her."

Vercingetorix walked slowly over to Alana and got down on his haunches to look her in the eyes. He reached out a dirty hand and placed it on her cheek tenderly.

"If you were mine," Vercingetorix said, "I would kill you right here where you kneel," he slowly stroked her cheek and chin, "you would already be dead."

"Then do it already," Alana said, "or are you afraid like Tiberius?"

Vercingetorix laughed again and stood up. "But you are not mine, my precious!" he said. "You are Scipio's, and he and I have a deal, so you go to him." He walked back into his tent, but turned before he went in. "I like her," he said jovially. "Let her eat."

Zara sat down at the fire with Tiberius and his men, eating what food they managed to beg off of their allies, and relaxing as best she could after the shock of today.

She looked at her son, jovially chatting with his men, and she saw all the parts of the boy she loved—his passion, his intensity, his love of order and precision.

But also, as she watched, she saw other traits, other things that she had never seen before. How his passion was unbridled. How his intensity led him to sharpness. How his love of order and precision led him to an unyielding temperament, where everything must be done in the way he demanded, or else there was hell to pay.

She smiled as she saw him for the first time in two years, and tiny tears streamed down her cheeks.

In the darkness Tiberius could only see the smile.

And Zara looking back could only see the cruelty.

Zara noticed a leather pouch in his things on the ground, and she picked it up to note with surprise the emblem of the silver cross. She carefully pulled the silver cross out of her bag and slipped it into the leather pouch. She held it close to her heart.

She looked at Tiberius, her tiny boy turned into a man, and saw how he had become warped and misguided. She looked down at the cross.

"I know what this will do to him," she whispered.

She thought of taking her seat as a mighty queen of Atlas. Wielding the silver cross, ruling over nations, dominating the world.

And she could. She could see herself doing all of those things. But she looked at her son and saw what that would do to him. To her child. She realized what that would do to Atlas.

Zara cried bitter tears that night, the love she had for her son.

"He meant we ALL could eat, not just Alana!" Ethan complained as they were marched to the outskirts of camp in the dark.

Alana smacked her lips loudly. "I'm sorry man," she said, "he only said me!"

Ethan grumbled. "There was plenty of food there, haven't any of you heard of a last meal?" he said.

"Shut up you idiot," Sahil grumbled this time. "Don't give them any ideas!"

Ethan looked at him with wide eyes. "Ohhhh yeeaaahhh," he said, remembering how Vercingetorix went to great lengths to specifically only clearly state that Alana and Alana alone was to be protected and go to Scipio, "riiiight."

They walked by a small encampment with only a single man sitting at a fire. The man briefly looked up at them as they passed, his eyes barely visible under his dark hooded robe.

"Wait," Ethan whispered to Alana, "that wasn't..."

"Shut up!" Alana shout-whispered back at him, then smiled.

And then she nodded.

It was.

The three of them were bound with their ropes staked into the ground to prevent them from escaping during the night.

Ethan's teeth chattered as the temperature dropped. He

was tired, cold, hungry, and could not remember a more miserable time in his life.

"Can you sleep?" he whispered to Sahil.

"No," Sahil replied, "I think I probably slept too much last night you know, I'm just all rested up over here."

Alana let out a loud fake snore just to bug Ethan.

"Oh, shut up," Ethan said, eyeing the tent with their captors just a few feet away. "I don't need them to have any excuse to hurt me."

They were all quiet for a few minutes, staring at the vast expanse of stars overhead to the soundtrack of the chattering of Ethan's teeth.

They heard a quiet rustle behind them.

"Now I want all of you to shut up, especially you Ethan," Etienne whispered quietly. "If you can, of course."

Alana's smile gleamed in the starlight as she mouthed, "Thank the gods you're here."

Watching the tent like a hawk, Etienne quietly cut their ropes, then silently retreated away from the camp, motioning for them to follow.

The three of them tip-toed away from their cut bonds and followed him. He walked by another few tents and then down a small rise away from the main camp to where he had set up his own tent. Alana recognized his two horses and went over to nuzzle for a moment before following the rest where they had gathered huddled low behind a rock.

"What took you so l-l-l-long?" Ethan said, chattering.

"I had to wait until I was sure everyone was asleep," Etienne said, "and then I observed the night watches on the perimeter, trying to figure how I was going to get you all out of here."

"Thank you, Etienne, you are such a welcome sight," Alana reached over and held his shoulder. "Thank you," she said again.

"Don't mention it," Etienne said, "besides, this is no way

to treat a princess, especially my princess."

"Thanks," she smiled. "Now what's the plan?" Alana asked.

"Always business with you Alana," Etienne said. "I've kept my eye on one of the night watches over that way," he pointed east along the line of the hill, "and if I'm not mistaken, we should be good to go in half an hour, maybe less."

At that moment they heard a rustling at the top of the hill, and the four of them froze.

"Who could that be?" Etienne whispered in confusion, then pulled his rifle around from where it hung on his back. He knelt and aimed it up the hill at a dark figure approaching.

"Hold on," Alana said, putting her hand on the barrel. "I think I know her."

"Her?" Etienne asked.

The woman approached the group, shaking from the adrenaline.

"Zara," Alana said with a smile.

"Leo's Zara??" Etienne asked.

"Yes," Zara whispered as she strolled up calmly to the group and knelt down next to Alana. "How does everyone know me?"

"It's a long story," Etienne said.

Zara shrugged and looked at Alana. "I saw you leave," Zara said, "I waited until I was sure it was safe, but I had to come to you."

"Zara, I am so sorry for everything, but please, this is not safe, you must leave. I don't want any part of hurting you again," Alana said.

"No, this was never about you," Zara said, "and I'm the one who's sorry. I have had to face some very hard truths today, but none of them are about you." She reached into her shirt and pulled out the case that hung on a leather strap around her neck. She unbuttoned it and pulled out the silver cross.

"Well I'll be," Etienne gasped, and backed away quickly

with wide eyes.

Alana was speechless as Zara showed her the silver cross, put it back in the leather case, and held it out to her.

"This tool is not for me," she said, "it belongs to you."

"But-but-but," Alana stuttered, "it is yours!" she said. "The crown too!" She gestured to the east, "come with us, and I will see you restored! The throne will be yours; we will see to it the wrongs are righted."

Zara shook her head. "No Alana," she said as she picked some wildflowers and wove them together. "I once dreamt of taking up the cross and following my father on some great foreign quest." She layered in more wildflowers, "and in another life I will, in another life I will lead nations to war. But in this life, I choose to seek peace for me and my family."

Alana knelt speechless next to Zara as she watched her slowly construct a beautiful crown of the wildflowers that surrounded them.

Zara held the crown of wildflowers up in starlight and held Alana's hand. "They crowned my father in the battlefield," she said to Alana, "with a makeshift crown of laurels. He too was hunted and attacked by those who wanted to deprive him of his right to lead; in his case it was a large rebellion. In their darkest moments when they felt that the rebellions would overcome them, Leo's brother crowned him with laurels in the nighttime and proclaimed him king of the five nations.

"Dad always said that was the moment that defined his life. The small ceremony in the southern hills with just a few loyal followers. It gave him the courage to rise and assume the role that was always there for him, prepared for him.

"And so I realize this doesn't have the grandeur that you probably expected to see someday outside the palace on capitol hill, but as my uncle crowned my father the true king, and gave him the courage to lead the nation, I hope that I can do the same for you."

Zara stood up next to Alana.

"Alana, daughter of Titus II, the assumed and phony ruler of Atlas," she said, winking to Alana, "with the power inherited by me, and as the once heir, I crown you queen of Atlas," she said, and placed the crown of wildflowers on Alana's head.

"I charge you with this burden: protect the nation. Honor the gods. Make war on our enemies," Zara said, and draped the silver cross around her neck. "Take this. You will need it to lead Atlas out of the dark place it has fallen into. You must return and destroy the evil that rose with your father."

Alana teared up and nodded her head. "I will," she said. "It ends with me."

Zara nodded. "Do this for me," she said, looking back up to the camp, "as I find that I am no longer able to, not if I want to salvage anything of my child who has been so terribly poisoned." Zara hugged Alana and whispered, "You must make the war, and I will find a way to make the peace."

Etienne whispered, "I hate to interrupt, but it looks like we're about ready to go!"

Zara pulled back. "Go," she said. "I will wait here until you are long gone so I cannot disturb anyone." She looked at Ethan, "oh, and your grandma says, 'come'."

"What??!" Ethan replied. "How do you..."

"Shut up," Etienne said, "we gotta go," and taking care to give the silver cross a wide berth, "let's get," he said.

"Thank you," Alana said as the others led the horses away. "I don't know what to say."

Zara smiled. "Just do your best," Zara said. "It will be more than enough."

Alana nodded and left. "I so swear." She said into the night. "Atlas will be restored."

CHAPTER 25

The four of them hustled through the tall grass at the edge of the camp, looking out for the night watches as best they could.

Etienne stopped and looked left, then right and listened hard in the dark. "This is the far line," he said, "we should be clear once we're beyond this."

He tapped Alana on the shoulder and pointed down the slope of the hill they were on. About two hundred yards away a watchman stood looking the other direction to the north.

"Time to move," he said, and they were immediately off and beyond the lines.

But behind them they heard a shout.

Ethan was the first to make out the words. It was far away at this point, but in the still of the night voices carry for a long way.

"They're gone!" he heard the call. "They're gone!"

Etienne cursed. "It was a one in a million shot for sure kids," he said.

Alana tugged at him, "Let's go, let's go," she said, "get a move on!"

"There's no chance," Etienne said, "we needed a few hours at least, but now..." he trailed off, "now there's only one way."

Etienne pulled all his bags off his horses and pointed at the three. "Get on, now," he said. Ethan and Sahil wasted no time mounting up.

Alana hesitated.

Etienne tossed a pistol at her. "Take this for emergencies," he shouted.

"Just come with us!" Alana said as she caught it.

"Get out of here!" Etienne yelled, "we don't stand a chance, somebody needs to give you the time, and time is all I have. If you don't go now, we're all dead."

Alana nodded. "Thank you," she said, and hopped up on Ethan's horse in front of him. "I'll be guiding now, thank you very much," she said, taking the reins.

I'll buy you the time!" Etienne yelled, then pointing at Ethan's chest, "you only need a minute," he said. "I know you can do it. Now fly!"

They were off in an instant, at a hard gallop just as the crescent moon rose in front of them.

Etienne looked at his gear on the ground. "Time to sing my friends," he said. "Time to sing."

"An eternity of time and now this," he muttered to himself. He didn't have much time, but he had to make every second count, and getting some armor on might help delay them just a little. He pulled out the remnants of his old uniform and threw off his giant black cloak for the final time. He placed his bright silver helmet on his head, fluffing the feathers that adorned the top. He tightened on his silver breastplate with his dark weathered leather straps and strapped his sword to his side. He was a cavalry officer of the old order: an age when cavalry stood for nobility, gallantry, and bravery.

We'd consider their uniforms highly unsuitable for

survival in any sort of modern battle, but that wasn't the point. He was the conscience of the entire army, the embodiment of hope that failed in men when the cannons fired their deep muzzling sounds and the shells whistled overhead. When the forces of the deepest blackest pit were unleashed on men like hail to a flower, and every heart froze in its chest and feet turned to run, there would be one man who refused the tempting embrace of fear. One man who could face down death with bright plumes of feathers and no thought for death.

He could strike fear into the hearts of his enemies as he rode across the battlefield like a falling star, his shining armor glinting in the sun and the plumes from his helmet flying behind him. He was the last cavalry officer of the old order, an order that didn't care for camouflage or self-preservation. It was an order that would recklessly charge booming fixed batteries on incorrect orders and refuse to ever acknowledge it had been a mistake. For him, the mere act of being in battle was enough. He was the actual living embodiment of the old glory.

"Consider this my atonement," Etienne said. He saluted Alana and the others as they faded out of sight, and then turned around to the west to face his doom.

To his everlasting frustration, he did not have a horse to mount for his final charge, and so he set about finding the best ground to harass the forces that were being marshaled.

"They're gone!" someone screamed in camp. "They're gone!" he shouted again.

Tiberius practically jumped out of his makeshift bed and looked around to see dozens of Carpathians doing the same.

"I want her alive!" he yelled out, "she's no good to us dead!" he shouted at the forces hastily mustering. "Medea wants her!"

Vercingetorix popped out of a nearby tent and looked at him with complete and total disgust. "You call yourself warriors," he said slowly, "and you say that you will rule the world, but how can a nation be afraid of a woman?"

Tiberius shook his head. "You don't know who she is," he said. "It is so much easier if we keep her." He raced off to the sounds of shooting.

Vercingetorix didn't bother shouting after him, but he said it for the benefit of any present. "It's easier if she's dead. It's easier if they're all dead."

Etienne lay down on the ground and picked off a few of them at long range. The riders fell to the ground in the darkness and forced the others to stop and regroup before they attacked. Nobody wanted to die on to capture a prisoner alive.

"Good job," Etienne whispered, "we've got to make every second count," he patted his rifle. "Every second."

He saw them debating and holding back.

"That's right," he said, "start discussing this at length. Take as much possible time as you can making your decision."

Raised voices from an argument wafted through the cold night air and Etienne laughed. "You children," he said, "nobody knows how to fight a war anymore."

He saw them split up into a few groups to encircle him. He didn't care, as long as it took as much time as possible.

Moving from position to position to cause maximum confusion, he fired off shots at each group as they approached, wounding a few more, delaying always delaying the inevitable. He couldn't lose track of the clock. They must be delayed.

Tiberius' horse was shot, and he tumbled to the ground and cursed. "How did they get weapons?" he grumbled. His hosts must be more careless than he thought. He picked up his rifle and crouched down and slowly advanced towards the firing.

Deep in his chest he could feel there was something not quite right.

Etienne shot through the darkness, bringing them to a standstill. He could shoot you dead from a horse at full gallop, and given that, shooting his targets from lying prone on the ground was cake. He fired and fired, repositioned, fired and fired.

Until he ran out of ammunition for his rifle.

"Well," he said, "time to start the fireworks," and he stood up and hefted his mechanical gun.

"I see one!" Tiberius said as he watched Etienne stand up. He dropped to his stomach to take a shot.

Etienne fired the mechanical gun wildly into the dark, aiming roughly where he thought the riders were coming from. The barrels swung around in a hot circle, blasting red spurts of anger wherever he pointed.

He grunted as he swung the gun and tried to keep it roughly on course. It was a herculean task, but one he could do for a few moments, for a few moments was all he needed. He only had a minute of ammunition left.

But that didn't matter because the bullet got him first.

The firing stopped as the man went down.

Tiberius cackled, stood up and ran towards him, yelling to the others.

The rest of them, teeming with anger, raced towards the fallen man to try and find the others.

But he wasn't done yet.

Etienne stood up, and lifted his last and best weapon, his old friend of so many years, his broken sword. The runes glowed red hot and could be seen glowing in the night, tracing fiery lines as he swung his strokes.

To never know defeat
To never taste death

Etienne charged.

He was shot once, twice, three times. He reached one of the riders and made short work of him, then attacked another. For a short-lived second time stopped. The ghosts of the cavalry of old lined up along the path and saluted him with their swords. A frantic desperate single old cavalryman ran forward towards an unstoppable innumerable enemy, both hands on his sword raised to his right side as he screamed the last oaths of the old order. The pageant and gallantry of the past came from the beyond and stood at attention and saluted his honor. He ran forward as a relic of the past, the last of his people, the last of his kind. And he died on that field like the rest of his people, the rest of his kind.

The ghosts of the past bowed their head and honored one of their own. The last great cavalryman fell.

Etienne lay on the ground, smoke curling about from the gunfire and the red glow from the runes on his sword, and as he paused there between realms and watched as the life drained away, a calm and peaceful woman from some far country appeared. She was arrayed in white and appeared to waft across an undisturbed pond as she approached him through the mists. He lay paused between realms. The angel came and rested her hand on his face. There was a warmth and a glow to her smile such as had not been seen in the land for many, many cold years.

"Come in my sweet boy, Etienne. How I've missed you," a warm voice resounded from the other side. "I told you that you would find me waiting for you at the end of your path. My love binds you to me forever." Etienne smiled as he felt an incomprehensible joy and entered.

Tiberius found him crying on the ground, enraptured as none had seen in this or any life. And as he passed, with his final breath, he heard him say, "Mother, how I've missed you." And Etienne released his soul into her arms.

Across ages and realms, Aaron the General, Aaron of the Cavalry, Aaron Prince of Ariens, sweet Etienne, was reunited with his people. His long white locks lay flowing on the ground, and he was at rest.

Tiberius cursed the day. He looked into the distance and saw nothing. He had failed.

The sun set in the west as he passed into the unknown kingdoms.

And thus the old ways died.

CHAPTER 26

In another life, Zara would have stood at the bleeding edge of hordes of thousands, holding the silver cross high above her head, its rays shining forth to excoriate any resistance, laying waste to all lands and people who dared oppose the five nations.

But not in this life.

In this life she stood alone and calm as she heard the shooting. She stood with just as much honor, just as much glory as any other, the heir apparent, and once future queen of Atlas.

She made her way through the chaotic camp, hearing reports and rumors floating in the wind. By sunrise the cross had still not shown up, and she decided she needed to make her way out before they started putting any pieces together.

She packed up her things from her abandoned site and slowly rode away from the fiasco the opposite direction. She rode calmly and resolutely, without fear of death or betrayal, and cried tears of pain as she left behind the guiding force behind her entire life until that point. "I will find a way," she thought. "I can find a way."

What that was, she could not see.

Through her tears, in the dark of the western skies with the sunrise behind her, she saw a bright streak of light and a thundering boom. The light fell to the earth due west of her, and she thought she could hear a dull thud.

She rode for a minute before Marie's words came to her mind. "A star will fall to Ariens and will raise up a peacemaker," she said, and looked down at her gift from Marie. "To make the peace."

"I can make the peace," she repeated.

She rode on, but now with direction.

Alana looked back and watched the thin smoke rise in the distance in the quiet light of the rising sun. "He's gone," she said. She was sure of it.

Alana stopped the horse, and Sahil followed suit. "I'm sorry," Ethan said.

They observed a moment of silence as the last great generation passed on. And, seeing movement in the distance, Ethan interrupted. "We'd better get out of here if we feel like living through the day."

"And I do," Sahil said.

They kicked it back into gear and headed off as fast as they could.

"What do we do now?" Ethan asked as they sped off by the light of the stars.

"What do you think we're going to do?" Alana said. "We are going to save Atlas with the silver cross," Alana said resolutely. "And then we are going to find some justice for Zara."

"Us and what army?" Ethan replied.

"My army," Alana said.

"Your army?" Ethan said.

"Well, not mine, but they will follow me," Alana said, "you asked me once what I told my commanders when we left them in Titan: it was to return to Atlas via Ithaca, and well, in my optimism I told them to prepare for me to return with the silver cross."

"Seemed unlikely at the time, but here we are," Ethan said.

"And they are finding the loyalists in the ranks. When they do, we will confront Jacques together and settle this petty matter of leadership," Alana said. "For far too long the conniving generation has suppressed the rising one, and we are going to make things right."

Ethan smiled. "Aye aye, captain," he said.

There were a few things my dad would always say impressed him about Alana: for example, her incredible ability to never give up. She could make things happen even when the odds seemed impossible, and long after Ethan felt it was time to try something else.[27]

But one of his favorite things about her was that she was never afraid to gamble big, and sometimes, like this time, it paid off. They were both thrilled to be returning to a hero's welcome.

Alana looked out across the dark plains that led into Atlas and felt a swell of gratitude. She loved this land, this people. She held the silver cross close to her chest and smiled. "I have no idea how you work little friend," she said, "but we are going to find out together."

She knew her commanders were waiting for her, and this time when she returned to Atlas, instead of walking into a trap, she was prepared to bring the heat herself. It wouldn't

---

[27] And as his daughter, I wish he would have stopped using that example on me whenever I was ready to give up on something. We can't all be relentless queens dad!

be long before she'd have Jacques jailed for treason and retire all those who would destroy Atlas through their hapless enabling of evil, to gain a few pennies for themselves while they gave the treasury away. It was time for change. Time for a regime for the rising generation.

A shot rang out from behind them.

"Not good, not good!" Sahil shouted.

Alana looked back. "Riders behind us!" she hollered. Another shot rang out.

"There's no way we can outrun them with two of you on the horse!" Sahil shouted. "These guys are really good at tracking!"

Another shot rang out, and the horses spooked, throwing Ethan and Alana to the ground.

"This is it Ethan, you have to do it!" Alana shouted. "This is what Etienne said, we only need a moment!"

Sahil jumped off his horse and picked up Ethan, "Let's go!" he said.

"No!" Ethan shouted. He pulled out his necklace, pulled the green gem out from the leather bands, and held it high, shouting in the ancient tongue. He pleaded and coaxed and cajoled and in the end, called out to his mother.

They heard the hoofbeats approaching, but Ethan wasn't paying attention. The green light exploded from the gem, and he drew a circle in the air, cutting out a portal into reality. The dark portal shimmered in midair.

"What in sweet hades is that?" Sahil asked.

"Go!" Alana said, and pushed Sahil through. He fell into the portal with Alana jumping through quickly behind him.

Ethan walked up to the portal and stopped as its tendrils reached out to him, and in a waking dream he saw Alana step up to the throne of Atlas with a crown of wildflowers and take her seat like her father before her. The throne immediately disappeared in the vision and he saw her holding the cross high and running across a long grassy field as she called down the arrows of Apollo. And as the vision melted away, Ethan again saw an old woman in a desolate desert. She looked at him and said, "Come!"

The vision left as quickly as it came, and he turned around to see the riders approaching. "I'm right behind you Alana!" Ethan shouted with glee, "you'll probably need a guide!" And he jumped backwards the portal, waving at the riders with a smile as he and the portal disappeared into thin air.

ABOUT ATMOSPHERE PRESS

Atmosphere Press is an independent, full-service publisher for excellent books in all genres and for all audiences. Learn more about what we do at atmospherepress.com.

We encourage you to check out some of Atmosphere's latest releases, which are available at Amazon.com and via order from your local bookstore:

Newer Testaments, a novel by Philip Brunetti
All Things in Time, a novel by Sue Buyer
Hobson's Mischief, a novel by Caitlin Decatur
The Black-Marketer's Daughter, a novel by Suman Mallick
The Farthing Quest, a novel by Casey Bruce
This Side of Babylon, a novel by James Stoia
Within the Gray, a novel by Jenna Ashlyn
For a Better Life, a novel by Julia Reid Galosy
Where No Man Pursueth, a novel by Micheal E. Jimerson
Here's Waldo, a novel by Nick Olson
Tales of Little Egypt, a historical novel by James Gilbert
The Hidden Life, a novel by Robert Castle
Big Beasts, a novel by Patrick Scott
Alvarado, a novel by John W. Horton III
Nothing to Get Nostalgic About, a novel by Eddie Brophy
GROW: A Jack and Lake Creek Book, a novel by Chris S McGee
Home is Not This Body, a novel by Karahn Washington
Whose Mary Kate, a novel by Jane Leclere Doyle
Stuck and Drunk in Shadyside, a novel by M. Byerly
These Things Happen, a novel by Chris Caldwell
The Dark Secrets of Barth and Williams College: A Comedy in Two Semesters, a novel by Glen Weissenberger

ABOUT THE AUTHOR

Chris Perry loves a nice long walk in the wilderness and telling stories along the way. This is his first novel; he started writing it while daydreaming during Statistics classes a long time ago. He lives in Northern California with his wonderful wife and three children.